To C. Cormier

The Red Bitch's Revenge

Enjoy!

Alberta is in my new book & I'm writing! Be there!

Jane B. Lee

Jane Lee

ISBN:

CONTENTS

1. GODZILLA MEETS STUMP

"Hey Stump," Ron called out as he and Moses ran Gina down. It hadn't taken long after Ron got out of prison to find Gina and run her down.

"Hey, Stump. Wait up," he called to Gina.

Ron and Moses quickly backed twelve-year-old Gina up against a chain-link fence.

"You got me two years in the slammer." Ron slapped Gina across the face. "You should have never called the cops." Ron angrily spat out the words. Slapping her across the face again, and again, he grabbed her by the throat, lifting her onto her toes. He then ripped open her blouse and pulled up her skirt.

The sudden pain of his little finger breaking caused him to release his prisoner. Turning, he faced a very tall, thin twelve-year-old Dana.

"What the fuck?" he yelled.

Moses grabbed Dana by her hair. Dana's well-placed stomp broke three critical bones. He quickly lost the use of his left foot, as he let Dana's hair go with a loud "Fuck!"

Gina had fallen to the ground when Ron turned to take a swing at Dana; she easily avoided the blow. Before Ron could complete the swing, he felt his sixth rib on his right-side break.

Moses pulled his gun from the back of his pants. Dana kicked in his right knee, breaking it at the joint. His gun flew across the street as he hit the ground. He was not going to stand for quite a while.

Ron tried to kick Dana. She pushed his leg even higher, dropping him on his back. As he hit the ground, Dana dropped a knee in his chest, breaking his ninth rib.

With both men down, Dana turned to help Gina up off the ground. Seeing Gina's eyes grow wide, Dana quickly pivoted to react to Ron pointing a gun at her head. She turned the gun backward toward the ground, breaking more of Ron's fingers in the process. She then threw a palm at his jaw, breaking it, and followed up with a blow to the side of Ron's head; his eyes rolled back as he hit the ground.

With the men down, Dana turned to Gina still leaning against the fence, her blouse torn open, pulling her blouse over her small chest. Dana asked, "Are you okay? You're bleeding." Dana saw blood coming out of her nose and lip.

"No. No, I'm okay." Gina's eyes, which were rolling around in her head, told Dana a different story.

"I'm Dana. They call me Godzilla at school, and you're Stump, right?" Dana said, putting her arm around Gina's shoulders. She walked her down the street, turning their backs on the two men lying on the sidewalk. "So, Stump what's your real name?" Dana asked calmly.

"Gina," she said, looking up at her protector.

"I've seen you around the school." Dana was talking to her in a calming voice as if nothing had happened. Gina's whole body was still trembling. As they rounded the corner two blocks down the street, they heard sirens announcing the arrival of the police.

“There they are,” the crossing guard announced pointing the police in the direction of the fight. The police approached the men with drawn guns. Ron was lying on his back on the sidewalk, out cold with his gun still in his hand. Moses was crawling across the street.

Standing over Moses, the officer asked, "Where are you going, buddy?"

"To get my gun and shoot that fucking kid who did this to me," was Moses's answer.

"No worries. I'll get it." The officer said with a chuckle. He had never got a confession so fast.

*

"Where do you live, Gina?" Dana asked as they walked along.

"Over off Piedmont. Those apartments. You know."

"Oh. That's like ten blocks. My house is just over a few blocks. Let's go there and fix you up." Dana guided her toward her house.

Eve was leaving her house for her shift at the hospital when she saw the girls walking up the sidewalk. The minute she saw the way her daughter was protecting the little girl; she knew something was very wrong. When she noticed the torn blouse and blood on the little girl's face, Eve rushed to meet them on the sidewalk. "What happened?"

"Mom, this is Gina. She goes to my school." Eve had gotten down on one knee and was examining Gina's bloody lip and nose. The wounds had stopped bleeding, but there was plenty of dried blood on her face. The bruises on her face and neck were just starting to get an ugly purple color. Eve then stopped to look at Dana and do a quick inspection. She didn't expect t see any blood or bruises.

"Come with me, honey," Eve said, taking Gina by the hand. "We'll fix you up.". As they started walking toward the house, Eve ordered, "Dana, talk!"

Dana started her story as they entered the house. With Gina in the middle, they headed to the kitchen.

"I was coming home from school when I saw these two men. One was beating Gina up," Dana started.

Gina was quiet as Eve sat her in a chair and carefully wiped the blood from her face with a wet towel. Eve checked carefully checked Gina's eyes, ears, and nose. Looking at the bruising on her throat, she stopped Dana and asked Gina a few questions. Eve was listening to her voice and breathing to determine if there was any other damage.

"Go on, Dana. Describe the men." Eve said, as Dana continued her description, Eve opened the refrigerator door, taking out an ever-present ice pack, used for moves gone wrong on the martial arts mat outback. She put the ice pack on the side of Gina's bruised face. "Honey, hold this, it will keep the swelling down. OK, Dana stay with Gina. I'll get her a new blouse," Eve said, on the way upstairs, she stopped and called the police, asking that they bring an EMS with them. Then a quick call to the hospital, telling her supervisor she had a family emergency and wouldn't be in today. Back with the girls, Eve explained that the police had to talk with them.

"Everything will be alright. Just tell the truth. Also, I asked for a nurse to give you a check-up." Eve was looking at Gina. "Gina, I'm a nurse. So, when I tell you that there is no damage and you will heal, you know I'm telling you the truth."

Gina nodded in agreement.

"Gina, I need to call your mom."

"I live with my aunt. She's a flight attendant. She won't be home till the day after tomorrow. I can't always call her. My sitter won't be at my house till five," Gina explained.

"We should call the sitter then," Eve said.

"Her name is Alice, and she's new. I don't know her number," Gina answered.

"Okay, what's your phone number? We'll call your sitter at five." Eve wrote down the number as Gina called it out.

Dana and Gina were still sitting in the kitchen when a plainclothes detective, a uniformed officer, and the EMS nurse showed up at the door.

Eve led everyone into the kitchen. The detective directed the nurse to check out Gina and document her wounds.

Stepping around the men, she noticed Eve, "Oh, Hi, Eve. These your kids?"

"Just the tall one, Susan. I think Gina, the shorter one, doesn't have any long-term trauma. Other than bruises and a split lip. But you make sure," Eve said.

"So, you're a doctor?" The detective asked Eve.

"No just a nurse. Susan and I work out of the same hospital...You're Detective Lawrence," Eve said, recognizing him, "You got shot in the left leg, maybe two years ago. I took care of you at the hospital."

The detective gave Eve a half-smile and shrugged. He had been too doped up to remember. "Okay, where is the guy who beat up those other guys? The ones we found on the sidewalk, over near the high school?" he asked.

"Oh, that was me," Dana said, her eyes wide.

"No, the tall one who beat up the bad guys?" The detective asked again.

"That was me," Dana stood up, showing off her five-foot seven-inch, still growing thin frame.

Detective Lawrence was shaking his head. He began again. "The crossing guard saw a tall kid beating up those bad guys. So, who was it?"

"That was Dana," Gina said, grabbing Dana's arm.

"Come on. Who was it?" the detective asked again, pointing his finger at Gina.

"I believe that was my daughter, Dana," Eve stepped in. "She's well capable of that."

"Come on; they had guns. Who was it?" The detective said, looking around.

"Dana, explain to the detective, please, what you did, move by move," Eve said to Dana.

Dana put her hands up in Karate attack pose, "No, Dana." Eve said, "Tell in detail. Do not demonstrate. Now sit down, please."

"Well, I was across the street when I saw this guy slapping Gina really hard," Dana started.

"Can you describe him? Was his partner with the guy attacking Gina?"

The nurse had finished up with Gina. She handed a report on a clipboard to the detective, who signed it. The nurse took off the top copy and gave it to him.

"It is just like you said, Eve. There's nothing that won't heal. See you at the hospital." The nurse gathered her things and made her way out the door.

"Okay, where were we?" Detective Lawrence folded the report and put it in his pocket.

Dana went on to describe, move by move, what she did and what the bad guys did. A lot of her descriptions used martial arts terms. Eve would come in and give a more generic description of her moves. After a few more questions, Detective Lawrence was finally convinced. He had to believe the unbelievable. This young girl took on two dangerous men, on purpose, and beat the hell out of them.

"Okay, I guess you're the man. Sorry, you're what? A tough, dangerous little girl," the detective said, looking for a description.

"They call me Godzilla at school because I'm so tall," Dana said. "I guess now I'll never live that name down."

"They call me Stump because I'm so short," Gina said, extending her hand to shake the detectives.

"Well, I'm delighted to meet you brave girls." Detective Lawrence said. "If I ever need help, I'll give you a call."

The girls giggled.

"No, really," he said with his eyes wide open.

The girls giggled again.

The detective stood, wrapping up his most unbelievable interview ever. Under his breath, he said, "They're never going to believe this at the station house."

"Detective, would it be okay if Gina stays with us tonight?" Eve asked.

"Yes, can she, Mom?" Dana asked.

"Can I stay with Dana?" Gina asked Eve, taking Dana's arm.

"That would be great," the detective said. "I'll send a car around to talk to the sitter. But I'm sure it will be okay. I guess the sitter can tell us how and when we can contact your aunt."

"Can I call my husband now?" Eve asked.

"Sure, Mind if I finish up a few notes before I go. I might have another question or two."

Christopher was home in less than fifteen minutes. Detective Lawrence met Christopher outside on the sidewalk.

"You have an amazing and brave little girl there. Have her describe how she took down two thugs with guns. She probably saved Gina from rape and death. Amazing." Shaking Christopher's hand, the detective instructed the other patrol car to wait here and to go to Gina's house around five, telling them, "Make sure they're not disturbed." Signaling the uniform officer that they were leaving, the detective handed Christopher his card. "Call me anytime."

As the detective and the uniformed officer got into their patrol car, the detective said, "I hope the press goes easy on them."

They didn't.

Dana met her dad at the door. She got a great big hug. "Are you okay?" he asked and then turned to Eve. "She's okay, right?"

"Yes. And this is Gina," Eve waved her hand toward Gina.

Christopher, with his arm still around Dana, led them all into the library. Eve poured two glasses of wine and handed one to Christopher before taking her seat.

"Okay, Dana, what happened?" Christopher asked, looking at Dana and Gina on the sofa.

Before Dana could get beyond, "I was across the street," Lars came crashing in.

"What happened?" Lars was confused. "That cop out there gave me the third degree, patted me down, and asked for my driver's license."

"Lars, this is Gina. Gina, this is my son Lars. Lars, Gina's going to be our houseguest tonight." Eve said.

"Hi, Lars," Gina said. Lars gave her a little wave.

"Okay, Dana. Start over," Christopher said as Lars took his seat.

Almost an hour later, Dana finished up by saying, "I don't see I had a choice."

Eve had been going back and forth, preparing dinner. Before Christopher could voice his opinion, Eve announced, "Dinner's on the table. Come on."

At the table, Christopher said, "I don't see you had much choice, either." He took a big spoon of rice and passed the bowl on, "But if there ever is a *next time*, please look for alternatives," He picked out a piece of chicken, from the plate on the table. "It could have turned out much worse."

With a little smile, Eve said, "You did good, Dana."

*

Dana dressed Gina in one of her nighties. It fell off her shoulders. She then gave her an old t-shirt. It came to Gina's knees. Gina joined Dana in her bed. Dana fell asleep almost as soon as her head hit the pillow. Gina looked at the back of Dana's head, put her arm on Dana's shoulder, and fell into a quiet sleep.

*

"Who the hell is that at this time in the morning," Lars looked over at the clock, it was just after six am. He threw off his covers. Wearing just his flannel pajama bottoms, barefoot, and bare-chested, he stomped his way to the front door, opening the door a mic was shoved in his face and a foot in the door. "I'm Tim Slaid. This is NBC can you..." Was all the reporter could get out before his mic went flying, and his wrist bent back as the reporter was forced out the door.

"You shouldn't do that. You don't come into my home unless you're invited," Lars said, his attention drawn to the front yard. His mouth dropped open as he saw three cameras filming him, then a dozen people in the yard trampling down the hedges and flower beds, digging up the grass. Television trucks with three different logos were blocking the street.

Lars slammed the door putting his back up against the door and his eyes wide, he yelled, "Mom, Dad!" as he ran up the stairs. Bursting through their door, he found Christopher and Eve already awake from the commotion.

Lars stood there, just waving his hands and arms. Words were not coming out of his mouth. Pointing at the window, he squeaked, "News."

Christopher and Eve were looking out the window as Lars came in, "Shit. They're digging up the yard. Trampling the bushes and flower beds." Eve grabbed her robe and headed for the door.

"Hold on," a sleepy Christopher said, slowing Eve down. "First, go get Dana and what's-her-name. We'll all meet in the hall."

Dana and Gina were still asleep when Eve entered. Dana was on her side, and Gina's arm was draped across her shoulder. "Girls, up," Eve ordered, shaking Dana's shoulder.

Two minutes later, they all gathered in the hall. Christopher had been looking out the window, summing up the situation.

"Okay, here's what we do. First, we all get dressed. I'll call the detective right now and find out what we should do and what we can or can't say." They just stood looking at him. "Move!" he ordered.

Ten minutes later, they were all gathered in the kitchen. Eve had started the coffee. Christopher came in just as the phone rang.

"This is NBC news. Can you—" Christopher hung up. The news called every thirty seconds or so until Christopher shouted into the phone, "Quit calling," Before he could hang up, he heard, "This is Detective Lawrence," The phone was already a few inches from his ear.

"Oh. Thank you. It's chaotic around here," Christopher said.

"So, I've been told. A patrol car is on its way. They'll back them out of your yard and have them park properly. Now, what?" the detective asked.

"What do we do? What do we say?" Christopher asked.

"Give it a half hour. We'll get everything in order. The press won't be easy on you." The detective was warming up. "Do not take the girls out there. Don't say anything about them. Don't answer any questions directly."

"They won't like that," Christopher pressed.

"I know," the detective said. "Just say please respect our privacy, da, da, da."

"Okay, we'll try. Anything else?"

"No. Those newsmen are experts at digging things out of you. Just don't give in." The detective had no other advice.

"Thanks." Christopher hung up and turned to the group and said, "So, here's what we do."

Thirty minutes later, Christopher, Eve, and Lars stepped in front of the cameras and mics at the end of the driveway near the sidewalk. Three newsmen shouted out the same question three different ways, all at once. Ten minutes later, Christopher, Eve, and Lars retreated into the house.

That day, the morning, noon, and evening news on every station had the same thing, just with a different newsman's name.

Tim Slaid said it best. "I'm Tim Slaid. This is your exclusive news." NBC had him standing in front of the Perssons' house. They then cut away to Lars opening the door, tossing the mic away and forcing Tim Slaid out the door. They then cut to a closeup of Lars standing open-mouthed in the doorway in only his pajama bottoms, his bare, muscular chest fully exposed.

After a short explanation about the twelve-year-old girl who took on the brutal bad guys and won, Tim Slaid finished with, "This is one family you don't want to fool with."

2. THE FIRST KISS

The two stood toe-to-toe, furiously throwing jabs, chops, punches, and kicks. Each blow blocked by the other. Each counterblow deflected or blocked. Not one blow landed.

Lars brought his left foot forward to attempt an ankle sweep. Dana sprang over his ankle sweep and flipped onto her back, falling to the mat. In mid-air, she threw her right leg out, catching Lars behind his left knee, bringing him down on his back. The instant Lars landed next to Dana; she threw her right-hand knife chop death blow to Lars' neck.

Lars had no defense.

Eve rose from her throne. Approaching the pair on the ground. Looking Lars in the eyes, she said, "What were you thinking? Throwing an ankle sweep off balance?"

Lars, lifting Dana's hand from his neck, said, "I thought it would work. It did before."

Eve leaned over, looking more intently into Lars' eyes. "It didn't, did it?" Glancing over at Dana, Eve gave her a slight smile.

Dana quickly raised herself off the mat. Her brother slowly pushed himself up to face Dana eye to eye. They politely bowed to each other.

Eve returned to her throne. The throne was nothing more than a large Adirondack chair with a leather back and seat. During Eve's pregnancy, it was where she sat and directed the boys; it soon became known as the throne.

Gina sat in a chair next to Eve's throne, her mouth open in amazement, her eyes fixed unblinkingly on Dana and Lars. Dana had spent most of Saturday morning trying to explain martial arts to Gina, using words Gina never heard and didn't understand. Judo, karate she had heard of, but hapkido and Wing Chun—even the pronunciations were over her head.

"Come on out here." Dana waved Gina onto the mat. "Okay. Stand this way," Dana had started when the doorbell rang.

"I'll get it. You girls keep going," Eve said, expecting the visitor.

Elizabeth was still in her tidy flight attendant uniform, and only her blood shot brown eyes showed her stress and lack of sleep. "I came as soon as I could. I was in Cairo when I got the message, and it takes two days to get here from there. I'm so sorry."

"Don't worry. Gina's just fine, a few bruises are all. Gina and my daughter are playing out back." Looking over her shoulder at Gina and Dana, 'Playing.' It was the only word she could come up for what they were doing.

"What happened? All I heard was that Gina got beat up by that bastard Ron." Elizabeth said, spitting out his name still standing on the porch. "Is she OK? He didn't hurt her, did he?"

"She got a bloody nose, and split lip, a few bruises, but she's OK. Please come in," Eve stood back.

"God, I didn't know anything. I got messages in three different airports," Elizabeth said, coming into the entryway, looking around for Gina, "I didn't find out Gina was here till the last airport."

"Maybe we could talk a little before you take Gina home." Eve showed Elizabeth into the library and offered wine. Elizabeth waved her off with a "No, thank you."

"I know it looks like I'm a horrible aunt," Elizabeth said, looking out the window at the two girls giggling and laughing on the mat. "I'm not a mother. I'm not even the motherly type. My drug-soaked sister dropped her off at my apartment. All Gina had was a paper bag for a suitcase. She said she'd be back for her in a couple of weeks. That was two years ago."

"I'm curious," Eve said. "Why did this Ron come after Gina?"

"Ron was beating up Helen, my worthless little sister. Gina dialed 911. Ron is—was a dealer. I thought he went to jail in Tampa for five years. Beating up a little girl, I guess he holds a grudge."

Looking out the French doors at the girls laughing and playing at judo on the mat. Eve smiled to herself. "You know, my daughter and

Gina get along really well. I have been thinking, and I talked it over with my husband, and we would like... let me say, and we would love for Gina to stay here when you're traveling. It would save you a sitter, and Dana needs a friend her age."

"I couldn't ask you to do that," Elizabeth said, looking away from the girls to Eve.

"You didn't ask. We offered. So, is it okay?"

Looking out the door at the girls who were laughing and pushing each other around, she could not ever remember Gina laughing. "I'll ask Gina."

*

"Hey, Godzilla, wait up," Gina called out to Dana, just after school.

"Stump? Stump? Where are you?" Dana called out with her hand shading her eyes as she scanned the horizon over the top of Gina's head. "I can hear you, but I can't see you," Dana said.

"Here, silly." Gina waved her hand in Dana's face.

Gina and Dana had become fast friends over the last two years. Gina always felt safe when around Dana. When Gina's Aunt was flying, Gina stayed with Dana and slept with her in her bed. It was the only place she felt safe at night. Gina had become part of the family. When Elizabeth was home, Gina felt more like she was visiting her aunt.

One evening, Dana changed into a kimono and met Lars on the mat. They were working on the lesser known, but effective Wing Chun moves. The discipline required Dana to wear a kimono. Her moves had to be minimal against her unimpeded attacker. She had to avoid all blows and, in the end, deliver a quick and decisive blow.

Eve was sitting in her throne, watching carefully. She would direct their movement with comments and commands. Eve stopped the match to adjust one of Dana's moves.

"Come on, Stump. Pick up a Bo staff," Lars called to Gina.

After two years of trying to spar with Lars, Gina knew Lars was just looking for a reason to land a playful slap on her butt.

"No way, Jose. Only if I'm on Dana's side." Gina taunted Lars back.

"Two girls against one manly man? No way, Stump." Lars knew his limit. Even at eighteen, he was no match for the fourteen-year-old

Dana. Lars thanked Gina, if only in his mind, for his bare-chested shot on the evening news. Overnight, he became the stud on campus.

"Positions!" Eve ordered.

"Hi, all," Christopher said as he walked on the patio. "Hi, beautiful," he said and then kissed Eve.

"Dinner is about ready," Eve said. "Kids, it's a draw tonight. Put away your Bo staffs."

"Aww. I was winning," Lars said. Then Dana tapped him on the head with her Bo staff.

"I win," Dana said

"No fair." Lars reacted by taking his Bo staff up in both hands like a samurai sword.

"Kids," Eve scolded. The tone always meant to stop now.

*

"Do you think we'll be asked to the Junior-Senior Prom?" Gina asked Dana over dinner.

"You're freshmen. What part of Junior-Senior do you not get?" Lars said teasingly, hoping for a response.

"Well, it could happen," Gina spoke up. "Dana's taller and sexier than any of the senior girls. And I got bigger ta-ta's." She shook her shoulders, making her breasts bounce.

"Gina!" Eve said with a scolding look.

"Yes, ma'am," Gina said apologetically. "But I do."

"Don't talk like that with boys present."

"Yes, ma'am," Gina said, this time with no follow-up.

Christopher just smiled and enjoyed his meal and the small talk. After dinner, the girls cleared the table and washed the dishes. Then they joined Christopher, Eve, and Lars in the library.

The phone rang, jolting everyone back from their adventures. "Hi, Axel. How are you doing?" Christopher answered the phone. "It's the boys," Christopher said to Eve.

Axel and Beau had left almost three years earlier for college at California State University at Long Beach. They called every Sunday. If they missed a call, they had to contend with their mother.

"Guess what? We got parts in a Kung Fu movie. We both did! We're going to be the bad guys," Axel said excitedly.

"And we're making money!" Grabbing the phone, Beau shouted out, "We're going to be stars."

Grabbing the phone back, Axel corrected Beau. "Supporting roles. They like that we both knew martial arts and that we're twins. So, they wrote us in."

"We were called in today. We got the part!" Beau shouted into Axel's face.

"What about school? Can you make room for this?" Christopher asked.

"Well, we have to take a semester... next semester off. We don't start filming for a month," Lars explained.

"I don't know. Is that good?" Christopher was not excited.

"No problem. We only have two semesters to go. And this will probably count towards our drama degrees," Axel explained.

"And it pays a lot," Beau again shouted in Axel's face.

"We got to run, Dad. We'll call Sunday." Axel pushed Beau away again.

"So, what am I supposed to tell your mother?" Christopher asked.

"I should have all the details by Sunday," Axel said. "Love you all."

"Love you guys," Beau said. *Click* was the next sound in Christopher's ear.

Eve had been listening with interest to Christopher's half of the conversation. "They didn't want to talk to me?"

"I guess they left that to me. The twins said they would call you on Sunday. They had to run," Christopher said.

"And what is this about school?" Eve asked.

"They are going to be in the movies. A kung fu movie," Christopher said.

"Hmm." With that, Eve went back to her book.

Dana had taken an interest in art. She liked spending time at her dad's gallery, at first to be with her dad and then for the art. She started to wonder what life would be like surrounded by beautiful, exciting, and motivational art.

"Here is where you start. At the beginning of art," Christopher said as he laid a huge book in her lap. "This will take you from the first known man-made images in the Chauvet caves of France to Babylonia." He settled back in his chair. "If you get through that, then we'll try early Greece and maybe a bit of early Rome."

Everyone was in their own world as Rod Stewart played in the background. Gina yawned and tapped Dana on the arm.

"Tired, Stump?" Dana asked.

"Yeah, it was a long day. Soccer practice and all." Gina yawned again.

"Yeah, me too." Dana closed her book and shelved it on her way upstairs.

*

"Wow, those are some big ta-tas," Dana said as Gina got out of the shower.

"I just graduated to size C," Gina said, picking up her bra from the chair and swinging it around in Dana's face.

"Show off." Dana had undressed for her shower. "Mine are small but pert," Dana said as she stepped into the shower.

Gina was sitting on the side of the bed in her nightie, waiting for Dana. Dana joined her, pulling on her nightie over her head.

"Do you think we might get asked to the Junior-Senior prom? At least one of us," Gina asked.

"I don't know. If anyone gets asked, it's you and your ta-tas," Dana joked. "Boys are afraid of me," she added in a more serious tone.

"No shit," Gina said. "But they all want to get into Godzilla's panties. I've heard boys talking."

"Well, they all want to feel you up," Dana countered. "I've seen the drooling. Really, actually drooling."

"Funny, but say we get a date for the prom?" Gina asked, hopefully.

"Then we'll go buy beautiful gowns, shoes, get our hair and nails done. We'll be beautiful princesses." Dana was on a roll. "They will pick us up in a limo. Your aunt will come over, and we'll take pictures. If she's in town."

"Sounds good," Gina said, nodding. "So, I'm just putting this out there. The boys are going to want to kiss."

"I know," Dana said. "I know."

"They are going to want tongue and everything," Gina said. "I've never kissed a boy like that. Have you?"

"Me? No. I'm Godzilla. They are afraid that I'll bite their tongue off." Dana was giggling.

"Ewww. Nasty." Gina made a face. "You wouldn't, would you?"

"No way. Not without tartar sauce." Dana giggled again.

"Do you think we should?" Gina thought for a moment. "Practice?"

"You mean together?" Dana was intrigued.

"No, with Lars." Gina made a face. "No. Us, silly."

"Well, I guess we should practice, even if we don't get asked to the prom. We are going to kiss boys sometime." Dana was warming up to the idea.

"Okay. Let's try," Gina said, and they both leaned in and touched lips.

"Wait." Gina drew back. "One of us has to be the boy, or it's not right."

Yeah, Dana thought.

"I'll be the boy first," Gina said. "I'll put my arms around you like this." Gina slipped her hands and arms around Dana's waist. She then pulled her closer.

"You just sit there. Like you're not expecting it." Gina leaned in for a kiss, and Dana just sat there.

"Well, you got to turn your head. You got to lean towards me like you want to be kissed," Gina said.

"Got it," Dana said.

"Sheesh," Gina said and started over again.

This time Dana leaned in, and they kissed. Gina probed Dana's mouth with her tongue, just to meet Dana's teeth. "When I do that, you have to open your mouth," Gina said.

"Not on the first kiss," Dana said in a serious tone.

"Okay. This is the second or third kiss. Whatever." Gina was a bit flustered. "Open your mouth, and your tongue needs to play with mine," Gina said and leaned in.

Dana backed off. "Where did you learn all this stuff about kissing?"

"I was watching Lars with one of his girls after school." Gina laughed. "I saw her later and asked if Lars was a good kisser."

"Well?" Dana asked.

"She said he was an excellent kisser." Gina shrugged. "I asked questions."

"Really?" Dana was amazed.

"Again?" Gina asked.

They leaned in and kissed, their heads moved in unison, as their lips and tongues played the game lovers had played since the beginning of love. They both felt feelings of desire, starting deep in their gut, spreading outward and downward. They had feelings they never felt before.

Gina moved her hand and cupped Dana's breast.

"What was that?" Dana pulled back.

"Boys are going to want to feel us up. They will; they're boys," Gina said. "Again, and this time for two minutes." Gina leaned in, and Dana followed. Gina caressed Dana's small breasts. Dana put her hand on Gina's thigh. Both had become more excited.

"Now, I'm the boy," Dana said, as they reversed roles. Two minutes later, they came up for air. "Wow," Dana said, a bit out of breath.

"Wow," Gina said, just as much out of breath. "Which way did you like it best?"

"I don't know. I liked it both ways," Dana said.

"I liked you rubbing my ta-tas," Gina said. "Want to do it again?"

"Okay, one more time. Then we have to go to sleep," Dana said, and this time it lasted a full five minutes. A little embarrassed and flustered, Dana said, "I think we got it now."

"I think we're good kissers now. At least you are," Gina said.

"And you're fabulous," Dana said, rubbing her hand up and down Gina's back.

They laid down in bed, as usual, Gina with her arm over Dana's shoulder. Both were quiet and wide awake. They were both wondering about the feelings that they were experiencing. That stirring feeling in their stomachs was their libido awakening.

*

"Auntie's coming home today," Gina said over breakfast.

"Well, then you'll be at her house tonight," Dana said, trying to act as if nothing had happened the night before. In fact, over the next few days, they avoided any mention of that night. They were both trying to forget the feeling, but they both wanted more. At night in bed in their separate houses, they both wondered what more was.

A week later, neither Gina nor Dana got invited to the Junior-Senior Prom.

"Do you think I should ask Paul? He's a junior." Gina asked over lunch, with a hint of desperation in her voice.

"No!" Dana's whisper was nearly a shout. "Are you crazy? That's the boy's job. What if he says no? It would be around the school in no time. And I won't be able to stand your weeping and moaning."

"Sheesh! It was just a question." Gina held up her hand.

"Well, there is only one other dance left this year." Dana has some hope, "It's not formal or anything. So, if we don't get asked, that's okay. We don't need dates for the pre-graduation dance."

Dana said, "It's the only dance left. It's the week before graduation."

"That's just a month away!" Gina said, back in the groove.

"Auntie's going to Paris. Want anything from France?" Gina was changing the subject.

"You mean like a French kiss?" Dana cracked the week-long silence about that night.

They both sat in shocked silence for a few seconds. Dana could not believe what had come out of her mouth. Then they both knew the joke and giggled.

"She'll be gone for a week. Two trips out of JFK," Gina said. "She'll leave this afternoon."

"Cool, I got you for a week!" was Dana's response. "I didn't want to put up with Lars gloating over the Junior-Senior Prom. Not all by myself."

"You know we can dress up for the pre-graduation dance," Dana said as they walked home. Gina was still in fear of walking home alone, the slightest out of place noise sent her running home. When she was with Dana, she was never afraid.

"Maybe we can get Mom to take us shopping?"

"That would be way cool," Gina said.

"New dresses and shoes. So cool." Dana said.

"You have got to get high heels this time." Gina shook her finger at Dana. "And not those wimpy one-inch heels." She gestured with her fingers. "Real heels this time, like six-inch heels." And she widened her fingers all the way.

"Oh God. Why don't you just tattoo Godzilla on my forehead?" Dana made a scrunched-up face.

"And we're getting miniskirts! Oh, they are so sexy." Gina said.

"Really? Guess what? The way you have me dressed," Dana was shaking her head, "even if I get to dance with a boy, and that's highly unlikely, his hands will be on my legs, not around my waist, and his head in my little bitty titties."

"Exactly!" Gina laughed. "All they'll see is legs and boobs," Gina said. "And the dance floor will be wet with their drool."

"Oh my God," Dana said, looking to the heavens for help.

"And you have to wear a push-up bra and a low-cut blouse," Dana came back. "Show off your new C-size ta-tas."

"Godzilla and Stump. Can you imagine? The two hottest girls at the dance," Gina said as they walked into the house. Both excited and apprehensive at the same time.

Lars was out back on the mat, showing off his moves to his prom date, Sally. Sally was sitting on the throne.

"Up!" Was all Dana said as she and Gina stepped onto the patio.

"What?" Sally said puzzled.

Dana looked at Lars with a *What are you doing?* Look.

"Up. That's Mom's chair." Dana stepped next to the chair, ready to throw Sally on her ass.

"What?" Sally said again, very confused.

"What's the big deal? Mom's not home." Lars spoke up.

Dana took two threating steps toward Lars.

"Okay, Okay. Sally, pick another chair before Godzilla here blows it." Lars knew that look. He also knew he was in trouble. He knew what Dana was capable of.

"Sorry," Sally said as she changed chairs.

"That's okay," Gina said. "It's kind of a rule around here." As she softened the moment, she could see that Dana was not entirely through with Lars.

"Let's go see what we can make for dinner," Gina said before Dana could say anything else, she took Dana's arm and pulled her toward the house. "If we have dinner ready when your folks get home, maybe, we can soften up your mom for that shopping trip."

Over dinner, Gina and Dana laid out their plans for the pre-graduation dance. They begged to go shopping for new clothes. They left out the part about push-up bras, heels, and miniskirts.

"Please, Mom, can we go this weekend?" Dana pleaded.

"No way. It's *Junior-Senior Prom* this weekend," Lars objected.

"Lars is right," Christopher chimed in. "It's his weekend."

Lars made a face that said, "See!"

"Awww." Both Gina and Dana sighed.

"You're right, dear," Eve said as she placed her hand on his leg.

Looking at Dana and Gina, Eve thought, *My babies want to go shopping for sexy clothes. They are growing up. I didn't notice. I miss the giggling little girls. How beautiful they have become.* Looking more closely, Eve thought, *Dana's getting curves, hips, and a bust. Look at Gina. She was flat-chested when Dana brought her home. Now she is full-chested. Big ta-tas, as she would say. When did all that happen?*

Eve flashed back to that day Dana brought Gina home. Taking Gina away from those thug, protecting her. She all but said, "Can I keep her, Mom?"

"You know, girls." Eve said, "How about the Saturday after the prom, we all go shopping?"

Both girls got great big grins on their faces.

"...And," Eve continued, after a long pause. "For you, Gina. We'll get you a push-up bra and low-cut blouse or dress. You want to show off your best. Ah—" Eve looked for the word. "Assets."

"And for you," Smiling, Eve turned to Dana. "Of course, a push-up bra. You have assets in there somewhere. We might have to mine for them, but they're there." Eve said with a chuckle. "And stilettos. I think you can handle them now. Maybe you'll need to practice walking in them. I know! You can do your martial arts in them. That should give you some confidence walking in them."

"Oh, that's a great idea." Lars saw a chance of besting Dana on the mat.

Dana and Gina were looking at each other wide-eyed, giggling.

"Don't forget miniskirts. They are all the rage now," Eve said, Christopher gave Eve a questioning look. Eve knew exactly what he was thinking, "Christopher, look around all the girls are wearing miniskirts now, join the modern age, like it or not."

Christopher just shook his head.

The girls were turning red and laughing. *How did she know what we want?* They thought at the same time. The girls were on top of the world, giggling nonstop

Later, they were all settled in the library. Lars was at one end of the sofa reading a romance novel, looking for clues for the prom. Dana, at the other end, was reading about early Greek art. Gina was cuddled up against Dana with her legs on Lars's lap. She was reading *Les Misérables*.

Dana yawned and tapped Gina on the arm. "Ready, girl?"

"In a minute, sweetie," Gina said, not looking up from her book.

Dana caught it. Eve did not look up from her book, but she got the drift.

"Wow, that's some story," Gina said as she put a marker in the book and closed it. "Does he escape from prison?"

"Well, yes. If he didn't, the book would be way shorter." Eve answered, adding, "Sweetie," and letting Dana know she heard.

*

Gina showered first, as was usual. When Dana came out of the bathroom, Gina was already in bed facing the wall.

Dana crawled in bed. "Goodnight, Gina." She said, kissing her on the cheek, and turned away from her. She wasn't sure if Gina was feeling what she was feeling.

Gina wasn't sure of her feelings, either. She feared Dana's rejection more than anything. Her mother had rejected her. Her aunt did take her in. But, if Dana rejected her, her protector, her love, she felt she would die.

Gina quietly rolled over and studied Dana's neck and hair. Finally, she worked up the courage.

"You awake?" she asked softly.

"Yes," Dana said over her shoulder. She then rolled over to face Gina. Face to face, their noses were just two inches apart.

"What are you thinking?" Dana started.

"Well. Do you remember," Gina paused, "us?"

"Practicing kissing? Yes, I remember." Dana finished her thoughts.

"Well, I liked it. Practicing," Gina said.

"I liked it too." Dana placed her hand on Gina's shoulder. "But," Dana took a breath, trying to think how to say how she felt.

Gina was fearful of what was coming next.

"But," Dana started again. "for me, it didn't feel like practice." Dana stopped and put her hand on Gina's cheek. "For me, it felt real."

Gina put her hand on Dana's cheek. "For me too. It was real. I got feelings I never felt before."

"Me too." Dana paused. "I got feelings, you know, down there." She waited. "What do we do?"

Gina leaned in and kissed Dana on the lips. Dana returned the kiss with even more passion. Rolling over, so her head and shoulder were above Gina, the kiss grew in intensity. Dana rested her leg between Gina's. "Wow," she said a little while later as she laid back. A tremble went through her body.

Gina lifted Dana's arm and put it around her. She rested her head on Dana's shoulder and settled in on her side with her arm over Dana.

A little while later, Dana spoke up.

"We can't tell anyone. Not your aunt, not my mom, not anyone."

"I know," Gina said.

"We can't kiss anywhere but here. Not ever in public."

"I know," Gina said again.
"We can't let anyone know," Dana said and added, "Sweetie."
"I know," Gina said in a soft, contented voice.

3. THE PRE-GRADUATION DANCE

"Is this too much makeup?" Gina asked Dana.

"Yes," Dana said. They were sharing the mirror in their bathroom. They were both just wearing their bras, panties, and pantyhose.

"Well, you need more," Gina said. "I'll do you, and you do me. Okay?"

"No!" Dana reacted. "You'll make me look like a slut."

"Isn't that the look we're going for?" Gina picked up the eyeliner. "Here, let me."

"No!" Dana said, taking the eyeliner away from Gina. "You just watch."

"A little more on the ends. Like mine," Gina said, showing Dana her eyes in the mirror.

Somehow, they managed to get their makeup on in about thirty minutes. Fifteen minutes later, they were dressed and coming down the stairs.

Christopher, Eve, and Aunt Elizabeth were waiting at the bottom of the stairs with cameras in hand.

"Wow. Beautiful." Aunt Elizabeth said. "And you both are so grown up," she said, shaking her head. She wondered where the last four years had gone since she inherited Gina.

"Sexy," Lars said involuntarily. "I mean for freshmen." He tried to play down his comment.

"Over here." Eve directed the girls to a place by the arched doorway into the library. "Pose."

Dana and Gina posed in various positions for full length and close-ups. Always together. Their favorite was a close-up with their heads together, blowing kisses to the camera.

"Okay, freshman. Climb in," Lars said, getting behind the wheel of his Dad's Cadillac. Gina in her four-inch heels and Dana in her six-inch heels, carefully made their way down the steps and across the walk to the Cadillac.

"Well, I should be going. I have a four-thirty get-up time for my flight tomorrow," Aunt Elizabeth said after the car disappeared down the street. "Thank you so much for having me over."

"Oh, we love having you over," Eve said.

"Thank you for everything you all have done for Gina. I am so thankful. I don't think I can thank you enough."

"You're family. Gina and Dana are like sisters, as far as I'm concerned." Eve said.

"I know I should have done more. I should have done better," Aunt Elizabeth said, holding Eve's hand.

"You're out earning a living, paying the bills. That's what you do. Don't feel bad about that," Christopher said.

Hugging Eve and Christopher, Aunt Elizabeth said, "Sincerely, thank you for all you have done." She then waved goodnight. On Elizabeth's way home, she could not help but think about the unwashed little girl who was literally dumped on her doorstep. Gina had been quiet, withdrawn, and afraid.

At first, she resented her. "What the hell am I going to do with a kid?" she complained to co-workers on many flights. A year later, she had grown used to her and sometimes even liked having her around. Gina did put a crimp in her sex life, but she worked around it.

Elizabeth had grown close to a pilot. During their six-month affair, she had felt he was the one. She was ready to say yes. He broke it off in a short, painful, unapologetic phone call. Elizabeth had dropped the phone on the floor, sat on the sofa, and cried.

Eleven-year-old Gina had heard the whole thing. She went over to her aunt and put her arms around her, her head on her chest. "Aunt Elizabeth, I love you. I love you so much. I will never leave you or hurt you. I promise."

Elizabeth held her tight and cried. She kissed her on her head. "I love you too, honey." And for the first time, she really meant it.

It struck her that night on her way home, having sent Gina off to her first dance, that she had become her daughter, with all the love in her heart a daughter deserves.

Lars stopped in front of Sally's house and honked the horn.

"Get out and get her!" Dana said, slapping Lars across the back of his head. "Be a gentleman for once."

"Ow. Okay. But here she comes." Lars pointed out the window.

"Get out and open the door for her." Dana slapped him across the back of his head again. "God, what a doofus."

"Okay!" Lars said. He dodged another slap to the head as he jumped out the door and opened the door for Sally.

"Hi, girls," Sally said as she settled herself in the front seat. "You all look great."

When Lars got into the car, she leaned over and gave him a big kiss.

"Such a gentleman," she said.

Dana and Gina looked at each other, rolled their eyes, and laughed.

"Drop us off at the front door. We'll wait for you to park the car," Dana said to Lars.

"Aw, okay, I guess," Lars answered.

"I'll go with him," Sally said, taking Lars' arm.

"Sally, we're all wearing heels. None of us are walking across that old gravel parking lot in heels. Come with us. Lars will hurry." Dana's words were followed by a *are you listening* look at lars.

"We'll wait for you by the front door," Dana said as Lars flinched, thinking he was in for another head slap.

Boy, this being a gentleman is tough work, Lars said to himself as he drove off to find a parking spot.

Lars and Sally entered the auditorium to "Hi, guys. You made it," and "Dude!"

Dana entered behind them to gasps and whistles; she was six-foot-three in her heels. She looked over the crowd, literately looked over the top of the crowd. Only two senior basketball players were as tall as Dana in her heels.

Gina, on the other hand, had better ta-tas than most of the girls. She was now five-foot-seven in her heels.

Gina guided Dana to the front of the dance floor.

"Dance, Gina?" were the first words they heard from one of the boys.

Dana stood in place. She watched and smiled as Gina danced. She looked around to see if anyone was going to ask her to dance. No one did.

"Gina, want to dance?" she heard from another boy as she was coming off the dance floor. He took her hand and turned her around and headed back to the dance floor. Gina looked back over her shoulder, with a *what can I do* look.

Dana started to drift back toward the wall. She was embarrassed by her tallness. *No one wants to dance with a Godzilla,* she said to herself with a plastered smile on her face. She was feeling more and more like Godzilla.

Lars and Sally disappeared after a few dances. They were escorted back in by a teacher, as were several other couples. No one was getting pregnant during the Pre-Graduation Dance. At least not on campus.

"You look great," Debbie, is one of Dana's classmates, said. "I love your makeup."

"Hi, Debbie. You look awesome in that dress." Dana looked her over from her ankles to her very short skirt and strapless top. Debbie and Dana chatted about the dance, and some couples for a bit, "You should wear heels more often," Debbie said as she wandered off. "Makes you look like a hot model."

Debbie drifted by a few more times, stopping to chat. She didn't seem to be with anyone in particular.

Gina was on the floor for almost every dance with a different boy, shaking her ta-tas. The boys loved that. Gina worked her way back to the wall. There were lots of "I'm sorry not this dance." She stood next to Dana. "Sorry," Gina said.

"For what?" Dana said, looking sideways at her. "Having every boy in school wanting to dance with you? I get it."

"They just want to see me shake my ta-tas, probably hoping one will fall out," Gina said as she pressed close to Dana and took her hand behind their back.

"Would you please have this dance with me?" Gina added, "Sweetie."

"Ah. No," Dana said. "Thanks. You don't have to feel sorry for me." She tried to let go of Gina's hand, but Gina would not let go.

"Come on. See? Girls are dancing with girls. Let's go." Gina started pulling Dana toward the dance floor.

"No, I said." Dana pulled back.

"Come on." Gina did not let go of Dana's hand. "I'll make a scene!"

"God, no," Dana whispered. "Okay. Fast dance."

Gina finally dragged Dana onto the dance floor. With her martial arts training wearing her stilettos, Dana was a natural and graceful dancer. Everyone took a minute to watch Dana's smooth moves. The next dance was the last dance, and it was a slow dance. Dana started for the wall.

"Dance, sweetie?" Gina said, grabbing Dana's hand again.

"No." Dana tried to pull away without it being too noticeable to the other couples who were wrapping themselves around each other.

"I'll make a scene." Gina held tight.

"You are making a scene." Dana turned back. "Oh, what the hell!" Stepping up to Gina's arms.

It was a few steps before who was going to take the lead was established. Dana took over.

"Thank you, sweetie," Dana said, pulling Gina closer.

Sally and Lars were waiting in the car. They were busy.

"Break it up," Dana said, knocking on the window.

Dana and Gina slid into the backseat. Dana reached for Gina's hand.

"Thank you for being my date," Gina whispered.

Dana went to give Gina a kiss on the cheek. Gina turned her head, and the kiss landed on her lips. Nobody noticed.

"I'll drop you guys off first," Lars said as they pulled up in the driveway.

"Be good," Dana said as she got out of the car.

"Have fun," Gina said as she got out of the car.

"It was great!" "Had a ball." "Awesome." "Wild." Were the words they gave to Christopher and Eve as they were greeted at the door.

"Come, tell us about it." Christopher pointed toward the library.

"Tomorrow. Too tired now," Dana said.

"Oh, yes. I'm beat," Gina said as the girls headed up the stairs with their heels in hand.

"Thank you again for the dances," Dana said, once the door to their room was closed.

"I only wanted to dance with you. You do know that? Right?" Gina said. "The boys only wanted to see me shake my tits."

"Well, you did a good job of that!" Dana said, "No one wanted to dance with Godzilla."

"They were all afraid of you because you are so awesome. Everyone knows you're way above all those boys." Gina grabbed Dana's hand as she saw a sad look on her face.

"Not just in height. But in class. And you were the most beautiful girl there," Gina added. "You were like a goddess."

She took hold of Dana's waist and reached up. She could not reach Dana's lips, so she put one hand behind Dana's head. Pulling her to her lips, she said, "Kiss me beautiful!"

4. YOUNG LOVE

"Okay, Okay, cool. I'll tell Mom and Dad," Lars said, hanging up the phone.

"What's that?" Dana said as she walked into the room.

"Oh, nothing," Lars lied.

"Yeah." Dana came close to Lars and leaned in. "Then whisper sweet nothings to me."

"No," Lars said. Then he said "Ouch" as Dana twisted his nipple.

"Okay, let go." Lars was squirming. "I'm moving in with Lars and Beau."

"That's it? That's nothing. We knew that months ago when you got accepted at CSULB." She twisted Lars' nipple a bit more. "What's up?"

"Jesus. Let go." Lars applied pressure to Dana's palm, turning her hand away.

"I'm going after the Fourth of July," Lars said, rubbing his twisted nipple.

"Hmm." Dana stepped back. "I thought you weren't leaving till mid-August."

"So? Just a little early. Figure out the lay of the land. You know?" Lars looked away from Dana.

"So what's Sally got to say about this?"

"Nothing." Lars looked down at the floor.

"Nothing?" Dana tapped him on the chest. "Really? Nothing?"

"She doesn't know yet," he said finally.

Dana shook her head and sat down beside her big brother. She put her arm around his shoulder and moved closer to him. "What happened?" she asked in a motherly tone.

"Nothing." Lars sighed. "We had another fight."

"About?"

"She wants to be all couple-ish. Like, get engaged or something." Lars shook his head. "I'm just not ready for that yet."

"Lars, my dear Lars. I don't know of a delicate way to ask this." Dana tried to look into Lars' downturned eyes. "Is she pregnant?"

"No!" Lars' head jerked up. "No! I don't think so."

"So, it's possible?" Dana asked.

"No. I follow Mom's advice." Lars tapped his wallet. "I always have protection."

"Always?"

"Always!" Lars was adamant.

"Okay." Dana and Lars sat for a minute.

"Were you, like, her first?" Dana asked.

"Yes," Lars said. "I don't know. She said I was. I don't know."

"You're special. Not just special, but really special to Sally. She gave you something she will never have again." Dana paused for effect. "Her virginity."

Lars let that sink in. *Oh. I guess so,* he thought. "But I'm not ready."

"She is, and you know you're a really arrogant ass. Treating her like, I don't know. Like she's got to chase you. Like you don't care. Like she's not important. Lars, you have a lot to learn about women. She's put up with your shit. You'll never find another woman who will do that." Dana put her head on his shoulder. "But if you got to get away, go. I'm behind you all the way."

"Thank you. I always knew that." Lars patted her head.

"So. What do you want me to tell Mom and Dad?"

"Nothing. I'll tell them over dinner tonight." Lars laid back in his chair.

*

Over dinner that night Dana gave lars a 'like so' look.

Lars got the signal, "Axel and Beau are going up to Canada to work on the movie. They're leaving early. So, I have to get out there and settle into the condo and learn the ropes, and I'll be leaving after the Fourth." Lars didn't lie. He just fudged the date by a month or so.

"Tomorrow's the Fourth!" Eve said, "I wasn't expecting you to leave so early."

"I got to go, mom, sorry." Lars put his head down, eating to cover not having to look in his mother's eyes. She could always read his thoughts through his eyes.

Eve put down her fork and looked at Lars for a long moment. She knew what he was up to, "If you say you got to go, you got to go. I'm sorry…you have to leave so early."

*

Sally's mom, Jody, dropped her off in front of Dana's house, kissed her goodbye, and drove off to her own Fourth of July celebration.

They squeezed all six people into Christopher's Cadillac and then spilled out in the parking lot at Stone Mountain National Park. They wandered around, looking for a good place to watch the fireworks and to spread out their blankets. Christopher and Eve, hand in hand, the kids following up with the blankets, picnic baskets, and ice chest. They spread out their blankets in a good spot and dropped the gear near the blankets. Even before sitting down, Lars and Sally started to wander off.

"Back in an hour!" Christopher shouted after them. "Got it?"

"Yeah, Dad," Lars called back over his shoulder.

"Let's see if we can climb up to the top of Stone Mountain?" Dana said to Gina.

"No, you don't," Christopher said right away. "That will take way too long."

"Want to wander around?" Gina said to Dana as they started to wander off.

"You heard what I said?" Christopher said. "Back in an hour."

Dana turned and, with her trademark, innocent smile, said, "Of course."

Sitting on the blanket, Christopher popped a bottle of champagne. Pouring Eve, a glass, he kissed her. "I thought they would never leave," he said.

*

The day after the Fourth of July, Lars called Sally. "I'm pretty busy today. Why don't we meet at Buckhead Mall? About noon. Okay?" Lars did not want to be stuck in a car with Sally after what he had to say.

"I didn't think you were leaving till mid-August?" Sally was close to tears or spitting fire. She just didn't know which one yet.

"Well, everything got moved up. I can't help it." Lars fudged the dates again.

"So, when did you find out?" Sally was looking for a direction. Was it going to be tears or fire?

"The day before the Fourth. I didn't want to ruin our first Fourth of July together."

"Oh," Sally said, knowing that it was going to be tears. "You know, I love you so much."

"I love you too." Lars did not get home till near midnight. It might have been later, but he still had to load up the Volkswagen Bug, complete with a luggage rack on the roof. It was another day before Lars was ready to leave.

Lars and Beau had found themselves with lots of extra cash from their movie gig. They had rented a condo in Marina Pacifica with a view of Alamitos Bay. It was perfect for them with lots of shops, bars, and restaurants within walking distance. CSULB was just up the hill, less than a mile away. Close enough to convince their mom and dad that they still intended to finish up their degrees.

"Little Bro," Lars said as he opened the door to find Lars had arrived near eleven Sunday morning. Almost a day early.

After they hugged each other, Axel shouted up the stairs. "Beau get your ass out of bed. Little Bro is here."

"Wow! This is quite the pad." Lars was blown away by the view of the bay and the homes that lined the opposite bank.

"Beau, Lars is here," Axel yelled again. Seconds later, Beau's door burst open.

"Little Bro," Beau yelled with his arms held out wide, dressed in only his boxers. He jumped over the rail and landed on the sofa five feet below. He jumped the coffee table and gave Lars a big hug.

"I need coffee! Then tell me everything." Beau headed for the kitchen just behind the breakfast bar. "How's Mom and Dad?" he called over his shoulder as he heated the water and prepared the coffee press. "And Dana?"

"You mean Dana-dash-Gina. They are like one girl," Axel said. "But no problems. Same old, same old."

Beau set out three coffee cups. "Were all black right?" he asked without waiting for an answer. "We haven't any cream anyway."

"By the way, I told Mom and Dad I had to get here early because you were going up to Canada next week for the movie. Please don't tell them you're not. Okay?" Lars pleaded.

"Yeah, about that. Mom called Friday," Axel said. "I kind of screwed things up there."

"Shit!" Lars said. "What did she say? No, don't tell me."

"You're really in trouble... she didn't say anything."

"Nothing?" Lars said.

"Just to call her when you get in," Axel said.

"That's all. Damn, I'm really up shit creek." Lars shook his head.

"When Mom says nothing, that means you're dead," Axel said. "She's saving it up for you."

"Who's Sally?" Beau asked.

"How do you know about Sally?" Lars looked up.

"She called," Lars said.

"Oh, damn. Oh shit," Lars said again.

"Don't worry. After Mom's call, we figured out what you did." Beau said. "We just said we needed you out here as soon as possible."

"Thanks," Lars said.

Beau pressed the coffee and passed the cups around.

"Let's get your stuff and get you settled in," Lars said. "Then you need to call Mom."

The call to his mom did not go well. Eve knew how to take her kids down a notch or two when they needed it. Lars was brought down three notches.

*

"Okay, enough freeloading. Lars, get a job." Axel was standing at the foot of Lars's bed at 4:30 in the morning, shaking his foot.

"What?" came from a sleepy Lars.

"Time to work." Axel pulled the covers off Lars. "You've been here for three days. Time to work."

"What?" Lars was trying to curl up and go back to sleep.

"Work. You got fifteen minutes to shower, shave, and get dressed," Axel said as he pushed Lars onto the floor. "And put on your good clothes. No shorts or Levi's." He turned to leave as Lars was picking himself up off the floor. "Hurry," He ordered.

"Here's coffee." Beau handed Lars a go-cup of coffee, pushing him down the stairs to the door.

"What the hell is happening?" Lars had a bewildered look on his face as they marched him to the car.

"We got makeup at six." Axel pushed Lars into the backseat.

"Really?" Lars yawned. "You got me up for this?"

"You're our goffer. We need something you go for it. Besides, you might get discovered. So, you just sit around with us while we're in makeup or on set, and we'll try to get you a part as an extra." Axel said.

*

Sally called every day. With the three-hour time change, sometimes she woke Lars up. Sometimes she called at seven am her time, which was four am Lars's time.

*

"You get your wish Little Bro," Axel announced on the ride home Friday evening. "Were leaving town Monday. We have a few days of filming. Then we get a week off to enjoy."

"Calgary!" the twins said together, slapping palms.

"So, what am I supposed to do?" Lars had never lived alone in his life.

"Whatever," Axel said.

"OK, " Lars said as he thought, *This might be fun*.

It took about three days before he was bored and lonely. Even Sally quit calling.

Lars' imagination started working overtime. He imagined that Sally was out with one of his classmates from high school.

"Is Sally there, Mrs. McKelvy." It had now been a few days since Lars had heard from her.

"No. Remember, she left for nursing school in Columbus a few days ago. I'm sure she'll call you when she gets settled in."

"Oh, okay. I knew that, thanks, Mrs. McKelvy." The phone clicked as the call ended.

'She was calling every day, now she's not calling. I'm sure she's seeing someone else," Lars was thinking. "Or just got tired of me. I didn't think she was leaving for nursing school for another week. " He dropped himself on the sofa. "I should have treated her better. Dana was right; I am an arrogant ass." Rolling over, he said, "God, I miss her."

He missed Sally, missed her calls. He missed her most at night, so much that it hurt. Why hadn't she called at least once? At least to tell him she wasn't interested. *I have no way of getting a hold of her.* That thought hurt his gut.

It was just after one in the afternoon. Lars was sitting on the balcony, his feet up on the railing. He was looking at the water and the houses on the opposite shore. Nothing was moving when the doorbell rang. *Who's that?* He thought. *I didn't order pizza. At least I don't think I did.*

No one had rang the doorbell since the twins had left. He leaned his chair forward, taking his feet off the railing and walking barefoot to the door. The doorbell rang again. "I'm coming. Keep your shirt on," he called out, then jerked the door open.

"Did you miss me?" Sally said, standing there with her suitcase behind her. She had doubts about this meeting since leaving Columbus, but she missed Lars so much, she could not stop herself. Then she became afraid. Afraid that he was with someone new. What would she find?

"Ah," Lars said, halfway thinking this was a dream. He reached out and touched her arm, to make sure she was real. "Oh God, yes," he managed to say, squeezing her so tight, she could hardly breathe, followed by a long, passionate kiss. "How did you get here?" Lars asked, looking at her but not letting go.

"Greyhound," Sally said.

"Really? All by yourself? Isn't that dangerous?" He reached behind her and, picking up her suitcase, walked her into the living room. He closed the door and dropped the bag.

"I wanted to take the Greyhound to Columbus. I never rode on the Greyhound bus, I always wanted to, it's safe, or Mom would not have let me take it. By the time I got to Columbus, well, I couldn't stand it."

Sally took a deep breath. "I missed you so much. I just took the next Greyhound bus. I didn't even leave downtown Columbus."

"Why didn't you call me?" Lars asked.

"Three days on the bus from Columbus. No phones on the bus." Sally had had a chance to call several times. She even stood with the phone in her hand in Las Vegas. She had dialed Lars but hung up before he could answer. In the back of her mind was the thought, *If he's screwing around. I need to know, and I need to know now.*

"It's been more than a month. You didn't seem to want to talk much on the phone. I was wondering if you found a young starlet." She finally said what she was thinking.

"I hadn't heard from you for days. I thought you started dating someone else," Lars said.

"Never," they both said together, then laughed and kissed again.

Sitting together on the sofa, the kiss became more intense. They soon spilled over onto the floor and took off each other's clothes.

Later, naked and wrapped in each other's arms. Sally's head was on Lars' chest.

"What did your mother say about you coming here?" Lars asked.

"I haven't told her yet." She petted his arm. "I haven't had time." She'd had time but was afraid of what her mother would do.

"Oh," Lars said.

"Oh, what? I'm eighteen," Sally started.

"Barely," Lars interrupted.

"Still, I'm eighteen. I can do what I want. And I want to be here." She looked at him. "Do you want me here?" She wondered if, now that she had satisfied him, did he still want her?

Lars answered her by wrapping his arms around her and giving her another passionate kiss. He became aroused again.

"I'll take that for a yes," Sally said as she came up for air. Later, they showered together, dressed, and walked across the bridge to the shopping center to a pizza parlor for dinner.

"What about nursing school," Lars asked, curious as to her plans now.

"They have a good one here at CSULB. I'll just transfer from OSU. No problem."

"Well, okay!" Lars said. "When are you going to call your mother?"

"As soon as we finish saying hello!" Sally giggled; her hand creeping higher on his leg.

*

"Hi, Mom. Sorry I didn't call sooner." Sally called her mom that evening.

"Where the hell are you? You should have gotten to school a week ago!" her mom started in "I was out of my mind with worry. They said you didn't check-in at the dorm."

"It hasn't been a week; it's been three days. And I didn't check-in at the dorm because when I was checking in at OSU, I found out I was accepted at CSULB and had to get here right away." Sally kept talking when her Mom didn't interrupt her. "You know I really want to go here."

"Humm," Sally's mom said. "And Lars had nothing to do with it?"

"Well, a little. I'll try and find him after I get a place and settle in." She winked at Lars.

"Sure. After you settle in. Sure." Sally's Mom wasn't buying it. "You know you should think your story through before you tell it."

"Really, Mom. That's my plan." Sally tried to sound sincere.

"If you had dropped the part about finding a place and settling in before you tried to find Lars, I might have believed you." Sally's mom had been eighteen once. That's how Sally came along. "Put Lars on the phone."

"Mom, really." Sally clearly was losing this charade.

"Yeah, really. Put Lars on the phone. Now!" Mom was having none of this.

"Here. Mom wants to talk to you." Sally tried to hand the phone over to Lars. Shaking the phone and her head, she got Lars reluctantly to take the phone.

"Hi, Mrs. McKelvy," was about all he got out. The conversation lasted an hour. Lars did most of the listening. At one point, he was directed to send Sally out of the room. Lars had some honest explaining to do out of Sally's hearing range. "Now remember what I said. You have an opportunity to win my trust and love. Please do that. If you don't, well, you won't like the alternative. Now put Sally on."

"Yes, Mom. I'm sorry but." Sally only got that far before she was ordered to shut up and listen.

That conversation lasted twenty minutes, again with Sally doing most of the listening.

"Sally, I love you so much. You're my life. Now please don't screw up your life because it will kill me."

"Yes, Mom. I promise. I love you too." Sally was almost relieved the conversation was almost over.

"Now, I know your eighteen, and you're in love. Be honest with Lars and demand that he be honest with you." Sally's mom had to take a minute. "If things don't work out, I'm always here for you. I love you so much. I pray your love for Lars is a forever love."

"Thank you, Mom. I know it is." Sally said.

Sally's mom knew from experience that eighteen-year-old love is rarely a forever love. But it is the most intense love you will ever experience.

*

"Hi, I'm Jody McKelvy. Are you Eve Persson?" She had driven over soon after hanging up with Sally. She wanted to find out if Lars' parents were in on this little love match. Jody knew she would find out; she was one hell of a prosecutor. She was the head DA in Atlanta.

Eve stood at the open front door, looking at an attractive woman of average-height in her late thirties. She was dressed in business attire: a gray suit, white blouse, and black leather heels.

"Hello." Eve was trying to connect the name. "Oh, you're Sally's mom, right?" she asked as the last name came to her. Then, without wasting time, she said, "Welcome. Come in." Eve stepped aside, waving Jody into her home. "I was just going to sit down with a glass of wine. Please join me."

Jody studied Eve for a moment. She was looking at a tall, attractive woman in her late forties, who had taken care of herself. She had long legs, a great figure, blue eyes, and long red hair in a ponytail. Eve had a kind, accepting, but strong face.

"I'd love to," Jody said.

Eve led the way into the library. "Have a seat." She gestured toward the long sofa.

"What's going on out there?" Jody said as she stopped. She was looking through the open French doors on to the patio, where two girls were fighting it out.

"Oh, that's Dana and Gina. My daughter is the tall one. Gina, the other one, she is like our other daughter." Eve walked over to close the doors. "They're practicing karate moves. Since the boys left, Dana has no one to spar with but me." Looking back at the girls, she said, "Frankly, she's faster and stronger than me. She has the moves."

"Why Is she wearing heels?" Jody asked, pointing at Dana.

"I don't know. She says she likes the balance." Eve shook her head. "Maybe they work for her?"

"We have all heard about the legendary Dana and the damsel Gina. But I've never seen them in person," Jody said, looking through the French doors.

"Oh? How is that?" Eve said with concern in her voice.

"I'm a prosecuting attorney. It wasn't my case. But, boy they were the talk of the office." Jody stood near the sofa.

"Really?" Eve squared off on Jody.

"She's an incredible girl. Ron and Moses's defense wanted to put them on the stand to try and throw a wrench in the case," Jody said, looking at the girls again. "We argued that it wasn't necessary. The detective. Detective Lawrence, wasn't it? His testimony and that of the arresting officers was all that was needed." Jody sat down, and Eve loosened up.

She turned and went to the small wine bar built into the bookshelves.

"I talked with Sally and Lars today," Jody said.

"Oh?" Eve said with her back turned to Jody, pouring the wine, turning with the wine glasses in her hands, she said, "And how was that?" Eve walked over to Jody; their eyes locked on one another. She handed Jody a wine glass.

Jody didn't answer the question until Eve had sat down.

"That's why I'm here now." Jody sat back a bit. "They are together in California."

"Now it makes sense," Eve said after a little thought. "A complete change of attitude on Lars's call yesterday. Lars sounded happy but elusive."

"I guess we're in this together. What do you know?" Jody took a sip from her glass.

"Not much. Lars had gone out with lots of girls. But he seemed to settle in with Sally. They were together a lot the last, oh, I guess six months or so. They didn't hang out around here much. I thought they broke up," Eve said without telling Jody that Lars left town early, just after the Fourth.

That conversation went on until seven-thirty. It included an entire bottle of wine.

"So, I'll have the twins keep an eye on them, and they will, for certain, keep me informed," Eve said.

"I guess that's all we can do," Jody said. "They're eighteen and of free will."

"I know. They are both on scholarships. So, the little control of the purse strings will go away soon," Eve pointed out.

"Yes, and if we try to separate them, we're just the bad guys." Jody was right.

"Just got to love them," Eve said.

"Yes," Jody sighed. "Just love them."

"Christopher will be home in half an hour or so. Please stay for dinner," Eve said.

"No, I should go," Jody said, setting down her empty glass.

"Please, I want you to meet my husband, and you really need to meet Dana and Gina. You'll enjoy them. Please stay." Eve was convincing.

"Okay. Are you sure I'm not going to be a bother?" Jody asked.

"Bother? No. You just might be family someday. Who knows?" Eve said as she got up and went to the patio door.

"Girls, time to shower up for dinner." Eve closed the door, then led Jody into the kitchen. "We eat dinner late here. Christopher doesn't close the gallery until eight, and we like to have dinner together.

5. IT COMES TOGETHER

The summer passed quickly. Dana's moves became quicker and more precise, in heels or barefoot. It got to the point that Eve had to take Dana up a level. She took Dana down to the dojo for the first time. “Dana, I would like you to meet Bobby Chew and Tommy Kong. They are the masters here. Bobby and Tommy, I would like to meet your next instructor, Dana.” They both gave her a slight bow.

“If you’re anything like your mom, I'm sure in a few years you'll be an instructor here," Bobby said.

“Actually, she can start teaching your black belts today," Eve said with a smile. Bobby and Tommy smiled politely.

"Give her a try," Eve said.

Tommy started to call over one of his black belts. “Why don’t you give her a try?” Eve asked again with a big smile and an emphasis on *you*.

“Well, I don’t think,” Tommy started.

“Afraid?” Eve asked quickly.

“Okay. I would only do this for you.” Tommy said, bowing to Eve. A few minutes later, Dana and Tommy were standing opposite each other. They bowed to each other. Dana waited for Tommy's advance. He just stood there in the typical judo pose. He waved her in. Ten seconds later, he was on the floor with Dana's foot on his neck.

“Tommy. What happened?” Eve asked, smiling and pulling Tommy up from the floor. “Let’s make this interesting. Dana do only Wing Chun. Bobby, want to give her a try?"

Bobby and Dana bowed. Bobby came at her with his best Taekwondo. Dana backed, ducked, and turned with her hands all the time behind her back. She did this for a full minute, then Eve lifted her pointer finger on her left hand. In one quick move, Dana grabbed his shoulder, and with a short leg move, Bobby was on the floor. Dana was above him, her palm ready to drive into his nose. Dana let him up and bowed.

It took a minute for the shock of what Dana had just accomplished to wear off. Tommy turned to Eve. "You said she can start today?"

"Yes, but she makes her own schedule. School and other things in a young teen's life. You know," Eve said, smiling. Then they all bowed. "Let's discuss salary," Eve said to the masters.

*

Their sophomore year in high school, Dana and Gina went to all the dances. Sometimes they had dates. Other times they went together. Dana was no longer the tall wallflower. She danced with those boys who would ask her. But mostly with Gina and Debbie. Debbie was not put off by Dana's tallness, and Gina made her laugh.

With the boys gone, Dana found herself at the gallery or at the dojo when Gina was at her aunt's. Christopher loved having her at the gallery. Dana soaked up the paintings, and information about the paintings and the artist, like a sponge. When Christopher was working with a client, Dana sat quietly, listening, and watching. She was trying to understand what her father called sales. It just seemed like talking to her.

Late in the spring, she had turned fifteen and loved talking to people about art. One evening, Christopher was busy in his office when one of his out-of-town regulars walked in. He finished up his work in a few minutes and went to meet his client, stopping in his tracks. He backed up and stood around the corner of the divider, just out of sight.

Dana had walked up to the client and had started a conversation about the piece of art she was looking at. Christopher was listening in as that conversation progressed.

"Yes, I love LeRoy Neiman. I think he is one of the best expressionists of our time. His bright colors and action are just awesome." Dana was standing at her side, just talking. Christopher decided to see where this went. After all, he could step in at any time. The conversation went on for quite a while.

"Oh, you live in New York," Dana said. "Do you know the Hotel Des Artist? It's on West Sixty-Seventh Street."

"Sure, on Central Park," the patron said.

"Well, LeRoy Neiman lives there with his wife." Dana fed her a little tidbit.

"Really?" she said. "I don't live far from there." She looked back at the painting. "This one would look great in my entryway. The other one over there would look good in the den. That's where my husband and I fight."

The client stood there, thinking for a minute. "Have your dad send them to me, dear." With that, she gave Dana a hug. "Be sure and let me know the next time you're in New York. We have to get together."

She began to leave. Christopher stepped in. "How are you, Mrs. Steinbrenner?"

"Wonderful. Your daughter is great! She knows her stuff, and I love talking to her," she said. "She'll show you what I want. I have got to run; George is waiting for me." With that, she was out the door and into her waiting limo.

"Wow," Christopher said, walking up to Dana. "You're quite the salesgirl."

"Thanks," Dana said then thought for a moment. "Is that all there is to sales?"

Christopher smiled. "You got the order. You get the commission. Which one did she buy?"

"This one with the sailboats." Turning, she said, "And this one with the wrestlers." Dana pointed them out.

"Both?" Christopher looked her in the eye.

"Both!" Dana looked back.

"Not the baseball one?" Christopher wondered aloud. "I would have tried to sell her that one."

"She said she had had enough of baseball. She said she didn't want any more of it in her house."

"Oh." Was all that Christopher said? He was thinking, *I would have blown it.*

"So, what's my commission?" Dana turned with her hand out.

"Before or after room and board?" Christopher laughed. Her commission was fair, what he would have paid any salesperson, and after that, Dana became a regular sales agent in the Gallery. She worked her own hours and cleaned, packed art for shipment, and sold paintings. Before long, Christopher rewarded her with her own desk.

*

"Christopher, you're going to have to eat your words. The boys are graduating," Eve said, hanging up the phone one Sunday afternoon. The twins did manage to get in their final semester and graduate. Aunt Elizabeth arranged all the flights for Christopher, Eve, Dana, Gina and Jody to Los Angeles for graduation week.

The graduation ceremony was outside on the quad. The speaker was boring. The twins secured the large patio around the pool of their condo for their graduation party.

"I never thought you guys would graduate. After all, it took you a year to complete the final semester." Christopher raised his glass. "To the graduates!"

"Congratulations," They all said, raising their glasses in a toast.

"I think we have several announcements." Beau stood with Lars.

"We go first," Beau announced. "Regency Films have offered us a four-year contract to make films."

"Fantastic!" Christopher raised his glass again. "To the new film stars. See, I told you that you had to get your degrees to get a good job."

"Yes, Dad." Lars and Beau rolled their eyes. "Now, for the good part. We're moving to Singapore. That's where the film company is based."

"Okay." Eve was the first one to speak up. "That's wonderful. I'll miss you a lot. But what a great opportunity."

Everyone excitedly talked over each other. There were lots of questions, and few answers beyond "The studio is taking care of that."

After the talk started to die down, Beau stood up and raised his hand for everyone to look his way. "Now, Lars, you have the floor." He gave a sweeping jester bowing, giving Lars the stage.

Lars stood up and took Sally by the hand, and they stood face to face. Lars dropped to one knee and took out a small box.

"Sally McKelvy. Will you marry me?" Lars opens the box to show her a ring.

"Of course, yes," Sally said.

"Sally!" Jody quickly and loudly said and looked at Eve.

Jody stood up. Eve stood up also. They both approached the couple. Standing in front of their kids, they drew long breaths.

Arms came out as they pulled their kids to them, kissed them, and said, "Congratulations!"

Everyone stood and surrounded the couple, clapping, kissing, and hugging.

Tears were running freely down Jody and Eve's faces.

"Welcome to the family," Christopher said, giving Sally a bear hug.

"Yes. Welcome to the family," Jody also said, reaching out for Lars.

"Well, that went off better than rehearsed," Lars said.

Eve slapped Lars's arm. "You knew?" she said, then looked at Dana.

"We just found out yesterday," Dana said, pointing at Gina.

"He actually proposed last week," Sally said, "But we wanted to do it in front of you all."

"Have you picked a date?" Christopher asked, again hugging Sally.

6. CARS AND CHANGES

"Driver's license issued by the State of Georgia," Gina goaded as she waved her driver's license in Dana and Aunt Elizabeth's face. Aunt Elizabeth and Dana for the last two hours had been sitting in the hard chairs provided by the Georgia Department of Motor Vehicles. They were happy for Gina, happier still to be getting out of that building.

Walking out of the building rubbing her numb backside, Dana said, "Cool. Now we can go get some martinis."

"Dana!" Aunt Elizabeth said, shaking her head.

"Well, she has a driver's license. That's all bartenders ask for," Dana joked.

"They ask for your driver's license to check your birth date." Aunt Elizabeth didn't get the joke.

"Oh, I knew that." Both Dana and Gina were giggling. "Congratulations sweetie," Dana said, giving her another squeeze. "By the way, you get to plant your butt in this chair. That particular chair there, in just three weeks, when I get mine."

"Let's go get something to eat. I'm starved," Gina said. "Let's go to that Russian place I've heard so much about."

Aunt Elizabeth put out her hand for the keys.

"Really? Auntie, can't I drive?" Gina asked.

"Let me see your license." Aunt Elizabeth held out her other hand. "Hmm, old enough to drive. But not to drink! So, I don't have to worry about DUIs." Aunt Elizabeth smiled and opened the driver's door, inviting Gina to drive.

After that, Gina got to drive the 85' Trans Am when Aunt Elizabeth was out of town, but only if she took her to the airport and picked her up.

Dana passed her driver's test, waving her license in Gina's face. Dana drove them to the Russian restaurant for their now traditional celebration lunch.

Dana didn't get a car. Christopher needed his vehicle at the gallery. Eve's hours varied so much that she needed her Nova with her at most times.

"Hi, Ms. McKelvy," Gina said as she opened the front door. "Come in." Then she called to Eve, "Mrs. Persson, Ms. McKelvy is here."

Eve came around the corner from the library, her arms open. "Hi, Jody." As they hugged each other, she said, "Wine, of course." As she showed Jody into the library, she said, "Guess what? I talked to Lars and Sally yesterday. They are in Barcelona. It looks like they are going to stay awhile." Eve turned and handed Jody a glass of wine.

"I talked to them yesterday too. I guess they just set time aside to call us." Jody thought for a second. "Maybe we should set this up as a conference call. That way it would cost less and more importantly, we will know when they are going to call."

"Great. No more missed calls. That sounds like a wonderful idea. How do we set that up?" Eve was all in.

"I'll take care of it. We do three-way calling all the time at work." Jody settled in. She then turned her attention to the two girls fighting in the backyard. "Am I wrong or is Gina getting better?"

"For sure. Dana is a good sensei. Gina has learned to never give up. That's a good thing." Eve settled in with her wine.

"Actually, I'm here for a reason." Jody took a deep breath. "Ron and Moses are up for parole. We just heard it today from a court clerk. My contact said it hasn't happened yet."

"When?" Eve asked.

"In the next month probably. I would like for you and Elizabeth to do a write-up. You know, on how dangerous they are. And how it might affect your daughter and Gina if they are let out early." Jody was very serious.

"What good would that do? They got ten to fifteen. It's only been four years since they went to prison. Why are they even being allowed a parole hearing?" Eve asked.

"The feds are encouraging the states to reduce the prison population. I hear that they have been good in jail. So they get a shot at early parole." Jody was clearly frustrated.

"Okay, I'll talk to Elizabeth. You'll have your letter by the end of the week." Eve drained her glass. She reached for the bottle and started to refill their drinks.

"The truth is, it probably won't help," Jody said. Eve stopped in mid-pour. "We are on the outside and have no standing. We just heard about it by chance. We asked to testify. I don't have much hope." Jody was shaking her head. "It's all politics. It's all shit."

Eve finished pouring the wine. They both sat quietly, thinking about what to do. They were quiet for quite a while.

"Ah. You're staying for dinner of course. Christopher will be home in forty-five minutes or so." Eve took a sip of her wine and stood up. "Do me a favor and call the girls in and tell them to clean up. I'm going to call Elizabeth and leave a message for her to call me. She has a London, Rome, and somewhere trip. I don't know when she'll get the message and have a chance to call me back."

*

Elizabeth called the next evening. She was in between flights in Berlin and only had time for a brief outline. She called back at four in the morning from Rome. They talked for an hour. Elizabeth got home from her trip two days later.

*

"I don't know?" Gina said into the phone to Dana. "She won't let me go to school. She's been on the phone nonstop. She's acting really weird."

"I'm coming over." Dana was about to hang up the phone.

"No. Wait. Let me ask her. Just a sec." Dana tried to hear what was going on while Gina talked to her aunt. "She said tomorrow after school. I still can't go to school. I got to go now. Auntie wants to use the phone." Gina blew Dana a kiss and hung up. Dana was even more worried than before she called.

Dana then called the hospital and asked for her mom. "Mom, Gina's aunt is acting weird. She won't let Gina go to school or let me come over."

"Stay in the house. I'll be right home," Eve said and hung up.

Eve checked the roads and around the house. She even drove around the block checking things out. When Eve got home, she sat Dana down and went over what Jody had told her.

Eve reached for the phone. "Elizabeth. What's up? Can we come over?"

"I don't know?" Looking over at a scared and depressed Gina, "Well ok, I guess."

Eve knocked on Elizabeth's door, with Dana standing behind her. "What's up? Is this about Ron?" Eve asked as soon as the door opened.

"Come in." Then Elizabeth all but dragged Eve and Dana through the door, then she checked the outside before shutting the door. They were standing in a nearly stripped room full of boxes. All the shades and curtain were drawn shut. Gina ran, crying into Dana's arms crying.

"What's going on?" Eve asked as Elizabeth took her by the arm and led her into the kitchen.

"Gina, take Dana to your room," Elizabeth called out. Eve sat at the kitchen table. Elizabeth searched the kitchen for clean glasses and set them on the table next to an already open bottle of bourbon.

Elizabeth started to pour the bourbon, but her hands were shaking so much that Eve took the bottle gently from her and poured. Elizabeth sat and covered her face with her hands.

"We're moving," Elizabeth finally said, looking up.

"So soon? What's the hurry? You got at least a month before Ron gets paroled," Eve said.

"Because Ron did get paroled. Jody was wrong. They already let him out. At least a week ago." Her shaking hand held her glass, but she did not drink.

"Wait. How do you know?" Eve asked.

"Because my sister is dead. She was killed. I know that fucker Ron killed her, I know. The Tampa police called just as I got home. They said they didn't know who killed her, but Ron was a suspect. I know that fucker Ron killed her." In a loud whisper, she added, "I know he did it. Now he's on his way here to kill Gina. To kill me. Maybe Dana. I don't know. The bastard is crazy."

Eve sat in shocked silence. As it settled into her brain, "I'm so sorry." Eve reached across for Elizabeth's hand.

"I know that crazy son of a bitch is coming after Gina and me. So we're moving. We're going somewhere that even if he knows where we are, we will still be safe." Elizabeth took a deep breath and a sip of her bourbon. "I got a transfer to our London base. It took some work and a lot of explaining, but we're moving Saturday."

"How is Gina taking this?" Eve asked.

"It's been rough on her, but Ron's after her more than me." Elizabeth looked around the room with boxes and everything laying around, waiting to be packed. "What I can't take, I'll give to the Goodwill. If they'll come to pick it up."

"Don't worry about it. I'll make all the arrangements. You just do what you got to do," Eve said.

"Is it okay if I give the Trans Am to Dana? Please. Elizabeth asked. Gina will like that."

When Elizabeth and Eve entered Gina's bedroom, Dana and Gina were in each other's arms, crying.

"Is it alright if Gina spends the night with us?" Eve asked.

"No! Absolutely not."

"Auntie please?" Gina begged.

Elizabeth looked at Eve, shaking her head. "It's going to take me two days to get everything organized and sent off. Gina is not much help right now." After thinking for a moment, she said, "Eve, can you do me a giant favor?"

"Sure. What?" Eve said. It was settling into her head that she was losing one of her daughters. Also, Dana was losing even more than a sister. She was losing her lover.

"Take the girls to the Hilton near Perimeter Mall. I get an airline discount there. Ron would never think of going there. Get two rooms. One for the girls and one for you and Christopher. Please." Elizabeth was begging. "Please. I'll pay for everything. Please, can you stay with them? Please."

"What about you? Are you going to be safe?"

"If I don't have to worry about Gina, I can take care of myself." Elizabeth reached behind her and placed her 9 mm Glock on the table.

Elizabeth and Gina packed a small bag, then they rushed to Dana's and packed for the hotel. They had checked into the Hilton by six. Dana and Gina were in bed by eight o'clock. Christopher joined Eve in the hotel bar at about the same time. Jody was on her way. It took several dirty martinis for Eve to explain the situation to Jody and Christopher.

"Maybe we should take a vacation? Maybe go to London? Maybe next week?" Christopher said mostly off the cuff.

"Not a bad idea. Give me a few days to find out what I can from the courts. They have got to be on parole. If so, we should be able to track them down." Jody face settled into s somber frown.

"Let's go further. Let's go to Singapore. See the twins," Eve said, looking to Christopher for agreement.

Saturday, Dana and Eve saw Elizabeth and Gina off at the airport. Dana would not see Gina again for almost two decades.

*

The following week, Eve, Dana, and Christopher left for three weeks in Singapore. It was a relaxing stress-free, three weeks for Eve and Christopher. Dana was quiet and depressed most of the time. She felt a hollow place in her heart that Gina had filled. The zoo and gardens did help her mood. By the time they headed back home, Dana had regained her smile and a healthy attitude.

Two months later, on a Saturday night, Eve arranged for dinner at the Russian restaurant. They all came in separate cars, Christopher from the gallery, Eve from the hospital, and Dana drove over in her inherited Trans Am.

After dinner, Eve kissed Christopher in the parking lot. "Love you, honey," she said.

"Love you too," Christopher said.

Eve followed Dana home. Dana parked in front of the house. As she parked, a car door across the street opened. A man got out with a shotgun.

Eve saw the man and sped up. He fired a shot at Dana's car. Eve hit the man and the car's open door with her left front fender, flipping the man into the air. He landed in front of his car on his head, dead.

Dana's driver's door would not open, having taken the full force of the shotgun blast. She crawled across the front seat to the passenger door.

Eve came to a full stop, brakes screeching. Looking behind her, she saw three men get out of the car with their guns blazing. Eve slammed her car in reverse, hitting the gas. They hit Eve in the left side of her neck, then again on the left side of her head. Her car drifted off, jumping the curb and hitting a tree.

By the time Dana got out of her car, and before she could cross the street, the men jumped back into their beat-up Chevrolet, even though it was now missing a door. They sped off, running over the dead man in front of their car.

Dana ran to the Nova and opened her mother's door. Eve fell sideways out of the car, bleeding, and unconscious. Dana pulled her the rest of the way out of the car and laid her on the lawn.

"Mom, Mom. Come on, Mom," Dana cried through her tears.

*

Eve laid in her hospital bed, her head and neck heavily bandaged. Tubes ran into her nose and mouth, and more tubes were in both arms. Wires were plugged into her everywhere, and three machines painted jagged lines on dark screens. They beeped every few seconds.

Christopher had sat for the last four days, holding his wife's hand. Every few hours, he would give her a kiss on the lips. Dana sat on the other side of her bed, holding her mother's other hand. She and her father didn't talk much.

Lars and Sally arrived first. Sally tried to get Christopher and Dana to go home. "Get some rest," she begged, but they were not leaving their mother and wife. Lars and Beau came in the next day.

A few hours later, the doctor called them into a separate room. He explained that the head wound had caused her brain to swell. Her brain had just stopped working. The machines were breathing for her and were pumping her heart. The most humane thing for them to do was to let her go.

They all kissed Eve goodbye.

7. SO, IT STARTS

Eve's four children stood on the mat, Bo staffs in hand. Looking over at the empty throne, they felt their mother sitting watching them ready for them to start.

They bowed to their mother, then to each other. They took their positions. Dana was fierce. Moving quickly, she dropped Beau in seconds. She lodged her Bo staff under Lars' arm, He grabbed it. Dana left it, turning to Axel. She took Lars's Bo staff in her forearm and dropped him with a clean ankle sweep. Dana moved quickly back toward Lars, placing her hand on his throat. He dropped both Bo staffs and bowed. The whole match had taken less than a minute. They bowed together, then fell into each other's arms, tears running down their cheeks. The funeral was that afternoon.

*

Two days after the funeral, Lars and Sally flew back to Barcelona. The next day, the twins left for Hollywood for a few days before heading back to Singapore.

A week later, the Nova with a smashed-in front fender stopped in front of Jody's house. As soon as Dana stepped through the front door, she asked, "Do you know where Ron is?"

"I'm doing fine," Jody said sarcastically. She led the way into the living room.

"What do you know? Tell me," Dana said.

"Sit, please." Dana took the seat nearest Jody. "I'm not allowed to tell the victim's family anything at this point. Understand?"

"How about family? There are no secrets between family." Dana gave Jody a smile designed to put her at ease. "Please. I just want to make sure my dad is safe. And of course, I need to know where I should be cautious."

"Well," Jody said, looking away from Dana's piercing eyes. "Just between family. The guy who got killed was part of a drug gang ran by a guy in Miami named Carlos. They hang out down around Sylvan Hills. In the stolen car, we found fingerprints that were Ron's, Moses', the dead guy's, and another guy's named Duston Hommer. Ron and Moses broke probation, of course. They most likely left the state. But if the cops anywhere happen to run across them, they will be arrested." Jody added, "That's just between family." She changed the subject. "Now, how's your dad?"

"Quiet," Dana said, shaking her head. "Really quiet."

"Now that you know what I know, what are you going to do? You're not going to do anything stupid?"

"No, no. I guess those guys are out of the state. Nothing much to worry about, I guess. I'll just keep watch." Dana cataloged everything in her head.

"I'm going to dinner with a cop friend of mine. Please join us," Jody asked.

"No. Thanks anyway," Dana answered.

"It's a cop. This one knows everything, I'm told. Please come." Jody hit Dana in her soft spot.

"Well, okay. Where are we going?" Dana asked.

"Downtown to Nikolai's Roof. It's in the Hilton. I'll drive." Jody started to lead the way to the door.

"Am I dressed okay? Sounds kind of classy." Dana checked herself out.

"You're young, tall, and beautiful. You could be wearing flip-flops and a sack, and you would fit in anywhere. Come on." Jody waved her out the door.

The maître d' showed them to their table by a large window in the far corner of the room. It had a great view of downtown Atlanta to the north and Stone Mountain to the east. The cop was already sitting at the table. She was fiftyish, with brunet hair cut square, just above her shoulders. She had green eyes that were set off by her green dress. She showed some cleavage. She had a martini in front of her that had hardly been touched.

Jody gave her a kiss on the cheek. It was returned. Dana held out her hand. As they were shaking hands, Jody did the introductions. "Dana, I would like you to meet Chief of Police Mason Janson. Mason,

I would like you to meet Dana Persson." Dana was a bit taken aback but held her composure. "Dana is my daughter's husband's sister. So, I'm thinking, but I could be wrong. Dana's my stepdaughter once removed. I think?"

"So, you're the famous Godzilla," Mason asked, breaking the ice.

"I guess I am. I can't seem to get away from that nickname," Dana said. "And you're the police chief. I'm just wondering—I don't mean to be rude, but do I call you Chief Janson or Ms. Janson?"

"Honey, when I'm in uniform, I'm Chief Janson. When I'm not, like tonight, I'm Mason... I know about your mother. I am so sorry for your loss."

"Thank you," Dana said, turning her head away and holding back tears. "Well, so, what are the police doing about it?"

"Everything possible." Mason gave the stock police answer.

"Really? What specifically are you doing about it, and what can I do to help?" Dana pressed the issue.

Mason sat back, studying Dana's face. She then looked at Jody.

"I told her almost everything. Sorry." Jody came clean.

"You can help by keeping out of the way," Mason said. Her eyes fixed on Dana's.

"I intend to. I just want to protect my dad. Chief," Dana lied.

"Okay, enough police work. We're here to enjoy ourselves," Jody said. Mason and Dana got the hint.

The dinner started off a bit frosty. Dana saw the signs that Jody and Mason were more than just friends. She leaned back and relaxed a bit. Throughout the meal, Dana measured Mason and counted her as honest. Maybe that and Mason's relationship with Jody was why she was so comfortable with them. Near the end of the evening, Mason gave Dana her card. She wrote her private number on the back. "If you ever need my help, give me a call."

Dana took out her Persson Gallery business card and wrote her number on the back. "If you ever need my help, give me a call."

Dana now had a loose plan. The next day, she took her inherited Trans Am to the shop. Not just any shop, but to Eddie's Speed Shop. After crawling across the seat to the passenger door. Taking in her surroundings, she saw the office on one side. It was small cluttered and dirty. A heavy man with what might have been described, at one time, as a beard, sat in a well-worn wooden desk chair.

"Hi," Dana said, taking in her surroundings. As the man turned in his chair, Dana noticed the name on his shirt. "Eddie. I would like you to do some work on my car."

Looking Dana up and down, he guessed that the job would not be in his area of expertise. He got up anyway and walked with Dana out of the office. Seeing the black Trans Am with the caved-in driver's door with nine bullet holes, he turned to Dana. "Take it to a body shop." He turned to leave.

"I need more," Dana called after him. He just kept walking off.

"Godzilla! Sorry. Dana," a young man called out and ran up to her.

"Oh, hi, Tommy," Dana said.

Eddie stopped and turned. "You're Godzilla?" he said. Tommy was Eddies, son. He was in the shop learning the trade. The three of them stood and chatted for a bit.

"You know bodywork is not what we do here," Eddie said.

"I know. But Tommy said you can make a car breathe fire. Can you do that?" Dana looked at Eddie.

"I sure can." Eddie looked at the car and then Dana.

"Then fix it. Make it breathe fire and roar. And make it not shiny, but black," Dana said.

"Not shiny." Eddie nodded. "Breathe fire and roar. Right up my line of business. A badass car. Now that I can do. Keys." Eddie held out his hand. "Tommy, take her home. See you in two weeks." Eddie was smiling.

Two weeks later, just after dark, Eddie explained everything he had done to the Trans Am. The paint job was just a coat of clear dull paint that made it not shine. It was still black. Eddie had taken off all the names and badges. No horse. No chrome at all. The grill was painted a flat black.

Dana only asked, "Does it breathe fire? Does it roar? Is it fast?"

"Fastest Trans Am in Atlanta. Hell, in Georgia. Maybe anywhere but a drag strip. And then I would not bet against her," Eddie said with a smile. "Tommy, get in and light her up." The engine rumbled to life like it was mad at the world.

"See. Hear that? Just a quiet rumble. I doubled the mufflers. But see here, just behind the front tires and low to the ground, see that pipe? Stand back. Tommy, flip the switch and give her some gas."

When Tommy hit the gas, it roared like a lion. A crazy angry lion and it spit fire like a dragon.

"You did it. Oh, yes. Way better than I thought possible," Dana said, dancing around the car.

Dana gave Eddie a kiss on the cheek and Tommy a big hug as he got out of the car. On the way home, Dana found a dark, quiet, empty street. She flipped the switch and hit the gas. She smiled all the way home.

Dana kept her school time at a minimum. She spent at least an hour a day teaching at the dojo in Buckhead. She only taught black belts. The rest of her time was spent at the gallery. Her dad let her do most of the work when she was there. He sat in the chair by the little table near the window.

Dana started bringing dinner to the gallery. That minimized her evening time at home. When they got home, Christopher began drinking, not wine.

It didn't take long for her to get her timing down. She was usually out of the house by ten. She started cruising, in her mother's Nova, around Sylvan Hills on her night trips. Her circle gradually expanded, looking for signs of gangs. Guys standing on corners with nothing to do and wearing heavy gold chains.

She became good at spotting hookers hawking their wares and the homeless sleeping in doorways. Everything was recorded on her map. She saw very few cops; that was fine with her.

If Christopher noticed her going out late at night, he didn't say anything.

After over ten trips into Sylvan Hills, Dana started to make her move.

She dressed like a hooker for a trial night cruising around Sylvan Hills. She wore her red stilettos, red minidress, a red wig in braids, and heavy make-up. This time, she took the black Trans Am, parking near Pete's Bar, the place she had picked out as being a place where people went to buy drugs.

"Hey. You Pete?" she called to the bartender standing at the far end of the bar as she walked up to the bar. Then she answered the guy standing next to her, "Sorry honey. I'm off the clock."

"What? No, I'm Richard. Let me guess vodka." The bartender walked over, looking her up and down.

Thinking quickly, Dana said, "No. What kind of girl do you think I am? Champagne. By the way, I'm new in town. I was told to find a guy named Duston something. Know him?"

"Maybe." He said, pouring her flat champagne and looking at her cleavage. "What's in it for me?"

"You'll have to ask Duston," Dana answered, taking a sip of her champagne. "Well, whatever. I'm tired and bored. I'm headed back to my room." Dana turned and headed for the door.

"Hey, that's ten dollars," the bartender called after her.

Dana just flipped him the finger over her shoulder and kept right on walking out the door. When she got in the car, her hands were shaking so badly, it took both of her hands to get the key in the ignition. She then lit up the street, leaving rubber, noise, and fire behind.

8. THAT WAS EASY

On the third night, she dressed as before. At eleven o'clock she parked next to a squad car sitting out front of the 7-Eleven. She got out and, swinging her hips way more than usual, she stepped into the 7-Eleven and bought a pack of Marlboros. No questions were asked. The cops waved and smiled as she got back into the Trans Am.

At the bar, she walked in, tapping down her pack of cigarettes.

"Hey," she called to the bartender.

"You owe me ten bucks, bitch," he called back.

"Put it on my tab, Dick," Dana said.

"No, it's Richard."

"Same difference. So where is my champagne?" She was slowly peeling back the paper on her cigarettes. The cigarettes were her prop, meant to make her look older and more like a hooker. But it was also the part she was most unsure of. She had never smoked. She was sure she would do it wrong and show her hand, so she went through the ritual as slowly as possible, mimicking what she had seen in the movies.

She felt a tap on her shoulder. Dana turned around with a *whatever* look on her face.

"I hear you're looking for me, bitch," Duston said, looking her up and down, settling on her tits.

"I am. If you're Duston?" She studied him for a second. *Yeah*, she thought, *he was one of them that night.*

"I could be." Duston tried to play the game.

"Well, if you're not, get lost." She took a deep, frustrated breath and started to turn around.

"I'm Duston. What do you want?" he finally answered.

"Well, I was told you could hook me up with some guys who need some of my supplies." She fiddled with her cigarette pack. "You know. From Miami. Carlos sent me."

"Hmm, is that all you're selling?" Duston was looking at her long, slim body.

"Maybe," Dana said, running her hand along her leg. "You're kind of short for me."

"Not everywhere," he said, rubbing his crotch.

"Okay. But you're not the guy I need. I need your boss. Ronny something," Dana said, turning her back to him.

"He's not the boss. I run things," Duston said.

"That's not what Carlos said," Dana said, turning back to Duston. "Well, anyway. I need to get things rolling. This town is boring. Can we go someplace to discuss business?"

"Yeah, sure. Follow me." They walked out of the bar and down the street. As they passed by an alley, he pushed her in and up against the wall. He pressed his body up against hers and grabbed her ass.

Dana grabbed his balls and squeezed them hard. With her other hand, she pinched a vein in his neck. "Fun and games are over. Carlos wants me to talk to Ronny. So where is he?"

"Okay. Let go. Jesus. He's at the house," he said.

"Good. Now we're getting along. I like that." She let go of his neck and his balls. "Come on, honey. Where is this house?" she cooed, putting her arms around his neck and stroking his hair. "Where?" she asked again.

"Browns Mill Road near the elementary school." He reached up for her right tit.

"Figures," Dana said. She pushed him away. He tried to grab her, but she backed down the alley, getting further from the street and deeper into the dark alley.

He came after her and tried to grab her. She slapped him. He tried to slap her back. She stepped back, raising a hand and breaking his little finger. "Fuck," he hissed and tried to punch her with his other hand. She pushed it aside and at the same time slapped his ear hard with a cupped hand, causing maximum damage.

"Fucking bitch. You fucking red bitch," he said as he reached behind his back and took his gun out of his belt. He stuck it in her face, inches from her nose.

"Mistake," Dana said. She quickly twisted his hand and moved the gun away. Holding his hand, she kicked him in the chest with her six-inch red stilettos. Her spiked-heel broke through his ribs and sunk into his heart. He had a shocked look on his face as he looked down, then back up at her.

She pulled out her heel, releasing the blood to flow down his chest. She watched him fall to his knees.

"Your first mistake was killing my mother." She pushed him over, dead.

Dana stopped at the 7-Eleven next to the same squad car. She bought a Coke. She waved at the cops as she got into her car. They smiled and waved back. They might not have noticed the blood on her leg and red stiletto.

*

"Don't be late for school." Christopher tapped on Dana's door.

"I'm up," Dana said. The lying was becoming easier, especially when it had a purpose. "See you at the gallery this afternoon," she called back to him.

She needed another hour's sleep. She wasn't going to get it. First, she wondered about what had happened just a few hours ago. Killing someone was not supposed to be easy. But it was. Especially when someone so needed killing. Duston needed killing. *One down, Mom,* she thought. Then Dana started going over what she had learned. *Now I have to develop a plan,* she thought.

If Ron and Moses missed Duston for some reason, they might go looking for him. I'm sure they would go to that bar. What was the earliest that could happen? Tonight, that's the earliest. So, whatever I do, I do it today. No nerves, no doubt, no hesitation. I must follow my training; the training Mom gave me. Draw them in, find their weak points, take advantage. A sexy girl brings out all the weak points in men. Use that. The end result is I kill them.

Dana showered and dressed in her red minidress, red spiked heels, and her red wig. This time, she took it up a notch with a red garter belt and red hose. The straps on the garter belt came down just below her skirt. Dana inspected herself in the mirror. What did Duston call her? "You Red Bitch." *I like that better than Godzilla,* she thought.

Dana backed the Trans Am out of the garage. When she got out to shut the garage door, she saw a squad car cruising down her street. Did he see her? Too late to worry about that.

The house on Browns Mill Road was an old run-down shotgun house from a century ago. A shotgun house is one story, and only about twelve feet wide. They are all laid out the same.

Dana drove up and parked her Trans Am in front of the house like she owned the place.

She didn't knock; she just walked in the front door. Two big men were lounging in the front room, watching television. Both thugs stood up. They both had 9 mm Glocks stuffed in the front of their belts.

Dana took off her sunglasses to reveal bloodshot eyes, a badge in the drug world. In Dana's case, it was just a lack of sleep.

"Who are you?" one of them asked.

"What's it to you? Anyway, Carlos sent me." Dana took her snootiest attitude.

"Who's Carlos? And who are you?" The other thug asked, stepping forward.

"I'm Red. You haven't heard of me? Duston said I could meet Ronny here. You know? Do some business."

"Duston ain't here," the lead thug said.

"I know that! Call him." Dana crossed her arms and tapped her foot. "He's probably at that fucking bar."

The other thug picked up the phone and dialed the bar. He talked to the bartender for a few minutes. He learned that a bitch in red met Duston there and they went off to do some business. That was enough.

"So, Right this way." He was all of six feet two and two hundred and seventy pounds. He winked at his partner, as he followed her down the hall.

He opened the first door for Dana. It only had an unmade bed in the small room. He picked her up and threw her on the bed.

"Oh. It's that way?" Dana said with a smile. "You sure? I'm deadly in bed."

"Oh yeah, bitch," he said as he put his gun on a small dresser under the window and unbuckled his belt.

Dana spread her legs and pulled them up to her chest. Smiling, the thug dropped his pants. As he bent over her, she kicked hard with her right foot. She felt his ribs break as the steel spike of her heel sink into his heart. He managed to throw a punch to the side of her head. It didn't have any force behind it. With her other foot, she shoved him off onto the floor. He had the same shocked look on his face that Duston had. He looked down as blood gushed out of his chest. "You red bitch" was the last thing he said. Then he died.

Dana got up off the bed. Looking down at the thug, she said, "You know you should take a girl out to dinner before you try to screw her. Oh well, lesson learned."

"Hey," she called to the other thug in the living room. "I'm too much for him. Want to help?" As he smiled and got up and walked around the corner, she threw a palm up into his nose, breaking it. A second punch drove the broken bone up into his brain. He fell dead on his face.

There was a mirror on the wall in the hallway. Dana stopped, pulled down her skirt, fluffed up her hair, and checked her makeup. She passed the bathroom and saw that the door was closed.

As she entered the kitchen, she saw three men. Moses was the furthest. It only took Dana two steps into the room for Moses to recognize her.

"Oh shit," Moses said and headed for the back door. "Kill her," he called back to the other two.

There was a butcher knife on the counter next to her. She picked it up and threw it at Moses. It hit Moses in the back of his right leg, and he went down. The guy next to her threw a punch, hitting Dana on the side of her face. She threw a chop to his throat, crushing his windpipe as he went down to his knees. She threw a quick knee to his head that snapped his neck. He fell over. The other guy came at her with a pair of scissors. She picked up a Bunsen burner and jammed it up into his jaw, flames going to his brain. That look of shock again, she thought. Well, what did he expect?

Moses was now up and limping out the door to the small porch. Dana caught up to him and kicked him in the back of his other leg. He went down on his face. She dropped a knee into his back, keeping him from moving. She pulled the knife out of his leg, giving it a twist as she did it.

"I see you remember me. Kind of like the last time. But, oh. You don't have a gun this time."

Moses turned his head to see her over his shoulder.

"You should not have killed my mother." Dana then slit his throat.

Ron pulling up his pants as he came out of the bathroom to see what all the yelling and commotion was all about. He had left his gun in the kitchen. The thug on the floor in the hallway was lying dead on his gun, and Ron didn't see it.

Ron first saw Dana on Moses back. He didn't recognize her. Realizing where his gun was, he turned and ran to the front door. "I'll get you, you red bitch," He yelled back as he jumped off the front porch.

Dana saw him as he turned and ran. By the time she finished with Moses and ran to the front porch, Ron was nowhere to be seen. "Red bitch? That's what Duston called me. I like that."

Dana walked back into the kitchen. There were three unopened plastic blocks, maybe a kilo each, and some white power in bowls on the table.

"Well, you wanted it so much. Here you go." She took the scissors out of the dead man's hand. Walking around the house, she dumped the white power on the dead men's bodies. Then she took a towel off the table and wiped down anything she had touched. As she was leaving, on the counter, she saw a pile of money. Next to it was a paper bag with more money inside.

"We can't just leave money laying around," Dana said, putting the cash in the paper bag and she left the house. In the Trans Am, she dumped the paper bags in the backseat. Flipping the switch, she announced her exit.

Dana was on automatic after that. She drove home and put the Trans Am in the garage, on the porch she sat in the chair next to the throne, inspecting the blood on her stilettos, her legs, dress, and hands. She touched the bruise on her cheek and looked at the empty throne, wishing she could see her mother.

"That's two down, Mom." She hung her head and cried.

*

"Hi, Dad," Dana said as she entered the gallery. Christopher was sitting at the small table near the window. Dana looked down to see a bottle of red wine and a half-full glass. Christopher never drank by himself at work. Only if he had a high-value client, and then it was mostly champagne or maybe white wine.

"Where were you today?" he asked, not looking up. He just continued looking out the window.

"Where? At home. I was tired and a little depressed," Dana said, sitting down.

"The school called. Said you weren't there today." He looked at her for an answer.

"Like I said, I was at home. By the time I got going, I had found I had an afternoon to kill." She tried to be a little bit honest.

"What's that on the side of your face?" Christopher said, pointing to the heavy makeup by her left eye.

"Oh, this?" Dana said, touching her bruise. "I was doing some martial arts moves, and well, I was a little off-balance. I need more practice. Are you expecting someone?" Dana asked, pointing to the glass of wine.

"No," Christopher said, taking a sip of his wine.

"You know, Dad, the traffic hasn't been so great lately." Christopher just looked out the window. "Why don't we get an artist and some of his paintings? Do a little advertising. Get some people in to meet the artist. Maybe do something at the Russian restaurant. You know, like we used to."

"Okay," Christopher said, still looking out the window.

"Really?" Dana said, a little excited.

"No," Christopher said, still just looking out the window.

"Dad, we got to talk. I'm almost seventeen. I'm going to be graduating from school in a year. I am trying to work here. What do you want me to do?" Dana was frustrated.

Christopher looked over at her. He tapped the table with his fingers. "I want you to go to college. Meet a nice man and give me grandbabies. That's all I want from you." He turned his head back to the window.

"Fine, let's not talk," Dana nearly shouted, stomping out of the room.

*

Two nights later, Dana was able to slip out of the house. Backing her Trans Am out of the garage, she saw the police cruiser passing by. Again? She thought. Something might be going on. *Just be careful*, Dana warned herself.

She drove down to Selvin Hills. The only thing different was that the gang bangers on the corner turned and watched her black Trans Am until she disappeared. They never did that before.

Dana then drove past the house on Browns Mill road. It had yellow tape all around. A police van and squad car were parked out front.

When she got to the bar, she parked out front. The bartender saw her walking through the door. He came over a lot quicker than before.

"Hi, Red. Champagne?" He reached down, coming up with one of those single pour bottles.

"Why not?" Dana said, looking around the room.

"Did you hear? They found Duston dead." The bartender poured her a glass.

"So?" Dana said in a bored tone.

"They found him in an alley about a block from here." The bartender waited for a comment.

Dana put her leg up on the foot rail. She turned sideways to the bartender. "Really? That's about where we finished our business," She said, looking around, distracted.

Turning back to the bar, she put both elbows on the bar, showing cleavage. "By the way, I'm trying to get in touch with Ronny. What's-his-name told me where to find him."

"Duston. That was his name," the bartender said.

"Oh yeah. Duston. Anyway, Duston said I could get him at that house on Browns Mill Road. I just drove by there. Cops all over the place. Must have been some kind of a bust. Anyway, I didn't stop. So, do you know where Ronny is?"

"No. Really no. No idea." The bartender wasn't lying.

"He wasn't arrested, was he?" Dana asked.

"No. I don't think so. I would have been told. I haven't heard." The bartender was backing off a bit.

"Well. Okay. I guess I need to find another buyer," Dana said. "Know any?"

"I'll ask around." The bartender saw some bucks coming his way.

"Don't bother. I'll just ask Carlos." Dana turned away from the bar.

"Next time you're in, I'll have someone for you," the bartender said as she walked out the door. "No charge, Red. On the house. Anytime." The bartender nearly bowed. "Tell Carlos we're cool. Okay?" he called after the red bitch.

Dana turned at the door and took a long look at the bartender. Her eyes narrowed. "Next time I see you, I want to know where Ronny is." She waved her arm around the bar. "Nice place. I'd like to see you keep it that way."

On her way out of Selvan Hills, she stopped at the corner where the gangbangers hung out. It was nearly midnight. They all turned to look at the rumbling black Trans Am. Dana rolled down the window and waved for them to come over.

They came over to the car, the boss in front with two others just behind him and to either side.

"What are you selling?" Dana asked.

"Nothing you don't have already," he answered, leaning over hands in his pockets.

"Hmm. Who do you buy it from? Ronny?" Dana asked.

"No, he's gone," he said.

"Do you know where I can find him?" she asked.

He shook his head.

"So, who's stepping up?" Dana probed his eyes.

"Nobody yet. But when they do, I'll tell them the Red Bitch is looking for them." With that, he turned away. Dana flipped the switch. She didn't jump on it. Instead, she let the loud rumble and small red flame do the talking for her. They all watched as the black Trans Am drove off.

"The Red Bitch was not to be fooled with" was the message she got that night. If anyone came after her, they would use all the power they had.

Dana went back a week later. She had the same results, except they all called her *Red*. If someone didn't recognize her, they were quickly whispered to. "She's the Red Bitch. You don't want to fuck with her."

*

Three weeks after the drug house hit, Dana got a call in the Gallery. "Dana. This is Chief Jenson. Mason would like to meet you this Saturday. Just you and Mason. Okay?" That was the clue that anything said would be off the record. Still, Mason was a cop and not to be trusted.

"Okay. Where? When? And why?" Dana answered.

"First, At Stone Mountain, at the food stand. Second, at one. And last, think about it. I think you know." Chief Jenson then hung up.

Damn. What did Mason know? Did it have anything to do with the police cruiser? If she wanted to meet in private, then she was fishing.

Dana drove the Nova to Stone Mountain and parked in the parking lot. A lot of people were wandering around, enjoying the day. Dana walked into the park, looking around carefully. No cops. Mason was dressed in Levi's and a blue blouse. No uniform. She was sitting at a lunch table as far from the lunch truck as possible. Mason got up and met Dana at the lunch truck. No handshake. Just, "What do you want?"

"A Coke and a hot dog" Was Dana's quick answer. No other words.

Looking at the vendor, Mason said, "I'll have the same."

They got their Cokes and hot dogs then sat at the remote table. Mason looked Dana up and down, unsure of how to start the conversation if she should start by accusing her or just layout her evidence.

"Did you know that Duston? The guy Jody told you about before our dinner. He was killed three weeks ago," Mason said, starting quietly but looking intently at Dana for some sign to confirm her suspicions.

"Good. Someone finally shot the bastard," Dana said.

"No. Stabbed through the heart. The interesting part is that the only other people who knew his name are in the department or Jody." Mason waited for her reaction.

"So, he was a bad guy. Lots of people probably wanted him dead. Don't look at me." Dana held up her hands, a hot dog in one of them.

"Well, there was no evidence. In fact, Duston had been dead for two days when we found him." Mason was watching Dana closely. "He was last seen at Pete's Bar. He left with someone they called the Red Bitch. Ever hear of her?"

"I can't say that I have." Dana looked back into Mason's eyes.

"We figure that less than twenty-four hours after Duston was killed; a drug lab was hit. It was in the same neighborhood. It looks like another gang came in and killed everyone. Five dead men. But maybe one got away. These drug labs get hit all the time. But here is the strange part. Not a shot was fired. The guys who were supposed to be guarding the place had guns. They both were killed. One was knifed in the heart, just like Duston. But with his pants down. The other had his face bashed in." Mason took a sip of soda, her eyes still on Dana. Dana looked interested but not fascinated. But she didn't say a word.

"It gets stranger. The other gang usually takes the drugs. Not this time. The drugs were spilled all over their bodies. The only thing missing was money. We found a money counting machine with five twenties in it. There must have been more. A lot more." Mason took her time. "Oh yeah, Moses was one of the dead men. He had his throat cut."

"Well, finally some good news," Dana smiled.

"The word is that the Red Bitch, who I told you about, directed the killing," Mason finished up.

"Great story. Especially the part about Duston and Moses getting killed. Is that why you asked me here, all secret and stuff?" Dana was not expecting what came next.

"Ever since your mother was killed, I have had a patrol car cruise by your house. Just to make sure everything was okay. Did you know that?" Mason asked.

"No, I didn't notice. Isn't that kind of normal?" Dana was thinking, *So that's it. What does she know?*

"Yeah. You're right. Kind of normal. Just another note of interest. You were not in school the day the lab killings took place. Why didn't you go to school that day? That particular day?" Mason had laid all her cards on the table.

"I was on my period. A little depressed. I went to the gallery on time, usually around five o'clock. But you knew that." Dana thought, *Is that all you got?*

"You didn't know that two of your mother's killers were killed? And you don't know anything about the Red Bitch?" Mason watch for any reaction.

"No. Why would I?" Dana sat back.

"Just so you know, Ron can't be found. He has disappeared. Vanished into thin air. The word is that he was running that drug lab for Carlos. We think Ron was even living there. The word is he's hiding out in Mexico. I don't believe that. But all we're hearing are rumors."

Mason took Dana's business card out of her purse. She was tapping it on her fingers. She looked Dana in the eye. "No one would believe that a sixteen-year-old girl could wipe out a drug lab, killing five men barehanded. Really, no one would believe that. Would they?" Mason tapped the card, doing some more thinking. "Then again, no one believed a twelve-year-old girl could take on two armed thugs and beat the shit out of them. No one would believe that either, would they?"

Mason looked at Dana's business card. She turned it over, looking at the number on the back. Mason put it back in her purse.

Looking at Dana, Mason said, "I'll call if I need help."

"Anytime. Happy to help. Well, I got to get to the gallery. Saturday is our busy day. You through with this?" She pointed at the plates.

"Yes." Mason kept her unblinking eyes on Dana.

Dana got up, gathering up the paper plates.

"Well, I'll just trash them, okay?"

As she, walked off Mason called out, "Moses was one of the guys you beat up when you were twelve. Wasn't he, Godzilla?"

Dana dropped the plates in the trash, turning to leave. "Yes, I believe so."

9. I MISS YOU, GINA

Dana was not surprised to see Debbie standing by her locker after her fifth-period class. She was more intrigued by the question. Why?

"Hi, Debbie," Dana said and stepped up to her locker.

"Hi, Dana. I miss you. I haven't seen much of you since Gina left." Debbie was leaning up against the locker next to Dana's. Dana turned from her open locker and looked at Debbie for a long second. Then Dana threw her arms around Debbie and gave her a long, tight hug.

In her ear, Dana said. "You know what? I missed you too." Stepping back, Dana said, "I don't have a sixth-period class. I'm out now."

Debbie broke in. "Me neither. I'm out now too. Want to go get some pizza?" she asked breathlessly.

"Oh yeah. For sure." Dana was happy to spend some time with Debbie. Life was getting too heavy, and Debbie reminded her of Gina. "Are you driving?"

"No. I kind of sideswiped a post that popped up out of nowhere." Debbie frowned. "Two more weeks without my car."

"No problem. I got Mom's Nova. It's got a dented fender too, but it's mine. Let's go." Dana slammed her locker.

*

"Hmm, that's good pizza," Dana said, taking another bite out of her slice. Dana smiled at Debbie across from her. It was only then that she realized that she hadn't smiled and felt good at the same time in a long time. Debbie looked up at Dana and smiled.

"Thank you for ambushing me at my locker. I so needed to get out of my killer rut," Dana said. Debbie reached out for her hand and gave it a squeeze.

"I know it's been rough," Debbie said and gave her another squeeze. She let go but didn't move her hand away. "You going to the pre-prom?" Debbie asked in a lighter voice.

"You know, I haven't even thought about it." Dana considered the question. "You're going, aren't you? If you're going, I'm going."

"Oh yeah. I wouldn't miss it. It's our last year. Are you going to get all dressed up?" Debbie asked.

"I haven't thought of it. Maybe? But not to the nines. Maybe to the sevens." Dana was back to her full girlish mode.

"Great. Can you pick me up? I don't get my car back till Monday after," Debbie said.

"I got a better idea. Can you get someone to drop you off at my house? We can go from there. Then you can spend the night. That might be easier for both of us," Dana suggested.

After some chatter about what to wear and what time, and who else might be there and gossip about their love life, Debbie asked, "Have you been asked to the Junior-Senior Prom yet?"

"No. Again, I haven't even though of it. I really have been antisocial at school. Just doing adult things. Helping my father with the gallery. I'm killing it at work," Dana said with a smile. "How about you? I'm sure you have been asked."

"Yeah. Casey asked me. He's a horny little devil. All hands. Anyway, I told him I promised someone else. I said they were out of town and I didn't know if they would be back in time. I can back out anytime I want. Anyway, the prom is still a month away." Debbie was looking down and was quiet for a bit. "So. You wouldn't consider going to the prom with me. Would you."

"Are you asking me to the prom?" Dana said. "Look at me. Are you asking me to the prom?"

"Kind of, well. Yes, I guess I was." Debbie said, looking for signals.

"Then ask me properly," Dana demanded.

Debbie cleared her throat, preparing herself for anything. "Would you please go to the prom with me?"

"Yes. I would love to," Dana answered. "Yes, this is perfect. We're both wearing dresses, right? You're not thinking of one of the crazy lesbian dressy things?"

"No, I'm wearing a formal for sure. This is our last high school prom. Let's make everyone jealous." Debbie hands going up in the air.

"Cool. We can shop for dresses together and get each other corsages. I'm driving," Dana said happily.

"No. I'm getting us a limo. I'll pick you up and everything." Debbie said.

"Perfect." Dana clapped. The last time she felt this good was before Gina left. *Oh, Gina. I'm so sorry. It's just that I need somebody just now. Sorry, sweetie,* Dana thought to herself.

The night before the pre-prom, Dana sat on the sofa next to her dad's big chair. He had a book in his lap. He was looking down at it but had not turned a page in an hour. "Dad, Debbie and I are going to the pre-prom together. Remember when Gina and I went to our first dance, the pre-Graduation dance? Lars and Sally were going too. And you took lots of pictures. Can you do that again? I mean, to take lots of pictures?

Dana waited for an answer. She was getting used to getting no response. "Anyway. Debbie's coming over, and we're going together. I'm driving the Trans Am. That's tomorrow, okay?"

"Yes. I remember," Christopher all but whispered. Dana waited, but no other words came, so Dana left the library, her head hanging in disappointment. Christopher whispered, "Your mom was there." A tear ran down his cheek.

*

The next day, Debbie's dad dropped her off at the front door. Dana heard her drive up. She threw on a robe and ran down the stairs. Throwing open the front door, she greeted Debbie with a hug. "You look fabulous." She admired Debbie in her white silky flowered dress. It was very short. She was wearing six-inch white heels.

They ran up the stairs laughing and giggling.

"So, this is the nest? That's what Gina called it," Debbie said, sitting on the side of the bed.

"Yep," Dana said, dropping her robe.

She was naked underneath the robe. She took her red Chinese silk dress off the hanger and slipped it on. It was tight and nearly floor length with a slit up one side nearly to her hip. The top came up to just under her chin. Dana sat on the side of the bed next to Debbie to put on her stilettos. Debbie sat open-mouthed. Her mouth snapped shut. "You are so beautiful," she said.

Dana was leaning over, strapping on her shoes. "Thanks. So are you," she said.

"No. I mean I have never seen anyone so beautiful naked," Debbie said.

"Thank you again. I'm sure you are beautiful naked too." Dana winked. She stood in front of the mirror to put her hair up, holding it in place with two painted and sharpened chopsticks.

"Ready to go?" Dana asked. As Debbie got close to the door, Dana turned to her. "First, this is something we don't do in public." Then Dana wrapped her arms around Debbie and gave her a long, wet kiss.

"Wow. I have been waiting for that for a long time. Ever since I saw you at our first pre-prom." Debbie wrapped her arms around Dana's neck and returned the long, passionate kiss.

As Dana opened the door, Debbie asked, "I'm curious. What is the difference, if any, between Gina's kiss and mine?"

"I didn't have to pick you up to kiss you." Dana smiled.

They were a little late to the party. Dana dropped Debbie off at the door. "Get us a place in line," Dana said. The student parking lot was full, so she drove across the street. Behind the school, she found a parking place near the back of a strip of stores.

They entered together. After giving the English teacher-chaperone their tickets, they stopped just inside the door. Most of the boys quit talking. Most of the girls whispered to each other. They all were jealous in one way or another.

They had just finished their first dance when Casey caught up to them. "So, this is who invited you to the prom?" He threw a thumb at Dana.

"No. I invited Dana to the prom," Debbie said, looking Casey in the eye with a look that said *Don't you dare say anything*.

Dana just looked at Casey; she just smiled.

Turning away, he said to Debbie and anyone else within earshot, "Must be nice?"

"It is," Debbie said with a smile.

They danced most dances with each other. Occasionally, one of the boys would ask for a dance from Dana or Debbie. But Casey was not one of them.

When they were leaving, Dana said, "Stay here, Debbie. No use us both treading across that gravel pit they call a parking lot." When she reached the Black Trans Am, two thugs were leaning up against it. Dana looked them up and down and quickly checked her surroundings.

"What are you doing with the Red Bitch's car?" the thug on the right said, not moving.

"What's it to you?" Dana took a step closer to them.

"We just want to talk to her. Where is she?" the other thug said. Dana took another step closer. The thug on the right started getting nervous.

"You mean my older sister?" Dana said, taking another step, putting her in striking range. She took the sharpened chopsticks out of her hair and shook her hair out. "My sister told me about you guys. You're from Pete's Bar. Right? I guess you didn't think there were two of us. Right?"

"You'll do. I guess?" the thug on the right said, taking a gun out from the back of his waistband. Before he could raise it, Dana pushed one of the sharpened chopsticks into his ear all the way to his brain. He dropped dead. The other thug was slower in pulling out his gun. Dana quickly punched the other chopstick through his wrist. Before he could yell, she pulled the chopstick out of the other thug's head and jabbed it through his cheek and tongue and out the other side of his mouth and pushed him up against the car.

"I'm going to ask you a question. After I do, I'm going to pull this chopstick out of your mouth. You're not going to spit blood on me. You will have trouble talking. But you're going to give me the answer anyway. Got it?"

He nodded "Actually, it's two questions. Maybe more. First. Why are you here?" Dana slowly pulled the chopstick from his mouth.

He was hard to understand, but Dana made out, "For the money."

"Who's paying?" she asked quickly.

He mumbled again. "Some Mexican."

"How did you find me?" was her last question.

It came out, "Car."

"You did good. Now drag your buddy out of here." Dana let him go, pulling the chopstick out of his wrist.

He leaned over to pick up the dead thug. Instead, he went for the dead man's gun. Her stiletto went through his throat. Pushing the bodies aside, she got into the Trans Am and wiped the blood off her hands with a towel and took off her shoes.

*

"Sorry, it took me so long. I had to park over behind the sandwich shop across the street," Dana said as Debbie got in the car. "I had to take off my shoes; they were killers."

When they got home, Dana parked the car in the garage. She waved at the patrol car as it came up the street.

In Dana's room, Debbie unzipped Dana's dress. Dana did the same for Debbie. It was a long and very satisfying night.

When Dana awoke, Debbie was still asleep with her back to her. "Hmm," she said aloud. She thought about Gina, who always had her arms and legs wrapped around her. That's what usually woke her up. She still missed her.

Dana used the toilet and then took a shower. Debbie was standing naked in the doorway with her arms folded when Dana came out of the shower.

"Beautiful," she said and walked up to Dana. She hugged her with her hands on Dana's ass. They kissed.

"What are you doing tonight?" Debbie asked without letting go of Dana.

"It's Saturday. That's our big day at the gallery. So I'll be there late." Dana leaned back and moved off to dress. "But what about tomorrow afternoon?"

"Sure," Debbie said, sliding the shower curtain back. Stepping into the shower, she turned. "We can go shopping for prom dresses."

"But of course," Dana said with a toothbrush in her mouth.

*

"Coffee, food," Dana said, rushing down the steps on her way to the kitchen.

"Coffee first," Debbie said, right behind Dana.

"How do you like your eggs?" Dana asked as Debbie was making a stack of toast.

"Over easy," Debbie said.

Before sitting down, Dana made an egg and sausage sandwich and a cup of coffee for her dad. She cut the sandwich in half.

"You up? Can I come in?" Dana knocked on Christopher's door.

"Yes," came the one-word answer. Christopher was sitting on the side of the bed, his head in his hands, still in his pajamas.

"Try this, Dad. I think you'll like it. Debbie and I are having breakfast. Then I'll take her home. I'll see you at the gallery this afternoon." Dana said, setting the tray on the nightstand. She gave her father a kiss on the cheek and stood there for a few seconds, waiting for a response. She turned and quietly closed the door behind her as she left him alone.

After dropping Debbie off and picking up her laundry, she came home to an empty house. She threw her red dress across her bed. Her dad's door was open. His bed was made. This was a habit Eve had instilled in him. "We can't mess it up if it's not made," she would say to him. Sometimes just after making the bed, Eve would get playful, and they would mess up the bed again.

Dana picked up the tray. She looked down at the empty coffee cup and half of a sandwich. "Well, at least he ate half," she said out loud. Dropping the dishes in the sink, she went out to the patio.

"Why is it so easy for me?" Sitting next to the throne, she asked her mother as if she was sitting by her mother's spirit.

"I don't feel sorry for them. I don't feel much at all. The only thing I regret is getting blood on my clothes. That's really cold. Right, Mom? Heartless?" Turning to the empty throne, she said, "I remember you told us not to use our skills out of anger." Dana put her hand on the arm of the chair, trying to feel her mother's hand. "Revenge is not anger. I'm not angry. I want revenge. My heart has been ripped out. Revenge doesn't put my heart back. It just helps fill that void."

Dana sat quietly for an hour.

10. THE PRICE ON HER HEAD

The Red Bitch backed the Trans Am out onto the street at eleven ten. That would be between the regular police drive-by.

When she got to the edge of Sylvan Hills, she flipped the switch and the fire-breathing dragon came to life. She didn't go directly to Pete's Bar. She made a wide path around the neighborhood, announcing her presence with an angry engine and fire.

When she got to Pete's Bar, she jumped the curb and stopped in front of the door. It was behind a six-foot-wide and four-foot-deep recess. The Trans Am blocked the exit. She revved the engine, announcing she had arrived with noise and fire. Loose paper and parts of the doorframe caught fire.

Dana got out of the still idling Trans Am, leaving the door open. She pulled her Bo staff after her.

Dana kicked open the door and strolled in with the smoke and fire around her.

One of the thugs sitting by the door was up and coming after her. The end of her Bo staff caught him in his mouth. Nearly all his front teeth were knocked out and his jaw broken. He went down, howling in pain and holding his bloody mouth.

Richard, the bartender, was trying to bring up a sawed-off shotgun, but the barrel was caught under the bar. The other end of the Bo staff caught him in the forehead, knocking him down behind the bar and dazing him.

Another thug was sitting at a table with three college kids; he was in the process of selling the kids drugs. He stood and tried to pull his gun out from behind his back. The Bo staff came whizzing through the air, hitting him alongside his head and knocking him down, his pistol still in his hand. Dana stepped forward and drove a heel through his hand. Pulling the heel out she watched him try to reach over with his other hand to get the gun. Dana smiled and drove her heel through the other hand.

Her Bo staff swept the table clean of drinks, drugs, and cigarettes. Then it went high into the air and came smashing down on the table. "Don't move. When I'm gone, you leave and don't ever come back." She reached over and pinched the cheek of one of the college kids. "Got it, cutie?" she said with a smile. Then she said, "Hands on the table," and she turned her attention to the bar.

Dana sat on the bar and winked at the college kids as she swung her legs over it. Richard was sitting on the floor, his back to the bar. His shotgun was a few feet nearer Dana than him. She strolled down the bar, her Bo staff knocking the bottles off the bar onto the floor, most breaking on one another. When she reached the cash register in the middle of the bar, she stopped.

Richard was still fuzzy when he reached for the shotgun. Dana drove her heel through his hand. With a scream, he pulled his hand back. Putting her Bo staff on the bar, she squatted and picked up the shotgun.

"Come on, honey. It ain't that bad. Now stand up for me. Please," she cooed, as he struggled to stand, leaning against the curve at the end of the bar.

"That's a nasty bruise on your head. It will probably give you a big knot." Dana handed him a dirty bar towel. Smiling, she said. "See, honey? I'll take care of you." With that, she put the double barrel in his ample gut.

"Now, who put the price on my head? Was it Ronny?" She pushed in a little extra at that.

"No," he said, wrapping the towel around his bleeding hand.

"Then who was it?" Dana asked politely.

"I don't know," he said.

Dana looked at him. "I don't ask twice," she said in a normal voice.

"A Mexican guy. Carlos. He was your boss, wasn't he?"

Dana cocked her head.

"Really, that's all I know," Richard said, looking up from his broken and bleeding hand.

"Okay, what's the price?" she asked.

"Twenty-five thousand dollars," he answered, looking back down at his hand.

"Is that all? I'm not worth much." Dana shook her head. Taking a breath, she continued, "Here's the deal. Anyone who comes after me dies. You will say to anyone asking that they will die. Don't try it, or you will die." She pulled back the hammers on the shotgun. "And if they come close to me or anyone I love—hell, anyone I know. They'll die. You're going to make sure they don't come after my friends or me or anyone else I know. Want to know why?" Not waiting for an answer, she said, "Because, after I kill them, your bar is going to burn down. And you're going to watch it burn down from right here. All tied up. Watching the bar burn. Your feet, then your legs and balls. It's going to take a long time. Got it, Dick?"

Richard nodded.

Dana stepped back toward the other end of the bar. She shot the cash register with the shotgun at her hip. Then the other barrel shot the bottles that were still behind the bar. Richard was sprayed with booze and glass that embedded in the side of his face and in his arm. She then opened the double-barrel shotgun, pushing the button to separate the barrel for the stock. She threw both halves toward the front door.

Dana hopped up on the bar, throwing her legs over. Smiling at the college boys, she showed more than leg. She took her Bo staff and started for the door. The thug on the ground was still trying to pick up his gun with two broken and bleeding hands.

"Well. Do you want your gun? Here, let me help you." Picking up the gun, she smiled. "I always try to help the handicapped." She tucked the gun into the front of his pants and pulled the trigger. Screaming in pain, his broken and bloody hand went to his crotch, "Whoops. I was never very good with guns," she said, seeing the blood coming out of his crotch.

The college students were sitting very still with their hands on the table. The other thug was sitting in a chair with blood coming out of his mouth and nose. His hands were in the air over his head.

"Good boys," she said as she left the bar to get into her rumbling, angry Trans Am.

Dana had only been in the bar for five minutes. The cops would show up in another ten minutes and would crash into a nearly empty bar. The college kids would be long gone. The thug without teeth drove the other thug without balls to the hospital. Richard was sweeping up the bar. He looked at the cops in their flak jackets with their guns drawn. "What? Didn't you feel that earthquake?" He didn't have much else to say for the rest of the evening.

When Dana left the bar, she drove down the streets on the wrong side. When she reached the corner with the four hoods, she revved the engine, throwing fire and noise in their direction. They jumped back.

Dana opened the door and raised her tall frame onto the sidewalk in front of them. Her blue eyes drilled into the main man's eyes. She straightened her dress. She then held out one hand and signaled with her finger for the main man to come forward.

"Honey, have you heard of the price on my head?" she asked with a smile. He put his hands in his front pockets and turned sideways, looking at his crew. That meant to do nothing. He looked back. "Yeah."

"Do you want to collect the reward?" she asked in a serious and cold voice.

"Ain't our thing. You ain't done nothing to us." He lifted his eyes to meet Dana's ice-cold stare.

She stepped forward, her eyes inches from his. He could feel that he was inches from death. Still, he didn't blink. For the first time in a long time, he was totally and utterly terrified.

"Okay," Dana said, taking the ice out of her voice. "But, if you hear of anyone trying to collect, please do this little favor for me." He knew this was an order. In a kind and calm voice, she continued, "At the Lenox Mall, in front of Macy's, in red spray paint on the curb, write their initials. You'll do that for me, won't you?"

He took his right hand out of his pocket and placed it on his heart. "For the Red Bitch. You have my word, I swear."

"Thank you," Dana said, then gave him a short, wet kiss on his mouth, biting his lip just enough to draw blood. Stepping back, she ran her tongue around her lips, tasting his blood.

Smiling, she turned her back and got into the growling, impatient Trans Am. She slowly left the curb and, a little way down the road, punched it, screaming noise and fire.

The four men watched her drive off, full-on this time and not trying to hide their faces.

Touching his sore lip, the main man said, “That is one fucked-up Red Bitch."

11. CONFERENCE CALLS

It was just after ten Sunday morning when Dana made her way downstairs. Christopher was sitting at the kitchen table, a cup of coffee in front of him. He was talking on the phone. Dana gave him a kiss on the cheek and poured herself a cup of coffee, then put bread in the toaster. She leaned against the counter and watched him.

"Yeah. I guess. Hmm-mm," was the most significant part of his side of the conversation.

Sunday mornings were when the twins, somewhere in Asia, and Lars and Sally in Barcelona called Christopher on a conference call with Jody on the other line. It would be nine or ten at night in Asia and four in the afternoon in Barcelona.

The calls had become shorter and shorter as Christopher became less responsive. Still, by eight every Sunday morning, Christopher was sitting in the kitchen next to the phone.

Dana buttered some toast and placed it on a plate in front of Christopher. She then sat down, waiting for her time on the call.

"Yeah, she's sitting here. Okay. Here." Christopher handed the phone to her.

"Hi, Dana," they all said at once.

"Hey, guys," Dana said quickly.

"How are you doing?" Beau asked.

"Tired but good," she answered honestly.

"Now, we have something important to talk to you about. Keep smiling, and don't ask *what*. Okay?" Lars said.

"Sure," Dana said through her teeth with a smile plastered on her face.

"We want to talk to you about Dad. But privately. Can you go over to Jody's at noon?" Lars asked.

"Yes, I love you guys too," she said, smiling at her father.

"This way, we can speak openly. You can just say yes." Lars waited for her answer.

Dana kept the smile on her face and acted like they were telling her something interesting. She was thinking it over. *What the hell is this shit,* she thought. Finally, she said, "Yes. I got it." Then, "Okay, here's Dad." She handed the phone over to him and got up to make some scrambled eggs and sausage. She put some extra energy into beating the eggs.

As usual, Christopher picked at his eggs. He might take a bite of sausage. Mostly he ate toast.

*

Jody met Dana at the door and led her into the kitchen. Mason was sitting at the breakfast table with a mimosa in front of her. Dana was not expecting to see Mason at Jody's, but she was not surprised.

Mason smiled and gave Dana a little wave. "Didn't expect to see me here, did you?"

"Well, yes, Mason." Dana put both hands up in the air. "And no, Chief Janson."

Jody poured herself a mimosa and then one for Dana.

"What? Jody, I'm only seventeen, and there is a cop sitting right, there." Dana pointed at Mason and gave the glass a little push away, but not too far.

"Chief Janson is at the office. Mason is here," Mason said. "And my guess is you're going to need something stronger by the time this conference call is over."

Jody gave Mason a sidelong look.

"Well, she should be prepared. The call is in less than fifteen minutes," Mason answered Jody's look.

"The kids have been calling me every Sunday morning for maybe the last ten weeks, usually about eight. Today, it was a long call. It has been all about you and Christopher. They just want to try and find a solution to his problems," Jody started.

Dana broke in. "It's a broken heart. I can't fix it. Believe me, I am trying everything I can think of."

Now it was Mason's turn to break in. "They are trying to not..." The phone, in the center of the table, rang. "Damn. They would be early."

Jody answered the phone. "Hi. Yes, she's sitting here. Yes, we'll stay here. No, we won't interrupt. No, we haven't told her anything." Then she handed the phone to Dana.

"First, thank you for doing this." Axel was taking the lead. "So, what's your opinion about Dad?"

"Not good. He's losing weight. He doesn't eat. He drinks bourbon at night, not wine. He barely talks. That's the long and short of it. Nothing you didn't know already." Dana waited.

"A quick question. Has Dad shown any interest in anyone special? You would know." Axel went on.

"He doesn't even have an interest in the gallery. Women? Definitely no." Dana didn't see where this conversation was going.

"Okay, then Dad's fading away. What are you going to do about it?" Axel asked.

"What am I going to do about it? Is it all on me? I'm doing everything. No help from the big boys? Shit. I'm doing everything. Plus trying to get some re...." Dana looked at Mason. "Never mind." Then she nearly shouted into the phone, "Damn you guys. You call once a week and think you have all the answers. You should try living with him. Hell, working with him. You're all out there having a ball, not a care in the world. Damn." Dana's eyes were tearing up. "Damn." She was ready to hang up the phone.

"We know it's hard on you. You're taking all the pressure." Lars tried to calm her.

"It's a killer," Dana answered.

"We don't think Dad should be left alone," Axel said quietly.

"No shit, but I've got a life, or should have one!" Dana shouted into the phone.

"We know. But here's the thing," Lars said.

"Now you're going to tell *me* what to do? Like you're in charge." Dana's hand came down on the table hard, nearly knocking the mimosa over. Jody and Mason were sitting quietly with their drinks in their hands, knowing what was going on and feeling the pain Dana was going through.

"Come on. Just give us a chance to explain. Please?" Axel begged.

Dana was silent for a moment. Then a quiet, "Sure."

"First, we have no interest in the gallery. You know art. You can sell art; hell, you're almost running the gallery now. We can't do any of that. We want you to have the gallery. It's yours one hundred percent, but that would mean you would not be able to go away to college." Axel was going over the agreed-on script.

"So, you guys went away to college, but I can't. Hell, you went all the way to California." Dana gave a little huff into the phone. "Shit."

"We didn't mean you can't go to college, just not away." Beau tried to clarify.

Dana put her hand over the phone, looked at the ceiling, and shook her head. Then, she said, "I want to go to college, I would love to get away from all this shit. But with dad the way he is, plus other things, I just can't see me going away to college."

There was silence on the other end of the line. Then Lars started. "Here's the other thing."

Beau broke in. "First, you get the Gallery and the house. Everything. We don't want anything from it. It's all yours, understand? We have all agreed on it. Jody has agreed to write up a contract covering everything. If Dad leaves us anything in his will, this contract will override that, and you get everything. It's a done deal."

"Really, a done deal?" Dana said sarcastically. "Before you even talk to me? You have been planning this for how long? And now you think it's a done deal?"

"Okay. Let Jody explain it to you. If you want to make changes, any changes, sight unseen, we all agree. It's all up to you. If I can go on now?" Axel asked.

"Now." Lars broke in again. "Sally and I can't have kids. We might adopt sometime down the road, but not now."

"And" Axel stepped back in, "I'm not having kids. Hell, women are just arm candy for photoshoots, and the only relations I have with them is public relations."

Beau came back into the conversation. "Besides, just a heads-up. Just to be honest here, if you didn't know, Axel is gay. So not much chance of grandkids there. I'm just not going to have kids ever."

"So, Dad has been on us about grandkids." Sally was taking the lead on this. "It seems to be the only time he perks up is when he's talking about grandkids. So, you see, that part is on you."

"And as soon as possible." Axel upped the ante.

Putting the phone down on the table. Dana looked up at Mason. "You were right. Can I have another?" She drained her glass in one gulp, then picked up the phone again.

“Are you still there?” Axel asked.

“You know I’m only seventeen.” Dana had almost had enough of this conversation. “I have never dated a boy. Only girls. You know that. So according to you, I’m supposed to go out and get pregnant. Just how am I going to do that? Never mind that. I know how to get pregnant. I know how to do it with a boy, but I never have.”

"Well, pick someone good," Lars said.

“Shut up,” Sally broke in, “Lars can be so insensitive sometimes. Look, this is not. Well, it’s just a suggestion. Something to think about.”

"Something to think about! What about me? Have you ever given a thought about me?" Dana asked.

"You still get everything. We're not taking that back. Whatever you do is up to you. We just want you to know what we have been thinking. Sorry if it came across so gross," Beau said.

“Yeah, well, it did. And how about including me in some of these conversations?” Dana was furious with her brothers. “Can I hang up now?” She didn’t wait for an answer. She just hung up.

Looking at Jody and Mason, she asked, “You knew about this?”

“Don’t look at me. I just found out today,” Mason said.

“Not all of this. Not till today,” Jody lied.

“I can’t go away to college or anywhere. I’ve got to have a baby fast. That’s what they want? And they are never around. It’s all on me. I could kill them.” Dana finished her tirade.

“You don’t mean that?” Mason said in a serious tone.

Dana just gave her a look that said, *You’re not serious, are you?*

"I've got to go," Dana said, getting up from the table. "Thanks for the mimosas."

Mason got up with her and signaled Jody to stay put. "I'll show her to the door." On the front porch, Mason took Dana by the arm. Looking her in the eyes, she said, "Honey, I know you're carrying quite a load. It seems like the world is gunning for you. I like you. If I can help, just ask."

"Thank you. I like you too. Thanks again." Dana waved as she walked down the driveway in her loose mini dress and black flats.

'Dana was a sweet, young, sexy sight,' Mason thought as she watched her get into her Nova and drive off.

Mason had her arms folded and was leaning against the railing, thinking. *Girl, I don't know how you got to this place. You are a seventeen-year-old tall, beautiful girl. I'm almost sure you're the one. The Red Bitch. Oh, I've seen what you can do. That drug house on Brown's Mill Road. Five men dead and not a shot fired. Revenge, I'm sure. You're at one time a sweet teen, and another time, you're a stone-cold killer. I hope I don't have to bust you. Just don't give me any solid evidence.*

Jody came out on the porch. She put her arm around Mason's waist, her head on her shoulder, watching Dana leave. "What are you thinking about? You seem so far off."

"Oh, just about that little girl. She's got so much on her." Mason turned to Jody. "Let's go see a movie. I need a distraction."

*

That afternoon, Debbie pulled up in her red VW with the right front fender painted primer. When she tapped on her horn, Dana came flying out of the house still wearing her loose-fitting mini dress and flats.

Debbie gave her a long, wet kiss.

Dana came up for air and shook her finger at Debbie. "I said, not in public."

"Like, everybody knows we're in love." Debbie ground the gears into first and, pressing the gas pedal, the VW engine rattled into life.

I didn't know that, Dana thought.

12. THE PROM

The long-line strapless bra was stabbing Dana in the ribs. But it pushed what she had up and together. *I wonder if they can make this out of Kevlar?* She thought.

She strapped on her gold sparkling stilettos. Dana checked herself out in front of the mirror. Her gown was a black strapless gown with a few gold sequins at the top, and they were ever-increasing until at the floor it was solid gold sequins. The sides of the bust were high near her arms and then plunged to show maximum cleavage. A simple gold chain with a small gold cross hung around her neck. She wore no other jewelry. Her hair was rolled in the back and held in place with two sharpened chopsticks, one gold, and the other black.

Debbie, her mother, and father and Jody had already arrived and were waiting in the entryway at the bottom of the stairway, cameras in hand.

When she got to the top of the stairs, everyone stopped to look. Dana slowly came down the stairs; her arms held tightly at her sides. When she got to the bottom, she signaled for Debbie to come over. "Please zip me up," she said.

With that done and everything moved back into place, Dana was now able to properly greet her guests.

Christopher was in the library entrance, camera in one hand and a bourbon in the other. He was staring at Dana. "You are beautiful, Eve," he said, a tear in his eye. Noticing the silence, he said, "I mean you look just like your mother. You look beautiful, just like your mother."

Debbie was wearing a floor-length pearl white gown with spaghetti straps and black and white folds starting at the waist. Debbie presented Dana with a white carnation corsage, which she slipped onto her wrist and then gave her a heartfelt but polite kiss. Dana returned the gesture with a black carnation corsage. She slipped it onto Debbie's wrist. Another polite kiss. They posed for dozens of photos, apart and together.

The pretenses of being just friends had melted away some time ago. Nobody said anything. It just now seemed normal. On the way out, everyone hugged and kissed. Christopher hung onto Dana a few extra heartbeats.

Jody was standing by the door and was the last one to give Dana a hug. She whispered in her ear so that only Dana knew a message had been delivered. "Mason says the coffee is great in front of the High Museum. Sunday at noon." Then she kissed her on the cheek. Dana smiled as if nothing had been said.

The limo was waiting for them at the curb, just as Debbie had promised. An unmarked police car was parked right behind it although the two men up front were not unmarked. As they pulled out, the unmarked police car followed. Dana was well aware of the police car following them.

When the driver opened the door at the Marriott ballroom, Dana quietly asked the driver, "What's with the unmarked police car?"

"I don't know. You got me."

This time, when they walked into the ballroom, they held hands. The crowd took notice but kept most of their comments between themselves.

They posed for three photos in the flower-covered archway. One with their arms around each other, another hugging and the third kissing. Not a polite kiss. For this kiss, Dana was in control.

Halfway through the evening, they were standing next to the refreshment table. Casey came up to them. He held his plastic glass between them as if it were a shield. "First, I want to say I'm sorry for the way I acted at the Pre-prom. I was way out of line. I'm sorry."

"Okay with me," Debbie said. "How about you, Dana?"

"Okay with me too."

"Great. Then, Debbie, can I have this dance?" he asked.

Dana swept her hand out, ushering them onto the dance floor. The next dance, he asked Dana. After that, he asked Debbie again.

"Sorry, Casey. We're together. So, it was very nice for you to ask but..."

Then Dana cut in. "It was very nice for you to apologize and to ask us to dance. I don't want to hurt your feelings, but we're here together tonight like Debbie said."

"Okay," he said with his eyes turned down. "It's just that. Well, I'm here alone. Prom night and I'm here alone."

"Really, don't be that way," Dana said, taking him by the shoulders. This was the first time Dana realized he was her height. "Please understand. It's not you. It's just that it's our prom night."

"Okay. Sorry," he said as Dana let him go.

"Honey, you have nothing to be sorry about. You are the only person here who has come up to talk to us. You did everything right. It's just, you know, our night." Debbie gave him a kiss on the cheek.

"Ditto," Dana said, giving him a kiss on the other cheek.

He backed off, walking away with his hands in his pockets.

"God, I feel sorry for him," Dana said.

"Me too," Debbie said. "May I have this dance?"

Toward the end of the evening, couples were wandering off. Dana and Debbie were ready to go back home. Their limo was parked right in front of the entryway, blocking everyone else from getting close to the entryway. The unmarked police car was parked right behind the limo.

The driver was holding open the back door of the limo. He was a different driver. Dana let Debbie get in and settle down and then stood at the door.

"What happened to our driver?" Dana asked quietly.

"He's off duty. It's my shift." Dana noticed a bulge under the left arm of his jacket. That could only be a shoulder holster.

"You have been watching us. Why?" The driver looked away. Dana patted his shoulder holster. "I asked politely why?"

"Chief Jenson ordered us to. She also said you're not supposed to know." He was looking around.

"Jesus, man. You got an unmarked police car on our tail, and you hog the entryway like we're the president. Who doesn't know? Tell him not to follow us." Dana jerked her head in the unmarked car's direction. The embarrassed driver began to wave them off. "Don't do that! Just go up to the car and ask them if anything is wrong. Out loud. Then quietly tell them to back off. God. Think, man."

*

The next morning after a little sex play, they dressed and went downstairs. Dana poured coffee for everyone and sat down next to Christopher. He was on his weekly phone call with the boys and Sally. Dana said a quick hello to the boys. "Yes, it was wonderful. I'm sure Dad will send you some pictures. I will send you copies of the prom photos." Then with emphasis, she added, "I still love you guys. Bye." She quickly gave the phone back to her dad.

Dana dropped Debbie off at her house and headed to the High Museum. The entrance to the museum was just off a large courtyard. Several tall buildings surrounded the courtyard. The coffee shop next to the museum had fifteen to twenty tables with two or four chairs at each. Only a few people were sitting in the courtyard with their coffee and pastries.

Mason was sitting at the edge of the cluster of tables. No one was sitting near her. She had two cups of coffee in front of her.

“Sorry, I'm late. It was a busy morning," Dana said, sitting down.

“No problem. Your coffee might be a little cold,” Mason said, pushing a cup across the table toward her. She then pushed several little cups of cream and several bags of sugar toward her. “I didn’t know how you liked your coffee. After the prom, I figured you might need some."

"Black is fine," Dana said as she took the top off her cup for her first sip.

“Did you know what happened at Pete’s Bar?” Mason started right off.

"Hold on. Me first. What's with the armed guards? Not to mention the not-so-smart cops last night. You know how oblivious they were? Changing drivers, an unmarked car with two cops in full uniform. Blocking the entrance. Watching us from the side door. Were you trying to advertise police protection?” Dana said all this with a note of anger in her voice, all the while sitting back with a smile on her face. Sipping her coffee. They both were intently eyeing each other.

Mason smiled and said through her smile, “Remember, I told you that whatever we discuss is between us and no one else."

"And what does the Chief of Police have to say about that?" Dana smiled back.

"She's not here. I'm here, and I keep my word." Mason put her hand on her heart. "My word," she repeated.

Dana looked at the doors of the museum and through them into the lobby, then casually around the courtyard. "No undercover cops?"

"I left them at the station," Mason answered. "Now. You know the Red Bitch." It was a statement, not a question.

"I've heard of her," Dana answered casually.

"Did you know she has a price on her head?"

Dana just looked at Mason. "So, what's that to me?"

Mason looked away and thought, *She doesn't trust me. Why should she? It's just my gut telling me she's the Red Bitch. If Dana is The Red Bitch and she doesn't work with me, she's going to die. Well, I got to warn her. So here goes.* She turned back to Dana. "Did you know we found two dead bodies outside of Pete's bar late Friday night?" Mason lost her casual look. "The bartender was missing three fingers."

"Didn't you mention that place before? I said I don't know the place. I'm too young to be going to bars." Dana smiled at Mason's serious face.

Mason could tell the message was getting through. *Now is the only time I can tell her the reason I'm here.* "My guys rousted a bum near there. He told them the trophy is now worth two hundred and fifty thousand."

"And what's the trophy?" Dana knew the answer.

"The Red Bitch's head."

Dana looked away, thinking. Looking back, she said, "You make it sound like a contest. Is it going to be on television?" She tried to joke.

I hit a chord, Mason thought. *Now the big information. The information Chief Janson should keep to herself.* "I'm not the Chief of Police now, just your friend Mason." She was the one looking around this time. "The detectives said one guy was sitting in the corner of the bar. He's from Miami. He said he just got into town. We checked him out Saturday." She was now deadly serious. "His name is Eduardo Estevez. The guy who pulls everyone's strings is Carlos Blanco. Big-time drug lord. That's all Chief Jenson knows, but she's not here, is she?"

"Why are you telling me this?" Dana now leaned forward to match Mason's pose.

"Because you need to tell the Red Bitch that they are gunning for her. She should lie low, maybe take a vacation. She should park her black car where it can't be found." Mason exhaled.

"Still, why are you telling me this?" *She has me pegged,* Dana thought. *Why is she telling me all this? What is up with her?*

Mason just looked at her. "Tell her to be careful."

"Tell you what. Don't make me look like the Red Bitch. Tell the cops to back off." Dana was emphatic.

Mason nodded then in a quiet voice. "Okay. Only from a distance. But please be careful."

Dana looked away. When she turned back, she said, "God, I'm hungry. We only had snacks last night."

"I'll get us some sandwiches. I'll be right back." When Mason got back, Dana's chair was empty.

13. SO, YOU WANT TO PLAY

On the curb in front of Macy's at Lenox Square, just like Dana demanded, was painted in red, the letters EE. "Well, I guess the bangers kept their word," Dana said aloud. She then drove to the gallery. It was closed on Sundays, but she needed to be alone to think.

She dragged a chair through the gallery to sit in front of the new Maimon. She studied the flat planes of color. Then the flowing lines of the two elegant women with their large sun hats, sitting in a Venice outdoor café, enjoying a glass wine. She let her mind drift. Soon, it found its way back to reality.

She began to contemplate her situation. The price had gone up from twenty-five thousand to two hundred and fifty thousand. *God, that's a quarter of a million. I must have really pissed someone off. I must be cutting into his profits. More likely,* she thought, *I got to his ego. He put up twenty-five thousand over a month ago, and I'm still here.*

This Carlos Blanco dude is used to getting what he wants. The guy he sent to get me, Eduardo, isn't like the other guys. Not like those two thugs lying on the ground behind the sandwich shop. My guess is he's experienced, trained, and hunting me. I need more information. I can't count on surprise. I am not going to intimidate him. I'm not going to seduce him. So what's left? Skill. I have got to get in close for that. Really close. Or find another solution.

What do I know? His name. His boss's name. He has got to be close to the top guy. So he is not cheap. He won't be staying down in the hills. I think he's staying in an expensive hotel downtown. He probably doesn't get up till lunch. Then he'll go to a nice local restaurant, Cuban, or a steak house. For sure, I do not make him nervous. He sees me as his weekend assignment. His weekend assassination. That's part of my advantage.

If I can string him out, make him run around, get some time on him, make him stay in Atlanta longer than he intended, maybe I can get his boss pissed off at him. I bet his boss gets pissed easily. Why else would he send him after me? I need both him and his boss to get pissed off.

Timeline? What's the timeline? I hit the drug house over five weeks ago. Then Pete's Bar. I have been quiet since then. Well, if you don't count the two guys behind the sandwich shop—that was two weeks ago. Then Pete's Bar again. I guess I have not been that quiet. I don't know if he knows about the two dead guys behind the sandwich shop. Maybe he does. But for sure he knew about the visit to Pete's Bar two weeks ago.

So, he came into town Thursday night? He was at Pete's Bar Thursday night for sure. I'm sure he killed those two guys up front. He was making a statement. Telling everyone, he was upping the ante. Thinking someone will rat on me. He's just waiting for me to show up. He is spinning a web, and like a spider is waiting in the middle. Waiting to kill me. He'll probably be at Pete's Bar. He only knows me from Pete's and the drug house. Maybe the two guys in the parking lot.

I guess Eduardo still doesn't know who I am. Ron doesn't even know I hit the drug house. He might not know about the limo. Then again, he might have paid some coop off. Shit, they might think Debbie is the Red Bitch! Debbie rented the limo. Damn, if they learned anything from last night, it's that. They most likely don't know about last night. But I can't take that chance. I have got to draw any attention away from last night and quick.

Tonight, first info. Then distraction. Then revenge. Tonight, is going to take some prep. The gallery has everything I need.

She spent the next hour putting together everything she was going to need.

Walking into the garage, Dana petted the Trans Am. 'You know sweetie, you need a name, a badass name. You need a name that is you,' Leaning over she whispered into the hood, 'How about the Black Dragon? Do you like that,' She turned the key, the Black dragon came to life with a roar, then purred its acceptance.

At eleven ten, she backed the black Dragon out of the garage. The patrol car would not be by till eleven-thirty. Around eleven-thirty, she stopped at the 7-Eleven just outside the Hills. She picked up the payphone outside and called 911.

"Yes. I'm not sure I needed to call. But, I thought, what if I didn't, and something bad happened," Dana said into the phone.

"What is this about?" the emergency operator asked.

"Well, I was driving down South Roberts Lane a few minutes ago. I saw two men in a car and two more going around the house into the backyard. They didn't look like they belonged in the neighborhood. They kind of hid when I drove by. Anyway, it was at 231 South Roberts Way. I know the people. They have a daughter. So, I guess I had to call."

"We'll send someone over. Who is this?" The emergency operator asked.

"Thanks," was all that Dana said, then hung up. That should give Debbie an alibi, police report and all.

The Black Dragon didn't breathe fire until it was rounding the corner up the block from the bangers. The Black Dragon snorted to a stop. It sat grumbling and breathing a soft yellow flame.

The boys had learned the routine. When the Red Bitch drives up, don't make any quick moves and put your hands in your front pockets. Dana stood slowly and walked to the head guy. She put a hand on his shoulder.

"I didn't hurt you last time, when I kissed you, did I? I can be a bit rough sometimes. You know?" she said, stroking the back of his neck.

"Nah. I'm tougher than that." He looked down.

"Honey. You heard that my price had gone up to two hundred and fifty thousand." Dana tilted his head up with her other hand and looked him in the eye.

"Ain't my business. Now, if another zero is added, I might have to talk to you about it." He did not blink.

"Are you sure?" Dana curled some of his hair in her fingers.

"For sure, bitch. You got my pledge. That's way better than my word." He smiled.

Dana put the other hand on his neck and her forehead against his. "Hey, thanks for the heads up. I got something else to ask you."

"What?"

"Where is the new Miami drug house?"

"Ain't no big deal. Anyone can tell you. It's back in that old shit house. Jesus. Not the smartest assholes around." He held her eyes and didn't move his head.

"Stay clear of them, honey. Bad news." Dana leaned in to give him a kiss. He backed off an inch. Then he accepted the bite on his lip. Their form of a blood oath.

The Black Dragon growled down Browns Mill road and stopped in front of the house. The Dragon breathed a great fiery breath.

Dana jumped onto the front porch and threw a planter pot with dead flowers through the front window. That was followed by a plastic bag of turpentine with a matchbook taped to it, lit. She kicked in the front door. The guards were both on fire, running into each other, screaming.

She then threw another firebomb into the bedroom. No one was there, but that wasn't the point. She kicked open the bathroom door. No one there either. She stopped short of the lab, seeing two guys run for the back door, and another got a shotgun blast off.

Dana tossed in another firebomb, hitting the guy with the shotgun in the chest and face. He fired another shot into the ceiling. Then he fell on the floor, rolling around and spreading the fire.

There was a bag of money by the counting machine near the door. "How nice of Carlos to pay me," she said as she grabbed the bag.

The whole time from car door to car door was just over a minute. Dana fired up the street and turned the corner. She calmed the Trans Am, turning on the mufflers and slowly drove over to Pete's Bar.

Eduardo did not expect to spend Saturday and now Sunday night in Pete's Bar. Thursday night, he had put out the word: two hundred and fifty thousand for her head. He figured he would have her head in two days at the most. Here it was Sunday, and Eduardo was still just sitting in the middle of his spiderweb. He was becoming less patient, waiting for word on the Red Bitch.

He had just lit another cheroot when the escapees from the drug house came crashing through the front door.

"The Red Bitch hit us. God, she just came crashing in."

Eduardo stood, throwing his cheroot on the ground as he approached the two guys. "What the fuck. When?"

"Maybe five minutes ago. We came straight here as fast as we could. Jimmy was waiting for her with a shotgun. I heard him fire both barrels. I think maybe he got her."

Eduardo pushed them out the door and into their car. They left a little rubber in the street. The Black Dragon, with its dark eyes, sat a half a block away quietly. As they turned the corner, the fire in its breath came to life. It stopped, blocking the front door.

Richard was hunkered down behind the bar at the far end. No one else was there.

"Up," Dana commanded, jumping over the bar. "You told him everything you knew, right?"

"I don't know anything. Eduardo cut off my fingers to get me to talk. I didn't know anything, or I would have told him. Wouldn't I?" Richard was white as a sheet, holding up his bandaged right hand with two fingers left.

"Sorry about your fingers," she was talking as if to a kid who skinned his knee falling off a bike. "How many people did you tell about the new price on my head?" she asked as if still talking to the hurt child.

"I didn't have to. Eduardo did. He's been sitting here for the last three nights. What could I do?" Richard was trembling.

"What does he know about me?" Dana folded her arms as if a mom asking her child.

"Nothing. I don't know anything. Just that you drive a black car."

"What do you know about this dude?"

"He's from Miami," Richard said.

"I know that. Everyone knows that. Tell me something I don't know, Dick, like, where is he staying? What is he driving?" Dana unfolded her arms and made a *come to me* gesture with her hands. "Give."

"A red Pontiac. Florida plates. He's staying at the Marriott downtown." Richard looking around for help.

"How do you know he's at the Marriott?"

"I saw his keys."

"Oh. Then what's the room number?" Dana was now within inches of his face.

"Room 815. I think," he stuttered out.

"I hope that's all true," Dana said as she jumped the bar and started out the door but stopped and turned to shake her head. "You should not have told him anything about me." She turned back and walked out the door.

Richard took a deep breath, happy to be alive. "Red Bitch," he said out loud.

Dana came back through the door with two flaming bags. She threw one at Richard, hitting him in the gut. The other she threw at her end of the bar, setting the whole place on fire. "I told you what would happen." This time, it took almost two minutes from Dragon to Dragon.

Dana pulled the black Trans Am into the garage shortly after midnight. "That only took a little over an hour," she said to herself as she stuffed the bag of money into the trunk under the workbench.

She patted the warm hood of the Trans Am as she walked out of the garage. "Good Girl," she said.

Upstairs in her room, she barely had time to undress when the phone rang. "I'll get it, Dad," She called to her father as she headed downstairs. She didn't need to say a thing. Christopher had passed out for the night hours ago.

"The cops have been here all night," Debbie said, breathlessly into the phone.

"Really? Why?" Dana said, feigning shock in her voice.

"Some guys were sneaking around here. Kind of scary. The cops just left a few minutes ago. You know they even checked my room. Can you believe it? Even my room?" Debbie said.

"Really?" Dana played her part.

"Yeah. The cops said they would park outside for a while and cruise by regularly." Debbie carried the conversation for a few more minutes. Then they hung up.

Dana went out and sat next to her mother's throne.

"Okay, Mom. Debbie's got her alibi; I've burned down the spiderweb. But I still have a price on my head. Did I tell you it's now a quarter of a million dollars? Now, what do I do?" Dana looked at the empty throne for an answer. "I know. I'll think of something. I've got to get some sleep. I got to go to school tomorrow."

The next night, she went to bed early. She was exhausted.

*

Eduardo drove around the Hills Monday night asking questions and reminding everyone of the bounty on the Red Bitch. "Hey," he said as he rolled up to the bangers. They walked over, standing on both sides of the car and looking in the windows. Their guns were at their sides just below the window level. They didn't say a word.

"*Vato*. Have you seen the Red Bitch around?" Eduardo asked of the head guy standing at his car door.

"Our corner, asshole. Buy or drive," the head guy said.

"You know there is two hundred and fifty K for her head?" Eduardo played his card.

"Nice car, asshole. I'd hate to see it get, you know, shot up and bloody." Eduardo heard the click of the hammer being cocked.

"I don't want any trouble, man. I'll be around if you hear anything," he said as he put the car into gear and drove off.

*

Tuesday, Dana sat across the street from the Marriott, dressed in her school uniform. Her hair in a ponytail. She wore no make-up. She looked to be fourteen or fifteen. Not a threat to anyone.

She had no idea what this Eduardo looked like. She just hoped he had gone out for lunch.

At noon she walked into the Marriott and took the elevator to the eighth floor. The maid was in the hall, her cart in front of the room she was making up. Just as Dana had hoped.

She knocked on room 815. There was no answer. *Good,* she thought and knocked at the door again, louder this time.

When her knock remained unanswered, she approached the maid, looking as pathetic as possible.

"I'm sorry. But I left my wallet in my uncle's room last night. It has my school ID and everything," she said, near tears. "Please. Can you help me? Can you let me in so I can get it?"

"I'm sorry. I can't do that," the maid said, turning away and heading back into the room she was cleaning.

"Please. It's my uncle's room, Eduardo Estevez. You can check it out. Please," Dana begged. "My mother doesn't like him for some reason. She didn't know I had dinner with him last night. If she finds out, I'm in deep *caca*."

"Well, maybe she has her reasons? Maybe she should find out?" The maid said in a stern voice, turning toward Dana.

"Oh please," Dana said with tears streaming down her cheeks. She was wiping at them with her knuckles. "We didn't do anything, I promise. My mom works at Macy's. She's at work now. Please, I got to get my ID to get back in school. Please."

The maid thought back to some bad experience she had as a teen. Foolish, stupid stuff.

"Okay, young lady. But don't let me catch you back here again," she said in a stern voice. She opened the door and stood in the doorway as Dana stepped by her, into the room.

She scoped out the room as much as possible. Finding the spare key next to the television she and palmed it. Checking the bathroom, she came back in the bedroom, she knelt down behind the bed and took her wallet out of the band on her leg under her dress.

"See, found it," she said to the maid, standing up.

The maid stopped her at the door. "I don't know what you were doing in his room last night. But I can guess."

"We didn't do nothing," she said innocently.

"Sure. Take my advice and stay away from this guy. He will mess your life up. Don't come back." She shut the door.

"Thank you," Dana said many times as she backed down the hallway to the elevators. She smiled and waved goodbye to the maid.

*

Dana sent Christopher home at seven as usual. She closed the gallery at eight as usual, then sat in the dark in front of the Marc Chagall, the light over the painting the only light in the gallery. For the next two hours, she worked on the details of her plan. She just didn't know if it would work. *So many variables,* she thought. She changed into a long-sleeve brown shirt and Levi's with black tennis shoes. She looked about as unnoticeable as she possibly could be.

At ten, she drove downtown, in the Nova and parked a few blocks from the Marriott. Suitcase in hand she entered the hotel taking the elevator to the sixth floor, then taking the stairs the rest of the way up. In the stairwell, she put her hair up in a ponytail and put on a baseball cap. She carried her bag down to room 815 using the stolen key to let herself in. *No one home,* she thought. *First variable out of the way.*

She searched the room, finding two suitcases, one on the little folding stand. It was open and had some clothes in it. The other was in the closet with a few hanging clothes and a safe. She hefted the second suitcase onto the bed and opened it. It had several automatic guns and what was that?" Damn. A grenade," she said aloud. She checked the safe; it was locked.

She went through the dresser drawers, nothing. Then the bathroom, the only thing she didn't recognize was the two prescription pill bottles. She memorized the names of the drug and noticed that the names on the bottles were not Eduardo's.

Last, she went through his suitcase. At the bottom, she found an address book. "Oh shit," she said and sat at the desk. She wrote down what looked like important names and their information. Carlos' name was at the top of her list, in the back of the address book she found a piece of paper. Handwritten was *Marriott Hotel,* the hotel's address and phone number, and a birthdate.

"A birthdate?" she said. "Bizarre. Why would he write down a birthdate?" She sat and thought about it. "Maybe," she said aloud. She went to the safe and dialed in the numbers. Click. It opened to reveal it was filled with bundles of one hundred-dollar bills. Ten thousand dollars to a bundle.

"Got you!" Dana said with a smile. Another variable out of the way.

She opened her suitcase and put on her Red Bitch clothing and wig. She didn't bother with the Red Bitch's makeup, no one was going to see her face. Spreading the bills out on the bed. Only then did she set up her camera on its tripod and angling it to show the bed, the open safe was in the background, along with his clothes and the suitcase with the guns and grenade.

The camera was set to take pictures every ten seconds. The Red Bitch crawled on the bed with the money. She played with it. She made love to it. She never showed her face.

Dana quickly changed back into her innocent clothes, this time with a black shirt. She put on a different baseball cap. She put everything back into her suitcase, laying the money across the bottom of her suitcase. Everything barely fit.

She wrote a note. *See you in Amsterdam soon. Hugs and kisses. Thank you, Master, for a wonderful weekend*. Dana then locked the note in the safe, making sure everything was as she found it, including putting the spare key by the television where she had found it that afternoon.

She retraced her steps and drove home. The next morning, she stopped at Walgreen's one-hour photo shop. Later, sitting at her desk in the gallery, she picked out five good photos. "Damn, I look hot," she said. "Maybe I should have thrown in some ropes or something? Oh well. Too late for that."

She put the photos and a short letter in a plain envelope and addressed it to Carlos. She mailed it from the downtown post office. The letter said, *Please thank Eduardo for me. I had a wonderful time. But please tell him for me that I'm not going to Amsterdam. Sorry. RB.*

*

Four days later, three thugs showed up at Eduardo's hotel room door. The hair on the back of Eduardo's head stood up. *This isn't good*, he thought.

"Ese. It's been a week and no head?" the big man said. "You know, El Jefe is getting worried that you can't do the job. He wants to talk with you."

"Now? I almost got her Sunday night. I got the word out. Half of Atlanta is hunting for her," Eduardo protested.

"Ain't nothing to worry about, Ese. He just wants an update from you," the big man said.

"I'm telling you, any time now I'll get the word. I just have to cruise by my snitches again tonight." Eduardo's arms were out begging. While the big man talked with Eduardo, the other two spread out around the room.

"Come on. We'll help you pack." The big man picked up the gun case and checked it. Closing it, he handed it to one of the other thugs. One of the other guys put the other bag on the bed, looking through it. Eduardo grabbed his clothes out of the closet and threw them to the thug. "Pack neat. *Vato*," he said as defiantly as possible.

"Is the money in the safe? Let's get it before I forget." Eduardo took the address book out of his case, taking the note out of it, he bent down to open the safe. It was empty. The leader took the 9mm pistol out of Eduardo's back holster. "Oh, Ese. Not good," he said.

"What the fuck? Where's the money?" Eduardo said, running his hands through the safe as if the money was invisible. He came up with the note.

Taking the note out of Eduardo's hand, the big man read it. "Man, we got to see El Jefe about this."

"It's that Red Bitch. She fucked me," Eduardo said as they took him by the arms and walked him out of the room.

Closing the door behind him, the big man said, "Yeah, man. In more ways than one."

At Eduardo's Pontic, the leader said, "I'll drive. You can sit shotgun. Sit back, Ese. It's a long drive." He already had the keys. The thugs put the suitcases in the trunk. One of the thugs got into the backseat. The other got in their black Cadillac.

Eduardo didn't make it to Macon. As soon as the traffic cleared, the thug in the back whipped a garrote wire around Eduardo's neck and pulled hard with his foot against the seatback.

"Jesus, man. You're bleeding on me." The driver pushed Eduardo's body over next to the door. They stopped at a scrap yard south of Macon.

They finished cutting off his head and put it in a bowling bag. His bags were transferred to the Cadillac. The rest of him was placed in the trunk. The red Pontiac was crushed, then loaded on a truck heading for a scrap mill, to be chopped up and melted.

Just a day later, Dana drove by the Macy's. The red EE had a big red X through it.

14. GRADUATION TRIP

Dana's and Debbie's graduation party was not very large. Mostly family; a few school and gallery friends; Bobby and Tommy, the masters from the dojo; Jody and Mason. Debbie's parents offered their backyard, complete with banners, balloons, sandwiches, pizza, munchies, and drinks. Dana and Debbie greeted each person as they arrived. They accepted their congratulations and gifts then thanked them, mostly with hugs and some kisses.

When Mason and Jody arrived, Mason first hugged Debbie and then Dana. She whispered in Dana's ear, "A word in private when you get a chance."

Dana smiled and said, "Thank you so much." Toward the end of the evening, Jody and Mason were sitting in chairs near the back of the yard. As Dana approached, Jody got up and gave Dana a kiss on the cheek. Then she went to talk with those few who had not gone home yet.

"Nice party. I'm so glad you invited me," Mason said.

"Thank you for coming. I think of you as part of the family now. It's hard to believe that I've only known you for a few months... It feels like we know so much about each other," Dana smiled, looking directly at Mason.

"You know it has been quiet now. No killings by the Red Bitch for almost two weeks. Just so you know. Carlos is looking for the Red Bitch everywhere but in Atlanta." Mason looked at her.

"How did that happen? Did someone leave town?" They were talking calmly as if they were discussing what Dana was going to do now after she graduated.

"More likely left the planet. From what I have learned, the Red Bitch did an incredible job of setting everyone up. I especially liked the way you, I mean the Red Bitch, had my men watching over Debbie while everything was going down. They'll never suspect her now. Good job. The only person who died was Eduardo. Masterful planning and execution. Pardon the pun."

"Eduardo died? How do you know that?" Dana asked, looking the other way.

"Oh, I have my sources."

Dana just looked at her and asked only one question. "Eduardo?"

"Did you know the plate and VIN number of all cars that are smashed have to be recorded and turned into the DMV? I had an APB out for any information on Eduardo's car. I got the info two days ago. It was smashed in Macon. My guess is that Eduardo went with his car."

Dana looked away, so Mason didn't see the small smile on her face.

"Just so the Red Bitch doesn't show up in Atlanta. And you get the muffler on your black Trans Am fixed. I think everyone will be okay." Mason was relaxed.

"I drive Mom's Nova. The Trans Am is just for special occasions." Dana looked up, then down. Finally, she said. "So, who else figured all this out?"

"I have information no one else has. No one will ever know what I know."

Dana was uncomfortable. It was all on the table now.

Sitting back, Dana asked casually, "So, what does this Carlos look like? Do you have any pictures?"

Mason's head jerked over to look at Dana, "Why do you want to know?"

"Just curious. No reason," Dana smiled.

Mason did not smile this time. She signaled for Dana to move closer. "The word on the street is that the Red Bitch is a force so destructive, so vengeful, so violent, so unforgiving that no one wants to cross her. Not even for a quarter of a million dollars." She looked Dana in the eyes. "The street cops love her. When she's busy, they are also busy, but somewhere else. She's doing what they can't do." Mason leaned over and whispered, "They are all gone now. If I need the Red Bitch, I'll call you."

They looked each other in the eyes.

"Where's Ron?" was all Dana said.

Mason, for the first time, did not see Dana. Her eyes were just as those who saw the Red Bitch described her. Cold, unforgiving, dangerous.

"I will use all my resources to find him." Mason did not blink.

"When you do, don't touch him. Just tell me. No one else," the Red Bitch said.

A cold chill went through Mason. She saw what dead men saw and turned away, now understanding what anyone who stood in the Red Bitch's way would face. "Yes," was her one-word answer.

Dana sat quietly, looking away for less than a minute. When she turned back to Mason, her eyes had calmed and changed back to the likable seventeen-year-old everyone knew. Dana spoke louder now. "You have been so nice. If I can ever do anything for you, let me know." Her eyes had changed, but not her meaning. "Oh, I may have a couple of things to talk with you and Jody about. It's about my personal life. It's complicated, but I've been thinking about the call we had with the boys. Please. I'll need Jody and you to help."

And just like that, by the time she finished her request, the teen was back, and the Red Bitch was gone. Mason was both relieved and disturbed.

Dana then said, "Okay. By the way, can you or Jody do me a big favor? Please, drop in at the gallery and check in on Christopher? Debbie and I are going to take a little post-graduation vacation."

"Sure. A trip sounds like fun. Where are you going?"

"Oh, I thought Debbie and I would take a drive down the coast to Miami." Dana smiled.

Mason took a breath and shook her head. She knew now that the Red Bitch would always be there somewhere. "Can I talk you out of that?"

"Why? I always wanted to see Miami. The place of my conception. It must be so," Dana paused for the right word, "informative."

Mason had a worried look on her face.

"Don't worry. We're traveling light. Bikinis and sundresses. Nothing exotic. Debbie will look out for me." Dana then added, "I'll take lots of pictures."

Two days later, Debbie and Dana loaded up the Trans Am. Then they kissed and hugged Christopher and Debbie's parents. They waved goodbye as they drove off.

They got to St Augustine before dinner. At the Casa Monica Resort, they literally threw their luggage on the bed, one of the bags missing the bed entirely. They quickly walked hand in hand the two blocks down to the shoreline. They walked along the sidewalk next to the bay taking in the salt air. Enjoying the feeling of the warm evening ocean air. They stopped to look at a restaurant that was built on pylons in the bay. The sun was setting behind them, the failing sun's rays first turned the water of the bay red as if the sun was angry to be leaving the bay. Then quickly almost a black with indigo blue swirls. The Red walls of the restaurant gave off a unique red brilliance as the sunset that sent the white roof off into a blinding glow. Almost as soon as the light show started, it was over. Dana led the way along the pier to the restaurant. They asked for a table by the window overlooking the quiet but choppy bay.

Just as they were ordering their meal, two young men took the table next to them, "Hi ladies," they said as they sat down. A few minutes later, one of them turned and asked, "Can we buy you, ladies, a drink?"

Debbie and Dana giggled. Debbie was quicker with an answer. "Do you guys want to get arrested?"

"Sorry. We were just offering you a drink," one of the men said.

"Yes. To underage girls," Dana said, laughing with Debbie.

Rolling his eyes, one said, "You look more mature."

"Thanks, I think?" Debbie said.

They all went back to discussions at their own table. Dana noticed that Debbie kept casting honey eyes at one of the men.

That night, lying naked in bed, Dana raised up on one elbow. "Did you want to have sex with one of those guys?"

"What? No, I got you. Why would I want a dick?" Debbie looked up at Dana. "Did you?"

"Hell no!" Dana said, flopping down on her back.

"Well then, do you want to have sex with me?" Debbie asked in a sexy tone.

"Hell, yes!" Dana gave her a long kiss as she rolled over on top of her.

The next day, they dressed in their bikinis and long loose t-shirts, which became their uniform most days till evening. That morning, they got into the Black Dragon and drove along the coastline. They got to The Pelican Hotel in South Beach an hour before sunset.

Parking in front of the hotel, Dana petted the hood of the Black Dragon and told the valet to "Put her in a nice quiet place where she can be alone."

Standing on the crowded porch, looking out over the sand and ocean, over the tops of people's heads, Dana took

Debbie's hand. "I can't tell you how many times Mom told me how much fun her and Dad had here in South Beach." Dana turned to Debbie, "I told you I was conceived here? Look how beautiful it is. I wonder why they never came back?"

"Probably couldn't handle another you!" Debbie said, pulling Dana inside.

"Very funny," Dana laughed.

They dressed in matching sundresses with black and white stripes and comfortable wedge shoes. They walked along the sidewalk, sometimes having to step into the street until they found a restaurant they liked with a deck above the sidewalk and a table open along the railing.

The sun began to set behind the buildings behind them. The wakes of the power boats caught and reflected flashes from the rays of the setting sun. Dana took a deep breath.

Debbie looked over to see tears streaming down Dana's cheek. "Why are you crying?"

"I don't know." Dana squeaked as she felt the warmth of Eve's love wrap her arms around her.

The next morning, they had breakfast at the News Café on the corner. Christopher had told them before they left that they must have breakfast there and with emphasis on *every morning*.

"Let's walk over to the other side. I hear that there is a cool island over there with houses of the stars."

Once over there, Dana picked a secluded spot with a view of the house she was interested in. It was large and in the Mediterranean style. It had a large deck along the second floor and a large raised patio under it. It had a pool and pool house next to a dock with a forty-foot boat and a smaller thirty-foot open fishing boat tied up on either side of the pier.

Dana twisted on the telephoto lens of her Nikon thirty-five-millimeter camera. Dana shot an overview of the house, then started to focus in on the details and windows.

"I thought we were going to walk?" Debbie said as they sat next to the sea wall.

"No, this is good." Ten minutes later, Dana said, "Okay. Let's go to the beach."

They laid on their towels on the sand in front of the Pelican Hotel. "Race you to the water," Debbie said. They both raced across the sand into the ocean, diving head-first. It only took about twenty minutes of splashing around for that to wear off.

They rubbed lotion on each other's back, arms, and legs, rubbing the lotion on the legs a little higher and more inside than necessary. They laid on their stomachs wearing their large sunglasses. Heads turned toward each other.

"Debbie. You know I've only had sex with you and Gina. Right?"

Debbie pushed her sunglasses down her nose and looked over the top of them. "Really?"

"Yeah. Well, we were only fourteen. Really young. We taught ourselves."

"Well, you did a good job. You're the best." Debbie smiled, and her elbow moved toward Dana's.

"So, what about you?" Dana asked as casually as she could and nudging back with her elbow.

"Okay. You want my history," she said, pushing her sunglasses back up. "Do you really want to know?" She looked directly at Dana.

"You know all about my sex life. I just told you. Your turn," Dana said, pushing her sunglasses down to look over them.

"Well, do you remember Kate Haskell, the gym teacher's assistant. You know, in fifth grade. She was in high school. You remember her."

Dana nodded. "Kind of? God, how old were you? Twelve?"

"Hell no. I was eleven. I was just on the receiving end, but I learned a lot. But you're better." Debbie was talking like it was about the weather.

"So, who else?"

"Penny. Tenth grade. She wasn't worth a dime. Ha, Ha. I made a funny. Then she met a guy, and that was that." Debbie sighed. "Then Ginger. Same year. She had a big island. Ha, I made another funny."

"I didn't get that last one about Ginger. But anyway, is Casey the only guy?" Dana asked.

"Yeah. Junior year. Casey and I sometimes, but it was very on and off. If you know what I mean." Debbie lost her sunglasses as a beachball hit her in the head.

"Hey, ball," a guy yelled. Reaching around, they hooked their tops back on.

"You want it? Come and get it," Debbie said, putting the ball behind her and leaning on it. They spent the rest of the afternoon playing on the beach.

They showered the sand away and made love, then showered again. Then Dana picking up the Nikon to go for another walk. "I'll be back in an hour. Be ready to go get something to eat," she said, going out the door. She knew that Debbie didn't want to join her. Besides, a little alone time would be good for them both.

It was about seven when they walked down to the beach hand in hand. Dana was lost in thought.

"What's up, Honey? You're not here." Debbie pulled on Dana's hand.

"Sorry. Let's sit down somewhere quiet," Dana said.

"Sure," Debbie said with a puzzled expression. She wasn't sure if it was going to be a good talk or bad talk. She began to think that being honest with Dana about her sex life was not such a good idea. They sat in the sand next to an empty lifeguard stand.

"I guess I'll just ask. How was Casey in bed?" Dana asked.

Debbie tilted her head back, not expecting that question. "He has a dick. I guess it's a big dick. It's the only one I had. It cums when you blow on it. So why?"

"Well, you have seen my dad since my mom died. He drinks too much. He's not interested in anything. If I weren't at the gallery thirty hours a week, it would be closed. He's just waiting to die. No, wanting to die." Dana paused. "I can't deal with his depression anymore. I've got to do something."

"How? I mean, what's that got to do with Casey?" Debbie asked.

"My brothers think he needs a grandchild to give him meaning to his life. That means it's up to me to give him one." Dana leaned over with her forehead on her knees. Dana went on to explain the conversations with her brothers, Jody, and Mason.

"So, I can't think of anything else to do." Dana slipped her head between her knees.

"That's it? Starting a family to make your dad happy? That's it? What about you? What do you want? Boy, you're something else." Debbie turned away.

"He's going to die. He's going to die if I don't do something. I'm the only one who can or will do something." Turning to Debbie with her hand on her arm, Dana said, "I need your help."

"Why, Casey?" Debbie turned back with intensity.

"He's tall. I'm tall. He has blond hair. I have blond hair. He looks good. I look good. And you say he has lots of sperm. What else do I need?"

"So, you're going to marry Casey?" Debbie looked shocked.

"No, not really. I can fake that part. All I need is his sperm."

"Oh God, now I have to get you pregnant? And you're dumping me." Debbie sat back.

"No, I'm not dumping you. I'm just getting pregnant. Will you help me get pregnant?" Dana asked, smiling at Debbie.

"If that's a proposal, I accept." Debbie gave Dana a kiss and put her head on her shoulder. "We're going to be a family."

*

For the next three days, it was breakfast, sand, and dinner with a magnificent sunset. The warm hugs of love from Eve, each sunset were just as comforting, but with not so many tears. Dana still took her walks twice a day, sometimes three times a day. She began to really unwind. Relaxing was not Dana's strong point.

"Mom said it all started right here. In this very spot. Perhaps this very chair," Dana said. They were sitting out in front of the News Café. It was very early. The wire chairs were made for durability, not comfort. The cast metal tables with their open flower design never needed wiping down. Well, maybe once a day they got wiped down. Dana was looking across the street to the sand and beyond to the ocean. She was looking but not seeing.

"What started here? I mean besides you. You told me that story the other night," Debbie said, looking over the top of her cappuccino cup.

Dana's eyes and thoughts slowly came back to the table. "Oh. The gallery. This is the exact spot where my parents met Angelo Vecellio. One thing leads to another and voila, Parsons Gallery of Fine Art was a social success. I was next."

"Very cool. Right here," Debbie said.

"I got an idea. Let's enjoy the morning, the beach, and the ocean. Then let's check out and go to Disneyworld. What do you think?"

Debbie put her cup down. "Really just like that?"

"Yeah. Who's going to stop us? We can do anything we want. I've never been there. It sounds like an adventure."

"I've been there a couple of times. You know Epcot has a whole land for that? Adventure Land. Oh, I'm so funny," Debbie said.

Dana had the Trans Am brought around. As she was putting the luggage in the back, she put white tape over the state and over two of the letters on the license plate. It now read D GON. There was no front plate.

Dana threw the keys to Debbie. "You drive for a bit."

Dana directed Debbie onto the causeway. Then to the first bridge to the right. "Take that bridge. Let's go see some stars' houses. That's Star Island. I think it got its name from all the stars living there." Dana handed Debbie a pair of large sunglasses and then put on her own pair. "They have a guard shack. We're going to have to fool him. Follow my lead, but this part won't be hard for you. Be ditzy." Dana directed; *Debbie didn't get it.*

As they rolled up to the guard shack, Dana said, "Roll down your window. But not all the way." The Black Dragon had heavily tinted windows and the guard could only see that they were cute young girls. The girls went into their ditzy act.

"Hi," Debbie said. "We're here for a party. They said to ask for someone. Who was that guy?" she asked Dana.

"Yeah, some guy. But it was at some gal's house. What was her name?" Dana said.

"Yeah, what was his name?" Debbie asked the guard.

"I don't know. You tell me?" the guard said.

"I don't know. Neal something. No, O'Neal something," Debbie said.

"No, no, honey. That was the guy who invited us. The tall black guy," Dana said to Debbie.

"No, the guy who invited us was his friend Lenny something. You know?" Debbie asked the guard.

"You tell me?" It seemed to be his stock answer.

"No, it was Gina's house. No, Gloria's house. That was it. I think," Dana said.

At this point, the guard just shook his head and opened the gate. "Dumb blonds," he said as they pulled away.

"Drive this way and really slow down." Dana directed Debbie to the right side of the road. The road ran down the center of the island. In the middle was grass and some plants and flowers, the perimeter was all huge houses. Dana pulled out her camera, rolled down the window a bit, sat as high in her seat as she could, and started to take pictures from inside of the car.

The house was the one she had been taking pictures of all week. It had iron gates and fence. Two guys sat on the porch at the entry. There was a three-car garage to the north and a black Lincoln in the driveway.

"Okay, now drive really slow," Dana directed Debbie. As they cleared the house, she said, "Now just drive around slow. Let's see if we can see some stars or at least their houses."

When they turned onto the causeway, Dana asked, "Please find a gas station before we get on the toll road. I got to pee and let's fill up and get some Cokes." She also needed to take the tape off the license plate.

In Orlando, driving down International Drive to the Sonesta ES Suites, Dana saw a Walgreens. "Stop here. I have some film to develop. I'll pick it up tomorrow. I know you're tired."

They spent the next day and part of the evening at Disneyworld. They seemed to spend most of their time standing in line for rides. That evening, Dana pick up her photos at the Walgreens. They were exhausted and sunburned and were in bed as soon as they turned out the light.

The next morning, after playtime, they checked out and went across the street to Denny's for breakfast. Dana took out her photos and started going through them, putting them in piles.

Debbie was looking at them from across the table. "Hmm. That's a congressman. I don't know who that other guy is."

Dana looked at the photo and then at Debbie with a puzzled look. "How do you know him?"

Debbie took the photo. "I saw his poster on a pole outside. He's running for re-election." Handing the photo back, she poked through the rest of the photos, moving the piles around. "This is the governor."

"Okay, how did you do that?" Dana asked, even more puzzled.

"I saw him on television. I just have a mind for faces and names." Debbie took a bite of her eggs.

"Okay, write their names on the back," Dana said, handing the photos back to Debbie. "Look through these and tell me who you know. Please," Dana said, pushing the pile of photos across the table to her. She watched her in amazement.

As Debbie went through the photos, Dana started putting together three piles. One with the people with their names on the back, another with special photos, and a third pile of photos that she might check out later. They sat there for two hours, looking through them.

In all, Debbie identified not only the congressman and governor but also the police chief, three television anchormen, and several movie stars.

Standing up to go, Dana gave her a big kiss on the lips. "Tonight, you get whatever you want and as often as you want."

15. THE PLAN

Saturday morning, Dana called Mason's private number. "We're back safe and sound. Nobody got hurt—except for Debbie. She got a nasty sunburn at Disneyworld."

"Thanks for calling. That's good to know. How was South Beach?" Mason asked with interest.

"Great. So relaxing. I don't think I've been this relaxed in a long, long time."

"Good. You needed something to take the edge off. You did take the edge off?" Mason asked.

"As much as I can. Can I see you and Jody Sunday? You know, at Jody's house? Any time that works for you, but noon would be best for me." Dana quickly added, "It's about our last conversation. Also, about the one we had with the boys. That seems so long ago."

"Sounds good. I'll make brunch." Mason thought she knew what was coming. Dana was just giving her time to prepare.

Sunday morning, she was up before her dad. She had coffee and croissants ready for him.

Dana regaled him with stories about their adventures on South Beach. He smiled, chuckled, and asked questions. He even told his own stories about Eve and his trip to South Beach, but mostly about the Pelican and the News Cafe. His tears would come and go, but it was all about happiness and remembering good times. He took out his wallet and quickly found the business card Angelo Vecellio had given him. It was discolored and worn around the edges, but his private number was still on the back.

"What room did you stay in?" was one of his many questions.

"Fourth floor, south end. They had a great view of the ocean and the side of the hotel next door."

"That was our room." His hand came slapping down on the table in amazement and excitement.

About this time, the boys rang in. Christopher once again dominated the conversation. He recounted stories Dana told him about South Beach. He told his own stories, and sometimes he mixed them both together. When Dana got on the line, everyone seemed happy. That had not happened in a long time. Dana asked if they could call Jody about one o'clock.

"We already received our instructions from Jody," Lars said.

At noon, Jody greeted Dana at the door with a hug and a kiss on the cheek. "I'm so glad you're alright. Did you unwind? Did you decide on a college? Did you?"

Walking into the kitchen, Dana put her hand up. "Stop. Stop. The answer is yes, yes, and yes."

"Sit," Mason said. She was setting plates of eggs Benedict on the table. The glasses of orange juice were already in place. The smell of fresh coffee filled the kitchen. Mason poured them all a cup and sat down.

"I would like to say a small prayer," Mason said to everyone's surprise. Prayers were not a regular thing. Thanksgiving and Christmas mostly. They all joined hands. "Thank God we're all safe. Amen."

"That was short," Jody said.

"But to the point," Dana said, knowing what Mason meant.

"Okay. Now talk. What did you decide while lying in the sun, getting a little sunburn?" Mason asked.

"Well, you all know Dad wants me to get married, have a baby, and go to college. I have decided that now is a good time to start that program. I mean, as soon as possible. But I'm going to need your help."

Jody and Mason looked at each other in surprise.

"Let me get this straight. You're going to get married? You're going to have a baby? You're going to college?" Jody asked.

"No. Yes. No. And I'm not straight," Dana said.

"What?" Mason and Jody said in unison.

"I'm a lesbian." Dana took a sip of her coffee.

"No. Not that. God, the other things," Jody said.

"No, I'm not really getting married. I'm just going to fake it. Cheaper and easier that way. Yes, I'm going to have a baby. No, I'm not going to college." Dana took a bite of her eggs.

"What the hell happened in Florida?" Jody asked.

"I figured it all out. But I'm going to need your help," Dana said, taking a gulp of orange juice and then turning her attention back to the eggs Benedict.

"What's your plan. And please, details this time." Mason said, pointing at Dana.

"Well, Casey's going to get me pregnant. And not marry me."

"What the hell?" Jody said again.

"Wait. I'll explain. Well, the not getting married and the getting pregnant part is really kind of one thing. Casey. You know Casey?" Dana looked up. "Debbie's old boyfriend? Haven't you been paying attention?"

"Who?" Mason asked.

"God." Dana looked for help. "In her junior year. Her boyfriend?"

"News item. We didn't go to high school with you," Jody said, her eyes wide.

"Anyway, he's tall, blond, and handsome. Also, smart, I think?" Dana looked down at her plate, then back up. "This is where I'm going to need your help." She took a sip of coffee.

Jody and Mason sat open-mouthed.

"Getting pregnant is the easy part. Girls get pregnant all the time. I don't need your help there." Dana giggled a little. "But—and here's the really big *but*—Dad and probably Casey's parents need to think we're married. So you guys got to get me a fake marriage license."

"A fake marriage license?" Mason asked. She was sitting back, her arms folded, shaking her head. "I guess I can get one."

"What?" Jody said. "Casey has agreed to this."

Mason cut in before Dana could answer. "So, what's going to happen to Casey after he has done his job? You don't expect him to just disappear?" Mason waved a hand at Jody, dismissing her question. Mason's question was directed at the Red Bitch.

"No, he's not going to disappear. He's going to join the Navy and go to sea; Dana took the last bite of her eggs Benedict. "Hmm, excellent. He'll just sail away. He might come back someday. So, I'm going to need something else from you guys."

"Has Casey agreed to any of this?" Jody asked again.

"He doesn't know yet. I haven't told him," Dana said matter-of-factly.

"What?" Jody said.

"I haven't told him," Dana said. She wanted to say *pay attention*. But she let her expression say that.

"I know that. How do you think you're going to pull this off is what I'm asking." Jody placed quotation marks with her fingers around asking.

"You know what? I think she can do it. I think she can do things nobody would ever believe," Mason said.

"Pshaw," Jody said, throwing her hands up in the air.

"Jody, I'm going to need divorce papers. Real ones. That says first, I keep my stuff. Second, no alimony. And third, I get full custody. No visitation rights."

Jody turned to her. "You're not going to be married. So you don't need divorce papers."

She looked worried. If Jody didn't go along, it was going to be difficult.

"What you need is a custody agreement. Let me think about it. I'll come up with something." Jody shook her head. "What are you getting me into?"

Mason had the last question on her mind. It was just one word. "College?"

"I'm not going. I'm going to run the gallery with Dad. I know a lot of artists. Hell, I grew up with them. I grew up in that gallery. I can sell art. I'm a better salesperson than Dad. I know more about art than any stuffy professor. So why should I go to college? What? For an art degree?"

Mason and Jody nodded in agreement.

"Besides, you'll have a baby to raise. With our help, of course," Jody said. "Are you sure you're a lesbian? I mean, you could be bi. Not unheard of for young girls to have lesbian experiences and then go straight.

"More to the point and I mean this in the most helpful way, did some boy scare you off? Did you have a bad or violent experience with a man or boy? You know you can trust us." Mason said concerned.

"No! I've never even been out with a boy. And once more, I don't want to. I was happy with Gina. Now I'm happy with Debbie. I don't see any of that changing."

"How are you going to handle it if you have a boy?" Mason questioned Dana.

"So? Boy or girl, they will have to decide for themselves. Nobody pushed me one way or the other. It just came about naturally." Dana looked at them. "How about you guys?"

"We're talking about you," Mason said as they peppered her with questions. Some were a little too personal.

The phone rang, giving Dana a break from the third degree. "It's the boys and Sally," Mason said, handing the phone to Jody.

"Hi, guys. Dana and Mason are here. I think Dana has something to say to you guys." Jody handed the phone to Dana.

"Hi, guys. How are you all doing?"

"We're all fine. Why this late-night call? It's one a.m. here," Lars said.

"Yeah. And I'm getting hungry. We were supposed to go out to dinner with friends," Lars added.

"Lars, it's only six. We don't go to dinner till eight. Lighten up." Sally scolded Lars on the extension.

"First, you've got to promise me you will not tell Dad anything. No matter what I tell you, you have to promise not to tell Dad. Come on, promise."

Promises were made all around.

"Okay. I'm going to have a baby," Dana said into the phone.

First, there was silence. "Oh, God, that's great!" Sally said. Her words were echoed by the brothers.

"When?" Lars asked.

"I don't know," Dana answered slowly.

"You don't know? Shit, you're putting us on," Lars said.

"No. I decided I'm having a baby." Dana defended her answer.

"No, you're not. I'll fly out there and kiss your butt if you do." Beau said.

"Deal. I'll have a baby within a year. Then you can kiss my butt, and not just a little peck either. A real wet kiss. Remember, you guys promised not to tell Dad anything until I do. Then you all have to act really surprised."

Soon after that, they all said their goodbyes and that they loved each other. Dana finished off the call with, "You promised."

"So, you're going to get laid," Jody said.

"I've been laid," Dana said, a little shocked.

"Not by a man. It's different. It's quicker. And it's not about you," Jody said with a knowing smile on her face.

"Jody, it's past one o'clock," Mason said. "You can buy liquor. Please, can you go down to the store and get two, no make that three bottles of Champagne? One for today and two for the mother to be. She'll need to be lubricated for her special night. He might need lubrication too."

"No problem." And within ten minutes, she was out the door.

"Now, alone time," Mason said and pulled an envelope out of her purse. "As promised. Here is a photo of Carlos," Mason said, putting it in front of Dana.

"He's kind of young here." Dana reached into her own purse and took out three photo envelopes, dropping one on the table. "He's a lot older here."

Mason looked at her wide-eyed. "How did you get this?"

"I took it. But here is a more interesting shot." She dropped another photo on the table. "Here is Carlos with the chief of police for Miami. He's the old friend who got you that old photo, right? I would say that's a good photo of him and Carlos."

Mason studied the photo.

"Oh, here's one of the governor. I think it's a good shot of him too. Don't you think?"

Mason's gaze was fixed on the photo of the governor. "I know him."

"Then perhaps you know this congressman." Dana dropped another photo in front of Mason, who was open-mouthed as she studied the photos.

"And well, these are stars and movie producers. I think they do movies in Miami. This is interesting: news anchors. I think there are three of them. I've seen this businessman on commercials." Dana finished dumping the photos on the table and pushed them across the table in front of Mason. "If you don't recognize them, their names are on the backs. Carlos is very popular. Don't you think?"

Mason was dumbfounded. "I'm not even going to ask how you got these photos."

"Oh, you can. I sat across the canal from Carlos' house two, sometimes three, times a day, just taking interesting photos. Most of this pile came from one big party." Dana dropped photos of the front and back of the house. "His address is on the back. He's on Star Island. A very private island."

Handing another pile of photos from the other envelope, she said, "I don't know who these people are. They were taken at different times. I was hoping you could find out."

Dana leaned forward, and the Red Bitch came out. Mason knew the look. "Honey, here is the deal. I don't need any trouble for the next two or three years. If you would please tell me if anything is coming my way. That's all. Just tell me."

Mason held her breath for a moment. "I won't let anything happen to you. You'll be protected."

"That's not what I asked you. I asked you politely to tell me as soon as you find anything out. Nothing else. You understand, don't you?"

Mason felt a chill go up her spine. "I understand."

16. SAVANNA

"What?" Debbie said. They were sitting on Dana's patio, sipping Cokes and laughing about their trip to Florida.

"Why does everybody answer me with *what*? I said, can you set me up on a date with Casey? That's like a yes or no answer." Dana looked at Debbie with wide eyes.

"Is this about sperm?" Debbie giggled.

"Yes. And keep July fourteenth to the nineteenth open. We're going to Savannah," Dana said.

"What?"

"Again? What? Keep July—oh, you heard me. I figured that my most fertile days are the fifteenth to the seventeenth. The extra days are so if I'm off. God knows I only want to do this once." Dana rolled her eyes.

"You crack me up. You're really going through with this, aren't you?" Debbie was serious.

"Yep. I got permission from Jody, Mason, the boys, and Sally. So it's a go."

"It's a go. Two weeks to launch. Houston, we have a problem. Oh, I am so funny," Debbie laughed.

"What's the problem?"

"You got everyone's permission, but Casey's," Debbie pointed out.

"Just get him on the phone. I'll take care of the rest." Dana handed the phone to Debbie.

Debbie dialed Casey. "Have you ever seen a dick?" Debbie asked while waiting for Casey to answer.

"Yeah. At school. They just show me without asking. Don't they show you?"

Nodding, Debbie spoke into the phone. "Hi, Casey. It's Debbie. How are you doing?"

"I'm doing fine. It's nice to hear from you. I haven't seen you since graduation. What have you been up to?" Casey was glad to hear from her.

"Well, Dana and I went to Florida, South Beach, and Disneyworld. We had a great time. But the reason I'm calling you is Dana wants to go out with you."

"Really? I didn't think she liked boys." Casey was surprised.

"Well, she's sitting right here beside me. She said I should call you and ask you to ask her out. I think she's hot for you. So, ask her." Dana rolled her eyes and waved her hands for Debbie to back off. Debbie just turned her back to Dana. "Yeah, she really wants to go out with you tonight."

"Sure, but why me?" Casey asked.

Debbie cupped her hand around the mouthpiece. "Because I told her you're great in the sack. You stud."

"That's it. Give me the phone." Dana struggled with Debbie for a few seconds before Debbie gave up the phone.

"Hi, this is Dana. Look, if you don't want to go out with me tonight, you don't have to." Debbie was making little kissy sounds in the background. Dana was rolling her eyes and waving for her to shut up with one hand.

"No. I mean, yes. Where do you want to go?" Casey eagerly asked.

"How about that Mexican place in the Lenox Mall? Say about seven?"

"Sure, sounds good." Casey was happy to be asked out. The truth was he was tall, good-looking, and very shy. It was Debbie who had seduced him, not the other way around.

Debbie was the only girl he had asked out, and that was only after they had sex. He had never built up the nerve to ask anyone else out.

"See you there. Don't be late." Dana hung the phone up. She looked at Debbie. "Thanks for all your help. NOT." They were both laughing.

"He's going to be in for a shock. Let's go figure out what you're going to wear." Debbie said, getting up.

*

Dana wore high wedges and a short, lightweight summer dress that was white with little red flowers. It was cut low. When she walked into the restaurant, with the sun low behind her, Casey could see the shadow of her legs under her dress. He had commandeered a table in the corner and was standing to wave at her. She had seen him as she walked in; he didn't have to wave. She walked up and gave him a kiss on the cheek.

"Thank you for coming," Dana said.

"No, thank you for asking me," he said, directing her to the seat across from him.

"I hope you like Mexican food," Dana said, picking up the menu.

"Sure, I love it." Casey said, "Just not too hot. And no beans."

Dana looked up. She thought, *not too hot is one thing. But no beans in a Mexican restaurant?* "Maybe we should go to another place?" she asked.

"No, no. This is great. Really, I love Mexican food. Really." Casey said nervously.

Dana put down her menu. "Casey, why are you so nervous? Do I scare you or something?"

He took a deep breath. "Mom says, I'm way too shy. She says I should be more forceful and outgoing. That's just not me." His hands were shaking. "Jesus, I should go. I'm sorry." He started to get up.

"Don't you dare get up." She reached over and put her hand on his arm so that he had to sit back down. "Now, we're going to have a nice dinner. We're going to talk. We're going to find out about one another. So think before you talk. But say what you think." She was forceful but with a kind smile on her face, a talent she had learned to put people at ease, even when they should not be.

They talked. They ordered their meals. They talked some more.

"Let's go to my Dad's gallery. It's just around the corner. I've got something I want to discuss with you in private."

"I don't know. It's getting kind of late." Casey's nervously looking at his watch.

How did Debbie ever get this guy in bed? Dana asked herself. "It's not even nine. Come on. Are you afraid of me?" She teased. "Come on." She took his hand and led him out of the restaurant.

Casey followed Dana in his mother's car. Christopher had left the gallery at seven Dana let them in and shut off the alarm and turned on a few lights, just enough to give the gallery an intimate glow.

"Pretty neat," Casey said, looking around.

Dana went behind the counter and pulled out a bottle of Champagne and two glasses. She had moved the table back into one of the side galleries, out of the view of the front window. Showing him to the table and chairs, she handed him the bottle and said, "Open it, please."

Casey fumbled with the foil, wire, and cork. It popped suddenly, giving him a start and Dana a giggle. Some of the suds fell on the floor and he looked shocked. "Don't worry. Happens all the time. Please pour." Dana indicated the glasses. He poured and sat. Dana held up her glass. "Toast to us getting along," she said, smiling.

Casey settled in, drinking most of his Champagne in one nervous swallow.

"I've got a proposition for you," Dana said.

Casey with a surprised look on his face. "What?" he chuckled.

"Yes. It's that kind of proposition. But not the way you're thinking. Want another glass, honey?" She leaned over showing as much cleavage as possible as she poured him another glass of Champagne. She was not wearing a bra.

"I need to get pregnant," Dana said with her smile well in place.

"What?" Casey said.

Dana took a breath. *What? Again!* she thought. "I need to get pregnant."

Casey let that sink in for a few seconds and drained his glass. When the light finally went off in his head, he put up his hands. "Oh, no. I'm not ready to get married and have kids. I've got plans."

"I know. This isn't that kind of proposition. It's not a hooker kind of proposition either. More of a business kind of proposition. Just listen for a minute." Dana held his arm so he couldn't get up. "Look, you're tall, good-looking, and smart. What girl wouldn't want your kids? But please listen. Here's the deal, and you're going to like it." It was all that Dana could do to keep him from bolting out the door.

"Please sip your Champagne while I explain." With her free hand, she poured him another glass. "We're going to Savannah from July fourteenth to the nineteenth. We're going to make a baby. When I'm sure I'm pregnant, I'm going to give you ten thousand dollars. That's one hundred, one hundred-dollar bills."

Casey was not sure what was going on, but he was not struggling as much. "But we got to make our parents believe we're married." Dana pulled out the marriage license. It was dated July fifteenth. "You just have to sign here."

Casey looked down at the marriage license.

"You'll join the Navy."

"What?" Casey said.

Dana let out a sigh. "Do I mumble or something? Everyone is saying, *What*?"

"Yeah, join the Navy. But why?"

"Because I want you to go away for years. After you join up and go to boot camp or whatever they call it in the Navy, I'll give you another ten thousand dollars. But that's got to be like the day after we tell our parents," Dana said.

"Well, I always wanted to join the Marines," Casey said, warming up to the idea.

"No. The Navy. I want you alive, just not here. When you go to sea, I'll give you another, and the last, ten thousand."

"Okay. The Navy sounds good to me." Casey did not see a downside here anywhere.

"Now, here is a separation and custody agreement. It says we were never married. You have no claim on me or anything I might ever have. And the big one: I have sole custody of the kid, and if you want to see the kid, see here." She pointed out the clause titled *visitation rights*. "You got to tell me at least a week in advance. Sundays only, and then from one p.m. to six p.m. and supervised by the person of my choice or me. I didn't want that, but Jody said it would make it more. What did she say? Reasonable."

Casey drained his glass again. He looked at the agreement.

"Here, I'll pour you another glass," Dana said while he looked at the agreement. "Any problems?" Dana asked.

"I'm just not really sure."

Dana let the straps fall from her shoulders, her top peeled away enough to show her breasts. "Really?" Dana said.

His mouth open, he thought, *What the hell, I get laid and paid. How can this be bad?* He signed the separation and custody agreement where Dana pointed. "Here is the fake marriage license. It's just saying we were married July fifteenth. Listen to me. We need to make your parents think we're married. Got it?" Dana said, pulling up her top.

"We need to seal this deal with a kiss," he said after signing.

Dana leaned across the small table, gathering up the documents. They kissed. Casey tried to insert his tongue into Dana's mouth, but she pulled back quickly. "Just so you know. I don't like the tongue thing. Okay?" *Except with Debbie,* she thought.

"Sorry," Casey said his eyes down.

"That's okay. You didn't know. No big thing," Dana said, and she pulled his head toward her. They touched foreheads and shared a light kiss on the lips. "Thank you. You're doing me a huge favor. You'll be part of my thoughts for the rest of my life. Let's go."

At the doorway, she wrapped her arms around his waist, facing him. "Thanks again. I'll pick you up at ten the morning of the fourteenth at your house. Drive home safely." She closed the door behind him.

She cleared the glasses, then poured what little was left of the Champagne down the drain and buried the bottle in the trash. She cleaned up the floor and put everything back into place.

"Yeah, we're going to do really well," She said, looking around before turning off the lights, Dana was talking about the gallery, not Casey.

A few days later, Dana pulled up in front of Casey's house and honked. Casey came running out ten seconds later with his backpack. Opening the passenger car door from the driver's side, Dana took his bag and handed it to the backseat.

Casey got in and closed the door. Looking into the backseat, he saw Debbie. "What? What is she doing here?"

"Going with us, of course," Dana said as she powered away from the curb. It was a four-hour drive from Atlanta to Savannah. Casey talked non-stop. Debbie napped.

They got The Hyatt in Savannah is on the Savannah River late afternoon. Dana dropped Casey and Debbie off at the lobby entrance with their luggage and parked the Black Devel in the garage. She covered it with a gray car cover. "Sleep tight." She patted the spoiler.

By the time Dana reached the lobby, their luggage was already pilled on the bellhop's cart. When they reached their rooms, Casey opened his door and stood back. Debbie opened her door and went in. "That bag goes there." Dana pointed out Casey's backpack to the bellman. "The rest goes there." She pointed out Debbie's room. Casey gave the bellman a fiver and gave Dana a *what happened* look.

"It's okay, lover. We're not married yet." She gave him a quick kiss and a pat on the butt.

No sooner had they shut their doors than they heard Casey knocking on the adjoining door.

"Come in," Dana said, opening the door. "Isn't this wonderful." She held out her hands, twirling around. "Oh, look. A freighter," she said, pointing out of the fifth-floor window. The freighter's helm was level with them. It was so close that they could easily see the crew.

"What's going on? I'm confused," Casey said.

"Oh, you thought I was sleeping with you," Dana said, turning to him.

"Believe me, you don't want to sleep with Dana," Debbie said. "She snores and smacks me around in her sleep. I'm used to it. I wouldn't want to put you through that." Debbie was gently guiding Casey to his door. "Now, go shower and change. Let's go find something to eat. I'll knock when we're ready," she said, slowly closing the door.

"Do I snore?" Dana whispered to Debbie.

"No, sweetie. But you do smack me around. That's the part I like."

They giggled, then tried to take a shower together. "This isn't going to work. Someone's going to get hurt in this small tub," Dana said.

"Then me first," Debbie said. "Then we can rub cream on each other."

They help each other get dressed and put on their makeup. Debbie sprayed Red Door perfume on Dana's chest and her newly shaven pubic area. "Hey! That burns," Dana said, rubbing herself.

"I'm sorry. I'll kiss it and make it better." Debbie bent down.

"Why did you do that? Not that, the other thing. Spraying me down."

"You want to turn him on, don't you?" Debbie asked.

"Well, now I'm not sure about this romance thing." Dana was getting cold feet. "Besides, he was ready to do me in the car."

"Come on. We talked about this. This is going to be your first time. Maybe your only time with a man. Let's put a little romance in it. For you. So, you'll know what it's like. Just this once."

"Okay," Dana said, pursing her lips together.

"Then follow my instructions. Trust me, he'll love this perfume," she said. Dana had to admit that Debbie was the authority when it came to Casey. "Now, when we're out in public, make goo-goo eyes at him. Pet him a little. Men are like cats. They love to be petted, and when they have had enough, they run away."

When they knocked on Casey's door, he quickly shut off the game on TV and opened the door. He had splashed on too much Polo aftershave.

"Ah," Dana said, looking at Debbie, who gave a little head jerk which meant compliment Casey. "You smell nice, honey," Dana said. She shrugged as if to say to Debbie, *Right*?

"You too," he said. They left the doors open between the rooms. Casey opened his door and ushered the girls out to the hallway. The ride down to the lobby, in the enclosed elevator, was a bit suffocating. Both Dana and Debbie coughed a little. Casey was the first one out of the elevator and led the way onto the street.

"Does it wear off?" Dana mouthed to Debbie. *Yes*, Debbie nodded as they walked onto the street.

"Hmm." Dana rolled her eyes.

They walked to the nearest square. Savannah is one of the very few pre-Civil War cities in the South.

"You know, when Savannah was founded, the Irish and lawyers were not allowed, because both meant trouble. That was a while ago. So, I think you're safe, Casey. I'm not so sure about lawyers." Debbie teased Casey about his Irish blood.

"Very funny." Casey got the joke.

They walked through the streets, checking out the shops and restaurants. Along the way, Casey noted that many of the buildings had brass plaques noting *Built 1811, Built 1851*. Many different dates most were pre-Civil War. There weren't any pre-Civil War buildings in Atlanta.

Hours later, they settled on a restaurant whose porch faced an interesting street. There were restaurants and shops on both sides of the road. All had been there for well over a hundred years. Dana could imagine horses pulling carriages up and down this street. Now it was just tourists carrying bags.

"I guess Sherman didn't get here during the Civil War," Casey said.

The waitress was standing nearby. "Oh, he was here. His army surrounded the town. Most of the men were gone. They were all dead, in the Confederate Army, or captured. There were only women, old men, and babies here then."

"Not much of a fight," Casey said.

"Oh, there was no fighting," the waitress went on. "The old folks went out and invited Sherman and his officers to see the town. They were ushered around town by beautiful women. They showed them how beautiful the town was. They had a great feast that night, and I'm sure the officers all got laid. The next day, they left. General Sherman left the town alone. True story."

"So, the town owes its existence to sex?" Debbie giggled reminded why they were in Savannah. Dana smiled a knowing smile. Casey didn't get it.

Opening the doors to their rooms, Dana gave Casey a kiss. "Take a shower. I'll be over shortly."

Dana dressed in a red peignoir set. It consisted of a thin short nightie and an equally thin red robe to her knees, then little red slippers with red fuzz across the toe. Debbie fluffed Dana's hair and touched up her makeup, then sprayed a little extra perfume in the necessary regions. She handed Dana a bottle of cold Champagne and two glass flutes. Then finally, a tube of Trojan lubricant. "Rub this on his dick before you get it on; you'll both like it. Guaranteed. Have fun." Debbie opened the door to find Casey standing naked in a towel just on the other side of the door. Dana took a deep breath. She thought, *Maybe I do need a little romance to get this done. Maybe some champagne too*. She stepped past Debbie and entered the room.

Debbie smiled and slowly closed the door, then leaned against the door and said aloud, "My little girl's getting laid."

Casey had the radio playing soft music. The light from the street below provided all the romantic light needed. Dana let him put his arms around her and gently give her a kiss on the lips.

Dana took a deep breath. "Remember how to open this?" she asked, handing him the Champagne bottle and dropping the lubricant discreetly on the bed. She set the glasses on the little table by the window and settled into the small chair. They sat across from each other Dana opened the conversation. "You look very sexy in that towel." They mostly complemented each other as they sipped their Champagne.

Dana stood. Turning her back to Casey, she dropped her robe. Then she lifted her arms over her head. One hand came to rest on the other upstretched elbow. She stretched, letting her hips sway to one side, then the other, her sheer nightie rising just enough to show a little bottom. All this had the desired effect on them both.

Casey came up behind her, placing his hands on her arms and letting them slide down to her breasts. He cupped them gently, then gently tweaked her nipples. His hands slid even lower, across her flat stomach. As he began to reach lower, Dana turned to face him. His towel fell to the floor. Dana rested her hands on his chest. She gently kissed him, guiding him step by step back to the bed. He felt the bed behind his knees and sat down on the bed, looking up at Dana's face, then her breasts. He put his face between Dana's small breasts.

She gently laid him back on the bed. She ran her hands down his chest to his very rigid dick. She retrieved the lubricant, then gently rubbed some of it on, starting at the tip. Moans and whispered *yes, yes* came from his lips.

Dana kneeled on top of him with one hand on his chest. The other found its way to his hard cock. With her face inches from him, she guided his cock into position. A little "Oh" came out of her mouth as he entered her. The lubricant did ease the invasion of her vagina.

She moved her hips once, twice, three times and felt him explode in her. She pressed down, taking all he had to offer. His body quivered in ecstasy. She lay on his chest for a little while. Then she kissed him and got up. Retrieving her robe from the floor as she left the room. Casey turned his head to watch her slowly close the door as she gave him a smile.

The next morning, he was gently awakened as she slipped between the sheets for a repeat performance.

During the day, the three of them explored Savannah. They took buggy tours of the city and night tours of the graveyards. The night ghost tours were the most entertaining.

At night, Dana would visit Casey's room several times. It was no longer about romance. It was about sex. As time went on, she found that she had to become more and more creative to get the results she desired.

The last evening, he had nothing left to give.

17. THE TEST

"How was your drive home?" Jody asked Saturday night.

"Just fine. Casey slept all the way and Debbie jabbered all the long way home," Dana complained into the phone.

"Would you like to come over for brunch Sunday? Mason thinks it should be a regular Sunday thing."

Dana thought about Mason's request. *A regular family social event? Less noticeable than a clandestine meeting in parks and coffee shops.* "Sure. Sounds like a good idea. Any special time?"

"Not really. Eleven or twelve or so. Anytime around there."

"See you tomorrow then." Dana settled on the patio next to the empty throne. "Well, Mom. I know you don't approve of the way I did this, but you know it's for the best. If you can help me out here, make sure those little swimmers hook up with my eggs, I would really appreciate it."

She put her hand on the arm of the throne, looking out at the unused mat, then closed her eyes and tried to empty her mind. But she kept seeing her mom on the mat, instructing the boys when they were still young. She could see her perfect body turning to her with a big smile on her face and coaxing her onto the mat, moving her arms for Dana to come to her.

Her eyes flew open. Seeing the empty mat and the vacant throne, she said, "Sorry, Mom," and went into the house and eventually to a sleepless night full of disturbing dreams, none of which she could remember the next morning.

Jody was making waffles and bacon when Dana got there. The grapefruit juice was already on the table. The coffee smell met her at the screen door and guided her into the kitchen. This time, there was no meeting at the door with hugs, just a "Come on in." And then hugs.

Jody served as Mason poured the coffee. As they settled in, Jody asked, "How was it? You know what I mean. How was *it*?" with emphasis on "it."

"Hmm. Well, the first time was over in seconds. Yes, I mean seconds." They all laughed. "The last time, he fell asleep." They all laughed again.

"How many times did you do it?" Jody asked.

"Only two to four times a day. Always at night."

"Poor guy," Mason said. "You banged him to death. No other woman will ever come close. Of course, when he tells the story, and he will tell the story for the rest of his life, it will be all about you going wild over him, and how he made you climax many, many times. All men are that way."

"So, I guess we'll know in what? About six weeks?" Jody asked. "By the way, I got you a present." Jody handed Dana a small but long box that Dana studied, puzzled, "What's this?"

"It's a pregnancy test kit. You pee on it. If it turns blue, you're pregnant."

"Oh." Dana looked at it and opened the end of the box to check out its contents.

"I'll be back in a few minutes," Dana said.

"No, honey. You kind of have to be pregnant for at least a month to find out. So, do you still have to pee?" Jody asked with a smile on her face.

"I guess not," Dana said, putting everything back into the box. "Thank you. Really, thank you."

They finished up their brunch with small talk and stories of Savannah.

"Well, I guess I got to go do something in the backyard. So, you can have your," Jody put her hand in the air, making claw marks with her two fingers, "private talk." She got up and gave them both a kiss on the cheek.

"Thanks," Mason called after her.

They sat for a minute, waiting to see who would take the lead. Mason finally said, "I'm working on it. The only real thing I have is that the chief of police lives in a two-million-plus dollar home in North Miami Beach. On a private island, no less. Tough to do on a hundred and ten-thousand-dollar income. I'm trying to dig deeper on that."

Dana said nothing. She just held her coffee cup with both hands.

"Also," taking the package of photos Dana had given her, she sorted through them until she pulled one out, tapping the photo, "he's a host on a Mexican television game show. He's possibly a pedophile. I'm working on any connection to the cartel."

Dana shoved the photos back to Mason without looking at them. The Red Bitch was just below the surface.

"I'm doing everything I can without showing my hand. I'm chief of police of Atlanta, not the world." Mason defended herself.

Dana softened. The Red Bitch moved back a little. "I know I'm expecting too much. But you understand Carlos came after me and raised the bounty tenfold when he didn't get my head. I'm just a tick on his ass. He could raise it again any time he wants." They sat quietly for a little while. "I know Ron is connected to them somewhere, somehow. I need to find that out."

"You have bigger problems than Ron. You've got Carlos and maybe the whole drug cartel after you. Ron is the least of your worries." Mason tilted her head. "Understand?"

Dana got that puzzled look on her face again. Something just hit her memory. "Let me see those photos again. The ones with the guys we don't know."

Mason shoved the stack back across the table. This time, Dana took her time carefully sifted through them, studying each one. "Here he is," she said, turning one over to Mason. "See him? The one in the back. The young guy sitting at the table. He's just behind Carlos. Him." Dana pointed.

Mason, examining the photo, pointed to a face in the background. "Him?"

"Yes. He was sitting next to Debbie and me in St. Augustine. He hit on us. That's a connection we can follow. The waitress acted like he was always there. See if you can find anything out about him."

Mason stacked up the photos, putting his picture on top. "Let's join Jody on the patio. I'll let you know if I find anything out."

The rest of the week went by quickly. Dana had a lot to catch up on at the gallery.

"I enlisted," Casey said on the phone toward the end of the week.

"In the Navy, I hope," Dana said.

"Of course. I go to the Great Lake Naval Training Station in about seven weeks. I'm going to be on subs. Isn't that cool?"

"Great Lakes Naval Training. Isn't that near Canada?" Dana asked again.

"Yeah. North of Chicago. Strange place to put a Naval training station, let alone a sub training base. I thought it would be in California or Hawaii. But no."

"That's great news. Do you want to meet for pizza tomorrow? Say, about eight-fifteen at that pizza place in the mall?" Dana said.

Casey was waving at her when she came in. They hugged, kissed, and he showed her into a booth. She took his hand and pulled him in beside her.

"Thank you. You kept to your part of the deal. I am so proud of you." She reached into her purse. "I always keep my part of any deal. You can trust in that." She handed him an envelope under the table. "Now, you can do anything you want with that. But, please remember, you have joined the Navy. You won't need a car. They are going to take care of everything for you for the next few months. The Navy will give you a place to sleep, food to eat, and they will take up your whole day. And for this, they are going to pay you too. Please put it away till you need it."

It was a one-sided conversation. Casey bought a used Nissan Z car and sold it sixteen weeks later at a loss. He had put less than a thousand miles on it.

*

"Well, pee on it," Debbie said, standing in the doorway of Dana's bathroom.

"I can't pee with you standing there," Dana said.

"Well, you have before." Debbie threw her hands up in the air.

"Out, damn it."

Debbie stepped around the corner. "I can hear you. You're still not peeing."

"Come on. Shut up."

A few minutes later, Dana came out of the bathroom holding a stick in front of her. "Nothing," she said disappointedly.

"Silly. It says here to wait ten minutes. Give it to me. Wait, you peed on it, right?" Debbie said.

Dana nodded.

"Then you hold it. But behind your back. Don't look at it."

It was a very long ten minutes, especially with Debbie chatting on about nothing at all, non-stop.

"Okay, it's ten minutes. Let's see," Debbie demanded.

It was blue. They both squealed.

"You're pregers. What names have you picked out? Boy and girl names, please," Debbie asked.

"I haven't really considered it. Okay, this is where my plan runs out." Dana was in slight shock.

*

The next day, Dana contact Casey as soon as possible.

"Casey. Good news. I'll see you at the pizza place at eight-fifteen tonight,"

"Sure. What?" he said.

"Yeah. See you there." Dana hung up, thinking, *why does he think I was calling? Good thing he'll be locked up underwater for six months at a time.*

Casey was standing at the same booth, waving. Dana rolled her eyes. *God, married to this man is not for me,* she thought and slid into the booth. Casey slid in next to her. "Good news?" he asked.

"Yes. How do you like your new car?"

"Oh, it's great, and it's only two years old." He was going to go into more description of the car, but Dana stopped him.

"Can you load everything you are going to need in the Navy in it? I'm guessing you don't need much." Dana said.

"Sure. No problem. But I don't have to leave for almost two weeks yet."

"Well, honey. You'll need to leave Monday. Take some time in Chicago. I hear it's a great city." Dana waited for him to answer.

He looked at her, confused. Then the light finally went off.

"You're pregnant! Holy shit. You're pregnant. And I did it." He pushed out his chest and grinned from year to ear.

"Yes, you did. Now, remember the deal. You remember the deal?" Dana passed another envelope to him under the table.

"I do." Casey was counting his money under the table.

"Casey, did you hear me?"

"What?" he said, not looking up.

Dana rolled her eyes. "It's all there. Count it later. Put it in your pocket."

"Yes, I do remember the deal," he said, looking up. He folded the envelope over and started to put in his back pocket.

"Not there. That's the first place pickpockets go. Put it in your front pocket."

"Okay, woman," he said out of frustration, stuffing the money in his front pocket.

"Here is how we're going to do this. Casey, are you listening?" She nudged him. "Pack your car up Sunday afternoon. Tell your parents—" Dana looked at Casey and reconsidered that. "Don't tell them anything. Just tell your parents to meet us at Bobbie's Steak House. Tell them my dad wants to meet them. I think five would be a good time. Then we'll go to the Holiday Inn off 85, in Roswell. The next day, you'll drop me off at home. And then you'll drive to Chicago."

"Ah," Casey started.

"Casey, did you get all of that?"

"Do I got to leave the next day?"

Dana wondered whose brain her baby was going to get. "Yes, you do. Remember the deal. I'll give you another ten thousand when you ship out. Casey, that's the deal."

18. THE HONEYMOON

"Yes, Dad. This is important. Please, I need your support," Dana said as they pulled into a parking spot at Bobbie's Steak House. She was ready for this meeting. She was dressed to impress, wearing an empire dress of red lace over satin, cut to just above the knee. The little extra the style afforded around the middle suggested a bump. A bump that wasn't there yet.

The only thing she couldn't control was Christopher's drinking. He wasn't drunk yet.

Casey and his parents were already seated at a table. Casey stood and waved at Dana and Christopher. Dana waved and rolled her eyes. *Why does he do that*, she thought?

She sat next to Casey and looked at him as lovingly as possible. Casey's mother suspected that they were going to announce their engagement. She was totally against that. However, she felt that with Casey going off to the Navy, any commitment would not last.

After introductions, Christopher signaled for the waiter. He ordered a bourbon for himself; Dana ordered a seltzer; Casey ordered a Coke. His parents already had martinis in front of them. His mother's glass was empty, so she ordered another. They had the usual small talk while they ordered dinner.

Dana squeezed Casey's hand telling him it was time to give the short speech they had rehearsed on the phone.

"Well, I guess you're all wondering why we invited you all here. You all know Dana and I are in love." That was the first time Dana had heard *in love* and *Dana* in the same sentence from Casey. "So, we got married when we went to Savannah."

Casey's mother's jaw dropped, nearly hitting the table. She sat in stunned silence. Casey's dad was the first to recover. "Congratulations. I'm so happy for you. Welcome to the family, Dana."

"Yes. Congratulations," Christopher said less enthusiastically, raising his glass in a toast "Welcome, Casey."

"What the hell? You're fucking with me!" Casey's mom said loud enough for the whole restaurant to go silent. Casey went dead silent as well. He let go of Dana's hand and kind of faded back into his chair.

"It's true," Dana said, taking over. "See." She pulled out the marriage license and passed it to her dad. "We got married in Savannah. Debbie was the maid of honor."

Christopher passed it to Casey's mom, who said, "Well, we'll get it annulled. You're way too young, Casey. We can't do this."

Everyone else remained quiet. Casey's dad visibly moved away from his wife. Christopher took Dana's hand.

"There is something else you should know," Dana said. She was looking in Casey's mom's eyes steady, unblinking, projecting control. Dana took Casey's hand back. "I'm seven weeks pregnant with Casey's child."

This time, everyone had a shocked look on their faces. "God, the hits just keep on coming," Casey's mom said. "Well, we're not paying for it. You pay for your own abortion. My baby boy is not old enough to have a kid. You will get an abortion, you slut." She tried to stare down Dana.

"Now wait a minute," Christopher started to say.

"It's okay, Dad." Dana said, looking directly at Casey's mom, "It's my baby. It's my body. It's my life. And it's my decision. My decision is I'm keeping my baby."

"Meg, please," Casey's dad said to his wife, putting his arm around her. She pushed his arm off.

"We're leaving," she said, getting up to leave. "I'll see you at home, Casey."

"You better say goodbye to him now. He's leaving with me." Dana sat and took Casey's hand and put her other hand on his shoulder as they also got up to go. "Then he's going to the Navy." Her eyes were as hard and deadly as her voice. "I'm in charge now."

Casey's parents left the restaurant in a huff. Dana gave her dad a kiss on the cheek and a hug. "I love you, Dad. Thank you." She stood up and pulled Casey after her. "Will you be okay?" she asked her dad.

"Sure," he said, waving them off. Dana led Casey out of the restaurant.

Christopher was now the only one left at the table. The server came by with a big tray of dishes full of steaks. He opened a folding stand and set the tray down, looking around. Christopher took a deep swig of his bourbon. "Mine's the one without potatoes," he said, holding up his empty glass. "I'll have another one of these, please."

*

Casey and Dana got in Casey's car. They could see Casey's mom staring at them from their car on the other side of the parking lot. "I got to go home," Casey said.

"No, you're not. You're in the Navy now. They got your ass. We are married, at least on paper, so the rest of you belongs to me." Dana smiled, gave Casey a kiss, and then waved at Meg. "Leave now, honey," she said lovingly.

In the Holiday Inn, they sat side by side on the bed. "I know it's hard, honey. Leaving your mom and all. It had to happen sometime." She was speaking in a soft and loving voice. "But you're doing so well. You're changing a lot of things in your life. You have so many adventures ahead of you. You just can't imagine." She put her arms around his neck and looked him in the eyes. "Remember, we have a deal. Tomorrow, you'll leave for Chicago. You're not coming home till after you graduate. That will be just before you ship out and you'll be free then. Everything will be okay, honey. Just don't you worry."

Casey was still sitting quietly, wringing his hands. His eyes were turned down.

"You just make sure you leave tomorrow morning. You won't be turning back. Honey, you'll need to do really well in boot camp," she said, still in her sweetest voice, "because if you don't, believe me, I promise you'll never use these again." And she patted his dick and balls, still looking him in the eyes.

"Now get some rest, honey. You have a long drive tomorrow." She kissed him on the forehead. "I need to get some air." Dana got up and as she opened the door, Casey said softly, "Bitch."

Dana stopped cold. A second later, she turned, throwing her hip out, one hand on it and the other arm high on the door frame. "That's Red Bitch to you," she said kindly and softly.

*

The next morning, Dana came out of the bathroom after her shower. She was wearing a towel, tied at the top of her breasts, and using another to dry her hair. "Wake up, sleepyhead," she said, shaking him awake.

He and sleepily reached for her with one hand. Dana stepped back. "Come on. I want lunch in Nashville. Get your butt moving." She turned to go back into the bathroom.

Words were starting to penetrate Casey's mind. "I thought I was going to drop you off at your house this morning?"

During the evening, Dana had decided to go with Casey to Chicago. She didn't trust him not to turn around and go back to his mama. "No, I thought we should have a honeymoon. After all, we're married. It will be fun. Now get up!"

"Honeymoon?" he said, sitting up. His feet hit the floor.

"Yes, honey. Honeymoon." She went into the bathroom. Casey followed her in. "Shower and get ready," Dana said, turning to the mirror. Casey slipped out of his boxers and into the running shower. Dana finished drying her hair and putting on a little makeup. Casey looked around for a towel from behind the shower curtain.

"You used up all the towels," he complained.

"Here." Dana took off her towel and, standing naked, threw it to him. She walked out.

"Damn," Casey said, looking down at his erection. He dried as quickly as he could and came out to see Dana already in her panties and bra. She was pulling on shorts.

Looking up, she saw Casey naked with his erection. "If you are going to do something with that, you had better go back into the bathroom and do it."

"I thought?" Casey said with a disappointed look on his face. "When you said honeymoon, I thought?"

"I know what you thought. I said honeymoon. I didn't say anything about sex." She finished pulling up her shorts and pulled on a t-shirt. "Don't worry, honey. We'll have lots of fun. Just hurry. We will have lunch in Nashville." Giving him a kiss on the cheek, she said, "I'll be out by the pool. When you finish your business," she touched his dick, "come get me."

She stopped at the front desk and placed a quick call to her dad. He was a bit fuzzy from the night before. "Yes, Dad, I'm taking Casey to Chicago. See you in a few days."

"Sure. Okay. See you later." He didn't get what was happening and would barely remember the short conversation.

*

In Nashville, they stopped at The Johnny Cash Museum and Café. They ate lunch and walked around the Museum. Then they spent an hour in the Country Music Hall of Fame and Museum. "I can't look at another guitar. Let's get on the road," Dana said, taking Casey's hand and guiding him out of the museum.

Back in the car, Dana's feet were up on the dashboard, the map across her knees. "When we get to Clarksville, look for State Road 79. That will take us to The Land Between the Lakes National Recreation Park."

"Why?" Casey asked.

"Because it's beautiful. And we have never been there. That's why," Dana answered and ruffled her map.

Just out of the park, they stopped in Calvert City. They walked across the street from the hotel to an Italian Restaurant and shared a large plate of spaghetti and meatballs. They talked of the day and of the sites they had shared. They were enjoying each other's company more than ever before.

*

"Nope," Dana said, taking Casey's hand off her breast. The grab had woken her the next morning. They were lying in bed, a standard size bed which didn't offer a lot of room for two people.

Casey moaned.

"Just what do you think you're going to do on a sub. With guys. For six months?" Dana asked.

"I don't know," he said.

"Well, learn to control yourself. If you don't, you'll come back without any teeth." Dana rolled over on her other side.

*

They drove through the Shawnee National Forest. They again took their time to see beautiful rock walls dropping straight into the crystal-clear, fast running water.

That afternoon, they got to Chicago and the Warwick Allerton Hotel on Michigan Avenue. Parking the car cost almost as much as the room. "We're on our honeymoon," Dana said, cuddling up next to Casey at the check-in counter. The lady behind the counter smiled and congratulated them. At the same time, she was changing their room from a standard bedroom to a small suite. "Enjoy your stay." She handed them the keys.

The room was comfortable with a small living space and spacious bedroom. "Oh, we can't waste this place." Casey turned to Dana.

"We won't! We'll enjoy Chicago." Dana turned and gave him a quick kiss. She knew that wasn't what he meant. She ruffled through his suitcase, coming up with a blue short-sleeved button-up shirt. "Mind if I wear this? This t-shirt is getting a bit stinky."

Just around the corner from their hotel was Geno's East pizza. They stuffed themselves with deep dish pizza. That night, full and exhausted, Casey for once rolled over and went to sleep.

"First, I need to go clothes shopping," Dana said over breakfast. "There's a huge mall only two blocks from here."

"I don't want to go. Clothes shopping is for women, it's not a guy's thing,"

"Okay," Dana said. "I'll see you back in the room when I'm finished."

Back in the room, Casey was relaxing on the sofa watching a baseball game on TV.

She dropped her bags in the middle of the bed, "Oh Casey, can you come in here? I have something for you."

"Oh yeah," he said hopefully, jumping up.

Dana was holding up a blue sports coat, white dress shirt, and blue and white striped tie. "See what I got you,"

It took a moment. "Great," was his only word.

"Come try them on. We're going to a nice dinner. No, a great, once-in-a-lifetime dinner tonight. It's on the ninety-fifth floor of the Hancock Building. They say we can see four states from there." Dana said, "We need to leave here at seven. I made a reservation at the concierge desk in the lobby."

Casey slipped on the jacket. He checked himself out in the mirror. "Looks really great," he said, modeling himself.

"I'm going to take a little nap." Dana said, "Then we'll get ready. Oh, by the way, it's a jacket and tie only. Kind of like a prom." She kissed Casey on the forehead and laid down to take a nap.

*

Casey looked spiffy in his new sports coat, white shirt, blue striped tie, and khakis. Dana wore her new designer red mini dress and new red strappy six-inch heels. Neiman Marcus, just across the street, was a trove of great shoes. Dana was tempted to buy at least ten pair. She kept it down to four.

The elevator shook as it went up ninety-five floors nonstop. Casey grabbed Dana's arm. "Are you okay?" he asked. Dana just smiled.

Dana introduced themselves at the desk.

"You're on your honeymoon. Congratulations. I have a wonderful table for you by the window."

They both were hypnotized by the view. There were no clouds in the sky and no wind. Lake Michigan did not have a ripple. It was a two-hour dinner.

"We are going to the Chicago Art Museum," Dana said at breakfast. Casey rolled his eyes. "Don't do that. Just start with me. If you get tired, I'll meet you somewhere. But please try?"

Dana was blown away. Casey was blown out in an hour. "Oh wow," Dana said as she threw herself down on the sofa in the hotel suite. "They have a Chagall stained glass window. Oh my God, if I could live there, I would."

Casey was watching another baseball game on TV. "Great," he said, not looking up. "Pizza tonight? I liked that place."

Dana rolled her eyes. All of Chicago to pick from and he wanted to go back to the same place. Shaking her head all she said was, "Sure."

*

The next morning, Casey woke up with Dana's head on his chess her hand was resting on his hip. Dana was wearing just a t-shirt and panties. He didn't want to move. He didn't want her to wake up. In just a few minutes, she moved. Running her hand up his chest, she kissed him on the cheek.

"Good morning," she said. "You're awake early." She rolled over on her back. "I want to thank you for everything. Really everything. This honeymoon has been, all I can say is wonderful." She kissed him on the cheek. "Now, the news. I have a three-thirty flight back to Atlanta today. And you need to get to the base tomorrow morning."

Dana got out of bed. She stretched that stretch he had seen before, she turned to see a tent pole in Casey's lap. "Oh sorry," she said and turned away to go to the small living room. She stopped and turned to Casey. "You know, honey, if you want to, I can stay and watch. You know, if that would help?"

Casey smiled. "The memories of our Savannah trip are all the help I need."

Dana smiled lovingly. "Thank you. You're special and will always be special to me."

"Go. When I get out of the bathroom, we'll decide what we are going to do today," Casey said.

Dana almost hated to go. She had found something in Casey she sincerely liked. For all his immaturity, he was still a sweet guy.

*

At O'Hare airport, Casey found a place next to the curb, not far from her entrance. He got out and pulled out two new suitcases out of the backseat of the car. Putting them on the curb, he said, "I thought you traveled light."

"I started out that way. I collected more baggage than I had expected." That was not just a reference to her suitcases. She turned to Casey and put her arms around his neck. "I hope this helps you get through boot camp." Then she gave him a long, wet kiss. She left him, breathless, standing at the curb.

The porter picked up her bags. She found her way to the gate. She was a little early. "I should not have done that," she thought. "He'll expect more. I don't want to hurt him. I guess all I wanted to do is just use him. God, I am a bitch."

19. THE THRONE

"No, darling, it's no problem. I can pick you up. What time was that? Oh, I remember. Five-thirty at the curb," Debbie said into the phone. Then added, "You know, I have nothing to do on my Saturdays except wait for you to call."

"I'm sorry, sweetie. I thought I would be home Monday, Tuesday at the latest. But you know how Casey can be. I'll make it up to you. Sorry; I got to run. They're going to close the airplane door. Love you."

*

Debbie stopped at the loading zone at the airport. "Three trips around the airport," Debbie said, getting out of her VW.

"You did some shopping, I see," she said, looking at Dana's new suitcases on the curb and folding forward the passenger seat on her VW to put Dana's bags in the backseat. Dana picked up a bag to put in the back seat, Debbie took it out of her hands, "Back off, Preggers." She held up her hand for Dana to back off.

Debbie stuffed the last suitcase into the backseat and folded the seat back into place. It was already set for the longest legs. Standing aside, she held the door open for Dana. "Nice blouse. You trying to look knocked up?"

Dana was wearing her new shorts, new white tennis shoes with no laces, and a loose-fitting black top. It slid off one shoulder or the other. When she pulled it up, it would challenge her authority and slide off the other side.

She stopped at the car door. "Come on, Debbie. Please?" She leaned forward and gave her a kiss on the lips. Debbie looked at Dana and shook her head. She leaned forward and started the VW.

"Let's go somewhere and talk. Maybe have something to eat." Dana put her hand on Debbie's hand, which rested on the stick shift.

"Bobbie's Steak House?" Debbie asked sarcastically.

"Hell no."

"That Mexican place in Lenox Mall?" Debbie was looking straight ahead.

"Double hell no." Dana thought, *I got it. She's jealous.* "Shakees Pizza parlor," Dana said. That was the first place they went after school, so long ago.

Debbie softened a bit. Looking ahead, she said only, "Okay." She ground the gears into first, pulling away from the curb.

They sat in the corner. Debbie brought their sodas back to the table and went back for their large pepperoni, sausage, and double cheese pizza. She sat and looked at Dana.

"I'm sorry. I should have called."

"Damn right!" Debbie said. Her eyes were straight on Dana. "I was worried sick. I called your dad about ten times. He said you called from fucking Roswell. He said all you said was, 'It's going to take a while.' Period. That's all. Shit."

"I'm sorry. By the way, you didn't want to be at that dinner. Did you know Casey's mom is such an asshole?"

"No," Debbie said, looking forward.

"Well, she is. Casey was going to run home to mama. I had to make sure he got to Chicago."

"That's a twelve-hour drive. What took you five fucking days?"

"One, I had to keep him there till I was sure he was going to check in at boot camp. Two, the truth is I wanted to see Chicago. I'm sorry. I was selfish. I'm really sorry." Dana said her head down her hands in her lap, she was totally submissive, which was uncharacteristic for Dana.

"Did you fuck him?" Debbie asked with her nose in the air.

"No! Is that what you worried about?"

"Well, I heard you two going at it in Savannah," Debbie argued with both hands on the table, leaning forward.

"With your permission. And only when you were next door. I came back to you every time. Come on. I wouldn't do that to you."

"Well, okay," Debbie said in a softer tone.

"I'll tell you everything. I'll answer all your questions. I have nothing to hide. Okay?"

"You would agree he's a horny little bastard," Debbie said.

"Oh, God. He had a hard-on every morning. I made him take care of himself. In the other room. I never watched."

"Really! You made him jerk off?" Debbie asked wide-eyed.

"No. Jerking off was all his idea. Or maybe just his dick's idea." They both laughed. "I see what you saw in him." Dana looked up. "He can be sweet in a naive, clumsy, awkward, mama's boy way. All that time together in the same bed, he kept his hands to himself. He does follow orders. I think the Navy is the perfect place for him."

"I agree."

*

Debbie insisted on carrying both suitcases up to Dana's room. She dropped them both on the floor and gave Dana a long, wet kiss. "I'm sorry I was so hard on you. But you had it coming."

"I did. I'm sorry. I'm the bitch here." Dana meant it.

"I've got to leave early tomorrow morning. I've got some kind of college interview thing tomorrow morning," Debbie said, sitting down on the side of the bed.

"On Sunday?" Dana was puzzled.

"Can you believe it? I can tell you it's not Marymount. Not a Catholic school, not on Sunday. Mom and Dad are taking me. I guess they have to talk to them too. It's at the Hilton downtown."

"I know that hotel well," Dana said, remembering her diner with Mason and Judy there.

*

She had lox and bagels, a side of fresh strawberries, and coffee ready for Christopher when he came into the kitchen for his Sunday call from the boys.

"How are you?" he asked after a sip of his coffee.

"A little upset tummy this morning. Not much." She had actually thrown up. Debbie had held her hair.

"Dad, before we talk to the boys, I want you to know Casey and I decided to get a divorce. We think it's best for both of us. Also, for the kid, since he's not going to be in its life much anyway."

"Oh." Christopher sat quietly sipping his coffee and looking down at his breakfast but not touching it.

Dana sat quietly, waiting for some signal from Christopher one way or another. About forty-five minutes later, the phone rang.

Christopher did not talk much. Dana did most of the talking. Most of that was reassuring the boys. Dana finished off with, "I expect to see you all here in about seven months. And Beau, get those lips all warmed up."

Christopher sat for a while, not saying a word. Then he got up and went into the library.

Dana took a deep breath, closed her eyes, and shook her head. She got up and put Christopher's breakfast and fresh coffee on a tray. She took it in to him.

He had turned on the record player playing Bill Joel softly in the background. He had poured himself a large bourbon, with no ice. She sat on the sofa and put the tray on the coffee table.

"Dad, I'm pregnant. I'm alone. I'm afraid. Daddy, I need your help."

He looked down into his bourbon.

"Daddy. Please. I really need your help. Please. I so need you sober, to help me." She was trying her best. He just sat there. "Please, Daddy. Mom would want you to help me. Mom would have helped me."

Christopher did not look up. He shouted down into his bourbon glass, "If Eve were around, you would not have gotten pregnant at seventeen."

Dana left his breakfast on the coffee table. Walking onto the patio, with tears running down her face, she sat down, putting her arm on the throne, her head down on her arm, she cried. She was sure she had lost her dad to liquor and depression.

More than an hour later, she gathered herself up, wiped the tears from her face, and walked back into the library. The record player was off. Christopher was still looking down into his bourbon. His glass was nearly full.

She picked up the tray, untouched by Christopher and took it into the kitchen and cleaned up. She looked up at the clock. Almost one.

At about the same time, the phone rang. "I'm sorry, Mason. I'm not coming over today. I got some thinking to do," she said. "Thank you."

She walked back into the library and leaned against the doorframe, her arms folded across her chest, thinking of all the peaceful, quiet, story time's she had spent there. Between her brothers, Gin's head on her lap, with her mom and dad in their comfortable chairs. She could not think of another word to say to her father.

Christopher had heard Dana's words at the kitchen table earlier. They didn't mean much then, but they slowly seeped into his brain.

Shouting into his bourbon had woken up what was left of his soul. He felt Eve sitting next to him, reading in her chair as she had done for years. It was if she put down her book and looked disapprovingly at him. "What do you think you're doing? You treat the boys like they are perfect gods. You have a daughter. A very special daughter. She alone has stayed with you. She alone has helped you. What are you thinking? You treat her like shit. You just ignore her."

"I'm afraid of her." He looked over at the empty chair. "I love her, I really do. But when I look at her, I see you, and I hurt. I miss you so much."

"You see her and see me. Yet you push me away? You are pushing me away forever."

"I know. I'm weak. Not strong like you, like Dana. I don't have your force, your strength, your unyielding will. How do I help her?" The tears were filling his eyes, then made warm tracks down his cheeks.

"The same way you helped me. By always being there."

He walked back to the patio. Dana was sitting next to the throne, her head hanging down. The pain in her heart had spread to her entire body. She said softly, "I'm sorry, Mom. I don't know what else to do."

Dana felt a hand on her shoulder. She looked up to see her dad. He came around and, taking both of her hands, he pulled her up. Wrapping his arms around her, he said into her ear, "I do. I'll help you."

They held each other tight, not wanting the moment to escape.

Christopher stepped back. "I bought this chair for Eve when she was pregnant with you." He leaned over and touched the chair, feeling Eve's presence; he could feel her wishes. "I know your mother would want this to be your chair from now on. You sit here." He lowered Dana into the throne.

*

Sunday was a rough day on Christopher, both physically and emotionally. He was wasted Saturday night, passing out before Dana came home. Sunday morning, he had left his vodka in his bed stand. He wanted to be as close to alive as he could be when he talked to the boys.

Christopher went to bed early Sunday. He didn't want Dana to see him with the shakes. The DTs were crashing in on him. They were going to get worse. He could not sleep. He was shaking, cold, and sweating at the same time.

He lay down on the bed facing the wrong way. Eve was sitting on the side of the bed in only her t-shirt. He reached for her.

Around midnight, he sat up suddenly. He took his bottle of vodka from his bed stand and walked into the bathroom. His hand was shaking as he opened the bottle. Just one sip, just one. That would rid him of the shakes, calm him down.

He raised the bottle to his lips. "Help me, Eve," he said aloud. "Just one sip, please." Then he tipped the bottle away from his lips and poured it into the toilet. "Thank you, Eve." and threw up. It was easier after that.

*

"What are you doing? You're sitting on the throne? You're going to Hell," it was Sunday evening. The sun was low, the last of the sun's red rays were absorbed by the wispy clouds low in the sky. Debbie said, coming on to the patio after letting herself in..

"Dad said, Mom wanted me to sit here from now on. He said Mom wanted it that way." Dana patted the chair next to her. "Sit."

"Oh. Alrighty then," Debbie said with a surprised look on her face. "Guess what?" She shook a piece of paper in Dana's face.

Dana reached out to grab it. "Wait. I got more to tell you."

"I've been accepted at the University of Indiana at Bloomington. I start in the spring semester. Isn't that great?"

"Great," Dana said, a little stunned. She could feel her heart sink in her chest. "I'm so happy for you." She got up and pulled Debbie to her.

"It's a great school with a great law school. I can't wait."

Dana tried to keep a smile on her face. She did her best, but it was a frozen smile. Debbie noticed.

"Oh, I'm not leaving till after the new year. I'll be back every holiday, and I'll call every day."

"I know. I'm so happy for you. This is a great opportunity. You'll be in your second semester, and I'll be in my second trimester. That's funny." Dana gave a forced laugh. "Besides, I won't be much fun then."

"I'm sorry I didn't think of that. You'll be all alone." Debbie hugged her again. "I know, I'll put it off till the fall semester next year."

"No. Thank you, but no. I didn't tell you yet. Dad and I had a long talk today. He's not going to drink anymore. He's going sober. So, he'll be around to help me. And in other news, he's going to make me a partner in the gallery. So, I'm going to be busy." Dana found her news less exciting than before she discovered Debbie was leaving. Dana knew that absence makes the heart go wander. She knew that Debbie had a tendency to wander.

"Boy. That's a lot of stuff at one time," Debbie said. "Now, you need to get ready. Mom and Dad are taking us to dinner to celebrate my acceptance. I suggested Bobbie's Steak House."

"You didn't! After all the shit you gave me," Dana protested with a soft punch to her on the shoulder.

"Oh, get over it. I did. Besides, you said the food was great there." Debbie was guiding Dana to the stairway.

"I know. But I have to confess, I never actually had anything to eat there."

Debbie gave her a sideways look. "Come on. I'll help you throw something on. Dad dropped me off. He went home to pick up Mom, and they will be back soon." She tugged on Dana's arm.

"I really shouldn't leave Dad." Dana was slowly and reluctantly being pulled forward.

"Where is he?"

"Upstairs sleeping. I hope."

"Come on. You need food; I bet you haven't eaten all day. You need some downtime. A little time away from drama." By this time, Debbie was pushing her up the stairs.

Dana left a note on the floor in front of Christopher's door.

Bobbie's Steak House was actually a good steak house. When Dana got in around midnight, she stopped in front of Christopher's door, picking up the note, she heard her Dad thank Eve and then throw up.

*

Jody called late the next morning. "How are you doing?"

"Good. Yesterday was quite a day." Dana took a deep breath.

"Well, we're coming over."

Debbie drove up just as Mason and Jody were getting out of their car. "How is she doing?" Mason asked.

"Quieter than normal. Otherwise, she's just being Dana. What can I say?" Debbie answered.

Debbie unlocked the front door. "What ho. I brought reinforcements," she called from just inside the door.

"In the kitchen," Dana called. "Good thing I made more coffee," she said as they all hugged and took a seat around the breakfast table. Mason was wearing her uniform. Dana joked on seeing her, "Yes, officer, I did it." She held out her wrists. That got some laughs.

"Where's your dad?" Mason asked.

"At the gallery. Monday is a really slow day, so Dad said he didn't need me. He said he was going to straighten up the books and do some inventory. I don't know. A day without booze. At least that's what he says. I'll smell his breath when he gets home."

Mason spoke up, "I've dealt with alcoholism and depression coming up through the ranks. I know this is going to be hard on him. Doing inventory? Well, I hope he pours the inventory down the drain. You know this is going to be hard on you too!"

"And I'm going to be hard on him." Dana lowered her head. "What am I doing? Am I just making things worse? There's so much other crap I have to take care of." That last part was directed at Mason.

"We discussed this, girlfriend. We all discussed this. We all decided this was the only way," Debbie said.

"Nothing else has worked. You got your dad to at least admit he has a problem," Jody said.

"If he stays sober a week, it will be a miracle," Mason said. "You've got to help him now. We're all here to help both of you."

. "Police Chef Janson has an announcement." Jody presented the floor to Mason.

"I'm making an announcement this afternoon to the press and everyone. I'm not running for office this November."

"What?" Dana and Debbie said at the same time. Dana felt a chill.

"I accepted a job with the FBI. I'm going to coordinate between the FBI and police departments. Mostly with police chiefs for the Southeastern US. I don't start until January. Hell, my replacement won't be elected till November. So, I got to stick it out till January."

Dana's brain started to do some calculations. Her eyes locked on Mason's. *We'll have more resources* was communicated without a word.

"The FBI is way less public. I didn't want to drag Jody into the news. And that was going to happen sooner or later," Mason said.

"Why now?" Debbie asked.

"Because we are moving in together." Jody smiled and gave Mason a kiss.

"Lesbian police chiefs are big targets. But it doesn't matter in the FB of I," Mason said. "I'm free at last. That's why I'm in uniform. I'm going to announce to the press I'm not running today."

"Congratulations. That's fantastic news," Dana said.

"I heard lesbians can marry in France. It won't carry over here, but what the heck," Debbie chimed in.

"I've written up power of attorney, guardian, and last wills, so it's like being married," Jody said, "By the way, Dana, what about your documents?"

"Probably time to file them. You just got me thinking about something. If Dad and I are gone, would you guys take the baby? Sorry, Debbie, you're the next in line, okay?"

“Of course. We’re honored,” they all said.

"Wow, what a day," Dana said. They all nodded. "Are you going to be on television?" Dana asked.

"I don't know. Maybe," Mason said.

“Of course, you will. If Lars can get on television for pushing a reporter, you can for quitting the Atlanta Police Department,” Dana said. “Just don’t take their mike. Although it did get Lars married,” Dana smiled.

“Oh, I think Sally had her eyes on Lars long before then," Jody said.

Christopher walked in at around six o'clock. Dana and Debbie had comfort food—pasta and meatballs—ready for him. When he came into the kitchen, Dana gave him a kiss on the cheek. He turned and blew into her face. "See? Clean. You can check me anytime. I promised. I always keep my promises.”

So that’s where that came from. Always keeping our promises. Between you and Mom, it had to sink in. Dana thought.

Sitting around the table, Debbie served up heaping portions of pasta and three meatballs each. They all picked up their forks at the same time. Christopher just looked at his plate as Dana and Debbie dug in.

“Mr. Persson. Please eat something. You’ll hurt my feelings,” Debbie said with a pout.

Christopher took a bite. It hit his stomach hard. He didn't eat much, but, eventually, the comfort food had a calming effect.

After dinner, they all sat in the library. "Did Mom say I can have the daisho?” Dana asked, pointing to the samurai swords on the wall.

“What’s that?” Debbie asked. "Oh, here comes the lecture. I shouldn't have asked."

"Well, you did. The little one is called shoto. The other one is twice as long and is call daito. Together they are called daisho."

Dana was going to go on, but Christopher interrupted her. "That means *big* and *little*. Lecture over."

Looking at Dana, he asked, "Why do you want the daisho?"

"No one will fight me at the dojo. They let me kick their asses, but they never throw a real blow. But Bobby Lee and Tommy Chin are both masters with the daisho. I could learn a lot from them."

"I see. Well, Eve gave you the throne. I'm sure those go with the throne." Christopher was not anxious to give Dana ancient weapons of war. He knew they were Dana's and not the boys. Eve always said they will someday go to the best. That was Dana.

Christopher knew that after Eve's funeral, when Dana beat all three boys in under a minute, she should have gotten the throne and the swords then. But he had not been ready to admit that Eve was gone.

The next morning, Debbie held Dana's hair. "It will go away soon, or so it says in the book."

"I know," Dana said, on her knees in front of the toilet. "It also says I'm eating for two. Well, junior is not keeping up his or her part. They keep throwing their food down the toilet." And then she gave up the last of what was left in her stomach.

Halfway down the stairs, they smelled coffee and croissants. Dana grabbed Debbie's arm and gave her a puzzled look.

As they entered the kitchen, Christopher was taking croissants out of the oven. "Those croissants in a tube worked. I just gave them a hard rap on the counter and out they popped," he said as he slid the croissants onto a plate.

Looking at the amazed expressions on the girls' faces, he said, "What? I bake."

*

Sitting in the gallery that afternoon, Dana said, "Dad, now that I'm a partner, I should get to make some decisions around here." That discussion went on for over an hour. Dana wanted a more prominent role; Christopher was reluctant. They finally agreed to bring in Jody to help negotiate a deal. She then wrote up a document making them partners. As if they needed a document.

Christopher had been running the gallery his way, but under Eve's direction. She'd had a way of making him think her ideas were his. Dana did not have that talent. The result was a verbal war.

At Sunday brunch with Mason and Jody, Dana said, "God, I didn't realize Dad was such a pain in the ass. I don't know how Mom put up with him. He's still operating like we're back in the eighteen hundreds. All his ledgers are done by hand. All of them!"

"Oh, so we're talking about the gallery," Mason said.

"Yes, the old-fashioned gallery. Nothing I say is right. God, I should have gone to college. At least I would be out of the gallery and away from that.... Anyway." Dana finished her tirade.

"Do you really mean that?" Jody poured another cup of tea for Dana. She wasn't allowed Coke or coffee.

"No. I just get so frustrated sometimes." She took a deep breath.

Mondays were short days, only noon to five typically, but longer if there was traffic. Less if they had a reason. It didn't have to be a good reason.

Debbie, Jody, and Mason came by that Monday to take them to dinner. They were all interested in seeing how this new arrangement was working out.

They were greeted nicely at the door. Then Christopher and Dana continued their discussion on how to promote the new Chagall. The debate quickly amplified into a shouting match. Neither side gave an inch.

"Okay, can you guys continue this some other time?" Jody broke in.

"Pack it up. We going to dinner. Hurry." Mason took command.

As they left the gallery, Dana and Christopher were walking arm in arm, laughing at nothing at all.

"What just happened?" Mason asked. "They were fighting like cats and dogs a minute ago?"

Jody said, "No referee, I guess?"

20. HANDSOME

The next few months raced by. Dana's life was becoming more routine.

Her mornings were spent at the dojo. The shoto and daito were becoming good friends with their practice swords in hand, Bobby and Tommy no longer felt like they had to hold back. The blows were sliding the practice blade across arms, necks, legs, and body armor. The more vigorous practice was with real blades was against a well-punished wooden post.

*

"How can you sleep until eleven?" Dana shook Debbie's foot. Dana began stripping off her clothes from her morning workout at the dojo, dropping them on the floor and leaving a trail to the shower.

"It's because you keep me up all night. God, you're worse than ever. Look, you gave me a bruise," Debbie said, pointing to her shoulder.

"I couldn't have done that," Dana said, looking around the open door. "I'm just a weak pregnant girl." She giggled and ducked back in to test the shower water temperature.

"Yeah, sure." Debbie sat up on the side of the bed and stretched. "Save some hot water for me." She joined Dana in the shower.

*

Dana usually stopped at the mall for lunch, most times at the same Mexican restaurant. She had to cut back on the chilies; she claimed it gave the kid gas.

Then to the gallery. After a short discussion on any activities for the day, Christopher would walk down the street to a small café. During his drunken wasted time, he never stopped in for lunch. Now sober, lunch usually consisted of a cheese sandwich and coffee. He would leave there at one forty-five, give a minute or two.

Ms. Dunn had lived close by for nearly twenty years. She was now approaching ninety, still, she carried herself well, looked, and acted fifteen years younger. A retired school teacher, she never married and had outlived all her friends.

She dreamed for weeks in a row about the collie she grew up with on the tobacco farm just south of Cary, South Carolina. She saw an ad in the newspaper for collie pups. She called, then took a cab the twenty miles to see the puppy. There were ten puppies in a small, low-fenced area in the backyard. The puppies were playing, roughhousing, or sleeping. One broke loose of the pack and ran to Ms. Dunn and braced its paws on the top of the fence. His tail wagged so hard, it shook his whole body. He seemed to be saying, "You're the one I have been waiting for." The breeder drove her and the puppy home. On the drive home, she held the puppy in her lap. It licked her face more than once. By the time she got home, she had named her little boy Rough Collie; Pretty.

Christopher met Ms. Dunn and the dog coming out of the café one warm afternoon. He stroked the collie's head and neck as the three of them walked to the gallery. They rarely missed their short walk. Christopher always invited them into the gallery. On occasion, Ms. Dunn and the collie would join Christopher in the gallery, usually when he had a new piece to show off and if things were slow, they would sit and talk.

It was just a few weeks before Thanksgiving. On a cold Saturday, Ms. Dunn did not show up at the appointed time.

Christopher waited on the sidewalk out front of the café. Looking up and down the street, he heard an ambulance, its sirens blasting. It gave him a chill.

Ms. Dunn had collapsed on her daily walk a few blocks from her apartment. A group quickly gathered around her. A nurse in the group checked her for a heartbeat and applied CPR until the ambulance arrived. Someone had taken Pretty's leash and held him back. The collie jerked and fought the leash till his collar came off. He ran to the ambulance as they loaded in Mrs. Dunn. Pretty tried to get in with his mistress. One of the attendants pushed him out the door. His collar was again slipped around his neck.

Another truck with cages arrived a half-hour later. The dog catcher tried to load Pretty into one of the cages. He fought again, this time with more intensity. He broke free of his collar again and raced down the street. He was too late. He had no clue where they had taken his mistress. Pretty went one way, then the other, trying to pick up his mistress's scent. There was no fresh scent of Mrs. Dunn. He went back to that place on the sidewalk where Mrs. Dunn had collapsed. He sat for hours. Then he went home and lay in front of the condo door for two days.

On Monday, he went for his walk at the appointed time. He strolled as if the ghost of Ms. Dunn was walking beside him.

Christopher saw the collie walking his way as he came out of the café. He kneeled and petted him. They walked side by side up the street to the gallery. Christopher opened the door and Pretty followed him into the gallery.

He looked around for a few minutes. Seeing Christopher had gone to his desk to make a phone call, the collie walked up and put his head on his knee. Christopher petted him. Pretty looked up into Christopher's eyes.

"Animal Shelter," said the voice on the phone.

Christopher looked down into the dog's eyes. "Sorry, wrong number." He spoke softly to the dog, he explained that Ms. Dunn was watching over him now and always. That it was important that he be strong. That he had a new purpose in life. Others were going to depend on him.

Dana stood back, watching her father and the dog communicate. This dog picked its owners, not the other way around.

*

"Dana, this dog is starving. Please go to that pet store around the corner. Get him some bowls, dog food, and you know, dog stuff. I think he's going to be staying with us."

Pretty laid down on the floor beside Christopher. Shortly after Dana left, the dog put his head up, ears at attention. The door opened ten seconds later. A couple came in. "Just getting out of the cold. Mind if we look around? Don't get up," they said.

The dog sat up, watching them. When the lady came over, she said, "What a handsome dog. What's his name?"

Christopher looked down at the dog. Pretty turned toward him and cocked his head. "Handsome," he said. Handsome wagged his tail in approval. He never liked the name Pretty anyway.

At the end of the day, Dana headed home with an extra set of dog supplies. Christopher started his rounds shutting down the gallery. Handsome followed him, learning the procedure. Finally, Christopher set the alarms and opened the door. Handsome stepped out and looked up and down the street. Christopher had not put him on his leash and they both had a moment's hesitation. Then Christopher walked the short distance to his car. Handsome stayed close by his side. Christopher opened the car door and Handsome jumped in and crossed to the passenger seat. He sat, looking over at Christopher as if to say, "Well, get in."

"Well, okay then," Christopher said.

Dana watched them get out of the car and walk to the front door. Christopher had stayed sober, but the drinking had taken its toll. His hair, what he had left of it, was pure white. So were his eyebrows; his skin was thin and blotchy. He was bent over, and his walk had gotten a little stiff. When she met him at the door, she noticed his eyes were once again alive. They sparkled as his sense of humor returned.

Christopher made himself comfortable at the kitchen table as Dana finished her prep for dinner. Handsome sat for a few minutes before beginning his inspection. Starting in the kitchen, he circled the room. Then into Lars' room, and each room after that. They heard him run up the stairs.

"Making himself at home, I see," Dana said.

"For his first day at the gallery, he was good. Not aggressive but vigilant. I think I'll take him tomorrow."

"You sure that's a good idea?" Dana asked, stirring the vegetables.

"Tomorrow is a long, slow day; slow days are probably okay." He sat back. Handsome came back to the kitchen and looked around, then sat in front of the kitchen door to the backyard. He looked over his shoulder as if to say, "Well. Let me out."

Dana opened the door. He ran the fence line, checked the tree, and carefully inspected the mat. His nose was going a mile a minute as he moved onto the patio, paying particular attention to the throne. Then he found a far corner of the yard and did his business.

Dana was clearing the table when Debbie's VW parked at the curb. Handsome's ears and head popped up. He went to the front door and gave out one bark. Dana beat Debbie to the front door. Opening the door, Debbie took a step back. "Who's this?" she asked.

"He's Handsome. He's going to live with us. Handsome, this is Debbie. Debbie, meet Handsome."

"So, you are." Debbie kneeled and petted him. "He is gorgeous." Handsome smelled her. Recognized her scent. He then knew she was part of the pack. She would have no problem coming and going. Handsome would meet her at the door and show her out when she left.

*

Jody and Mason had decided on getting a new house, one that appealed to both of them. They agreed on the house that had been for sale for a few months, just next door to Dana and Christopher.

The driveways were next to each other, divided by an ancient hedge. A narrow sidewalk ran down beside each garage, separated by a short white fence. At the back end of the fence, a gate would soon be added.

Their move-in date was November nineteenth. Dana and Debbie spent the next few days helping them move in. Dana's tummy was starting to round out. She wasn't allowed to pick up anything heavier than a table lamp.

"Not that. I'll get it." Was the phrase she most often heard.

"I fight with swords," Dana protested. "I'm stronger than wimpy Debbie."

"Maybe. But get out of the way and sit down," she was told. She pouted a lot.

Mason insisted on having Thanksgiving dinner at their new house. Mason never had a real family. Her parents were both killed when she was young. That was the main reason she joined the police department. She now adopted Jody's family as her own. Any suggestion that Thanksgiving dinner be held at Dana's or Debbie's was met with the Hand.

Dana managed to convince a reluctant Mason that she would make a few dishes for the Thanksgiving dinner.

"It's oyster stuffing," Dana said as Mason turned up her nose. "Mom always stuffed the turkey with oyster stuffing. It wouldn't be Thanksgiving without oyster stuffing. Now help me." Dana pointed to the bird on the chopping block in the middle of the kitchen. "Turn it on its head and spread its legs."

"What's this?" Mason put her hand down inside of the turkey and a puzzled look crossed her face as she pulled out a neck and a bag of giblets.

Dana started to laugh, "Mason meet turkey, turkey meet Mason, I see you have never been introduced." Dana could not stop laughing, "It's the makings of gravy."

Handsome lay near the dining-room door, facing the front door, expecting Debbie at any time. "Debbie will be over after her Thanksgiving Diner." Dana patted his head. He still didn't more.

They reached out to each other and said a short prayer for everyone's health. "Do you mind if Mason and I have a glass of wine?" Jody asked Christopher.

"Please, do. But no wine for me. I have had my fill long ago," Christopher smiled.

*

Five days before Christmas, Jody and Mason had the spare room ready for Lars and Sally. The boys flew in from Singapore the next day. Lars had brought a new beau; his name was Chad. They got the bigger bedroom downstairs at Christopher's. Beau was relegated to the last remaining bedroom upstairs.

As each of them arrived, Handsome met them at the door. With one sniff, he knew they were part of the pack. This is one big pack, he thought. This pack seemed to never end. Still, all their scents were securely registered in

Handsome's nose in order of importance. First, Christopher, then Dana, Debbie, Jody, Mason, and so forth. His nose had room for more.

Handsome had found his pack and his purpose.

The boys commandeered the Nova. Dana was forced to take the Black Dragon out. She had missed its power.

*

On January third, everyone lined up next to the Cadillac. The trunk was overflowing. Dana sat on it till she heard it click shut. They all hugged and kissed. Beau called shotgun and parked himself in the passenger seat. The rest of them packed themselves into the back seat. Sally sat on Lars's lap, with her legs stretched out across Lars and Chad.

As the car backed out of the driveway, Dana called out, "See you all in April. Beau, keep those lips warm." She turned and smacked her butt, giving him an exaggerated air kiss.

Dana and Debbie walked down to the VW at the curb. They hugged and kissed. "I'll call. Love you." Debbie said as she smashed her gears into first. She then left for the University of Indiana at Bloomington. Dana was left on the curb, watching Debbie drive off, till she was out of sight.

Dana turned to Mason and Jody, still on the front lawn, Dana put her arms out and let them fall to her side.

"We'll bring over leftovers later for dinner," Jody said as Mason wrapped her arm around Jody's waist. They walked back to their house. Dana and Handsome walked back in through her front door.

Dana shut the front door and leaned against it. The house had gone from laughter and chaos to silence with a taste of loneliness.

*

A few days later, Mason started her new job at the FBI. Inspector Janson was given a badge, passes, passwords, and an office. The next day she started orientation. She didn't see her office for a week.

Dana and Mason saw each other practically every day. Toward the end of the month, Dana and Handsome came through the never-closed gate one evening. Dana joined Mason at the patio table, placing her bottle of Coke on the table.

"Bad girl. Coke? Distilled water, that's what you should be drinking," Mason said. Dana rolled her eyes as Mason collected the Coke and headed for the kitchen. She returned with a glass of ice cubes and water.

Dana had not said a word since entering the patio. They now sat looking at each other, not saying a word. Dana's eyes were demanding answers.

"You don't have to say anything. I know what you're thinking," Mason said, breaking the silence. "I'm working on it. I've only been on the job for two weeks."

Dana's face was frozen. Not a word came out.

Mason slid a photo across the table. "A present."

Dana picked up the photo. "That's Manuel Ortigas."

Mason slid another photo across the table. "Here's a better photo. Same guy. His address is on the back." Dana turned the photo over and memorized the address. "We have Jody to thank for this. She had a drug dealer on trial for murder. He dropped his name during questioning." Dana put the photos down. "Well, anyway, he lives in Puerto Vallarta. He's not so much Carlos's boss, he's more like his sole supplier."

Dana slid the photos back across the table. "Anything else?"

"Ah. Thanks. That was quick would have been nice to hear," Mason said.

Dana sat back, putting her hands on her baby. "Thanks," she said, turning her head away.

Mason could see the wheels spinning. She let them spin.

"Well, I'm grounded for the next year or so," Dana said. "We need to collect as much information as possible. The more information we collect, the more dots we'll find. The more dots, the better the connections. Eventually, they will lead to Ron." She looked at Mason. "Can we do that?"

Mason tapped the table. "We can use our third bedroom for an office. That way, if anything sensitive makes its way home, it's contained. I can always say it's part of my investigations, which it is. Jody can have the den downstairs for her office."

Dana nodded in agreement.

"But I have told you this before. Ron is the least of your worries."

"The Cartel. I know. But they haven't hurt me or mine. Those that have tried are dead. Except for Ron."

"The cartel has put a price on your head. We need to factor that in. The FBI is really working on getting info on the cartel. Information I can tap," Mason said. "Look. It is my objective to keep you and ours safe."

"That was my objective. I failed. Mom's dead. Ron will pay. I promise," Dana said.

21. THE OFFICE

Right around Dana's birthday in February, the kid started a growth spurt. The kid pushed on her uterus, then pumped up her breasts. At first, the skirts didn't fit. Then bras didn't fit. Loose clothing and bras two cup sizes larger were now all she could wear.

At the dojo, Dana adopted a loose-fitting long red satin Japanese dress. It came up to her neck and had two dragons on the front and one large one on the back. They all breathed fire. It hung easily from her increasing breasts to her knees. It somewhat hid her pregnancy. Her movements were only encumbered by the kid.

*

"Happy Birthday," Debbie shouted as she came through the front door. It was now impossible to surprise anyone with Handsome around. He knew she was coming before she parked the VW in front of the house. He was sitting at the front door waiting for her. Mason and Jody followed her through the front door with a birthday cake. Eighteen candles burned in honor of Dana's eighteen years on earth.

Dana's bed was just big enough for the three of them. Dana getting up every three hours or so to pee made Debbie look forward to going back to school the next day.

Dana and Debbie, the next day had lunch at the Mexican Restaurant. Dana thought she saw someone staring at them out of the corner of her eye. Not with healthy curiosity, but with intense interest. When she managed to get a better look, all she saw was his back going out the door.

"Honey, here." Debbie snapped her fingers to gain Dana's attention.

"Did you see that guy looking at us?" Dana asked, turning back to Debbie.

"No. As I was saying, my roommate is a totally straight girl. Once she found out I was a lesbian, she won't even get dressed in front of me. So, naturally, I'm naked a lot of the time."

"Really? Naturally." Dana said, trying to pay attention.

"Yes, but guess what? I came back to the room early one afternoon. She was fucking her boyfriend. And she was on top."

"So, let me guess. You joined in," Dana chuckled.

"Hell no. All I said was 'nice ass.' Then I stripped down to my bra and panties and sat at my desk to do my homework. He came before I could click my pen." Debbie laughed. "He wrapped a sheet around himself, picked up his clothes, and left without saying a word. She had nothing to cover up with. So, I said, 'Nice tits, Lue Ann.'" Looking at her watch, Debbie said, "Look at the time. I won't get back to the dorm till late. Love you. Got to run."

Dana walked her out to the VW. They hugged and kissed their goodbyes. Dana was looking around to see if that guy was around. She didn't see him.

*

Dana was having her roughly once-a-week lunch at the Mexican restaurant. The kid was getting so big, Dana had to push the table back a little to make room. She always sat in the corner booth with her back to the wall.

"Hi. Don't I know you?"

Dana looked up to see the guy from St. Augustine. He was the same guy in the background of the Miami photo, too. Dana looked at him with a blank expression on her face. He was in his late twenties, tall, fit, with dark, styled hair, and was good looking. He dressed nicely but casually. Dana said nothing.

"Yes, sure," he said. "From that restaurant in St. Augustine. Remember me? I offered to buy you and your friend a drink."

"Okay. If you say so." Then, as if it was just coming to her, she said, "I do remember that. Was that you?"

"May I sit down? I promise not to buy you a drink." He pointed at the other side of the booth.

"Okay. Just don't push the table. I'm kind of taking up this side." She put her free hand on her baby.

"I'm Tom." He put out his hand.

She slowly put down her fork. "Dana," she said shaking his hand.

"You like Mexican food. My dad is Mexican," he said.

Dana didn't say anything. She knew that he would try to get a conversation going. The more he talked, the more she learned. All she had to do was look mildly and politely interested.

"Yes, my last name is Garcia. A real Mexican last name."

Dana just nodded in acknowledgment.

"Yeah. I remember your friend. What was her name? She looked like she was interested in my friend Hernandez. I think she had the hots for him."

"I don't think so," Dana answered.

"You sure? I'm a pilot. We're trained to notice everything. So, your friend, what's her name?" He waited but got no answer. "Well, she looked interested. Anyway, I fly jets. Lear jets. I get to travel all over."

"Is your friend Hernandez a pilot also?" Dana asked as if to be polite.

"No, I just deliver stuff to him in St. Augustine when he needs me to. But I prefer to fly people, I'm a piolet, not a delivery service," he said.

"Stuff?" Dana asked.

"Just stuff." Realizing what he said, he quickly added, "But I mostly fly people. I could fly you and your friend. What's her name?" He waited a second. "I could fly you and her just about any place. So, where is she?"

"At school, I guess. I don't see her much." Dana smiled. "So, you live in Atlanta?"

"No, I live in Corpus Christi. But my grandpa lives in San Diego, so I spend a lot of time there. I could take you and your friend there sometime. You guys would like it."

"No, thanks. I'm sort of pregnant if you haven't noticed." Dana put her hand on her baby again.

"Well. Nice to have met you again." He stood up. "Say, would you like to join me for dinner tonight? I only have tonight. I'm flying to Miami tomorrow."

"Sorry. No," Dana said.

He put out his hand again. "Another time," he said.

Dana shook his hand. She turned back to her meal but watched him out of the corner of her eye. Dana saw him signal someone who followed him out the door. She recognized his back. 'I got ya,' Dana thought, 'I know you are connected somehow. But why now? Is there a connection to Carlos?'

*

"Here is his name and his contact in Saint Augustine." Dana had a folded sheet of paper in her hand. She tried to pass it to Mason, who just stood up, not taking the note.

"It's chilly out tonight. Let's go inside. I've something to show you in our new office." She led the way into the house. At the stairway, she stopped and asked, "Oh, do you need help up the stairs?"

"Come on, I got a few more weeks to go." Dana scrunched up her face.

"I thought not." Mason gave a little laugh.

"Okay, why are we here? It's not that cold outside," Dana said as she followed Mason into the new office. "Oh!" Dana said, looking around the room. A table was set up in the middle of the room, with a chair on either side. A four-drawer file cabinet with locks was set up against one wall in the corner.

There were two maps on the wall, the world map and a much larger map of North America. The only window in the room had been changed out. It had two panes of bulletproof glass, with nitrogen gas in between. No signals were going to be picked up through that window.

On top of the file cabinet was an electronic device to detect any listening devices in the room.

Dana was drawn to the North America map. It had pins in it.

"Red is for the known locations of Ron, including prison. The notes are possible dates."

Dana nodded in approval.

"Green is Carlos. Black pins with numbers correspond to the photos on the wall over there." Mason pointed to the other side of the room. The wall was covered from ceiling to floor with corkboard. "Those photos and notes are the cast of characters we have identified. They may or may not be innocent and/or dangerous. If we find out for sure who is not innocent, they will get orange pins and moved over there." Mason pointed to the left side of the wall that held pictures of Carlos and a few others.

"I'm impressed," Dana said as she studied the wall. She sat down.

"Feel under the desk," Mason said. "That is a nine-millimeter pistol, loaded and cocked. There is one on either side, just in case. Here is a set of keys," she said, holding them up. "House. Office. File cabinet." She handed them to Dana. "Don't keep them on you. Put them in your key can with all the old keys. Hiding in plain sight is always the best way."

Dana took the keys and put them in her new size D cup bra.

"A set is in the refrigerator under the vegetable drawer. They are painted white. Don't use them unless you have to." Mason sat, taking a breath after all the instructions.

"What about Jody?" Dana asked.

"She knows more than she's letting on, but she's not coming into this room for lots of reasons."

"Here." Dana then passed the paper to Mason. "He is the guy in that photo." She pointed to the wall. "His name is Tom Garcia. He's a pilot. Flies a Lear jet. I think he should go to the left side of the wall."

Mason looked over the note. It appeared to be very complete, including times, dress, physical appearance. Dana had also written a synopsis of their conversation. On a separate sheet was the little she knew of the other guy.

"He's mixed up in this somehow. That's all I know. Not much," Dana said. "This Tom guy really wanted Debbie's name and location. He asked me several times. It makes me nervous," Dana explained.

"If this Tom guy is a pilot, that's a break. We can get his tail number, and that will lead to copies of his flight plans—at least the old ones, and I'll see if I can get tied in somehow for his new flight plans. That's going to be more difficult." Mason took the notes over to the file cabinet. She put them in folders and filed them alphabetically.

"Oh," Dana said.

"What?" Mason quickly turned around.

"Nothing. The little shit is kicking me again." Dana rubbed her belly. "Watch. You can see it's moving around."

Mason watched for a second, then moved her chair around the table and put her hand on Dana's tummy. "Wow," she said as she felt the baby moving.

Dana studied Mason. "Mason, why?"

"Why what?" Mason asked without looking up.

"Lots of whys. Why didn't you arrest me? That's the biggest why. Let's start with that."

Frozen in time, Mason looked up at Dana, not moving her hand from her tummy. She sat back in her chair, bit her lip, and gave a short laugh. Not a funny laugh, a time's up laughs.

She got up and walked away a few steps. Turning back to Dana, she said, "At first, I didn't know. A sixteen-year-old single-handedly taking on the cartel, without a gun no less. And if I did know, I probably couldn't arrest you without the press having a field day. I mean, a sixteen-year-old. Besides, I only had intuition. No proof."

"I was almost seventeen," Dana said.

"I stand corrected. God, has it only been a little more than a year?" Mason was wandering around the room. "Jody and I started dating about a year before all this happened. Not serious dating. But, still, we had to keep it, as they say, on the downlow. Not just the lesbian thing. But, mostly the police chief and the prosecutor dating. That's a no-no in the department."

Mason stopped to look out the window. Dana sat quietly. "We didn't talk business much. We tried to keep away from it." Turning back to Dana, she pointed at her. "You were on my list. Not in a serious way. Just on a long list of names. Jody noticed. That's when I found out that you and Jody were related by marriage. Sally to your brother."

She walked over to the North American map. She was avoiding eye contact now. "Over dinner one night, Jody told me about your history. About saving Gina at twelve. This all kind of started there, didn't it?" Turning back to Dana, she said, "About you being Gina's protector. Godzilla and Stump."

Dana gave a little laugh. "Would you please forget those nicknames?"

"Well, yes. You got a better nickname now, Red Bitch." Mason sat down and took Dana's hand. "She told me about how your mother died. How she was killed in front of you. I'm so sorry."

Dana took a deep breath. A tear formed in each eye. It was still hard to be directly confronted by that day.

"I studied your file. Yes, you have a file. It goes back to when you were twelve years old. Somewhere along the way, I started putting Duston's death in the alley and then the dead guys at the drug house together. Moses was one of those dead in the lab. There was a connection there. But I still couldn't believe you did it. Maybe if you had some serious help. That kind of stumped me. Even after the Stone Mountain meeting, I still could not believe it. Not that you said or suggested in any way that you knew what was going on."

She studied Dana's face. "You are so good at looking innocent." Mason shook her head in disbelief, she said, "Only after the two dead guys behind the stores next to the school and a report from the patrol cars—only then was I pretty sure you did it. Still no proof; just my gut. It would have been enough to bring you in for some serious questioning. But I didn't."

"So again, why didn't you arrest me?"

Mason got up again. She walked to the window. She turned around and sat on the ledge, her hands supporting her. "My dad was a cop. A good cop. He was breaking up a mob of gangsters and their Cuban drug dealers. Those he couldn't arrest, he shot." She took a breath. "Those he arrested usually got off. The mob owned most of the judges and a lot of the prosecutors. And of course, some of the cops. The fix was always in."

She walked across the room, thinking. She leaned up against the door, her arms folded across her chest. "I was eight when they broke into the house late one night. Dad made it to the bedroom door. He shot one of them. He was then shot by a shotgun taking one in the right side, blowing off his right arm. He landed up against the wall. I was coming down the hall. I saw everything."

She held a shaking hand to her head, silently asking for a minute. "One of them grabbed me. They dragged me into the bedroom. One of them was ripping off my mom's nightgown, beating and raping her. It took the cops more than half an hour to respond. And then only after a neighbor eventually called in the gunshots next door. The cops had been paid off. When they heard the sirens, they slit Mom's throat. Dad had already died. Someone said something to the guy holding me in Spanish. He took out his knife and put it to my throat. But then he decided to just throw me up against the wall."

Mason's energy was spent. She sat, laying her head in her arms on the table.

Dana felt the rage in Mason, but knew she had no one to direct it against. Dana put an arm around Mason and put her head on her shoulder. She didn't have to say anything.

"With all that," Mason said, patting Dana's head and taking a moment for Dana to sit back, "with all that," she said again, "your history. My history. You were doing what I wanted to do, what I never had the skills to do. Maybe I never had the guts." She looked at Dana, "I have not told anybody about that night since I was a kid." Then she put both hands down on the table and leaned forward. "Almost thirty years in the police department and so few of the cartel in jail. You know the judges are the easiest to buy off? So are some of the cops. The cartel owns so many. Look at our conviction rate." She shook her head in frustration. "Most of the cartel guys are let go on a technicality. Technicalities that don't really exist. At every turn, the courts use the law to stop me from getting those assholes. I want to do what my dad did and shoot them. But I can't." Looking directly at Dana, "I'm selfish. I'm using you to do what I can't do."

Throwing her hands up in the air, she said, "You're a seventeen-year-old pregnant girl. Sorry, eighteen-year-old pregnant girl. What am I doing?"

Pointing a finger at Dana, she said, "I want to kill them. I can't. You did." Backing off a bit, she said, "We really used each other, didn't we?"

Dana found her voice. "You cleared the road for me. Probably nothing illegal. Maybe. I don't know."

Mason gave a shrug.

"So here we are. The killer and the cop. What do we do now?" Dana asked.

"I'm not a real cop anymore. And you're having a kid in a couple weeks. Together, we will find them and a way to kill them. Somehow. Law or no."

Dana sat back, her hands on her baby, who was kicking her for attention. She had a lot to think about.

Just then, there was a knock on the door. Jody called to them through the locked door, "Christopher is here. So is Handsome, who brought his own bowl. Dinner in ten minutes."

"Great," Mason said. "We'll be down in a minute."

Dana got up and looked at the maps and the photos on the wall. She turned to Mason and said, "I'm a whole lot deadlier now than I was last year."

Instead of going to her regular lunch after the dojo and her shower, Dana started getting a hamburger and the forbidden coke for lunch. She found a place to park where she could see the entrance to the Mexican restaurant without being noticed. It took a few days until she saw the guy walking into the restaurant. About a half-hour later, she saw him walk out. She got a good look at his face this time and took a photo.

He looked around and headed for a car parked not far from the entrance. It was still about four rows of cars over from where she was. He stood outside of the driver's window, talking, gesturing like he didn't know what was going on. The car was white, but it left so quickly she couldn't even see what kind of car it was, much less who was in the car.

The guy she was watching made his way to a beat-up Dodge Monaco and left the lot. She followed him at a distance. In a few miles, she figured out what part of town he was heading to, so she took an alternate route and caught up to him again as he exited the freeway. In a few blocks, he turned into a dumpy motel, the kind of motel druggies and drunks lived in on a day-to-day or week-to-week basis; in those places, rent was always cash. The dirty beat-up Dodge parked in front of room 12. Dana took a few more pictures from the parking lot across the street.

She stopped at the one-hour photoshop and got the roll developed.

"This one, I have seen at one of the field stations," Mason said as she looked at the photo. "I'll have a file on him in a few days; I only go to the Sylvan Hills field station on an as-needed basis. I'm sure that's where I saw him. He must have been there a lot for me to recognize him."

"He talked to someone in a white car. Like they were together or something," Dana continued. "Anything on Tom?"

"Quite a lot." Mason got up and went to the file cabinet. She took out his now very large file "He is a pilot. He qualified in single-engine land, Cessna. 172s and 182s, so little planes. The 182 is a four-seater with a cargo capacity of one hundred and fifty pounds. Altogether, it could carry about eight hundred pounds with just the pilot. He qualified about seven years ago when he was only twenty-two."

"Not jets?" Dana asked.

Mason held up a hand as she read the file. "Someone paid for his training and license in the Lear 25. Much bigger and faster, it carries more cargo and passengers. That was two years ago. It was paid for by Tandem LLC, an offshore company. I'll find out more about them."

She flipped through a few more pages, mumbling to herself as she did. "Oh, here it is. Tandem LLC had a pilot named Charles Goody. He crashed trying to land a twin-engine Cessna 310 in the Everglades. The feds didn't get to it till the next day, not till noon, it looks like. It was partly burned. It had been carrying pot, and most of it was gone. Charles was lying next to the plane with a bullet hole in his head."

"And?" Dana asked.

"And Tom took over for Charles at Tandem LLC the next day." Mason put down the folder.

"Forced retirement," Dana said. "So, a bigger, faster, more expensive airplane. They are not landing that one in a swamp."

"You are so right." Mason went to the map. "I got his tail number and his flight plans for the last few months, at least. Here are his routes. Each pink pin represents an airfield, mostly private. Each string is a trip. He is based in Corpus

Christi, Texas, where he has a private hangar. But he goes to Brown Field Municipal Airport near San Diego a lot. From there, he makes trips to Mexico City and Puerto Vallarta with passengers; at least some had passports. I'll try and run down the passports. He only goes to these airports in the US," Mason said, pointing to the map. "Executive Airport near Miami; Atlantic Aviation, St. Augustine, Chesterfield Airport near Richmond, Virginia; Front Range Airport near Denver; and Lakefront airport near New Orleans." She stepped back. "Here is the interesting part. Just recently, he flew in twice to DeKalb- Peachtree Airport here in Atlanta."

"Good work," Dana said, looking more closely at the map. "Only these cities?"

"Yep. And your name might as well be right here." She pointed to Atlanta.

"So now what do we do with this?" Dana asked.

"Information." Mason shrugged. "I don't know yet."

*

Two days later, Mason stopped into the gallery around seven, having just left work. It was a late day for her. She asked Dana quietly, "Can you get off early? I need to see you in our office."

"Sure, I guess so. Dad, is it okay if I go home early?" Dana asked.

"Sure. It's kind of slow anyway."

Handsome was at attention. He was not letting Dana go without him. He knew where he was needed. It's a pack instinct.

As Dana headed for the door, Handsome was at her side.

"Well, I guess he wants to go with you. See you in two hours or so." Christophe went back to his paperwork.

In the Nova, Dana had her hand on the armrest. Handsome put his paw on her hand. She picked up her hand and put it on top of Handsome's paw. Handsome pulled his paw out and put it on her hand. They played this game all the way home. It made Dana giggle.

Dana pulled into the driveway just after Mason arrived. "See you in the office. Jody's still at her office. Some molestation case."

Dana took Handsome to the front door to let him in. She waved him in, but he just sat down. His answer was "No." He turned around to head over to Masons and Jody's house. He looked over his shoulder as if to say. "Well, come on."

As Dana entered the office with Handsome at her side, she said, "Sorry. He's being difficult today. Ever since noon, he has had to be at my side."

"Smart dog," Mason said and shut the door. Handsome walked the room, then lay down in front of the door.

"So, what can't wait?" Dana asked.

"I got a heads-up note from one of my old crew. It offered one million for the Red Bitch's head." Mason sat down with one of her ever-present files. "I've been following up all afternoon."

She flipped to another page. "Here is a report from a restaurant in Miami. Carlos was cussing loudly; you are his favorite cuss word. He called a Korean male waiter a "fucking red bitch." Another report from a golf course, about him throwing a fit and calling the ball a "fucking red bitch." He drove the golf cart into the water. He called that a "fucking red bitch" too."

She closed her file. "You got to him. You are the tick up his ass alright. He knows you're there, but he can't rub you out."

Dana just cocked her head. "So?"

"I finally got a contact in the Miami FBI station. She says the word has gone out. Your head is now worth a million dollars. Nothing else specific. I'm working on her." Mason put down her file with a puzzled look on her face. "

She wants on a date. Now, how do I explain that to Jody?"

"A lunch is a date. I don't know. That's the only excuse I have."

"Speaking of lunch, your lunch partner is a small-time drug dealer and user named Raymond Ray. They call him Ray Ray. My guess is he's being paid to watch you. Possibly by the pilot."

Dana took a deep breath. "Where is his file?" Mason dropped it in front of her, Dana studied it for a few minutes. "Not much of a guy. No one ever bailed him out. Doesn't look like he has lots of friends."

"The bigger question is why is he circling around you? And who is this new guy, in the white car?" Mason asked with intensity.

"I don't know. I guess I'll ask him," Dana said.

"Oh, no you don't. Young lady, you're almost nine months pregnant. You're literally days away from having a baby. You're not the Red Bitch right now. You can't be going out and beat guys up. Let's just calmly figure this out." Mason was standing across the table from her.

"Sure. Let's work on that." Dana said to calm Mason down. She already knew what she was going to do. Not right now, but soon.

*

Dana cruised by the motel the next day even though she did not see the white car, Ray Ray's car was there. She parked across the street and waited. Ray Ray did not leave his room till after one. Dana saw the manager go to another room and pound on the door, yelling at the guy who came to the door, "Rent money! Now!" Dana thought that was interesting.

"Guess what?" Mason said quietly as she came through the kitchen door. "My girl in Miami is now hooked up to get to see some of the transcripts from a wiretap. It's not on Carlos, but it is on one of his lieutenants. So, some inside info."

"Should we be in our office?" Dana asked. "Dad's in the library."

"Can he hear us?" Mason looked over Dana's shoulder. "Let's just go outside."

"Dad, going over to Mason's for a minute. Do you want a Coke or something? We're all out."

Mason gave Dana a dirty look. "Not me. Dad drinks them like water." Dana thought that was at least partly true.

Handsome was sitting at the kitchen door and followed them to Mason's kitchen, where Mason retrieved a six-pack of Coke from the pantry, handing it to Dana Mason said, "The word is that they are tracking the Red Bitch in New York, LA, Chicago, and even Paris. The only description they have is a redhead, young, and attractive."

"Well, that narrows it down," Dana said.

"Yeah, really. But it's interesting to note that Atlanta was not mentioned. I don't know if that is good or bad?"

Dana eased herself into a chair. "Maybe because they didn't have to. Maybe because they already have a line on me. Where is our pilot?"

"Oh, other news. I got access to Tom Garcia's flight plans on a regular basis. I've got to be in the office to get them, but that's an improvement. He is in San Diego, by the way, this morning, anyway. I'll check up on him first chance I get tomorrow."

*

The next morning was Friday morning. Dana was dressed for the dojo. Christopher was getting ready to leave for the gallery. As they were leaving the house, Dana bent over and said quietly to Handsome, "You need to go with Daddy today. Make sure he's okay." She petted him and gave him a kiss on the head, then pointed to the Cadillac.

"Daddy, I might be in a little late today. I've got something to do that might take a little while. Love you." Dana gave him a kiss on the cheek and watched Christopher and Handsome drive off.

Dana took a deep breath and reached behind the door for her swords.

22. I'M NO MY WAY

Dana had no intention of going to the dojo that morning. Instead, she headed down to Sylvan Hills. She parked the Black Dragon in the lot across the street. Grabbing her Daito, long sword, she walked the short distance to the motel.

She knocked on room 12 with her eye up to the peephole so he could not see who she was.

"Who's there?" he asked.

In a heavy accent, trying to match the manager's accent, she called, "Rent money."

"I paid," he yelled back.

"No. I call the cops." Dana kept her eye at the peephole. She could see shadows.

"The hell I haven't," he yelled as he jerked open the door. Dana threw a palm up into his jaw. He dropped like a wet sack.

Dana rolled him over and duct-taped his hands and arms. She taped his knees so he could not kick or run.

She went through his room, throwing things around, pulling out drawers, and dumping stuff on the floor. The medicine cabinet had only a bottle of aspirin in it. Back in the room, she noticed an envelope taped to the bottom of one of the drawers on the floor. It had three thousand dollars and a note with a phone number on it.

Dana got a glass of water and threw it in his face. "Quit faking it," she said, kicking him in the side.

"Fuck." He looked around. "Who the fuck are you? Shit. What the fuck?"

"Get up," Dana said.

"I can't. I'm all fucking tied up. I can't."

Dana kicked him in the ribs again, this time hard enough to break a rib. He screamed. "Honey, no one cares if you scream. Now get up." Then in a soft sexy voice, she said, "I really don't want to hurt you again." She blew him a kiss.

He struggled to get up. Dana pulled a chair to the middle of the room and behind his legs. "Honey, please have a seat." She ran the back of her hand softly down his cheek. "Relax," she said as she sat on the side of the bed facing him, her long sword in her lap. It was still in its scabbard.

"We're going to have a nice, friendly talk. I expect honesty. Lies always hurt someone," Dana said as she settled herself in.

"What the fuck are you doing here?" He spat out some blood.

"Oh, sweetie, I just have a few questions." The sugar was dripping from her words. "Now, where did you get this money?" She fanned the bills in his face.

"I earned it," he said, then screamed again in pain as the end of her scabbard broke another rib.

"Now, honey. What did I say about lying? Someone always gets hurt." Dana spoke to him as if he were a child. "Now let's try this again. Your answer is?"

"Fuck you."

The scabbard jabbed into his side, broke another rib.

As he was trying to catch his breath, Dana said, "I was never very good at anatomy. How many ribs does the human body have? You don't know? Well, maybe we'll find out."

"Tom." He spoke up, "Tom, the guy you were talking to in the Mexican restaurant."

"Now, isn't that nice that we can communicate. You know communication is the basis of all good relationships.

So, what is this?" Dana held up the paper with the number on it.

"Tom's contact number," he said, now more cooperative.

"Why?"

"If I see or hear anything about the Red Bitch, I'm to leave a message. If she shows up again, I'm to leave a message. Even if you do anything that makes it look like you're contacting the Red Bitch, I'm to call." His head was hanging to one side, completely dominated.

"Hmm. Why me?"

"Leverage, I guess. Tom thinks you know the Red Bitch." He looked up with a little grin on his face. "Frankie said we should take you and your dad captive. Kill one of you to draw out the Red Bitch."

"Frankie is your friend in the white car?"

Raymond nodded.

Dana stood up. "You know it's a bad idea to threaten me or mine."

"We don't have to anymore. Tom's getting the Red Bitch tonight. I get five percent of a million." He just kept grinning.

"What? Haven't you figured it out yet? I'm the Red Bitch!" Dana nearly shouted.

"No, you're not. The Red Bitch is in Indy."

Dana got a chill up her spine, then throughout her body. "I told you it's a bad idea to threaten me or mine."

"Too late. I win," he smiled.

The sword came out of the scabbard. His head bounced four times before landing on his right ear.

*

Dana stopped at the 7-Eleven using the outside payphone at the corner of the building she called Debbie's dorm.

"McNutt Hall. Who do you want?" Someone picked up the phone.

"Is Debbie Reid there?"

"I saw her leaving for class about ten minutes ago."

"Okay. This is very important. Tell Debbie to stay at the dorm. Not to leave. To wait for me and only me. Okay? I should be there around seven o'clock. Please write her a note not to leave. Is her roommate there? What was her name?"

"Lue Ann."

"Yes, is she there?" Dana asked.

"No, she went home for a week. Not really; she told me to say that. She's somewhere with her boyfriend."

"Okay, please leave her a note. And if you see her."

"I know. Don't leave," the voice said.

"Thanks."

The next call was to Mason's office. It rang over ten times before Mason picked it up, breathless. "Chief Jenson here. I mean Special Agent Jenson here."

"Mason? Thank God, it's you. They think Debbie's the Red Bitch. The pilot thinks Debbie's the Red Bitch," Dana said.

"Shit. I just got a flight plan in. Tom left San Diego two hours ago. Going to Chicago's Executive Airport," Mason said.

"I bet he is really going to Indianapolis. I can't get a hold of Debbie. She's in class. Can you send cops to her dorm? Better yet, arrest her. Or just find her anyway. Something," Dana said nervously.

"I will." Then Mason quickly added, "You're not going to Indy."

Dana wanted to say, "Try and stop me," but instead said, "See what you can find out."

"Sure. Dana, promise me"—Dana hung up—"you're not going," Mason said into a dead phone.

Dana ducked into the 7-Eleven and grabbed a big box of diapers and a six-pack of Coke. She was peeing, it seemed like, every hour or so, and she didn't want to stop to pee that often.

Getting into her car, she slipped out of her panties, laid a diaper on the seat, pulled up her dress, and headed for the freeway.

*

Four hours later, Mason picked up the phone on the first ring. "Did they find her?" Dana asked.

"No, not yet. I've got the Bloomington cops on the lookout for her. You don't know her class schedule, do you?" Mason asked.

"No, but here is her dorm number. Call them. The girls know everything." Dana read off the number. "And here is Tom's number. I just tried to call it. Some guy with a Mexican accent answered. He asked a lot of questions. I said I was an old girlfriend and need to talk with him and hung up. Can you please stop by and check on Dad? I'll call the gallery when I get to Bloomington."

"Sure. But I want you to—" Dana hung up before Mason could finish her sentence.

"Damn that bitch," Mason said, worried about her.

Dana filled up the Dragon, emptied out the wet diapers, and Coke cans.

*

Mason parked near the gallery, walking by a dirty white car. She turned quickly to look in the window of the gallery. Christopher was holding back Handsome, whose teeth were bare, his attention locked on someone. Mason got up to the glass front door and looked in cautiously. She saw the back of a man with an automatic in his belt. His right hand was on a gun. She drew her nine-millimeter handgun. As quietly as possible, she opened the door, then pushed it in.

Hearing the noise, he drew his gun and pointed it at Mason. Handsome was in the air and bit down on his arm, sinking his canines to the bone. As they came down, Handsome shook the arm as if to rip it off. The guy dropped his gun and fell to the floor, spinning around, trying to get the dog off him.

Mason put her gun in his face. At the same time, she was calling to Christopher, "I got him. Call Handsome off."

One command from Christopher and Handsome let go of the man's arm and slowly moved back a step. His teeth were still bare, a low growl warned the guy to stay put.

With her gun steady in both hands and aimed at the guy on the floor, Mason asked Christopher, "What the hell did this guy want?"

"He just walked in and asked where Dana was. Then Handsome got all defensive. That's when you came in. He wasn't even here a minute." Christopher had not moved a step.

"That's all?"

"That's all. Why did he want to know where Dana was? And where is Dana? She's not at home. I have not heard from her since this morning. Something about shopping." He was still in shock and as yet had not moved a step.

"Call 911, okay? And then wait for the cops outside. Please."

As soon as Christopher was out the door, Mason put the barrel of her gun in the guy's mouth. "You have one minute to tell me what's going on or one minute to live. Your choice."

Nodding he made his choice. Mason pulled the gun out of his mouth.

"Tom sent me here to find Dana."

"Why?" Mason put the gun to his head.

"I don't know. Tom just wants her."

"Where is Tom?"

"Indianapolis."

"Where exactly in Indianapolis?" Mason said. "Where?"

"Beach Grove. On the east side."

"Your minute is almost up." Mason pressed the gun harder to his head. "You'll be dog food."

"1522 Churchman Avenue. It's an old house."

"Why would he be there?"

"It's a safe house," He answered.

Mason backed off. "Okay, Handsome. Go see Daddy." She backed up to open the door and let Handsome out.

The half-second she turned to open the door, the man took the opportunity to go for his gun with his left hand. Mason turned to see him raising his gun. She fired two shots, the first to his chest and the second to the head.

"I was hoping you would try that," She said under her breath.

Less than three minutes later, the first police car arrived. The second came just behind it.

Christopher was standing just outside, holding Handsome by the collar. Mason opened the door wide and put her gun down on the floor. She was standing just inside the gallery with her FBI badge in one hand. When the police arrived, she raised her hands.

"Chief Jenson. What the hell's going on?" the first cop asked as he came through the door, his gun drawn.

"It's a short story. Can you put your gun away?" Mason asked, flashing her badge and giving the cop an *alright* look. He picked up her gun and handed it to the second officer through the door.

Turning to look at the body, she said, "Shit, thirty-some years on the force and I hardly ever even drew my weapon.

Then just a few months at the FBI and I shoot someone. Actually, I killed him."

The third cop was checking the body and moving the gun away from it.

"I guess he was holding up the place. Mr. Persson is my next-door neighbor. I was just stopping by."

"God, you're lucky," one of them said.

"Can you call Detective Glen Thompson? Get him over here to take our statements, et cetera." Mason pointed out the door. "I'm going to take Christopher, Mr. Persson, his dog's leash and a chair. I want to make sure he's okay."

The officers stepped aside as she picked up the leash from the table near the door. Once outside, she handed it to Christopher. She knelt and petted Handsome. "Good boy." Handsome's muzzle and chest hair were still wet with blood. "What's your most expensive picture in there?" she asked, not looking up.

"A Dali, why?"

"What's it worth?" She was still petting Handsome and not looking up.

"Maybe two hundred thousand?" he said.

"Then that's what that guy was here to steal. Do not say anything about Dana. Tell everything else just like it happened," She said, standing up. She gave Christopher a hug. "Got it?"

He nodded.

"You stay out here. I'll get you a chair. This might take a while," Mason said, heading back inside, she turned at the door. "Need a drink?"

"Oh God, I do." He took a deep breath. "No, thanks. I promised Dana."

Mason chatted with the officers as they waited for the detective.

"Chief Jenson. They told me you shot a guy." Detective Thompson said, coming in and shaking Mason's hand.

"First time ever. And just a few months with the FBI. God, I hope it's not always going to be like this all the time."

The detective was looking at the dead man. "Nice shooting. Was the head shoot the first or the second shot?" He asked.

"Second. I think. He had the drop on me. Then the dog jumped in and grabbed his arm. Shook him hard." They both looked over at the bloody arm. "If you ask me, Handsome should be made an honorary police dog."

The detective noted the dog's name in his notebook.

"When I went to let the dog out, he went for his gun. He had it pointed at me when I shot him." Mason said matter-of-factly.

About then the phone rang. "Mind if I take that? I'm expecting a call."

"Sure. I've got some detecting to do." He smiled.

She picked up the phone, and before Dana could say a word, Mason took over.

"Hi, Jody. I was expecting your call. The cops are here. Some guy in a white car tried to hold up the place. I shot him. In fact, I killed him."

"Is Dad okay? Is everyone okay?" Dana asked quickly.

"Yes, everyone is fine. Well, except for the dead guy. Seems like he was trying to steal a painting. The one you took care of. You know, your Dali."

Dana was decoding the conversation. She was calling from Debbie's dorm, no one had heard or had seen Debbie since she left for class that morning.

"Still, I think you should know about the party." Dana got a chill. "They are expecting you. In fact, everyone is expecting you. Look, the party has moved. I just found out. Those guys from Tandem came in and moved everything to the other side of town. Sorry about that. I wish I could help. They are at 1522 Churchman Avenue. They paid for the party crashers. You know, that band who always dress in blue. They're always way late. Sometimes they never show up. So, you're going to have to take charge. Don't get there late."

"Got it," Was all Dana said.

23. EXPECTING ME

It was just getting dark with a chill in the evening air. Dana passed by the house on Churchman Ave. The porch light was on. The rest of the house had just a faint glow through the newspaper taped over the windows. It was a small, nondescript house. Cars were taking up the parking spaces on both sides of the narrow street. Dana parked four or five houses down and on the other side of the street.

Before leaving the car, she taped the shoto, or small sword, in its scabbard to her right forearm, under the loose sleeve of her red silk dragon dress. She dropped the scabbard for the daito, or long sword, on the bus stop bench as she walked down the dark street to the house. She was holding her child with her left hand and the long sword in her right.

The house was only two steps from the sidewalk, with only one step up to the shabby wooden porch. The door was open a crack, telling The Red Bitch knew they were expecting her. She took hold of the daito sword in both hands.

The Red Bitch kicked open the door. In a split second, she not only judged the four men facing her but also how they were going to die. The tall, thin guy standing in the hallway to the right would be last. The guy with the Uzi would be first. The one with the two revolver pistols would be next. Then the short guy with the sawed-off shotgun.

The Uzi gave the first guy way more confidence than he deserved. "We've been waiting for—" Was all he said before his head fell back. His body, still holding the Uzi, fell sideways. The blade continued till it struck the next man with the pistols in the side of his head. The blade stuck in his skull halfway through his brain. He fell to the left, taking the sword with him.

Before the third man could completely raise his shotgun, the shoto came out of the Red Bitch's sleeve. With a quick swing, it sliced through his neck. He did manage to get off a shot. It went under the Red Bitch's outstretched arm, grazing her left rib cage. He looked surprised, then he joined the others on the floor.

The tall guy in the hallway turned to run. The Red Bitch threw the shoto javelin style, catching him in the back. The sword severed the aorta and pulmonary artery. The tip of the blade came out of his chest. He took two steps forward before falling face down. He had a few seconds left to live. He thought of his mother for the first time in years.

The Red Bitch pulled the daito out of the one guy's head. On her way down the hall, she pulled the shoto out of tall guy's back. He said, "Mommy," and died.

The Red Bitch pushed open the door at the end of the hall. Tom was holding Debbie's head up by her hair, holding a gun at her temple. There was another man standing just inside the door with a rifle pointed at Dana's head. In one motion, The Red Bitch pushed the rifle barrel aside, then drove the shoto down his neck to his heart. He fell, dead, on his knees, leaning up against the wall. She shoved the shoto back into its scabbard in her sleeve.

The Red Bitch took two steps forward with her daito long sword at her side.

"Stop, or I will kill your little cunt friend." Was as far as he got. The daito came up right between his legs. Tom's eyes crossed and both hands, one still holding the pistol, went to his crotch. He fell to his knees. "You cut off my balls, you Red Bitch."

"I've heard that before." The Red Bitch then took the classic Samurai pose. She held it for a second. When he looked up, she cut off his head with a clean sweep.

Dana sat on the side of the bed next to Debbie. Debbie's eyes were less than half open.

"Honey, is that you?" She asked in a hoarse whisper.

"Yes, lover, it's me," Dana said, quickly looking her over. A syringe was sticking in her right arm. "I'm going to take this out, okay?" Dana carefully removed the needle.

Debbie had been severely beaten; her red minidress was torn and ripped. Her red hose had been ripped so badly, they hardly existed. She had no shoes, and her feet were bloody. She had blood in her red hair and her nose was bleeding and broken. She had bruises and cuts on her neck, arms, and legs.

Dana gave her a soft kiss on her forehead. "Yes, sweetie, I'm here."

"Take me out of here," Debbie said in her coarse whisper.

"You're really bad. I don't think you can walk. I don't think I can carry you."

"No, I can walk. Please get me out of here." Debbie's hand found Dana's arm. "Please."

"Okay, I'll get you up. I'll hold you up, but you have got to do the walking. Can you do that?"

"Anything. Just get me out of here." Debbie gave Dana's arm a squeeze. She had no power behind the squeeze.

Dana sat Debbie up on the side of the bed, pulling her up and maneuvered her into a standing position. She then put Debbie's right arm around her neck. Dana's left arm went around Debbie's waist. Dana picked the bloody daito up off the bed and used it as a cane.

"Okay, one step at a time. We can stop whenever." The first few steps were very shaky for them both. As they neared the door, Dana reached out and, with one quick swipe with the daito, cut the thin, flexible gas line feeding the wall-mounted heater. When they reached the body in the hall, Dana guided Debbie around it. She walked on the body.

When they left the house, Dana shut the door behind her. The steps were difficult, but with Debbie's other hand around Dana and by leaning heavily against her, they made it. During the ordeal, Debbie had felt Dana's chest. "Bigger tits," she said.

"Yep. Ds," Dana said as they slowly walked down the sidewalk.

When they reached the bus stop bench, Debbie said, "Sit, please."

"It's just over there, the car." Dana wanted to get her to a hospital as soon as possible.

"I got to sit. Please, sweetie." Debbie slowly sat with Dana's help. Sitting next to her, Dana put her arm around her in a protective, loving way. Debbie rested her head on Dana's shoulder. She reached out to Dana's tummy. "How is she doing?" she asked.

Dana put her hand on Debbie's hand. "She kicks a lot. She also pees a lot. But she's doing just fine."

"I can feel her moving. I love our baby so much." Debbie just closed her eyes. With her hand still on the child, she went limp.

At that moment, the gas reached a spark and blew up the house. Parts of the house fell all around them. The blast took out parts of the houses on both sides. The cars in front of the house were rolled over and burning. Pieces of everything fell short of the bus stop bench.

Dana didn't move; her tears were streaming down her face. The first fire truck arrived in less than ten minutes, its sirens screaming. It was followed by a police car. Then another fire truck. A police car. A few minutes later, an ambulance.

The ambulance driver noticed Dana and Debbie and the blood all over them both. She stopped and got out of the truck. Two other EMS workers joined her. Dana did not look up; she was still holding Debbie's lifeless body. One of the EMS people felt Debbie for a pulse. He turned to the others and shook his head. "Are you hurt? Let me check you, okay?" He said to Dana, who only shook her head no. One of them opened the back of the ambulance, taking out the gurney.

The driver put her hand on Dana's shoulder. "She's okay. She not hurting now." She tried to lift Dana's arm off Debbie, but Dana would not move. "We're going to help her. Please let go." The gurney was now in front of them. "Please help us. We need to take your friend to the hospital, okay?"

Dana loosened up as two of the EMS guys lifted Debbie onto the gurney. They laid her out and covered her. Dana got up and pulled back the cover from her face. She gave Debbie a good-bye kiss on her lifeless lips.

The EMS people took over, rolling Debbie into the ambulance. They closed the doors, the driver again asked, "You sure you're okay? We can give you a ride to the hospital."

Dana took a step back, shaking her head again.

"Okay, dear. Please see a doctor," the driver said as she stepped into the ambulance and took off with the sirens blaring as if Debbie was still alive. Dana was left standing in the middle of the street.

She watched the ambulance turn the corner. She turned to see the firemen putting out the fires. The police were putting up yellow tape. The house had disappeared. There was lots of noise, Dana heard none of it.

Dana picked up her daito and slid it into its scabbard, getting into her car. As she left, she could see the policemen in her rearview mirror, putting up more yellow tape. This time, they used the bus stop bench as the place to tie off the tape.

She drove for about an hour. The tears dried on her cheek. She stopped at the first rest stop and parked as far away from everyone as possible. Her screams of anger were muffled by windows and distance. She pounded the steering wheel and the dashboard.

After a while, she got out of the car and, cradling her baby girl in her hands, made her way to the ladies' room. She peed. She washed her hands. Only then did she feel the pain from the shotgun. She lifted her dress to find two long cuts in her rib cage, one about four inches and the other half that size, about an inch apart. They were well away from the baby. She took out her little sword, which was still taped to her arm, and cut off a chunk of the towel from the towel machine. She wet it and dabbed away the blood. The wounds had not stopped bleeding yet. Wet and dried-up blood running down her side to just above her knee. She wiped it off cutting some more material out of the hand dryer and wrapped it around her chest.

Back in the car, she again screamed and cursed herself out, taking the whole blame for Debbie's death. About midnight, she stopped at a gas station to fill up the Trans Am. In the minimart, she found peroxide, tape, and some gauze. The clerk commented, "You have blood on your face." He was disinterested.

"Yeah, you should see the other guy," Dana said, turning away.

She went into the ladies' room and poured some peroxide on her wounds, then on the gauze, which she taped in place. She looked at herself in the mirror as she washed her hands and her face. She studied herself, then smashed her fist into her face in the mirror. She wrapped gauze around her bleeding knuckles.

That was when she felt her water break.

Coming out of the ladies' room, she asked, "Where is the payphone?"

The clerk, reading a *Penthouse* magazine, jerked his head toward the phone on the wall near the door.

She made a quick call to Mason's. Jody answered.

"Hey, I'm on my way home. I should be there around six, I guess. Oh, by the way, what does it mean when my water breaks?"

"Holy shit. Get to a hospital now," Jody demanded.

"No, I don't have any labor pains. I think I got a while. See you." Before she hung up, she added, "Oh, tell Dad I'm on my way home."

She cried, she yelled, she pounded the wheel. At about three a.m., she felt the first labor pain. "Oh well. Debbie said I shouldn't worry until they are three minutes apart. Debbie said." Then she cried some more.

After the next labor pain, she started to time them. When she pulled into the driveway just before six a.m., they were three minutes apart.

Handsome was barking and was the first one out of the houses, followed by Mason, Jody, then Christopher. They had all sat up all night waiting for Dana.

Dana got out of the car and leaning on the front fender, making quiet sounds of pain. Mason got to her first. "Okay, baby. How close are they?"

Dana puffed and puffed. "Three minutes."

"Christopher, start the car," Mason commanded. Dana was helped to the front seat. Jody jumped in with Handsome right behind her.

"Handsome, out," Mason said. "Oh, to hell with it. Let's go." She jumped in and shut the back door.

They stopped in the emergency lane of the hospital.

The receptionist was looking at a familiar scene as Dana, and the others rushed into the hospital. Except for the very large Collie dog. Recognizing Mason, the receptionist called out, "Chief Jenson."

"Oh." Mason turned. Dana, a doctor, a nurse, Jody, Christopher, and a dog were rushing down the hall to the elevator, taking them to the delivery rooms. "Christopher, throw me your car keys and send Handsome to me," She yelled over the din.

Christopher threw the keys to her. He took Handsome by the collar and told him to go see Mason.

"Here, Handsome" she called. The elevators doors were closing. Handsome was pushed to the outside. He reluctantly trotted down to Mason's side but looked at the elevator doors, hoping to see Dana.

"Chief Jenson, dogs are not allowed in the hospital," the receptionist said.

"It's okay. He's a police dog." Mason then thought, *Well, an honorary police dog, almost.*

"Helen, isn't it? It's been a while. I haven't seen you since Officer Charles was shot. What? Over a year ago?" As chief of police, Mason always visited any member of the department who was brought to the hospital. She saw no reason to give up the chief of police title at this moment.

"I'll leave Handsome with you, and I'll move the car. Then we can start the paperwork." Mason brought back Handsome's leash and hooked him up. She gave Helen

Dana's full name and address. "Father?" Mason repeated the question. "Just put John Doe." Then Mason and Handsome headed for the elevator. Mason was directed to the waiting room. The nurse hardly looked up until she heard Handsome's paws clicking on the tiles. Then she just shook her head.

Jody hugged Mason. "Everything is all right. She was going into final labor in the elevator."

The nurses helped Dana out of her red Japanese dress and into the hospital gown. They noted the bloody gauze covering her wounds as they unhooked her bra. She still wasn't wearing panties. Her legs were hoisted and spread apart.

"Push," the doctor said only once. The baby girl entered the world in one big rush. "6:19 am," the doctor said, holding the loudly crying little girl. "Lungs are good," he said as he did a quick exam and removed the umbilical cord.

She was placed on Dana's chest. Dana wrapped her arms around the child, looking at the new life in her arms with love, Dana said, "Debbie, see what we did."

24. PROTECTORS

"Smile," the nurse said, holding up a camera. Dana smiled. The baby let out one last yell then smiled, putting her hand in her mouth." Okay, give her to me. We have got to clean her up and check her out," the nurse said as she set down the camera.

"Okay, what do we have?" the doctor asked, rolling Dana onto her side. He carefully took off the gauze and took one look as he said, "Did I see Chief Jensen downstairs? I'm going to need to talk to her. Bring her up here please." To the other nurse, he gave instructions on what he was going to need to take care of the bullet wound on Dana's side.

A few minutes later, Mason with her surgical mask on was taken to the doctor and Dana. "See," he said, pointing to the stitched-up wounds on Dana's side. "Okay, nurse, you can finish up here." He walked Mason out to the hall. "Are you here because of those bullet wounds?"

She quickly slipped back into her detective mode. "What can you tell me about them?"

"Those are shotgun wounds, and at really close range. There are powder burns all up and down her side. Also, they are at least six hours old. She has lost a lot of blood," the doctor explained as if he was giving a detailed report to the real chief of police.

"Well, that confirms her story," Mason said, thinking quickly. "Thank you, Doctor. I'll put all that in my report. Just until we finish the investigation, please keep all this to yourself." Shaking the doctor's hand, she added quickly, "I'll need to be spending time with her to get the whole story if that's okay?"

"One more thing you should know. She has hernias on both sides. I'll have to take care of them before she leaves. But not today. To tell the truth, I'm beat and need some sleep." He waved as he headed down the hall.

Mason looked through the window into the operating room and said, "What did you get into, girl, and how did you pull it off?"

Mason walked with the gurney as they took Dana to a comfortable room. On the way, Mason asked if the family could be brought up to meet the baby.

"Here's your little special package," the nurse said, handing a clean and swaddled baby to Dana.

Handsome was the first one through the door, closely followed by Christopher and Jody.

Handsome put his paws up on the bed. He smelled the baby and licked Dana's hand, then sat quietly by the bed. *New baby to protect and love.* He thought.

Dana was smiling and exhausted. As they all chattered on, she closed her eyes. The chattering faded away.

Suddenly her eyes popped open. Christopher, Jody, and Mason were standing by the door some distance away, talking to the doctor. They appeared faint, as if she was looking at them through a white silk stocking. They seemed to fall farther and farther away.

Handsome was clear and as real as ever. He was sitting near the bed. He was looking at Eve and Debbie, who were also standing by the bed. They were as real as ever. Both were talking to the baby. The baby cooed back in little sounds. Sounds of love.

"Mom, what are you doing here?" Dana found it strange that her mother was standing there for some reason.

"Why, I'm here to meet Alyssa," Eve said.

"Who's Alyssa?" Dana was getting more confused but was strangely comforted.

"Why, Alyssa is my granddaughter. Isn't she beautiful?" Eve leaned over and kissed Alyssa.

"Debbie. How are you?" Dana saw Debbie dressed in her white prom dress and heels.

"I'm great. Isn't our Alyssa beautiful? I love her so much." Debbie also kissed Alyssa.

Dana looked down at Alyssa. She was lying in her arms, but the swaddling blanket was gone. She was waving her arms and kicking her legs. Dana looked up at her mother. "Mom, I thought you died." Everything was swirling around in her head, yet still felt so normal.

"Oh, honey, of course I died." Eve gave Dana a kiss on the forehead. Dana could feel the warmth and love from her mother coming through that kiss. "But I never left you. I'm still here, protecting you. Just like the day I died, protecting you."

Dana could see her mother just like the first time she ever saw her, looking up from her arms just after being born. Then she changed a little. Dana could see her looking lovingly at her from her throne. Then she changed a little yet again, more like when Dana was a young teen, now with both pride and love.

"You didn't think you got this far by yourself? You have done some very dangerous stuff. I am always with you. I am always protecting you." That seemed to make sense to Dana.

"Debbie? You didn't die, did you? They saved you, didn't they?"

"No, I died. Oh, you took such good care of me. It was so peaceful, so loving. Now, I am here for our Alyssa. Now, I'm her protector. I'm going to help you watch over her. From what I can see, we are going to have a lot of work to do."

Handsome made a little dog sound that meant *What about me?* Debbie patted him on the head. "Yes, you get to help too." Handsome wagged his tail.

Debbie looked down at Dana, putting a hand on her heart, "You know I loved you from the first time I saw you. That was at the first freshman dance in high school. I complimented you on your heels, remember?" Dana remembered. "I will always love you. You'll find love again. It's going to take a while, and it's not going to be easy. And your true love will also be my true love." Debbie paused. "Love adds. It doesn't subtract. Remember that." Debbie then gave Dana a kiss on the lips. It was warm, as loving and exciting as their first kiss.

As Debbie turned to Eve, they both started to become transparent, fading away.

"Don't go!" Dana called to them. "I need you!" she called in a panic. "We need you."

"We're not going anywhere. We're going to always be with you and Alyssa. See you in your dreams." Eve and Debbie blew both Dana and Alyssa kisses, and then they faded off, laughing.

Dana slowly opened her eyes. She heard laughing coming from two nurses in the hall outside her door. It was the same laughter.

"So, sleepyhead, you finally decided to join the world of the living?" Mason said, sitting in a chair next to Dana's bed. She put a marker in the book she was reading and put it on the bed stand. "How are you feeling?"

Dana looked around as if she had never seen the room or even knew she was in the hospital. Then suddenly it all came crashing back to her.

"Where's Alyssa?" Dana looked around the room.

"Who's Alyssa?"

"My baby. Where is she?" Dana felt her heart reach her throat.

"She's in the nursery. She is being well taken care of." Standing up and putting a hand on Dana's shoulder, Mason leaned over and studied the screens with wiggly lines and numbers. "Alyssa. When did you come up with that name?"

"I didn't. Mom did," Dana said, falling back.

"Good name," Mason said, thinking it was an old thing between mother and daughter. "You were asleep for twenty-five hours. Do you feel rested?" Mason took Dana's hand.

"I don't know. What's this thing in my arm?" She reached over to pull it out.

"No, no. Let's let the nurse do that. You were so emaciated, and you lost a lot of blood. That's helping rehydrate you." Mason moved Dana's hand away from the needle.

"Twenty-five hours. Really?" Dana asked.

"Let's see. What time did you get up Friday morning?" Was all Mason got out before Dana grabbed her arm tightly.

"Oh God. Debbie's dead." Dana went all white. "She's dead. Those bastards killed her." Dana pulled hard on Mason's arm with her free hand. Tears were already leaving trails down her cheeks.

"I know," Mason said. Her free hand patted Dana's hair. "I know." Mason let her grieve for just a minute or so. "But, honey, I need your attention right now. Can you look at me? We only have a few minutes to talk."

Dana looked up through wet eyes.

"You can't know that Debbie died just now. You can't say anything or act like you know Debbie's dead. Carlos thinks Debbie was the Red Bitch. He has to keep thinking that. It's the only way we can keep you and the baby safe for now." Mason looked intently into Dana's eyes. "I don't know if he thinks you're involved. Now, what did you do when you left town?"

"I went to find Debbie and save her," Dana said.

"You went to the dorm, right?"

"Yes," Dana said. She slowly let Mason's arm go.

"We have to explain you being missing for seventeen hours or more." Mason bit her thumbnail as she thought. She paced for just a few steps. "Okay, here it is." Turning to Dana, "You went to find Debbie because you wanted her with you when the baby was born. You went to the dorm, she wasn't there, so you came home." Mason thought for a moment, "Not much of a story. We can make up more later. But it covers some bases."

Dana lay quietly, then said, "Okay."

"No, say it. Tell me the story," Mason was holding Dana's hand.

"I went to the dorm to get Debbie so she could be with me when Alyssa was born. I couldn't find her, so I came home," Dana repeated in a dead voice.

"One last thing for now. What happened to Ray Ray? We don't need him showing up."

"He won't. I cut off his head," Dana said without emotion.

"Good. He hasn't been found yet. I'll make sure people I trust in the police department get there first and cover up that he lost his head." Mason said softly, "Is there anything else I should know?"

"The ambulance crew saw me," Dana said. "With Debbie." The tears started again.

"I know. I talked to the EMS commander. I saw the report. They didn't say anything about you. Just someone sitting at the bus stop bench. That's clean. Anything else?" Mason asked.

Dana shook her head.

"I'm sorry to keep quizzing you. But did anybody at the house get out? How many were there? Did anybody else see you?"

"Six were there. Tom was one of them. They all died," Dana said quietly. "Then I blew up the place. No trace of me, I'm sure."

"The rest we can talk about later." Mason looked around.

"Okay."

Mason handed Dana a tissue. "Ready?"

Dana blew her nose and nodded, yes.

"Oh, by the way, I cleaned out the Trans Am. I got rid of all the Coke cans, all eighteen of them, by the way." Mason gave her a condemning look. "I saw nothing indicating you had anything to eat."

"I ate a Twinkie," Dana said.

"Nice." Mason rolled her eyes. "I cleaned your swords with bleach. I found your panties in the car. What were the diapers for?"

"Me," Dana said, trying to smile.

"Okay. You'll explain that to me later. Honey, I know this is going to be hard, but act like you're happy." Mason pushed the button for the nurse.

"Also, I burned your red dragon dress. It was covered in blood and all torn up," Mason finished as the nurse entered the room.

"Well, is our sleeping beauty awake?" the nurse said, coming over and checking the machines.

"Can you take this out of my arm?" Dana asked.

"Sure, just a minute." She automatically checked Dana's pulse. Just habit; the machines told her everything she needed to know.

"I'll go get your dad and Jody. They are down in the cafeteria having breakfast," Mason said. "We all have been here most of the time. Just going home to take care of Handsome and make some phone calls." Mason turned to leave.

"Take your time," the nurse said as she removed the needle from Dana's arm. "We have to do some things to make the new mother more presentable. Have some breakfast, yourself."

Dana was washed, she had her catheter removed and replaced by a diaper. She was shown how to work the bed.

The doctor came into the room to talk with Dana. "You have two hernias. Left and right," the doctor said, gently touching her lower abdomen. "Do you feel them? I'm surprised they are not hurting you. We are going to have to operate on them. It's minor surgery. I have you scheduled with Doctor Shaw. As soon as we know his schedule, we'll let you know."

*

An hour later, Dana was sitting up. She was given a bowl of Cream of Wheat and a glass of apple juice.

"Hi, mommy," Jody said as she went to Dana's bedside.

"Hi, sweetie," Christopher said, going to the other side of the bed.

Mason hung back a little, watching.

Dana started to push the tray away. "Oh no, you don't. At least finish your apple juice," the nurse said. Two gulps, and the juice was all gone.

Everyone started talking at once. Then a nurse entered with Alyssa, who was placed in her mother's arms.

"Alyssa, meet your family. Family, meet Alyssa." Dana introduced Alyssa to her new family.

"Lars and Sally will be here at noon. Lars and Beau around four this afternoon. They were in Hollywood on some deal." Jody had gotten all their schedules just after the baby was born. "We haven't heard from Debbie. Her parents have been calling the school and dorm. They called my house and your house. No one has seen her in a day or two. We are all worried."

Dana started to tear up. Mason moved in quickly, taking a tissue from the bed stand. "Oh, look at that. You have some Cream of Wheat on your face." She got between Dana and the rest so they could not see that she was really wiping tears from Dana's eyes. She looked at Dana with compassion.

"Alyssa. Interesting name. How did you come up with that?" Mason asked to change the subject.

"That's a beautiful name. For a beautiful girl," Jody said.

"Yes. How did you come up with Alyssa?" Christopher asked. He almost told the story of how Dana got her name on his third date with Eve, but he held back.

"Mom told me," Dana said.

Everyone nodded and said, "Wonderful name."

Christopher had a puzzled expression. *How could that be? Dana was only sixteen when Eve died. Grandbabies never came up in any of their conversations,* he thought as he joined in the celebration.

"You guys can go home and get some rest. I'll sit with her. I mean them. For a little while," Mason said.

"I could use a little nap before Sally and Lars get here. They are renting a car, so I don't have to pick them up." Jody yawned and smelled her clothes. "And a shower would be nice."

Christopher looked at his watch. "The boys don't get in till four. I've got a few hours before I need to go home and change."

"Oh no, you don't." Mason took him by the arm and led him to the door, following Jody out. "You have been up forever. You need to go home and get some rest. Follow

Jody home. Pick up the boys and come back here. Get some rest and please shower."

By this time, they were out in the hall. Mason gave him a hug. "Jody, make sure he gets home okay." Then she closed the door.

"Nice going, chief," the nurse said. "Now, Dana, are you going to nurse your baby or bottle-feed?"

"Nurse, I guess." Dana had not thought about it much, except when her oversized breasts hurt.

"You don't know how to, do you?" the nurse asked.

She got the baby moved around and into a comfortable position. Alyssa followed her instincts.

"Ouch, oh. Wow." Then Dana giggled, looking up at Mason.

Mason was not much help with this part. She never had kids. Soon, her eyes began to go to half-mast.

"You know you can kick your shoes off now. Maybe take off your gun. Perhaps lie down in that bed over there." Dana pointed to the other bed in the room.

The nurse looked away. "They are for patients only, but no one is scheduled for that bed. So, I see nothing." She started to walk out of the room.

"Well, okay. If you insist." Mason passed out with her gun under her pillow. Over three hours later, she woke up.

"Did Alyssa get full?" Mason asked, working her way to sitting up on the side of the bed.

"Yes, twice since you took your nap." Dana was cradling the sleeping baby.

"Aw," Mason said, looking over at Alyssa. They just chatted about Alyssa for the next hour.

The nurse came in, pushing the food tray. She wheeled the tray in front of Dana and removed the metal covers off the dishes. "Soup. Wedding soup, I think. Turkey sandwiches. And milk." Pointing to the tray. "Oh, look at that. They made a mistake in the kitchen and gave me two of everything. Oh well." She winked at Mason. The lunch was more than welcome. Dana's stomach took a second to get used to solid food.

Lars and Sally cracked open the door about an hour later. Sally peeked in. "Are visitors welcome?"

"Sure." Mason opened the door, letting them in. Mason was wearing her gun, but her shoes were neatly parked near the other bed. Her coat was still on the bed.

"Oh, look at her," Sally said. "I love the name, Alyssa. Mom told us. She's parking the car." Then almost right away, Sally said, "Can I hold her?"

Lars was looking over her shoulder, waving his little finger at Alyssa and throwing air kisses. "She's smiling at me. She knows her favorite uncle when she sees him."

"She's pooping, Lars," Dana said.

Oh, Lars thought. "Well, anyway. I'm sure I'm her favorite uncle."

Sally cooed and whispered to the baby. She knew she would never have a baby of her own. That just made Allyssa more precious. She carried her around the room. She sat with her, seldom took her eyes off the little life in her arms. When she began to fuss, Dana reached over.

"She's hungry again. Like every two or three hours, she wants to suck on me." She hooked up Alyssa and looked over at Lars and Sally. "How are you guys doing?"

"The dojo has really taken off. I've had to hire help. Sally's been promoted at the hospital and has better hours now. So great."

"Not that. How are you guys doing?" Dana gave a questioning look.

Sally spoke up. "We have had some rough times. Nothing tragic or anything like that."

Lars was looking out the window. He turned around. "The problem is we are not the usual European married couple. We are an American married couple. That's different. Maybe."

"Both of us get flirted with a lot. I'm expected to put out at work. Not happening. Women in the dojo are just way too forward. They'll get undressed in front of Lars like it's nothing," Sally said.

"We made a deal. At night over dinner or in bed, we tell each other about all the, well, all this stuff going on with us. Made me mad at first," Lars said.

"Me too," Sally interjected.

"So now we just laugh about it. Sometimes it makes us horny. So not all bad. So, we're doing okay." Lars finished up by giving Sally a kiss.

Just as they finished up and Alyssa finished her snack, the door crashed open. "There are our girls," Lars said. He was the first one in the room.

"There she is. My beautiful girl." Beau followed Lars in. "And hello to you too, Dana." He nodded at her.

Christopher followed in with a big grin on his face and a vase filled with flowers.

"Hi, guys," Dana said. She received kisses and they took turns looking at Alyssa. "Sally, please take Alyssa for a few minutes."

"She smiled at me," Beau said as Dana passed Alyssa off.

"No, she is pooping at you," Lars said with a grin.

Dana rolled over on her side. Pulling back the covers and pulling open her gown, she exposed her butt. "Beau, it was a bet. You lost, so you owe me a big fat wet sloppy kiss right here on my ass," she said, pointing to her ass.

"Oh my God," Beau said as everyone laughed. "Well, with a butt that big, how could I miss?" And he planted one.

He finished it off by giving her a hickey. Everyone cheered and slapped him on the back. He went to kiss Sally.

"You're not kissing me with those lips. No way." Sally said to even more cheers and laughter.

25. HELLO, GOODBYE

"Yes, she's out of surgery. No, she's still out," Mason said, into the phone as Dana was rolled back into her room. The others had been standing around her, listening to the conversation.

It took a while for Dana to fully recover from the anesthesia. When she was feeling more like herself, the nurse invited the family back into the room. Mason was still in the hall, talking on the phone at the nurse's station. The family was trying to be happy. Trying too hard.

"Okay, what's up?" Dana asked. She already knew.

They all waited for someone else to step forward.

"Well, sweetie," Christopher started when Mason came into the room. Everyone turned to her.

"Oh," Mason said. "Okay," she said, looking around at the faces in pain. She sat on the side of the bed and took Dana's hand.

"I need to tell you. Debbie has been killed." Everyone else held back.

Dana, with both pain and relief at not having to hold back the pain, gave out a long cry of anguish.

Dana went home late the next morning with a bottle of sedatives and a newborn baby.

She's here. She's here, Handsome thought as he heard Christopher's car drive up. He could not hold back and jumped up and down. Beau had to push him back to get the door open. He quickly checked the scent to make sure Alyssa was there in that bundle of blankets. *I'll always make sure you're safe. I'll stay with you always.* Handsome tried to project his thoughts to Alyssa.

*

"Look what we did while you were kicking back in the hospital." Beau showed Dana into the upstairs room next to hers. It was painted light pink with white trim. There were big rockers in the baby's room and in Dana's room. Later, Dana would find two more identical rockers, one in the library and another in Mason and Dana's office.

Dana stood looking at the photos on the wall. "Here, mama. Sit down." Lars pulled the rocking chair up close to Dana, who sat down, cradling Alyssa. Lars took on his stage voice and pointed to the pictures one at a time. "Here, Alyssa is your Grandma and Grandpa. And this is us on the mat. You'll find out all about that later. This is your mommy and your other mommy." He pointed to a picture of Dana and Debbie at the prom. "And this one is your very first picture." He pointed to the middle of the wall and a picture of Alyssa just seconds old, in her mother's arms. Hospital pictures tended to be in black and white.

*

The first night Christopher was at the gallery, the whole family was in the kitchen helping to make dinner.

"How is Dad doing?" Lars asked.

"Good," Dana replied quickly.

"You know what I mean," Alex tilted his head back like taking a drink out of a bottle.

"Dad's sober. He has not had a drink in months. I believe he will never take another drink. He promised me he wouldn't, and I trust him," Dana said.

"Is it me or does he look older? A lot older from the last time we saw him. It wasn't that long ago," Sally said.

"It's the alcohol, drinking, and depression that aged him. Sometimes, I'm surprised not to find him dead in his chair in the library. But I have not seen him this happy in a long time. Thanks, guys." Dana looked down at a sleeping Alyssa. "For everything."

The dining room was full that night. Both Christopher and Jody were all grins. It was not often the whole family was together for dinner.

*

The next day, everyone was starting to make plans to go home. During the discussion, Handsome quickly went to the door long before the doorbell rang.

Jody answered the door and led Debbie's parents into the library. Dana began to silently cry.

“We came to see the baby.” Frank, Debbie's dad, said. “Here. This is for Alyssa,” he said, handing Dana a teddy bear. “That was Debbie's teddy bear when she was little. When you got pregnant, she said she wanted to give the bear to the baby. Debbie talked so much about her, we just had to come over. I hope you don't mind.”

“Of course not. You are always welcome here. You're, after all, Alyssa's grandparents,” Dana said.

“Oh, she is so beautiful,” Sofia, Debbie's mom, said.

“Do you want to hold her?” Dana offered her to her grandparents.

“No, well, yes.” Sofia held her and rocked her looking lovingly at tiny life in her arms.

“Debbie's funeral is Saturday at the James Church of Christ. We want you to give the eulogy,” Frank said, tears in his eyes.

Dana could no longer hold back the tears. “What do you want me to say?” she sobbed.

“Say whatever you want. You and Debbie were so close. It needs to be you. First, the padre will perform a short service. We will then greet the assembled guests. Then you will speak. No one else will speak. Is that okay?” Frank had been standing the whole time. He was afraid to sit down. He was worried he couldn't get back up.

"One other thing," Sofia said. "Please help me pick out Debbie's clothes for burial. I don't know what to pick out."

Dana could do no more than whisper through tears, "Yes."

She cleared her throat and took a deep breath. "Well, if it's okay with you, my best and most beautiful memory is of her in her white prom gown." After they all agreed that was best. "And if it's okay with you—you can say no to this, and I won't mind—can I wear my prom gown? I think she would like that."

"Agreed," Frank said at once, looking at his wife.

*

The church filled mostly with Debbies friends. Some students from the university, who mostly wanted a reason to go to Atlanta. The rest was the regular church people, most of them older.

The church went silent when Dana came down the aisle in her strapless black prom dress with gold sparkles. She had on a white orchid. Alyssa was in her arms.

Dana sat by Debbie's parents. Jody sat next to Dana to provide childcare as needed. After Dana had settled in, the minister came down to speak to the front row.

"I'm sorry for your loss. She now sits with God." His hand went up, as if praising God. "I'll say a small mass, only five minutes or so. Just giving God's blessing to those here and those who have gone before us." Gesturing to Debbie's parents. "You will then be given the floor to speak to the congregation." He then zeroed in on Dana. "I understand you will give the eulogy. This is a Church of Christ. None of your lesbian sexual stuff. Keep it clean. These are churchgoing people that believe in the Bible. Keep it straight." He turned up his nose and walked to the front of the church.

Frank leaned over. "Say anything you like. Debbie loved you."

The minister said his short mass, then blessed the dead and the congregation.

Frank and Sofia then stood in front of the coffin. They looked at their only daughter. They then held each other and turned to the silent flock. They welcomed those in attendance. That was just about the end of their composure. They then introduced Dana and took their seats in the front row.

Dana stood in her black and gold prom gown, wearing her stilettos. She handed Alyssa to Jody and approached the casket. Dana had a black orchid in her hand. She placed it in Debbie's hand. She told her she loved her, kissed her fingers, and placed them on Debbie's lips, returning Debbie's kiss to her own lips.

The crowd whispered to each other. It became quickly apparent that they did not approve of what they were seeing. "What's with her? Wearing that gown." and "A black flower?" were audible throughout the church.

"The first time I met Debbie was at the pre-prom our freshman year. I was there with my friend Gina. All of you avoided me. After all, you called me Godzilla because of my height. That was my first dance. My first time in heels. I was standing by the wall. I wanted to be the wall. Then Debbie came by. 'You look beautiful in heels,' she said. She came by several times to talk with me. I tell you this to show you the depth of her compassion. She wanted to speak to *Godzilla.* That's something." Dana turned to look at Debbie. "Recently, she told me she fell in love with me that night." The congregation began shaking their heads. "She kept her distance because I was seeing someone else. You all remember Stump, my friend Gina." The rumblings became louder.

"I was having a rough year. I was all alone. Gina had left." Dana was talking over the noise. "One day, Debbie showed up at my locker. We went to Shakiees Pizza Parlor. She talked me out of my depression. She made me laugh and smile. I fell in love with her that afternoon." The righteous flock was getting louder and angrier.

"She had so much to give." Dana got fed up. "You guys knew we were lesbians. So, shut up. Especially you Bill, Tommy, and you too, Tammy. I'm trying to tell you how loving and caring Debbie was. Again, shut up."

The crowd was stunned into silence. The anger grew again louder this time. Bill stood up to say something, just then a tall, well-dressed man in a black suit in the back of the hall stood up. "Everyone. Shut up and show some respect for the dead and for those of us who loved her." Pointing at Bill, who started up again. "Bill, sit down and shut up, or I will meet you outside. You won't like it. I can promise you that."

Dana took a breath, recognizing the man. "Thank you, Casey." She smiled. "Yes, we were lovers. We are lesbians and lucky to find each other. I just hope every one of you finds as much love in your life as we found in our short time together." Dana pointed at Alyssa. "Debbie was a big part of bringing Alyssa into the world. I'll see some of Debbie every time I look at Alyssa.

"She was there every, shall we say, stop along the way." She winked at Casey. "Alyssa is as much Debbie's child as mine."

Turning to Debbie, tears in her eyes, Dana looked at her face. A face she would never see again. Dana thought of her laugh. Closing her eyes, she could see Debbie making funny faces. She turned back. "I can still see her funny faces, her never-ending smile. I'm going to miss her stupid laugh. So, we're here to say goodbye to my love. My Debbie."

The ceremony at the gravesite only took about fifteen minutes. Those who came soon began to wander off.

Dana saw Casey standing off to one side. He had turned his back to everyone to hide his tears. He just could not watch anymore.

Dana handed Alyssa off to Mason and walked over to Casey. Tapped him on the shoulder, he turned to see Dana just as she had looked at the prom. It brought back vivid memories of that night with Debbie and Dana. He had told the guys on the base that he took two girls to the senior prom. Anyway, he kind of always felt that way.

"Thank you again," Dana said with real sincerity.

"For what?" Casey dried his eyes.

"For standing up for Debbie and me. No one else did. So, thank you again." She took his hand.

"I was just quicker, that's all." Casey came back to reality.

"You are coming to Debbie's house for the wake."

"No. I don't think so." He looked away.

"Yes, you are. You need to." Dana caught herself. "I'm sorry. There I go again, bossing you around. Sorry. But please come. I want you to meet Alyssa. Please. Besides, wakes are an Irish thing. Right?"

"Well, okay. Just for a little bit. I just got into town this morning. I haven't even told my folks I'm here yet and I got to be back at the base by noon the day after tomorrow. I'm just on a seventy-two-hour emergency leave."

Christopher was calling her name. Dana started to turn. "Okay."

"I'll see you there," Casey said. Dana squeezed his hand, then let go.

At the wake, Casey mingled with the guests and friends. He eventually worked his way around to Dana, who was sitting on the patio with Alyssa in her arms. "Hi," he said as he walked up.

"Alyssa meet Casey." Dana presented Alyssa. "Want to hold her?"

"Oh no." He backed off a step.

"No. Here hold her," Dana insisted.

"She's not heavy," Mason said with a smile.

"Really. No. The only thing I have cradled in the last few months are artillery shells. So, no, thank you. I'll just look. Okay?" He stepped a little closer.

"She won't explode. Well, except for her butt." Jody chuckled.

"I can see her perfectly fine from here. She is beautiful. Blond hair? Blue eyes," he asked.

"I think all babies have blue eyes. But, considering you and I have blue eyes and blond hair, it's a good bet." Dana held her out so he could have a better look at his daughter.

"Oh. There goes the bomb. Mason, would you do me a favor and change Alyssa? I think she dropped quite a stink bomb." Giving a head signal, she wanted to be alone with Casey.

"Come on, Jody," Mason said. "Christopher, could you get me those extra plastic bags out of the car?" They all accepted their assignments.

"I'm so glad you're here. But how did you find out?" Dana motioned for him to sit next to her.

"Debbie's dad called the base to see if I knew where she was. It took a while for me to get the message. By the time I called back, well, that was yesterday morning." He took a breath, looking down and shaking his head. He cleared his throat. "He invited me to the funeral. I got emergency leave and got here as fast as I could."

"Thank you again. I'm sure it means a lot to all of us. By the way, you are looking quite handsome. That suit fits you much better than your prom suit."

"Thanks. Bought it this morning. New shoes too." He lifted his leg to show off his new shoes.

"I think I still owe you ten grand. I can have it for you tomorrow morning if you stop by," Dana offered.

"You have no idea what you have done for me, do you?" Casey looked Dana in the eye. "You got me in the Navy. You practically walked me up to the gate. If you hadn't, I know I would have skipped. It's the best thing that could have happened to me. I'm not the shy kid I was in high school. I now have confidence in myself, and I'm developing skills I never thought of. I have friends and make a good income. You were the only person pushing me in that direction. So, I thank you for all you have done for me."

"But a deal is a deal. I still owe you ten grand. You have more than kept up your end of the deal."

"The money you gave me... Well, I squandered the first ten thousand. God, I did silly things with that money. That was a lesson I needed to learn. The next ten thousand is now invested. I make good money and have hardly any expenses." He thought for a moment. "Here is what I want you to do. Get a broker. Open an account in Alyssa's name, with both you and me as account custodians. Don't tell her till she's twenty-five. Okay, here is the other thing. We are working a lot with computers now. Computers are going to be really big. So, put it all into Microsoft. Just let it roll. That's what I want you to do with the money."

Dana gave Casey a kiss on the cheek. "I knew there was a good reason I picked you."

26. NO ONE WOULD EVER BELIEVE

Two weeks after the funeral, Dana walked into Jody's kitchen with Alyssa in her arms and Handsome by her side. "High baby girl," Jody gave Alyssa a kiss and went back to cooking. "She's up in your secret map room. I'm cooking dinner for all of us, so you'll have to take her up with you. Christopher will be coming home in a little while, so hurry it up."

"You got it," Dana said, closing the door behind her and Handsome. Handsome walked the room then lay down near the door.

"Yep. It's a Microsoft 486. I'm still learning, but it's cool." Mason was sitting at her new desk up against the wall. The screen took up most of the desk space. "I've had one in my office since I got to the FBI. I really tried hard not to use it. You know, they have a computer class in the building just for us FBI types. It's a three-day class. I learned a lot, and I still have to call them with questions, but it's coming around."

Dana pulled up a chair, looking over Mason's shoulder at the screen. Alyssa began to fuss. Dana knew that particular type of fuss. It meant she was hungry, so she opened her blouse and her bra. Once Alyssa calmed down, Dana gave Mason and the computer her attention.

"We can do a lot with this, just wait and see. We'll be able to put the whole Carlos gang together and cross-reference their activities. You'll see." Mason turned back to her computer screen.

Handsome stood up and stepped back from the door as Jody pushed it open. She had a beer for Mason and a glass of milk for Dana. She gave Handsome a dog biscuit. "Wrap it up. Christopher is on his way home. Dinner will be in thirty minutes." She turned and walked out, closing the door behind her. Handsome resumed his position by the door, his biscuit between his paws.

Dana gave a surprised look and cocked head at Mason.

"What? We sleep together. Maybe I talk in my sleep." Mason looked away.

"Yeah, maybe," Dana said slowly.

"Don't worry. She doesn't want to be involved. Not unless it involves legal work. Then she doesn't want to know too much," Mason said.

"I guess she was going to figure out what we're doing here sooner or later. She's not stupid," moving Alyssa over to the other breast Dana said, looking down. "Is that one dry, sweetie?"

"Okay. Now tell me what happened. In detail this time." Mason had turned and put her hands on Dana's knees.

"What?" Dana said with a fake questioning look on her face.

"Start," Mason said forcefully.

"OK," Dana said with a sigh. "I staked out the Mexican restaurant for a few days and finally was able to follow the guy."

"I know that part. You cut off his head, and I shot his pal in the head. What next?" Mason said moving along Dana.

"Next I drove to Indy," Dana said.

"Right, hours before you gave birth," Mason said.

"I was trying to save Debbie," Dana said, in her own defense and more than a little upset.

"I know. I'm sorry. In fact, I gave you the address to go to. So, I had your back." Mason was sorry she had brought it up that way. She said, "Now, what happened in detail when you got to the house?"

Dana told her in detail what happened. She told her the order of killing the six men. How she picked up Debbie and then cut the gas line on the way out to cover her tracks. When she got to the part about sitting on the bus stop bench with a dying Debbie in her arms, Mason asked her to stop. It was way too emotional for both of them. Tears were now finding their way down Dana's cheeks. Mason had sat back without saying a word. Then after Dana regained her composure, she continued up to the time she got home.

"You killed six armed thugs in, what? A minute? And they were waiting for you! And you were about to have a baby." Mason continued to study Dana, who was nursing her baby.

Mason finally shook her head. "You look so innocent. You act like a little young girl. You look and act so vulnerable. No one would believe what you just told me. Even when I put two and two together back when, even then, I didn't believe it." Mason studied Dana some more. Then said, "And."

Dana was now rocking a sleepy, full Alyssa in her arms. "And what?" She asked, looking up from Alyssa.

"And you are the most perfect, talented stone-cold killer who ever lived."

*

The next day, the Sunday call was at Mason and Jody's house. Lars and Sally had made it back to Barcelona. Lars and Beau called from the Haneda airport in Tokyo, they had spent some extra time in Los Angeles getting new headshots and attended some Hollywood parties. Photos and cocktails are how actor's market themselves.

They didn't talk long; Christopher went back to his library. He fell asleep a book in his lap in just a few minutes. Jody was fussing in the kitchen.

"Dana, I have been thinking. We have got to make some decisions," Mason said.

"So, let's go up to the secret map room," Dana said, Alyssa in her arms and Handsome at her side.

"Here. Let me take her," Jody said, coming around the corner to the stairway. Mason had been stewing about something all day and Jody wanted Dana and Mason to have it out. Jody and Alyssa headed to the kitchen. Handsome made a U-turn and followed Alyssa.

"So, let me guess. From our conversation yesterday, I'm a talented, heartless killer," Dana said, closing the door behind her.

"That's not exactly what I said, but in a way, yes. You attack with extreme effectiveness. As they say in the FBI, you are deadly. Nothing gets in your way or your head. They killed yours, they die. It's that simple for you."

Without expression, Dana turned away from Mason and went to the window. "It's not that I'm heartless. It's that my heart has been broken."

"I understand." Mason came up next to Dana. "Another unusual thing about you. They don't see it coming. They only hear your sweet, comforting words—if you say anything at all. Then they die."

Not turning to Mason, Dana's said, "If I have time, I tell them they are going to die, and why." In a cold, even voice, she continued, "They are going to die. Ron and now Carlos."

"I believe that. I just don't want you to die in the process." Mason turned Dana toward her, putting both hands on Dana's shoulders. "You're a tool. The most precise killing tool ever made."

Dana took a step back, going back to the table. She sat down and just looked at Mason. "You believe that?"

Mason walked over to Dana, her hands out. "I'm not going to hold you back. I'm going to help you." She wanted so much to shake Dana or hug her. "We. You and I are going to kill everyone and anyone who had anything to do with your mother or Debbie's deaths." Mason sat in the chair across from Dana. "The night Debbie died. Remember, I helped you." Mason understood the killer was in the room.

"Yes, you did," Dana said, looking up at Mason.

"Everyone, Carlos and his gang, thinks the Red Bitch is dead. That buys us some time. That gives us an advantage. We have got to be smart with the time we have." Mason looked at Dana, but her expression did not change. "Look at it like I'm a planner. You're a killer. For the next year or two, we will connect the dots. I will use my FBI connections. We will use your insights. Together, we will find and kill Ron. We will close down Carlos' operation; that will cause him a lot of pain. Then, we will kill him—and anyone who gets in our way."

Dana sat quietly. For the first time, she felt someone understood her. She slowly began to nod and said, "Okay. For the next year or so, we plan."

"You're nursing. No killing for a while." Mason shook her head. "Oh, God, what am I saying?"

"What you're saying is you and I, together, are going to work out a plan to kill these fuckers, these assholes." She sat very still.

"Dana. You're the killer. I'm the organizer. I uncover things. You can then take them apart. Then I can cover them up again."

Mason reached out with her hands open on the table. Dana looked at her hands, then reached over and put them in Mason's. Mason understood that Dana was putting her trust in her hands. She could feel the young girl come back into the room.

"Somehow I have come to love you. I know I can't replace your mother. But, would it be okay if I think of you as the daughter I never had?" She waited for a response from Dana, who sat quietly, looking intently at Mason. "At least sometimes?" Mason begged looking down.

"No," Dana said, she lifted Mason's head up. Looking Mason in the eyes, Dana said, "All the time."

*

"Well, she did it," Mason announced, coming into the library. Jody was following behind. "Go ahead. Tell them what you did."

"I retired," Jody said with a big grin. "Of course, it doesn't take effect till July one. But I put the years in, and now I'm out." Coming over to Alyssa, she picked her up. "Hi, Bo-Bo. We're going to be spending a whole lot more time together." She gave her a kiss and cuddled her in her arms.

"Great! Congratulations," Dana said, closing her book and setting it aside.

"We're here to celebrate," Mason said, pulling two bottles of Champagne from behind her back, holding one bottle out "Bubbles and alcohol." Holding out the other bottle, "Bubbles only."

"Wonderful, Jody. I'll get the good Champagne glasses." Christopher opened the glass doors, displaying the fine crystal.

"Your timing is perfect. Alyssa should be on the bottle by then. I can't wait to get back to the galley and straighten out whatever mess Dad has made of the place," Dana teased her dad.

"Watch it, girl. We're doing just fine." Christopher came back holding out the glasses. It was a quiet celebration. Alyssa slept through it. Handsome laid under the crib, his eyes closed.

Dana was in the dojo within a month of having Alyssa and her hernia surgery. It took her another month to loosen up after the surgery.

"Are you ready for this?" Dana said one morning to Bobby and Tommy. She set her daisho swords on the floor near the wall. "Come on." She took her position on the mat, her hands out, waving them in. "You're not afraid of a little mama, are you?"

Bobby looked at Tommy, who nodded. "You asked for it. No holding back." The three bowed.

Handsome and Alyssa had to wait in the office. Its sliding window opened a little to hear Alyssa if she needed something, but she usually slept most of the time. Handsome sat with her. He could not be allowed into the fighting room. His urge to protect was too strong to remain in the sit position, even under command.

Handsome was wedded to Alyssa. If they were separated, he whimpered loudly.

*

Dana had reserved several books at the library. It was about a twenty-minute stroll from home. On a beautiful day, Dana preferred to walk with Alyssa in her stroller and Handsome at their sides. The problem at the library was the doors were up nine steep concrete steps.

Dana had left Alyssa asleep in her carriage at her base of the steps. Handsome sat down between Alyssa and the sidewalk and stairway traffic. It took less than three minutes for Dana to collect her books from the librarian. She stopped at the glass doors, looking down on Handsome and Alyssa. They looked so cute there together. Handsome watched as people passed by. If they came a step too close, he bared his teeth.

Dana was just about to go down the steps when one woman ventured closer. Looking in the carriage, she saw

Alyssa and said, "What's your mama doing leaving you out here alone? I need to call the cops. I'll have your mom arrested for child endangerment." She took another step closer, try to take control.

Handsome's eyes narrowed, he bared his teeth and lowered his head, emitting a low, dangerous growl. The lady stepped back a little in shock. Handsome did not back off.

Dana came down the steps, her book bag in hand. "What are you doing?"

"You shouldn't leave a baby alone on the streets. I'm calling the cops on you." she said with an air of righteousness.

"Lady, as you can see, she wasn't alone." Dana petted Handsome's head. "If you had taken a step closer, you would be bleeding. Then I would have to call the cops. I would tell them you tried to kidnap my kid and got bit by her nanny."

The woman threw her nose up in the air. "You just try it," she said as she walked away. Her kind always had to have the last word.

Dana looked in at Alyssa, she was chewing on her hand. Dana giggled all the way home.

Most nights, Dana and Mason connected the dots. They developed more files on suspects and crooked cops, politicians, and other officials. The computer began coming into play more and more often. Most everyone was connected to Carlos in some way or another. Ron's name only came up once, and when it did, it was about the raid the Red Bitch did on his drug house. No news there.

The day after Alyssa came off Dana's breast, Dana made her first real trip to the gallery for her afternoon shift. Dana parked out front and made four trips to her car.

"What the hell is this?" Christopher questioned, seeing Dana put down the first box by the office door. She just put up a finger, meaning wait, and left for another box. After she deposited her last box, Christopher spoke up. "It's a damn computer. What the hell are we going to do with a damn computer?"

"Join the modern age," Dana said, heading to her desk in the office. She began to quickly clear off her desk.

"In all the years I have run this place, we never needed a damn computer." Christopher was standing by as Dana unloaded the boxes and set up the computer, screen, and printer.

"You'll see it will help our business so much." The printer, screen, computer, keyboard took up most of her desktop. After she got everything plugged in, she started the computer. It blinked and made funny sounds and different flashes on the screen. Most were so fast, Dana and Christopher could not even think about reading them.

The screen went blank. Christopher was looking over her shoulder. "See, it's broke," he said, pointing to the blank screen. Then it flashed *Welcome*. He took a step back.

Dana spent the rest of the day installing programs and getting online.

Christopher talked with customers who had come into the Gallery. He sold a Larry Icart print to a couple. He had to write the sales receipt on the small table upfront. Dana was taking up all of the office space. She punctuated her efforts with an occasional *Damn* or *shit* under her voice.

The next day, she brought in a deluxe pizza with everything on it and a six-pack of Coke. She set the open box on the slide-out shelf at the far side of her desk. She took out a slice and began to eat it. Then she opened a Coke. Christopher came over to receive a slice. This was his favorite lunch, and dinner, for that matter.

"No, you don't." Dana pushed his hand away.

"What?" Christopher complained and reached in again, just to be pushed off, again.

"Do you want some? Then sit here." Dana said, spinning in her chair to face Christopher and getting up.

With a cross expression on his face, he sat down with his back to the computer. Taking a slice and opening a Coke, he smiled. The smile didn't last long.

Dana twisted the chair around to face the screen. "What's the hardest thing you have to do here?" she asked.

"Put up with you," he answered.

"Besides that. I'll tell you. Write thank you letters. I know because you always make me do it." Dana pointed to the mouse. "I'm not going to write your thank you letters for you anymore. Move that." Then she said, "Click here. Press down with your right finger." A new screen popped up. "That's the tutorial," Dana said, smiling. "Have all the Coke and pizza you want." She walked back into the gallery, leaving Christopher to study the screen.

*

The next afternoon, Dana brought in another pizza and six-pack of Coke. Christopher met her at the door, with a smile on his face. Holding up a letter, he said, "See. I did it, and in a lettering style called freestyle script, so it looks like I wrote it."

Dana took the letter from his hand and read it. "That's beautiful, and unlike your handwriting, I can read every word. That fabulous, Dad."

Before she could hug him, he held up an envelope. "See. I even did the envelope. I might say so myself: I'm brilliant."

"Yes, you are, Dad. I'm so proud of you," she said, hugging him.

It was amazing how fast kids grow up. It wasn't long until Alyssa began to crawl. Sitting in the library one evening, Christopher, Jody, Mason, and Dana could not stop giggling.

Alyssa would start crawling toward a door. Then Handsome would get between her and the door. She would run into him and try and crawl over him. Then she would take off for another door. Handsome beat her there and lay down again. Alyssa would run into him and try to crawl over, then head as fast as she could for the other door. This game went on for longer than anyone thought it could.

Finally, Alyssa was getting tired. She lay down in the middle of the floor, Handsome next to her. Alyssa nestled up against his fur with her head on his chest. Dana got up and gave her a bottle. She was soon asleep. Handsome put his head down and closed his eyes with a big sigh. They both were content.

With everyone settled in, Mason asked Jody, "Mind if Dana and I slip off to the secret room for a little while?"

Jody waved her on. Mason signaled Dana, and they headed off next door.

"So, what's up?" Dana asked, coming into the room.

Mason closed the door and sat down across the table from Dana. "Do you remember Jessica? My contact at the Miami station? Sure you do. Well, you know we are working together to put the case together against crooked politicians in Florida." She pointed to a set of photos on the wall. "The problem is, we haven't told anyone at the FBI. We're flying solo."

"Yeah. What has changed? Why do you keep telling me things I know?" Dana said, a little frustrated.

"Sorry, I'm just being clear. But there is a conference in Miami in two weeks. The department wants me to go. So, I got to go." Mason was building up to something.

"So?" Dana wasn't getting the point.

"Jessica wants to meet me." Mason waited for a reaction that didn't come. "Wants to meet me. Like in my hotel room."

"Oh," Dana said, getting the picture. "And you haven't told her about Jody. You've been stringing her along, haven't you?"

"I was trying to get Jessica's trust and cooperation," Mason said defensively.

"And it's flattering to have a girl who is, what? Fifteen, twenty years younger than you are interested. Right?" Dana pointed her finger at her.

"What do I do?" Mason let her air out.

"How should I know? You're the one with a hundred times more experience than me."

"But you have only been in monogamous relationships. Jody is my first real monogamous relationship. We have been together for about four years or so. That four years without cheating. I don't know if I can help myself around Jessica. She's so cute."

"So who's the mom now?" Dana asked with a snicker.

"Listen, kiddo. I've got, well, a lot of years on you. So, it's Mom asking her smart daughter what to do." Mason's shoulders stiffened up.

"Let me think about this for a minute." Dana took her time trying to look thoughtful. That was hard with her suppressed smile.

"Start by bringing Jody up in your conversations. Then add some more intimate details; this Jessica isn't all that young. She's been around. She probably isn't expecting anything. She's just playing around, having fun and trying to keep it secret. She's like you were fifteen or twenty years ago," Dana said.

Mason nodded a little smile of remembrance, then a more serious look.

"If you want to keep Jody? You do want to keep Jody?" Dana asked.

"For sure. One hundred percent," Mason answered.

"Then you invite Jody to go with you. Like right away. Then about a week before you go, you tell Jessica you're bringing your wife. Give her time to assess the situation and still be cooperative." Dana finished off.

"You know she's closer to your age than mine. Why don't you come with us?" Mason smiled. "You know. Kill two birds with one stone. Or trip, in this case."

"No, thanks. I'm not any good at those casual relationships." Dana said, then looking in Mason's eyes. "Honestly. I'm off the market till Alyssa starts dating."

"You said honestly. You did not say you promised," Mason said with a sparkle in her eyes.

Dana suppressed a smile. "You're right."

27. IT MIGHT BE A PLAN

The wheels came up, signaling they were really on their way to Miami. "Jody, sweetie, about that girl in Miami. Jessica is her name." She went on to explain her phone relationship with Jessica, figuring that on the airplane, Jody would not yell or scream at her. Also, she would have time to calm down, especially after numerous "I'm sorry; I should have told you sooner. But it's only business. Really only business." Jody had only known Jessica as the FBI girl in Miami. Not anything more than that.

The cab ride from Miami International Airport to the Fontainebleau Hotel and convention center seemed to take forever. By the time they got to the hotel, Mason was running behind. Jody didn't care; she was enjoying the trip. The one exception was their conversation on the airplane, in flight.

After they finally registered for the convention, they wandered out into the lobby with their ID badges hanging around their necks. They were looking around, trying to decide which direction to walk.

Mason noticed her first. She wasn't quite sure, but she fit the image she had of her. She was five-foot-five and slim. Her hair was dark and cut short. She wore a white shirt with a black tie, black slacks, and black polished men's shoes. Mason took Jody's arm and wandered over in her direction. Once she was close enough to read the name on her badge, she knew it was her. Her badge name said, Jess.

"Jessica?" Mason asked.

Jessica turned, and her eyes widened. "Mason!" She took Mason's hand and shook it vigorously. "God, it's great to meet you at last. And you must be Jody?" she said, releasing Mason's hand and grabbing Jody's, shaking it just as vigorously as she shook Mason's. "I have heard a lot about you in the last few weeks."

"Really," Jody said, looking over at Mason. She gave Mason a look that said, *We'll talk more about this later.*

"Really, Jessica, it's great to finally meet you too." Mason could feel Jody's cold jealous shoulder.

"I go by Jess. Everyone calls me Jess. Not much is going on anymore. Everyone's is just wandering around. The bar is probably full by now." Jess had a habit of talking fast and looking around a lot. "Let's go to a nice quiet restaurant and catch up." She had maneuvered herself between them both and took them by the arms. She walked them toward the front door. "I'll have them bring my car around." As they walked out the doors, she called out, "Hey, valet guy. Here is my ticket. Can you bring my car around? And make it snappy. Thanks," she said as she handed him a fiver.

At Sylveno's, they settled into a quiet corner booth. Sylveno's is a dark, elegant restaurant with soft background music supplied by a smooth jazz piano player. Jess continued chattering non-stop and only slowed down to order drinks.

"So, how long have you two been together?" Jess asked as their drinks were set in front of them.

"Four years this Friday," Jody spoke right up.

"What? How?" Mason was confused. "How did you decide it was four years this particular Friday?'

"That was the day I turned down a date from Jenifer. You might remember her, Mason: cute young thing, a little butch." Jody looked intently at Mason, "I decided then and there I was yours. How about you? When did you decide I was your one and only?" Jody was ignoring Jess. That way, Jess would get the full impact that they were a committed couple.

"Ah, about the same time, I guess. So, why don't we just always use this Friday as our anniversary?" Mason gave Jody a kiss on the cheek. It was not warmly received.

Jess had been silent throughout the entire discussion about Anniversaries.

Feeling boxed in, Mason said, desperate to change the topic, "Okay. What have you learned about the chief of police?"

Jess tipped her head toward Jody, meaning *What about her?*

"Oh, I don't keep anything from Jody." Jody gave Mason a look. "Not anymore," Mason added quickly. "She is a retired prosecutor for the state of Georgia. She not only knows where most of the bodies are buried, she buried a lot of them."

"Now that you brought up prosecutors, there seems to be more than a professional connection between Walter, the police chief, and the city prosecutor. No slight intended," Jess added, nodding to Jody.

"Who's this prosecutor?" Jody asked.

"Patrick McMann. Do you know him?"

"I don't know much about him. I never met him. We never ran in the same circles. But I do know that he went to Northwestern University in Chicago. I believe he was born in Warsaw, Indiana. His parents were killed in a car accident when he was about twenty. He got plenty of money from the insurance company. After he graduated, he moved down to Ft. Lauderdale. He went to work for a law firm there for a few years. He lost all his money. I don't know how. What surprised everyone is that he was hired as a head DA for the city of Miami out of nowhere. I guess that's about all I know." Jody sipped her Manhattan martini.

Jess's mouth was open. Mason put her hand on Jody's leg, meaning *you did well*. Jody smiled.

"Prosecutors talk, too." Jody smiled over the top of her glass.

"Let's talk," Jess said, leaning forward with great interest.

"Let's order first," Jody said, picking up her menu.

*

The conference ended on Thursday. Mason and Jody decided to extend their stay and celebrate their anniversary in Ft. Lauderdale.

On the way up to Ft. Lauderdale, they stopped at the Aventura Mall to do some shopping. They were no longer young hotties, but they still looked good in sexy swimming suits and big straw hats. They bought a swimming suit for each day of their planned three-day stay. They also dropped into Victoria's Secret and bought sexy nightgowns, again one for each night. They spent their time at The Sheraton On the Beach, relaxing and soaking up the afternoon sun. Late evening drinks were at The Baha Cabana Across the street. It was open-air, casual, and looked out over the bay and boat docks of the hotel next door. Sometimes they had live music. There were always interesting people to talk to. Never a word about the business.

Dana picked them up at the airport late Monday afternoon. By the time they got home, Christopher had snacks ready and dinner on the way. By nine, the only one who was not ready for bed was Alyssa.

Tuesday morning, Dana packed up Christopher's car and sent him on his way to Lanier Island Legacy Lodge, at Lake Lanier.

While Mason and Jody were gone, Dana had convinced Christopher to take at least a week off and relax. Dana had booked him for a week at the lodge. Dana really wanted some time to redo the gallery. She didn't want Christopher looking over her shoulder. Accepting changes was difficult for him. Also, she hoped he would find someone interesting at the lodge, anyone.

Christopher's lake stay lasted five days.

The next morning Christopher dressed for the Gallery, "No, you don't. You're not allowed anywhere near the gallery till Tuesday." Dana all but took his car keys away. "Cook or clean or do something."

Alyssa was happy in the gallery. Handsome helped entertain and corral her. Jody showed up every afternoon. They chatted, and Jody played with Alyssa and usually took her home, leaving Dana to her tasks. Dana had lots of plans to modernize and update the gallery.

Dana was consumed. She was up early mornings with Alyssa, then down to the dojo. After a quick shower, she was off to the gallery till eight at night. Then Dana played with her daughter for a little and then to bed for two to three hours of sleep at a time.

Mason was busy with the meeting notes, reviewing papers from the conference for information, and Jess's notes. Then the magic moment of insight finally came. "Aw so," Mason said aloud.

The next evening, she got Jody to help her mount a large chalkboard to the wall of the secret room. Then she started connecting the dots.

*

"Look at this," Christopher laughed. "Handsome and Alyssa have started a new game."

Handsome would lie down and Alyssa would craw up and grab two handfuls of fur. Handsome would slowly stand up, taking Alyssa to her feet. He would take a step, and Alyssa would take a step or two. Then she would sit down, laughing. Handsome would lie down beside her again, and the game would start over.

The smiles on everyone's faces were so broad, they began to hurt.

Christopher was playing with Alyssa in the library. Jody was cleaning up in the kitchen. Dana and Mason were sitting on the patio.

With everyone else busy that Dana asked, "What did you learn in Miami?

"Well, Jody and I have been an exclusive couple for four years as of last Friday," Mason said with a straight face. Then she got a small smile on her face. "Honestly, I don't know how long it has been. Could have been before, could have been after. But whenever we are still an exclusive couple. I intend on keeping it that way." She reached for Dana's hand. "Thank you. Everything is great now. Thank you for getting me to take Jody to Miami with me. If I had not taken her, well, I might have stumbled. And if I had stumbled, well, I would not be as happy as I am now."

Dana got up and checked in on Alyssa, who had curled up against Handsome. Jody had given her a bottle. Jody and Christopher were trading stories of Miami and Lake Lanier.

Dana headed to Mason's house. She gave Mason a shush finger to the lips.

"Oh," Mason said, getting the message and following her to the secret room.

"You have been busy," Dana said, looking at the chalkboard. "Now, again, what did you find out in Miami, besides it's your anniversary?"

"I did see Carlos's house. Didn't look like anyone was home. Still very well guarded. I've got Jess collecting info on the comings and goings."

"Jess? Who's Jess?" Dana asked.

"Jess is Jessica. The FBI girl in Miami."

"Oh her," Dana said with a smile on her face. "Did you take her to lunch?"

"She goes by Jess; she's very butch. Nothing like Jody. And no, we took her to dinner several times."

"Okay, happy to help," Dana said.

"What I have learned this past few weeks is that we have been thinking too small. Carlos only has his own little spiderweb. There are lots of spiderwebs. But they all answer to the same US supplier. It turns out that Tom the pilot was only a delivery boy, working for the supplier. He called him grandpa. Not true; he just says that to get some kind of advantage."

As Dana studied the chalkboard, she saw what Mason was talking about. Carlos had a big circle that took up all of Florida, and parts of Georgia and Alabama. There were three other circles, all touching Carlos' territory.

"Oh. Something interesting. About the time you were giving birth, the grandpa—we'll call him that for now—sent someone to pick up the Lear jet. He flew it to Miami. He only spent a few hours on the ground. Then he flew to San Diego." Mason leaned forward, pointing her finger at Dana. "Here is my theory. Grandpa was collecting the million dollars on the Red Bitch's head. They all think the Red Bitch is dead. That gives us an advantage."

Dana got up and looked at the board. "An advantage over what? We're no closer to Carlos. Ron is bound to pop up if he isn't dead, and I don't think he is." Turning to Mason. "And who is this Grandpa anyway?"

"His name is Joaquin Pablo. One of his kids is in prison; he'll be out soon. The other is in Mexico somewhere. He has a daughter. We don't know where she is."

"Interesting. So, the kids supply the drugs?" Dana asked.

"No. They just deliver it to the US. Their supplier is the other cartels." Mason let out a sigh of frustration. "This is almost too much to take on."

Dana looked at the board again. "We only want to get Carlos, and of course, Ron. No one else is a threat."

Mason said standing beside Dana, looking at the board. "You know these territories are always changing. They are always fighting each other for territory. We might be able to take advantage of that. You know: Get them to fight each other."

"How sure are you of this?"

"I'm not sure of anything. I think Carlos is the biggest and most powerful of all the drug lords. All these guys only deal in coke, heroin, and crack. This guy is a big-time grass dealer plus some crack and heroin," she said, pointing to the circle west of Carlos's territory. "Grass is not Carlos's big thing."

"How did Carlos get so big?" Dana asked.

"He takes over part of the other guy's territory. Killing off the competition literally. He does it a little at a time. If he takes too much, the other guys would get mad and gang up on him. Carlos keeps it in balance."

Dana's eyes got big. She pushed Mason's shoulder. "I got it."

"What?"

"We play them all against each other. We hit drug houses, distribution points. Let them know the Red Bitch is back but make them think she's working for Carlos. Maybe make Carlos think she's working for Grandpa. I don't know. Shake thing up." Dana looked at the board again. "We need more information, more planning on these three guys and, of course, Grandpa."

Mason looked around. "Looks like it's about time that the Red Bitch comes back to life."

28. WINDY TALKER

"Jess, honey. You said you're going to D.C. When?" Mason and Jess talked several times a week.

"Monday. Why?" Jess asked.

"Get a layover in Atlanta, at least two hours. I'll meet up with you at the airport. Please don't ask why. You'll find out."

"Should I plan on spending the night?" Jess giggled.

"Nice try, Jess. Let me know what time you're getting in. I'll meet you at the gate."

"Well, can I at least meet this Dana chick?" Jess tried again.

"Jess!" Mason said in frustration and hung up.

*

Mason got Jess off into a quiet corner at the airport. "Drug lords are not supposed to be my purview. Some in my department are starting to look over my shoulder, some of them, I don't trust," Mason whispered.

"It's not my area either. Unless it involves elected officials," Jess followed up.

"Duly noted. Now, here are some photos that were taken about three years ago. I can't identify the people in the photos. They were taken at a big to-do at Carlos's. We think they are drug lords. While you're in D.C., see what you can find out about them. I don't want this taken away from me, so don't let it be traceable back to Atlanta or, for that matter, South Florida. Please."

"Okay. But you owe me a date with this Dana chick."

"Oh, Jess." Mason shook her head. "I'll ask. No promises."

"Cool. I'll see you on Friday. I'll spend the night." Jess stuffed the photos in her briefcase.

Jess called Mason from the Dulles Airport. "I'm leaving here at four-fifteen. I should be landing in Atlanta about five-thirty."

"Good. I got you a room at the Holiday Inn in Princeton Lakes. It's just west of the airport. Take a cab and don't leave a trail or get followed, for that matter. You're already booked in under the name of Windy Talker. You don't have to show an I.D. It's paid for."

"Really? Windy Talker. Okay, just how should I take that?" Jess asked.

"Descriptive," Mason chuckled. "See you in the lobby."

Jess was checking in at the desk when she heard, "Is that you, Ms. Talker?" Jess turned to see Mason and Jody standing near the front desk.

"Why yes," she said, picking up her key. She stepped over to Mason. "Thanks, loads for the alias. I hope no one else finds out." She hugged Jody. "How do you put up with this smart mouth?" she said to Jody as she turned to hug Mason.

"Oh, I give more than I get," Jody said.

"Well, here you go." Jess handed Mason a heavy briefcase. "Believe me, it wasn't easy. A lot of it I got early in the morning. There are just a few people around at four a.m. It's fairly complete, I think."

"Great. Thank you. You didn't raise any suspicions, did you?" Mason asked, hefting the weight on the briefcase.

"Nah, just part of the job, ma'am." Jess gave her best detective voice. "So, where is this Dana chick?"

"Right behind you," Dana said in a low, sexy Marilyn Monroe voice.

Jess turned to the voice, and her jaw dropped. Before her stood a six-foot-seven-inch Dana. She was wearing white strappy six-inch heels; her legs led up to a short white lace minidress. The light through the door outlined her legs under the dress, making Her legs look even longer.

She wore a white silk long-sleeve fitted blouse. Her breasts had shrunk back to their normal firm size B cup, and she wasn't wearing a bra. Her blond hair and blue eyes were set off by her bright red lipstick.

"Meet the chick, Dana," Jody said. As she walked by Jess, she reached over and with her right two fingers closed Jess's jaw.

"Hi, Jess. I've heard a lot about you." Dana held out a hand with freshly painted bright red nails.

"Hi," was all that Jess could manage as she gently took her hand, not shaking it, her eyes glued on Dana's face.

"Why don't you take your things up to your room? Then we'll head out to dinner," Mason said.

"Ah, sure," Jess said, backing up to pick up her bag, not taking her eyes off Dana.

As soon as Jess left the lobby, Jody turned to Dana. "I think you did your job by just standing there."

"You think!" Dana said. "I'll drive her over to Marc's Restaurant. You guys get us a nice, quiet table. I want to take a quick look at these files." Dana pointed to the heavy briefcase. She had just a few minutes to quickly scan the contents of the briefcase. It looked formable. She concluded that Jess was on the up and up.

When Jess got back down to the lobby, she realized that it would be ridiculous to try and take Dana's arm, since Dana was more than a foot taller than herself. Jess held the driver's door for Dana, Dana swept into the car showing a bit of everything, "Thank you," Dana said.

'No thank you' Jess thought as she closed the driver's door, a big smile on her face.

During dinner, they chatted about work, Alyssa, and life at the gallery. During part of the conversation, to get Jess's attention, Dana put her hand on her thigh. That warmed Jess up considerably. After a long, enjoyable dinner, they all left the table laughing and smiling.

"I'll drop Jess off. See you guys tomorrow," Dana said, walking Jess to her car. Dana handed Mason the briefcase with a wink.

Dana, as usual, parked in the driveway and came around back to go into the house. She saw Mason sitting on the patio. She had a Bug Away candle burning and a half a bottle of wine and two glasses. Her glass was half full. Dana walked over and sat in her throne, next to Mason, without a word.

"You know, young lady, it's almost two a.m. on a work night," Mason said.

"Yes, Mom. I know. I can't say as I'm sorry," Dana said.

Mason reached over and poured her a glass of wine and topped her own glass off. "Should we have that mother-daughter talk?" she asked.

Dana laughed. "It's a little late for that, I think."

"Yeah, I thought so as well." Mason laughed.

*

The next evening Dana, Alyssa, and Handsome were over at Mason and Jody's. Jody took Alyssa out into the backyard to play. Handsome followed.

Dana and Mason could hardly wait to get upstairs. As soon as the door closed, Mason said, "I can't wait to get into these files." And they divided the stack into two piles.

In a few minutes, they both started talking at the same time. "Did you know?" and "Listen to this" came flying out of their mouths. After a few more minutes, Mason put up her hand. "Stop. We'll never get through this pile if we keep this up. Take notes. Then we'll talk."

A few hours later, Jody stuck her head in the room "Christopher is here. Dinner is in a half-hour." Neither Mason nor Dana looked up. "I said dinner in half an hour."

"Sorry," Mason said, looking up. "Could you just bring us up some sandwiches or something? We're kind of deep into this."

Jody looked to heaven for help. "Of course not. I cooked us dinner. For all of us. Dinner is served in half an hour. After dinner, you can bury yourselves up here till morning for all I care," she said and shut the door.

Around one in the morning, Mason finished, and she studied her notes. Dana finished up twenty minutes later.

"Wow, we have a lot of work to do," Dana said as she looked up.

"Okay, we'll work on this tomorrow after the boys' call. Go get some sleep, honey," Mason said.

Dana left a note on the floor in front of Christopher's door to please make brunch and take care of Alyssa. She was exhausted and in need of some sleep.

*

At eleven, Mason came up to Dana's room. "Good morning, sunshine," she called as she entered the room.

"I'm here." Dana came out of the bathroom with a towel wrapped around her. "Thank you, thank you, thank you. Oh, I needed that sleep. Let me dry my hair and get dressed. I'll be right down."

"Christopher's baking. Jody was at the stove; it all smells good. The boys call in an hour," Mason said over her shoulder as she left the room, shutting the door.

The call with the boys now included Alyssa. She had not seen her uncles and aunt since birth. But she knew their voices and names. This call was mostly about Alyssa's upcoming second birthday. Every other word was spelled out. After brunch, Jody took Alyssa and Handsome out to the backyard to play. Christopher sat in a chair on the patio, soaking up every one of Alyssa's giggles, laughter, and antics.

Dana and Mason retired to the secret room. "We have drug lords and hitmen, their families, possible political ties, addresses, phone numbers, and possible distribution channels. We have too much," Mason said after several hours of discussion of their notes.

"We're after Carlos and Ron. Anything that doesn't help us with that, we put aside." Dana started dividing her pile. "Oh, and this Grandpa character. He could be the key to something. I don't know. Let's find more out about him."

After a few more hours, they came up with a basic plan. It involved the three drug lords who bordered Carlos's territory. Carlos was stronger than anyone of them, but not all three together. Grandpa was going to be involved in here somewhere. Just where they didn't know.

"Hmm," Mason said as she drew some lines on the map. "This kind of makes more sense now." She was referring to the pins and lines she had accumulated on her map over the last two years.

"You know, I have really done some good prep work in the gallery. Maybe I should get serious and do some scouting around. I mean, for new artists. Right around here, to begin with." Dana was pointed to San Diego on the map, and the two orange pins, one was a private airport, the other was labeled 'Grandpa.'

29. A REAL DRAGON NOW

Dana flew into San Diego, California. The flight had left Atlanta early that morning and landed in San Diego just after nine that morning.

She first drove down to the Brown Field Municipal Airport and located the hangar that belonged to Tandem LLC. The Lear jet sat in a mostly unguarded hangar. She took pictures.

She then drove over to Grandpa's house in La Jolla. It stood on a cliff overlooking the ocean and had twelve-foot walls, palm trees, and steel gates. The house was almost completely hidden. She took pictures.

Dana's next stop wasn't till that afternoon, and that was in Laguna Beach. From a client, she had heard of an artist who did beautiful jumping bronze dolphins, so she made an appointment to see him. This was her first real road trip by herself. This new artist, Robert Wyland, perfectly fit into her plans.

"Okay, Robert. I'll take these four dolphins. Now, you promise to send me photos of all your new work. I can't wait to get these in my gallery." Dana thanked him, shaking his hand to seal the deal. He invited her to dinner with him and his girlfriend as thanks. Robert's girlfriend did make Dana smile. She was bright, funny, and dressed in 1960s hippie garb. The local restaurant overlooked the ocean and was only a few blocks from her hotel. The view was breathtaking. It was the first time that Dana had seen the Pacific Ocean. If the Atlantic Ocean was female, the Pacific

Ocean was defiantly male. It seemed to Dana to be bigger, bolder and a bit wild.

"You are the first gallery to carry my work," Robert said over dinner.

"You do beautiful work. I know lots of galleries are going to be after you. Just remember, I'm your first. I'll get you out to the right crowd. So, from now on, you need to give me first shot at your new work." Dana smiled, knowing he would keep his word.

She spent that night in her Laguna hotel. She could hear the waves crashing on the rocks below her balcony. Opening the sliding glass doors, Dana took in deep breaths of the fresh night air. She had not been away from Alyssa this long before, and she really missed her. When she landed in San Diego, she called her, and again when she checked into the hotel before dinner. She was only going to be gone four days and was due back Friday evening.

She had heard that Pismo Beach was beautiful. She had scheduled to see some galleries there. However, the three-hour time difference had taken a toll on Dana. The next morning, she left the hotel two hours later than she had planned. She had also misjudged LA's size and congested traffic. It took her much longer than she had planned, and it was late afternoon when she checked into her hotel on the beach.

The weather was a bit chilly, and it was overcast. Still, Dana dressed in her bikini and a long, warm sweater. She walked the beach, watching the small waves come in. Several sand crabs scurried back and forth with the waves. She stopped and took a deep breath, breathing in the clean, fresh sea air, cleansing her lungs and soul. She sat in the sand, her knees up to her chin, her sweater pulled over her knees. She cleared her head. The setting sun found a crack between the overcast clouds and the sea. It cast its red and yellow light on the underside of the clouds and on to the tops of the white waves. Her thoughts slowly turned to Debbie and their time in South Beach. The belief that she didn't do enough to keep her safe bit into her soul.

With the sun gone and the crush of loneliness entering her heart, she headed back to the hotel room, wiping the tears from her eyes.

Wednesday, she visited the galleries she had scheduled for Tuesday. She came away with names, styles, and prices. "Take advantage of your travel. Collect names and information. You never know when you'll discover a new but talented artist." Christopher had drilled into her before she left.

The next morning, she drove down highway 1. She took the cutoff to drive by the federal prison in Lompoc. Dana wanted to see where Grandpa's son was kept. She stopped in a diner just off the highway for breakfast. It was late morning, and she was the only one there. She sat at the bar and made conversation with the waitress. Dana wondered if it was always this slow.

"Hell no. On visiting day, this place is full. Lots of visitors for the cons," she answered. The conversation went on for an hour, mostly about her odd customers on visiting day.

On her way down the road toward the prison, Dana passed two prison trucks and one police car setting up a roadblock.

The prison itself was huge, with lots of fences, gates, towers, and buildings. It was very stark by design. There was a lot of activity around the front gate. She did not have an opportunity to take pictures.

About two miles further down the road, she was stopped in a line of cars. The prison guards and police had set up a roadblock. As a guard approached the car in front of her, she watched with idle interest as the guard questioned the girl in the car. He stepped back, and she got out of the car. She was tall, slim, and young, sixteen or seventeen, wearing tennis shoes, a tight miniskirt, and a brown t-shirt. *Cute,* Dana thought. She opened her trunk. The guard closed the trunk. Then he had her stand facing her car, her hands on the car and feet spread. He felt her arms, then lingered on her chest. "My god he's feeling her up," Dana said aloud. She honked her horn, getting the guard's attention and also that of the cop beside the road. Dana wagged her finger at the guard.

The cop quickly called the guard over. In just a few seconds, he was back, letting the girl get back in her car, getting in her car, the girl turned, smiled, and waved to Dana.

Dana was next. "Hi there. Do you want to feel me up too?" The guard backed off and waved her on.

It took her most of Thursday to get back to San Diego. Her flight was Friday morning.

Dana was comfortable leaving Alyssa in Christopher's care. Jody was over early to help with Alyssa and breakfast. Breakfast with Alyssa sometimes was an adventure of its own. The four of them, Christopher, Jody, Alyssa, and Handsome went to the gallery and opened it up at ten in the morning every day.

Jody was bored at home and enjoyed the gallery. She was even selling a few pieces. The extra commission money usually was spent on Alyssa.

Sunday afternoon, Dana and Mason were upstairs in their secret room when the phone rang. "Hi Mason, what's happening?" Jess was rushing her words as usual. "Guess what I found out yesterday? Come on, guess? You'll never guess it, so I'll just tell you."

"Jess, slow down. Let me put you on the speaker. Dana's here." Mason pressed the button for the new speaker in the center of the table and hung up the phone.

"Hi, my gals. Guess what? You'll never guess." Jess said.

"I've heard all that. So please, just get to the point," Mason said in her irritated voice.

"The kid in Lompoc prison. He's dead. Shot dead. Along with one of his bodyguards." Jess was excited that she had some real news.

"Really. Was there a riot or something? Did one of the guards shoot him?" Mason asked.

"When was it? It wasn't last Thursday, was it?" Dana asked quickly.

'It was last Thursday. How did you know?" Jess asked.

"I was driving by there. I wanted to see the place while I was out in California. They were checking cars." Dana was puzzled.

"Okay, but here's the bizarre part. He was shot with a World War One rifle, an Enfield 303. Strange, isn't that? Like someone came back in time from World War One and shot him."

"Really strange," Mason said, shrugging at Dana as if to say, *What does that mean?*

"I got it. Here is another strange part. I was talking with this waitress at the diner up the road," Dana started.

"Was she cute?" Jess asked.

"Jess! No. Come on." Dana stopped her. "What she told me was on visitors' day, lots of people stop in for breakfast before going to see their cons. She was telling me about this one Mexican girl, who comes every visitors' day. Never misses one. She sits in the same corner booth every time. She always has this black notebook, and she looks like she's memorizing a list of things. I mean every visitors' day."

Mason got the drift. "Notes for and from the drug boy."

"Yep. That's my guess. I think she's the sister. No way to know for sure she if she has anything to do with the drug boy," Dana said.

"If that's right—and it might be—their operation is going to be screwed up. Maybe? It's a long shot. Did you hear anything about Grandpa?" Mason asked.

"No, I didn't check. Give me a few minutes; I got a source in the office downstairs. I'll call right back." Jess hung up.

"If there's anything here, we're not ready to take advantage of this. Dana, you need to get your scouting done as soon as possible. Like, every other week or so," Mason said.

"We need to study this, figure out where, when and how?" Dana said as they began going over the maps and chalkboard.

It didn't take more than fifteen minutes for Jess to call back. "Yes, lots of activity at Grandpa's house. I'll see if I can get info on that woman from the prison's visitor's log. Got to run. Kisses," Jess said.

"Something's up?" Mason said, looking at Dana. "How long has it been since the Trans Am has been out of the garage?"

"Oh." Dana's head jerked back. "A couple of years. More. The last time I drove her was when Alyssa was born. Really, more than two years."

"If we're going to bring the Red Bitch back, we're going to need the Black Dragon," Mason pointed out.

*

A few weeks later, Dana drove the Trans Am down to Eddie's Speed Shop. Walking into the office, she saw a much slimmer guy sitting in the same old chair at the same old desk. It looked like the same old pile of paper on the desk. The only thing that had changed was the calendar. It was now a Playboy calendar.

Dana knocked on the doorframe. The chair spun around. "Dana!" Tommy said. He got up and came to Dana as if to hug her. At the last second, he backed off and put both hands on her shoulders. "How have you been? Long-time no see."

"I know. Not since high school. How have you been?" Dana reached over and gave him a hug.

"Good. Dad passed; you know." Tommy said.

"I'm sorry. I didn't know." Dana said.

"No. It's alright. It was about a year ago. He was working under a car and just died. He was doing what he wanted to do. You know It took us over an hour to figure out he had died. He died happy," Tommy said.

"You took over the shop?" Dana looked around.

"Yep. He had been training me for it most of my life. Enough about me. How about you?" Dana was leaning up against the door frame. Tommy was standing across from her.

"Same old thing. Working with my dad in the gallery, but he has made me more of a partner. I do the buying and books and stuff. Oh, I had a little girl. Alyssa." Dana took out a picture to show him.

"Oh, she's a doll. Looks like you." Tommy handed the picture back.

"Ah, my car. I haven't driven it in over two years. Can you look at it?" Dana followed Tommy out to the front of the garage.

"Still looks great. I loved working on this car. Dad directed me every step," he said, walking around it. "The last time, all you said was make it dark, fast, and breathe fire. What do you want now?"

Mason stopped in front of the shop and waved at Dana, who waved, then turned back to Tommy, "Make it darker, faster, and breathe more fire."

"Oh yeah," Tommy said, rubbing his hands together.

Dana hugged Tommy again. Backing her way to Mason's car, she said, "Let me know when you're done. No hurry. I'm at the same number."

Three weeks later, Tommy called Dana into the shop. She and Mason stood looking at a completely flat black car. No chrome or color anywhere.

"I lowered her. She is stiffer. See, you can sit on the hood and she doesn't move." Tommy demonstrated. "You can hit a corner at a hundred, and she'll just slide around it."

Opening the door, Tommy got in. "See this red switch?" He pointed to a switch on the dash. "Nitro. Do not flip it in first gear, and maybe even second. Then pull this lever. When you do, you'll go to twelve thousand RPM. It will cut off after thirty seconds. Otherwise, it would burn up the piston rings and probably the crank bearings."

"We don't want to do that. Do we?" Dana asked.

"No, we don't," Tommy said in a matter-of-fact way. "If you need to hit it again, which I doubt, you'll need to wait for about one minute. When you hit it, I'm talking close to two hundred miles an hour in less than thirty seconds. I really don't know how fast, but that's a good estimate."

Tommy was all smiles as he started up the engine. "Stand back," he said as he closed the door. "Stand back farther. More." He flipped the switch opening the header valves. The Trans Am rumbled, its hot breath coming out behind the front tires. He revved the engine, and it threw flames six feet out on both sides of the car. "I installed a little gas line at the tip of the pipes. So it really breathes—no. Throws fire. It's a real-life flame thrower."

Shutting down the engine, Tommy got out of the car. He signaled for them to follow him to the back. Bending down, he pointed to the tires. "Thirteen-inch wide tires, all inside the fenders. You're going to need that meat to keep this beast on the road." Straightening up, he said, "What do you think?"

"Oh, my God." Dana walked around the car; her fingers softly petting the paint. "You are an artist. A speed artist. Fantastic." She hugged him and gave him a kiss on the cheek. "Thank you."

30. HELLO MY LOVE

“Dana, stop! We got too much. My God, we have got paintings piled upon one another. The new cabinet you bought is full. Statues are everywhere. Just stop," Christopher complained as she walked through the door carrying lunch.

She stopped in mid-step and looked around. For the last five months, she had been on scouting trips, two sometimes three times a month. She didn't always line up an artist. But she did often enough to fill the gallery.

Paintings, prints, statues made of brass and glass were everywhere. The paintings were stacked two and three together, leaning against the wall. Unique jewelry and figurines filled the cabinet.

"You are so right, Dad," Dana said, setting lunch down on the table. She wandered around the gallery a bit. "Dad. You are so right. I have way overdone it."

"We have got to get rid of at least half this stuff," Christopher said, waving his arms around.

“You’re right, Dad. We have to sell a lot of this art.” They sat across from each other at the front table. “We are going to do what you taught me. But, with a twist.”

“A twist?” Christopher did not like twists.

"Jody, drag a chair over here, we're going to sell a lot of this stuff. We are going to need your help. Are you in?" Dana said.

“Sure. How are we going to do that?” Jody was part of the business, not an owner, but emotionally invested.

"First, I'm going to do what I do best. I'm going to get the artist to come in and meet and greet. People are more interested when they can meet the artist. They are more likely to buy." Dana got up and retrieved a calendar from the office and laid it on the table.

"Jody, I want you to take pictures. Categorize them by artist and style. Then make a catalog we can send out."

"I can do that. I got an idea: Alyssa and Handsome will help me. We will create cute pictures with Alyssa and Handsome in the photos. Not just the static shit I always see. Something new, something to catch their eye and make them smile." Jody was excited.

"Excellent idea. How did you come up with that?" Dana was puzzled and pleased at the same time.

"I don't know. I just guess with Alyssa and Handsome around all the time, it seemed natural, I guess." Jody smiled.

"Dad, get out your phone book. Just make calls. Just talk to your contacts. You're a natural bullshit artist. We'll feed you with photos, artist dates, anything you need. Just get your bullshit out there." Dana turned a page in the calendar and pointed to a date. "We'll start here for the first show. We'll do Friday, Saturday, and Sunday."

"We're closed on Sunday," Christopher objected.

"Not during an artist sale. We need people to come in. I know this is news to you, Dad. But most of Atlanta is open on Sundays nowadays." Dana patted his hand. "Only Sundays on artist weeks. I promise," Dana said to calm Christopher's feelings.

"I'll have Robert Wyland come in as our first artist. I'll get him to bring in some new statues." Dana was excited. "Well, any questions?"

Jody raised her hand.

"Jody, this isn't court. You don't have to raise your hand. What's your question?"

"Which ones are the Wylands?"

Dana let out a little laugh. "This is going to be fun."

*

Dana got the artists lined up for every other weekend. Christopher got the right people coming for the right styles of art. Jody had a ball taking photos with Alyssa, or Handsome, and sometimes both in the photos. The catalog soon became a trademark of the gallery. People were calling for appointments and photo albums. The boys had to adjust to every other Sunday calls. Everyone had to make some adjustments.

Dana kept scouting, and Mason kept track of each mission and every detail. On one of the odd Sundays off, Mason and Dana were sitting in the secret room.

"The Red Bitch is dead." Mason looked up from her notes.

"What? I'm dead? What have I been doing all this scouting stuff for if I'm dead?" Dana was frustrated.

"She's dead. Carlos and everyone believe that. So, the Red Bitch is going to come back as a ghost. A ghost out of Miami. She's the Red Bitch's ghost." Mason waved her arms twirling around in the room. "She'll appear in her fire-breathing Trans Am, sorry Black Dragon, to take the money and drugs, leaving destruction behind. Then she just disappears, but always leaving someone behind to tell the story."

"Oh." Dana thought for a moment. "I like that. But how am I going to appear and disappear?"

"I'll work on that. Give me a couple of weeks. It takes time to alter time and space." Mason smiled.

*

"Jess. Hi honey," Dana said into the phone one evening a week later.

"Hi, dear. I got to tell you it's getting kind of hard keeping all the bribery and shit under wraps. I need to bring the department in soon. I think they think I'm doing something sneaky. It's getting sticky."

"I know. We're almost there. I'll let Mason give you the details. In the meantime, I'm going to need Miami license plates that say DRAGON. They must be untraceable. Can you do that?" Dana asked.

"It will take a while." Jess hesitated. "Three or four days anyway."

*

"Sure, honey. Thanks."

Just as she was hanging up, Mason walked into the kitchen. "Get the Trans Am and follow me," she said, then she led Dana a mile down the road. Mason led the way through the combination lock gates of the public storage yard. She drove to the back of the yard. There under a canopy sat a truck with a vacation trailer attached.

"Ta-da," Mason said as she got out of her car.

"What? We're going on vacation?" Dana asked.

"In a way. Stand back. No, over here. To the back and side of the trailer."" She then took out some keys and opened the door of the truck. A few seconds later, the whole back of the trailer came down into a ramp.

"Pretty cool, right?" Mason said, walking back to Dana. "I got it from Johnny Thompson. He was going to use it to move his race cars around but decided it was too small for all the extras he needed."

"Neat," Dana said as Mason lead her up the ramp into the trailer. She turned on the lights and pushed a button on the wall. The ramp closed in fifteen seconds.

"See the little door." They both had to squat down to get through. "See, it's a real trailer. Table, stove, icebox. Cabinets. This wall makes it look like the inside of a real travel trailer. The beds are above the car." Turning toward, Dana, she said, "What do you think?"

"Cool." Dana looked around. "Really cool. So, this is how I appear and disappear."

"Yep. I drive you near and drop you off, then pick you up. No one will know where you came from or where you went. Okay. Drive the Trans Amin here." Mason pushed another button and the ramp dropped.

*

Two months later, the 'Meet and Greet the Artists' series was finally over. The sale had been an enormous success. They sold some art that had not even been produced yet, just described by the artist. The gallery was thinned down to a reasonable supply of art, and a steady stream of buyers was once again coming and going.

Tuesday was still always quiet. Even so, Christopher, Jody, Alyssa, and Handsome opened as usual at ten in the morning. At noon, Dana came in with lunch: a large everything pizza and a six-pack of Coke. She set it on the table in front of Christopher and took a large slice and a Coke. She gave her dad a kiss on the cheek and went to her desk.

Jody came over and got her piece of pizza and a Coke. She patted him on the back. Alyssa came over and crawled up in his lap. "Grandpa help," Alyssa said as she tried to get a piece of pizza. Christopher took a small slice and helped her eat her fill, which was three bites. She had red sauce all around her face. As he wiped it off, she turned her head away and shook it to make it as difficult as possible. Then Alyssa gave him a big hug with both arms and her head on his chest. "Thank you, Grandpa," she said as she crawled back down and went back to her pile of toys.

Handsome came over and put his head on his leg. Christopher petted his head two or three strokes. He felt tired and put his head down on his chest. Soon, he felt a familiar warm hand on his hand. He looked up to see Eve sitting next to him at the little table as she had done so many times.

"The gallery looks wonderful," she said, looking lovingly at Christopher.

"Oh, thank you. Mostly it's our daughter's work. Have I told you how much I love you?"

"Yes, you have every day. Have you felt how much I love you?"

"Yes, every day."

"Remember that Louis Icort print we first kissed in front of?" Eve asked.

"Yes, I do. It still hangs in the back here. I look at it every day. I've had many offers for it, but it's not for sale."

"Let's go see it." Eve rose up and took Christopher by both hands to help Christopher leave his tired old body behind and raise from his chair. A young Eve and youthful Christopher walked to the back of the Gallery. Handsome followed.

They stood looking at the print. Handsome sat, looking at them. Eve put her hands around Christopher's neck and gently pulled him close to her. Her lips were close enough for Christopher to feel her breath. He took her in his arms and kissed her.

Handsome sat and watched as they faded from sight. He walked back to Dana, passing by Christopher. He licked Dana's hand. Dana patted him on the head. "What is it, boy?" She leaned over. Handsome gave her a kiss on the face, then gave Alyssa the same thing. He laid down next to Alyssa.

"Dad." Dana, called. He did not move. "Dad, what's wrong?" Dana stepped over and put her hand on his arm, "Oh God," Dana dropped to her knees, looking in her dads quite face, he had a slight smile on his face. "Oh dad," she said stroking his arm, the tears running down her face.

"What's wrong mommy?" Alyssa said, getting up to come over to her mother.

Jody looked up from her work seeing Dana crying, "Dana, Christopher," Jody said, getting up quickly, picking up Alyssa before she reached her mother.

"He's gone." Was all Dana could say the tears taking over her ability to speak. Taking Alyssa from Jody and hugging her tight, rocking back and forth.

Jody, check for a pulse, knowing she would find none. Shaking her head, she didn't know what to do next.

"Grandpa," Alyssa said with her arms reaching for her Grandpa. "Grandpa," she called again confused that he didn't reach for her as he always did, "Grandpa," she said again and struggled to get down.

Dana held her tight and fought to find her voice. Taking Alyssa into the office leaving Jody with Christopher. Dana found her voice but could not stop the tears. "Alyssa honey," Dana said, sitting Alyssa in the desk in front of her. "You know we talked about my mommy, your Grandma. How she went to heaven before you were born, remember?"

Alyssa nodded her head.

"Well, Grandpa has gone to be with Grandma in heaven." Dana held both of Alyssa's hands.

"But Grandma's dead," Alyssa said, not understanding.

"Yes, she is dead. And now Grandpa is with her." Dana's tears, now joined Alyssa's tears.

"No, I want my Grandpa." She shouted, and pushing her mother away, trying to get down.

Alyssa stood behind her mom, holding tight to her skirt. They were standing on the porch as Jody drove Christopher's Cadillac up the driveway. She peeked around her legs as four strangers got out of the car.

"Is that my Alyssa I see hiding behind her mom?" Sally asked. Alyssa's eyes got big as she recognized the voice. She came running out to Sally to be scooped up in both of her arms. Sally squeezed her and gave her a kiss. "Hi, baby."

Alyssa turned in Sally's arms and put her arm out. "Uncle Lars," she said.

"How's my sweetie?" Alyssa received another kiss on the cheek.

"Uncle Beau."

Behind him, Axel pushed Beau aside. "My beautiful Alyssa." He received an "Uncle Axel."

Alyssa was so excited; she didn't know which way to turn. She struggled to get down. She ran in circles, trying to see everyone, stopping putting her arms around Handsome's neck. "This is my friend. His name is Handsome."

Jody had gotten out of the driver's seat and was leaning up against the front fender of the car, smiling. Mason was standing in Dana's front door. She winked at Jody; they both smiled.

The four of them came up to Dana and put their arms around each other. "It's okay. It was his time. He went peacefully," Dana said as they hugged each other.

"Okay guys let's get organized," Dana finally said, pulling back from the group hug. "Sally and Lars, get your bags into your room." She pointed at Jody and Mason's house. "Axel and Beau, it's just like the old times. You two get to share the downstairs bedroom. No fighting, or no dessert."

"Dinner's in an hour," Mason announced.

Dana took Alyssa by the hand to guide her into the house but turned and said to the boys, who were getting their bags out of the trunk, "Oh, guys. Just in case you need a beat down, I put out the mat."

"Oh shit," Beau said, lifting his bag out of the trunk. "You think we're going to beat down a mommy?"

"No. But you can try," Dana said as she and Alyssa with Handsome following went into the house.

Everyone sat at their places at the dining table. Christopher's place at the head of the table was set. Dana stood and announced, "Now you all have to behave, by that I mean to kid, argue, laugh, and have fun. Behave just as if Dad was sitting here in his chair. Because he probably is, and he would like that."

Two days, later the funeral was held at St. John's Church, the same church where Eve and Christopher had gotten married.

Christopher was lying in front of the altar. Huge bunches of flowers were at either end of the coffin. The Louis Icart print of a beautiful woman with rough collies on a windy day, with clouds and a blue sky hung behind the coffin.

The four children stood at the door, welcoming each person coming through the door. Every person from celebrities to wealthy executive, waitress, and janitor all received hugs, handshakes, and a few kind words. The church was full. It took nearly an hour to welcome everyone. As they settled into the pews, they found at either end a bucket with a bottle of Champagne and glasses.

When the doors were closed, the four children went to the front of the church. The stood in front of their dad. Alyssa sat in a small chair in front of them all, facing the pews. Jody and Mason sat close to her in the front row. Beau, Axel, Lars, and Dana all held hands.

"Welcome all. We are here to celebrate Dad's life," Beau started.

"I don't think Dad worked a day in his life. He surrounded himself with what he loved. Beautiful art of all kinds," Axel continued.

"He had his dark times, as most of you know. But little Alyssa here grabbed his heart and pulled him back to the bright side," Lars said.

"So, we're going to celebrate Dad's life the way he would want it celebrated. We're each going to tell a short story about Dad. Then you all are invited to step up to the mike and tell your own story about Dad. Warning: one story only, and keep it short," Dana said.

"But first," Beau said as he turned and took a bottle of Champagne out of the coffin. "Thanks, Dad," he said.

"Everyone take a glass. Those of you who know how to pop a Champagne cork, get a bottle. When Beau pops his cork, you pop yours," Dana said.

"On three," Lars announced. "One, two, two and a half," he said as Beau struggled with the cork. "Two and three quarters. Three!" As Beau's cork flew, all the others went off, filling the church with flying corks.

They waited for all the glasses to be filled. The four of them turned to the coffin and held their glasses high. "God bless Christopher," they said in unison. The church rang out with those words repeated by the assembled crowd. It was heard through the doors out to and across the street. Passersby repeated. "God bless Christopher." However, some said Christ instead.

Starting with Beau, each told their story to laughter and applause. When it came to Alyssa, she stood up, and Dana held her mike for her. "Grandpa told me lots of funny stories about the pictures and the art, art"—she stumbled with the word *artist*—"The people who painted them." She substituted for the word artist. "But Mommy said I can't tell them here." Dana started to take the mike away to laughter and clapping. Alyssa reached up and took the mike back. "But Grandpa gave me lots of pizza." More laughter.

"Okay, the mike is yours," Lars said, as he took the mike stand down to the front of the church. A line formed. For two hours, stories were told to laughter, applause, and some tears.

When the last cork flew, and the last story was told, Dana took the Louis Icart down and brought it up front to the mike. "Both Mom and Dad told us, more than once, that this the print, aptly named *Joy of Life* is where they had their first kiss."

Beau stepped forward. "Mom always said she had to start the first kiss."

Axel replaced him. "Dad always said he planted the first kiss."

Lars took over. "It takes two to kiss. So, it was them both."

"Anyway," Dana continued, taking back the mike, "we didn't know until today, when we were bringing the print over here, that Dad had written a poem on the back of the print. He didn't date it, so we have no idea when he wrote it." Beau held the print so Dana could read the back. "I'm sure he wanted it to be read here today. He entitled it 'Epilogue,' and here it is."

As my spool of thread unwinds
And shadows cross the day's sunshine
I slip beneath the worldly wake
To a breath, my last to take

I journeyed through somber lands
Of goblin kings and roving bands

And flee before the hunting hordes
Pursuing with blackened swords

Summer stretches into winter
Against the clock, no man's the winner
And thus, I drift through wasted space
In search of beauty's face

I have visited her, here in my sleep
And felt her ringlets upon my cheek
Her face is that of every woman
Her skin is soft, her body silken

We blushed and grabbed, laughed and loved
Dressed only in the rays of the moon above
And danced the dance that lovers do
Upon the lawn, wet with our love's dew

I have found this corner of my heart
And from this place, I can't depart
My journey's through, my test is done
And your love is the heaven to which I've come.

31. ROAD TRIP

"Help!" Dana heard when she picked up the phone. "Mason is stomping around the room, cursing. I need you to take over. Please," Jody begged from next door.

"What's the problem?" Dana asked.

"Okay, okay," Jody said over her shoulder to Mason. To Dana, she said, "Let's switch places. I'll take Alyssa, and you take Mason."

"What is it?" Dana asked as they passed each other in the backyard.

"What made me happy makes her mad." Jody threw her hands up. "Good luck."

Sure enough, Mason was stomping around the house. She couldn't settle down. "Those rotten bastards," she yelled to the ceiling with clenched fists. Seeing Dana, she said, "Do you know what those rotten bastards did to me?"

Dana folded her arms across her chest, leaned against the door frame, and shook her head.

"Forced goddamn retirement. That's what. Those assholes."

"What did you do? Did you make them mad?" Dana held her ground as Mason turned on her.

"Age, that's what."

"Age. I didn't know you were that old?" Dana had a slight smile on her face. That only made Mason madder.

"I'm not old. I'm only sixty-two. Shit. I'm classified as a field agent. Got to retire at sixty-two, they said. Goddamn it. That's two weeks away. Shit. They said they just found out I'm turning sixty god-damn two."

"Happy birthday," Dana smirked.

"Shut the hell up," Mason said slowly and loudly.

Jody heard the yelling next door. "Glad I'm not there," she said aloud, covering Alyssa's ears.

"But you wanted to be a field agent. Right?"

"Yes, sure I do. But I'm anything but a field agent. They keep me locked up in my office all the time. So why the hell retire me?" She turned her hands into fists and lifted them in the air.

"Maybe they retired you so you could be a field agent. Ever think of that?" Dana sat down on the sofa and crossed her legs. "You know, partners with the Red Bitch's ghost."

Mason stopped dead in her tracks. She turned to look at Dana and tilted her head.

"We're ready? Are you ready? I'm ready." Mason stood still.

"We're ready," Dana said.

An hour later, Mason called Jody. "Dinner's ready. Bring Alyssa. We're setting the table now," She said calmly.

"Okay," Jody said slowly. "You okay?"

"Sure. Why not?" Mason said, hanging up the phone. "I was a wild woman. Wasn't I?"

"Yep." Was Dana's one-word answer as she placed the dishes on the table.

"Jody, thank you so much for helping at the gallery. And, of course with Alyssa. Especially for the last few weeks," Dana said over dinner.

"Oh, no problem. I love it. You and your dad trained me pretty well."

Putting her fork down, Dana thought for a second. "I need to do something to make sure you'll always love it at the gallery."

"Oh, I don't know what else I would do with my time. Certainly not sit and knit doilies with this old lady." She ducked her head.

"You'd better duck," Mason said, raising her hand, then smiling.

"Well. I'm going to give you ten percent. No. Twenty percent of the gallery. Is that okay?" Dana asked, watching Jody wipe Alyssa's dirty face.

"You don't have to," Jody said, turning her attention to Dana.

"I want to. Enough said." Dana had the last word on the subject. When Jody tried to say something, Dana held up her hand. When she attempted to thank her, Dana held up her hand again.

"And now that I'm retiring from the FBI, I can help too," Mason said. "Mostly with Alyssa. I don't know anything about the gallery. I guess I can learn. Maybe this retirement thing won't be so bad," she said, winking at Dana.

With that, the family unit was sealed.

*

Sunday morning, they called Jess and gave her the news.

"So, what now?" Jess asked.

"So we start burning Carlos's web. We're starting the plan," Dana announced.

"Finally. I can't wait to get these assholes. When do we start?"

"We're starting the first Monday of next month. When can you start?" Dana asked.

"Next Thursday. The big guys will be in town for updates. I don't trust these locals. If I lay out everything we have collected and get it in front of the big guys, I can make it run. Guaranteed." Jess's mouth never slowed down.

Thursday morning, Jess, with an arm full of files, waved off the secretary and opened the door to the big conference room. The three top guys from Miami and the big guys, one from Virginia and the top boss from DC, were sitting at the conference table. She froze at the side of the table. She could not speak.

"What is it?" Chuck, her boss, asked.

"Ah. As you know. I am the only agent assigned to the elected officials investigation unit," she said slowly, hesitating between each sentence. "Well," she said, taking a deep breath. Then the words flowed swiftly. "Here are the files on the Miami chief of police. He's taking bribes from all directions. These three files are on judges. They are either being bought off or blackmailed. This file is on the head district attorney for Miami. These are for two city councilmen." She said dropping each set of files on the table as she called out their position, then the rest of them all at once. "These are for a dirty mayor in Tampa and a bunch of dirty cops. I know cops are not my purview, but they were just there."

Jess had not taken a breath. The room was in shocked silence.

"You don't come in here and just drop files on our desk without approval. You don't even have them corroborated." The station boss, Frank, spoke up. His face was red.

The big boss from DC reached over and opened the chief of police's file. Frank started to speak again but Mr. Thomas, the big boss, raised his hand to silence him. He then spent several minutes flipping through the file. "And you did this all by yourself?"

"Yes, sir," Jess answered in her best military style.

"This is good," He said, laying the open file in front of him. "Let's take a look at the judges."

They spent the next five hours going over the files. Lunch was brought in. The door remained shut.

"Okay, Frank," Mr. Thomas said, "let's form a task force. We will bring in some help from DC and Virginia. I will use these files to get court orders. Federal court orders, not a state court order. Jess, you're going to run the Florida operation. What's your clearance level? Never mind. Frank will make it what it needs to be. This does not get out. Need to know only. Jess, I want you to pick your team carefully. You assign two or three, more if needed, to each target. Keep the teams apart as much as possible. We are not going to piecemeal this. We take them down all at once. Coordinate it so we can arrest them all in one morning." Mr. Thomas spoke almost as fast as Jess. "Frank, move Jess up here as soon as possible and give her as much help as you can. Jess, you report to me. Well, let's get going," he said shoving the files to Jess. Jess gathered up the files and gave Frank, a 'got ya' look.

*

"I know it's Dad's room," Dana said to Jody. "I have bought new sheets, blankets, pillows. Everything is new including the mattress. I hope you like firm." Dana was trying to convince Jody to stay in Christopher's room when she and Mason were in the field.

"I know. But still." Jody was apprehensive. "Why don't you move in here?"

"Maybe someday. I'm just. You know. I've lived in my room all my life. So?" Dana held out her arms. "Please. Alyssa needs to sleep in her own bed."

"I guess," Jody said slowly. "It will make it easier for us to get to the gallery in the morning."

The next Monday morning after breakfast, Mason left to pick up the truck, trailer, and the Black Dragon. She was back in a half hour. She drove up and tapped the horn.

"You be a good girl for Aunt Jody." Dana hugged Alyssa and gave her a kiss. "Handsome, watch over them." She hugged him and kissed him on the head. Dana ran to the truck and jumped into the front seat. Mason blew a kiss to Jody.

"Are you sure you're ready?" Mason asked for the hundredth time.

"Yes, Mom. Drive." Dana pointed out the front window.

*

On the way to their first stop near Richmond, Virginia, Dana again studied the photos, maps, and notes for all three scheduled stops.

That afternoon, Mason stopped at a rest stop on Interstate 95 just south of Richmond. In the trailer, Mason nervously went over the layouts and the plans yet again with Dana.

"Mom, I got it. I don't need to go over it again. Please give it a rest," Dana said, leaning back in her seat at the table.

"Just." Mason started up again.

Dana took a deep breath. "I know you're worried. But I got it. Get some rest please. Just take a deep breath and relax please."

It took every ounce of self-control for Mason to just shut up. She didn't relax; she just closed her eyes. At one-thirty in the morning, Mason fired up the truck and headed for Richmond. Mason said, "Be careful, honey. I know, I know, you got this." she said as Dana jumped out of the truck and got in the trailer. Mason stopped in the back of a supermarket. Dana hit the button dropping the ramp. The Black Dragon roared to life and moved powerfully down the ramp. Once on solid ground, its eyes opened, and fire matched her roar.

The first target was a taco stand. At night, they cooked meth in the back. The back door would be locked and guarded. The front of the building had glass windows and a glass door wasn't guarded.

The Black Dragon slid down the sidewalk and stopped in front of the taco stand. Getting out, the Red Bitch threw a four-foot sharped steel rod at the front door. She followed it in with her long sword in hand. She quickly made it to the door leading to the kitchen. The kitchen door swung open by a tall bearded guy with an automatic in his hand. The sword cut off his gun hand at the wrist, then pierced his heart. He looked at his missing hand, then Dana, and fell backward into the kitchen. As she entered the kitchen, she saw two women at the stove, cooking meth. A man was rushing toward her, fumbling, trying to get his gun out of his shoulder holster. Her left palm came up, smashing his nose bone into his brain. It was a large nose, an obvious target.

The two women standing at the stove squatted down, making themselves as small as possible.

"Where's the money?" the Red Bitch asked.

"I don't know," one woman said. Her head fell to the floor but her body fell sideways. The second woman pointed to the freezer.

"Please get it and don't forget your stash," the Red Bitch ordered in a soft voice.

The girl opened the freezer and took out a stack of money. She held it out to the Red Bitch.

"Please put it in a to-go bag," she said in a soft, kind voice as if she was ordering tacos to go. "And please put the meth in another bag. Thank you." She reached over and cut the gas line to the stove. "You should leave now. It would be best to take the back door."

In the Black Dragon, she revved the engine, blowing flames into the taco stand. A mile later, she quietly rumbled behind a closed gas station. The ramp came down. The Black Dragon rolled in and the ramp came up as the truck drove off. Mason headed back to the highway. Police cars raced past them on their way to the burning taco stand.

Dana cleaned herself up, washing off the blood and make-up, changing out of her Red Bitch dress and heels. By the time they stopped at a truck stop outside of Charlottesville, a much more normal Dana was ready to join Mason. The sun had just come up, but Dana knew that Alyssa and Jody would be up and into their day.

"Hi sweetie," Dana said as Alyssa beat Jody to the phone.

"Hi, Mommy. Guess what? Aunt Jody's making pancakes for breakfast."

Dana and Mason passed the phone back and forth. Then they sat down for breakfast. "How did it go? Tell me the details," Mason said over her eggs.

"Not much to say. I was only there for two or three minutes. They didn't put up much of a fight," Dana casually said.

"More? How many were there? What did they do? Did you kill anyone?" Mason pushed Dana.

Dana yawned. "Four. You said to let one live. I did that. Can we go to bed now? I'm tired."

"Oh, God. You're going to give me all the details." Mason's adrenaline was still flowing.

"Later. I'm dead tired," Dana said, pushing her plate away.

*

They slept all day in the trailer. Over dinner, Dana gave her a two-minute rundown as to what happened in the taco stand. Then they drove to a Walmart parking lot and parked in the back. Mason pulled out her file and laid the drawings and notes on the table. Dana glanced over them. "Looks like nothing's changed. Now let me get ready." Dana got up but Mason continued to study the files. "It looks like it's been abandoned for years."

"Nothing new there. We're leaving here at midnight, right?" Dana said, turning her back to Mason, who gathered up the notes and drawings, putting them back in the file.

"Be careful, honey," she said, taking the files to the cab of the truck with her.

*

The next stop was an abandoned warehouse just outside of town on a side road off Interstate 64. It was back about a half mile. After dropping the Black Dragon off, Mason moved the truck and trailer near an off-ramp to Interstate 64. "Damn, I'm never going to get used to this," she said as she sat nervously, looking out the windows and into the mirrors for any movement. Her thumbs involuntarily tapped the steering wheel.

The Black Dragon sped its way down the country road. She broke through the warehouse doors. Flipping the switch, she gunned it down one side of the warehouse, setting walls, boxes, wooden flats, and trash on fire. She stopped near the back-office doors. Revving the engine, she set them on fire.

The first guy was waiting for her. Her sword pushed the barrel of his shotgun to one side as it went off. She death chopped his throat, then brought her sword down and across his neck.

A second guy picked up an ax and was running toward her, yelling. She planted a heel in his heart. That shocked look again. The thought went through her head.

Two other guys were cutting coke. They put up their hands.

"Money, honey," the Red Bitch cooed. They pointed to a shelf on the other side of the room. "Please scoop that stuff up and put it that plastic bag. Use your hands. Thank you." She backed to the shelf. The money was in a duffel bag. "Thank you," she said as she opened the duffel bag. One of the guys took the opportunity to go for the gun in his belt. Before it cleared the table, her sword, thrown just six feet, went through his throat.

Quickly pulling the sword out of his neck, she pointed to the plastic bag. "Is that mine?" she asked politely of the last guy.

A squeaky "Yes" made it over his lips.

"Thank you so much," she said as she backed out of the office. The left side of the warehouse was burning nicely. She drove down the right side, setting it in flames. Then she was gone into the night.

Mason met her alongside the road just off the interstate near the overpass. An hour later, Mason pulled over and Dana closed the trailer and climbed into the truck.

Dana decided to just answer the questions she knew were coming up. "Four men this time. I let one live. Two minutes at the most. Oh, one tried to kill me with an ax. That's new." Then they were quiet for hours.

*

They parked at another truck stop well outside of Winston-Salem. They followed the same routine of calling home, having breakfast, then sleeping in the trailer.

At the next drop-off point, Mason said again, "Be careful, honey." Driving to the pick-up point, she said to herself, "This is not getting any easier." She felt her stomach turn inside out again.

The target was an office building in downtown Winston-Salem. The Black Dragon parked near the front doors. They were locked. A pry bar quickly popped the lock. She took the elevator one floor down to the basement. Getting out of the elevator, she saw a fat man with a shotgun up against the wall. He was sitting in a chair leaning back on two legs. The doors he was guarding said *Shipping and Receiving*.

She rushed toward him. Before he realized what was happening, blood gushed from his throat. The Red Bitch pushed through the swinging doors. Three men were cutting heroin and mixing it with flour. They intended to package it and ship it out the next day.

The guy standing closest to her grabbed his gun off the table and fired a shot at her, just missing her head by an inch. She split his head in half.

The other two men froze in their tracks. The Red Bitch, using her sword, swept the guns on the table onto the floor. "I'm sorry. You won't be needing them. Will you?" she asked with concern. They shook their heads.

"Good boys. Now, where is Carlos's money?" she asked politely. They pointed to a pile of envelopes; each was open. Each had money and return address shipping labels ready to go.

"Could you please put the money in that mailbag? Thank you." They hastily scooped up the envelopes and put them in the mailbag. "Oh. Could you please put those unopen kilos in the mailbag also? I'm sorry to be such a bother." One of them handed the mailbag to her.

"Are there drawings in that mailing tube over there?" She pointed with her sword.

"Yes," one of the men said.

"Please take them out." The other guy took them out and started to hand them to her.

"No, thank you. Just light one end on fire with that lighter there. I know I can be demanding. Sorry." She was backing to the swinging doors. "Now, one more thing before I go. Hold it up to that fire sprinkler. Thanks." The water started spraying all around the room, washing what was left of the heroin and flour onto the floor.

She took the stairway, mindful of the warning in the elevator, *In case of fire use stairs*. Back in the Black Dragon she pulled onto the street. She had only gone a block when she passed a police car, it alarms blaring lights flashing, as it sped to the office building to answer the alarm on the front door. Another block away, she passed a fire truck answering the fire alarm.

Two blocks later, she drove into the trailer behind a closed fast food store. Mason drove off toward Interstate 40. Just after they got onto Interstate 77, Mason pulled over and Dana jumped into the cab. "Four men; I let two live. I dropped Carlos's name this time. I should have done that earlier."

Mason's eyes opened wide. "Good idea. I should have thought of that earlier."

They drove silently to Lake Norman Park Campgrounds outside of Charlotte. It was four in the morning when they shut off the lights to the truck near a parking space next to the lake.

"Okay, time to dump the dope," Mason said, taking out the bags from one cabinet.

"The coast is clear," Dana called back, having checked the surroundings. They quickly emptied the bags into the lake. They would burn them in a few hours, in the fire pit next to the trailer. Maybe heating up some coffee for themselves at the same time.

Soon they were lying next to each other in the trailer. Dana looked over at Mason. "You okay with everything?"

"Oh." Mason let out a long sigh. "I didn't think it would be so quick." She turned to Dana, who faced the ceiling. "I mean, you're in and out in two, three minutes tops, leaving dead guys all around, not to mention the total destruction. It's scary what you can do."

"Things happen fast," Dana said to the ceiling.

“What do you feel? If you don’t mind me asking?” Mason said, rolling onto her side and facing Dana.

"Nothing. Nothing at all," Dana said to the ceiling.

“Nothing?” Mason asked.

"Nothing," Dana said, turning to Mason. "Do you know what those men felt when they killed my mother or tortured Debbie to death? Do you know what they felt?"

"I don't know," Mason said seriously.

"It gave them a thrill. They loved it. They couldn’t wait to do it again. Killing and torture is a powerful drug for them. It’s a thrilling drug for them to snuff someone’s life out.”

Mason slowly nodded in understanding.

"Given the chance, they would happily kill you and me. What would make it better for them is if they could beat us, shoot us, or cut us. Stretch it out as long as they can before killing us." Dana looked back up at the ceiling. "I'm not like them. I kill quickly. I feel nothing.”

32. BAD CHECK

"Hi, baby," Mason said, coming through the front door of the gallery, the next afternoon.

"Hi, honey," Jody said.

Alyssa ran up to Mason, "And to you, Jody," Mason said as she scooped Alyssa up in her arms.

"Hi honey," Alyssa said to Mason.

"Where did you learn that?" Mason asked.

"From Aunt Jody." She hugged Mason with both arms around her neck, then kissed her.

A few minutes later, Dana came through the door. Alyssa reached out for her. Mason handed her over, almost tripping over Handsome, who ran over to greet Dana.

"Hi honey," Alyssa said to Dana.

Dana gave Mason a questioning look.

"Jody taught her."

"No, I didn't. She has just started mimicking me." Jody hugged and kissed Mason.

"How's business, partner?" Dana asked.

"Nothing till noon today. Then I sold the Tyka oil," Jody said with pride.

"How much?" Dana asked.

"Full price. Forty-nine fifty. He said he would pick it up next week and gave me his payroll check for six thousand two hundred and ten dollars He's from Cincinnati and asked if I could give him the difference in cash since he's from out of town."

"Oh, honey, that's a scam. Get that check to the bank. Tell the bank you think it's counterfeit. Have them check it out. Let's have a look at it," Mason said. Jody retrieved the check. "Well, I can't tell. Take it to the bank. They can call and find out if it's genuine. Better yet, take it over to the bank now."

*

"We need to work out a schedule. I mean, when we're all here, and you guys are not on a trip or something," Jody said, getting back from the bank. "I mean, we keep bumping into each other, and I'm afraid Alyssa will get left somewhere."

"You're right. We need to work out a normal daily schedule," Dana said, looking over at Alyssa and Handsome.

"No, normal is when I do everything," Jody said. "I'm talking about when you're both home."

"Okay, what do you suggest?" Dana asked. Mason got out a tablet and made notes.

The schedule ended up on magnets on both refrigerators and pinned to the corkboard in the gallery.

"We'll just see how long that lasts," Jody said.

"Till Tuesday," Dana said.

"Another road trip?" Jody asked, shaking her head. "Why do I even try?"

Sunday was spent at Dana's. With Christopher gone, the boys' calls came less and less often. They didn't call that morning. Sally and Axel did. So did Jess.

"Hey, Jess, honey. What's happening?" Dana said into the phone.

"Hi, baby. I'm the dude. I got nearly fifty guys working for me. They moved me to a big office on the top floor. I've got two assistants working for me. God, you should see the ass on Angie. I always have her get my files. Anyway, I can't even tell you about my security clearance. And by the way, I'm no longer Jess. I'm Inspector Rizzo. Beat that. Oh, and by the way, that alias you gave me, Windy Talker? Thanks for nothing. I was in DC, and they wanted me to have an alias. I said under my breath, 'As long as it isn't Windy Talker.' My boss heard me and said it's a perfect name for me. I'm to use it when I leak things to the press or whatever. Shit, now it's in my permanent record."

Dana and Mason could not stop laughing. Every time they tried to say something, they broke up laughing.

"So, Inspector Talker," Mason stopped to giggle, "with your sky-high security clearance, what can you tell me? Something, please, of interest."

"Of interest? Sure, your trip north did not go unnoticed. This guy Felix, he's the boss up there, and he is pissed. He was on the phone with Grandpa all week. And don't call me Inspector Talker."

"What did he say? I'll only call you Windy Talker when I need something leaked," Mason giggled, "Oh God, I've been laughing so hard I think I'm leaking."

"Really? Now that's funny." Jess giggled this time. "Ok, back on subject, I don't know what was said. I just got the information secondhand. Hang on a second." She took the phone away from her mouth. They could hear her ordering a hamburger, fries, and a Coke.

"Where are you?" Dana asked.

"I'm in my car. I just ordered a late lunch at McDonald's drive-through," Jess replied as she drove off.

"Are you using a car phone?" Mason asked.

"Or one of those big walkie-talkies. I think they call them bricks," Dana asked, puzzled.

"That's old hat. The department gave me one of those new flip phones. You know, like the ones on the old *Star Trek* TV show. Except when I say *Scotty, beam me up,* nothing happens. I got a holster on my belt for my phone. You guys should get one. Warning: They charge by the minute, and they don't work everywhere. Well, I got to go.

My batteries are running low, and I got to plug in the charger. Love you guys."

"Let's look into this when we get back," Mason said to Dana's agreement as they hung up.

That Monday afternoon, Mason and Dana made their way out to Ashville. They pulled into a truck stop near the North Carolina border.

Just after they had left, Jody got a call from the bank. "Yes, the check is real, the company is real. But," the bank manager said to Jody.

"But? I'll bet it's a huge but," Jody said.

"You got it. It was issued by an electronics firm in New York six months ago. He managed to change the name and date. Some kind of new technology. We've got people studying it now."

"Shit. Mason was right. Thanks for working so fast." Jody hung her head.

"Thanks for the heads up. We usually wouldn't find this out for at least ten days. Longer, if the original electronics company didn't call it to our attention," the manager said.

"Well, thank you." Jody hung up. "Mason won't let me forget this," she said to Alyssa.

Alyssa said. "Hun?"

*

"Be careful, sweetie," Mason said as she closed the door to the trailer. At one in the morning, the Black Dragon rolled into Malvern Hill Estates. It was a nice middle-class neighborhood, but the house closet to the entrance on the corner was her target. It had an attached garage, and the black Dragon rolled up to it. With a revved engine, it busted through the door, blowing fire on the car on one side and the workbench on the other.

The house was soundproof. If any of the neighbors were awake, they would have seen flashes of gunfire but no sound. The Black Dragon backed out of the garage three minutes later. No one called 911 till the fire had taken over the house. By that time, Dana and Mason were well on their way to Knoxville.

This time, Mason was more relaxed with the Red Bitch. She was less apprehensive and more confident in Dana's abilities. Still, Mason was a basket case when the Red Bitch was out in the Black Dragon. If the Black Dragon wasn't back within fifteen minutes, she thought the worst had happened.

Mason picked up the Red Bitch, then finding a convenient truck stop just a few minutes down the road, she pulled over and went back to the trailer.

Dana had just put the drugs and money away when Mason opened the trailer door. She walked into the trailer to see Dana's face, arms, and legs covered in blood. "Oh, my God. Sit down. Where are you cut?" Was her first reaction, rushing to Dana's side.

"Oh, this. It's not my blood. I'm fine." Mason's face had gone white, "You had better sit down before you fall down." Dana helped her onto the seat by the table. "I'll just clean up now," she said as she took off her clothes. "Whenever you're ready, we can head for Knoxville," Dana said, washing the blood off her face and looking in the mirror.

"What happened?" Mason said.

"Not much. Six guys and a maybe twelve-year-old girl. Two of the guys had Uzis. They make a lot of noise. Two guys were naked; so was the little girl. I cut their balls off before killing them, which is one of the reasons they got so much blood on me. I gave the money to the little girl and told her to get out of there." Dana pulled off her bloody wig. "I spray-painted RB on the wall. Do you think they'll get it?"

Mason headed out the door, shaking her head. She turned to say something to Dana but instead just shook her head again and got into the truck.

They stopped at a truck stop in the hills not far from Knoxville. They had breakfast and called home.

"Hi, honey," Jody said to Dana. "I'm sorry, but Alyssa can't leave the table until she eats some of her omelet." Turning from the phone, she said, "Do not give any of your breakfast to Handsome. You'll just get more." Turning back to the phone, she said, "Sorry; difficult morning."

"Yeah, and sometimes we never know why. Do you want to talk to Mason?" Dana handed the phone over.

"You were right; it was almost foolproof," Jody said, "the check was genuine, and so was the company. He used a new technique to forge the name and date. The bank is having it studied now,"

"Well, if he shows up, just tell him the check hasn't cleared yet. Then call 911," Mason said. "Be careful; this type can get violent."

Over their own breakfast, Mason asked, "So, are you and Jess going to become a thing?"

"Jess? No. She's fun. I like her, but I've only seen her that one time. We just talk," Dana said.

"Are you sure?" Mason asked.

"We've talked like I said. No commitment on either side. You've been there. Especially at my age."

"I know. Boy, do I know. It was more about being satisfied, not about being happy. I didn't know what real happiness was until I met Jody. Even then, it took a while. I'm happy with Jody. It's right for us." Taking a bite of her eggs, she said, "I wish I had met her earlier."

"Maybe you weren't right for her earlier? And maybe the other way around also. Remember, she was married."

Dana examined her skinned elbow, then took a sip of coffee.

"Maybe someday you'll find the right girl," Mason said over the top of her cup of coffee.

"I already did. Twice. One left me. The other died." Dana took a deep breath. "I'm just not going to see anyone till Alyssa starts dating." Then she quickly added, "Anyone in Atlanta, that is."

"Why are we drinking coffee when it's time to get some rest?" Mason asked Dana as they made their way to the trailer.

That night, they headed for the auto repair shop just out of town. The Black Dragon pushed its way through the garage doors into the shop. It was a transfer location, drugs in one direction, money in the other. They were mounting boxes under pickup trucks.

"Hi, guys! Sorry to disturb you. But I'm going to take Carlos his money and his drugs," The Red Bitch said as if she were helping children with their chores. "I'm going to save you so much trouble." The Red Bitch turned just in time to duck a swing from a huge guy. The boxes went into the Black Dragon less than a minute later. She was out in about three minutes.

That night, three were left dead, two in the garage and one in the gallery.

*

It was just after five at the gallery. Alyssa was sitting in her highchair, eating her dinner. Handsome laid at the foot of the chair, cleaning up the droppings. Some were intended.

Jody was at the door, showing a new couple who had an interest in two Robert Lee pencil drawings out the door. The bad buyer walked in just as she was closing the door. He had a big smile on his face. "Hi, Jody. Boy, I can't wait to get that Tyka on my dining room wall."

He was standing just inches from Jody's face, so she took a couple of steps back. "Well, there is a problem. I called the bank. Your check has not cleared yet."

He took several steps closer. "Really? That's not possible. It's a paycheck. It should cash in a day or two. It's been like five days." He kept walking Jody back into the gallery.

"I'm sorry. I can't help you." Jody kept backing up.

"Well, I'm leaving tonight. I'll just take the Tyka and that painting, too." He pointed at the painting next to the Tyka, and his voice was threating.

"I can't do that. I'll send the Tyka to you when the check clears. Just leave me your address." Jody tried to head for the office. He cut her off.

"I'll take them now." He pulled out a switchblade. Pressing the button, the blade sprang out. He put the knife in her face.

Handsome's ears came up. He rushed in between Jody and the bad buyer, jumping in the air at him. The bad buyer swung the knife, burying it deep in Handsome's side and pushing him to one side. Handsome landed on his side with a yelp of pain.

The bad buyer took another step closer to Jody and held his bloody knife near Jody's throat. Handsome struggled to his feet. He sprang another time, higher and faster than before. His lower jaw sank into the bad buyer's throat, his upper jaw into the back of his neck. Handsome pushed him down on his side. The bad buyer tried stabbing Handsome. He managed to inflict several superficial wounds.

Handsome shook him by the neck like a toy. When the bad buyer stopped struggling, Handsome let go. He knew the smell of death. Then he laid down on his side.

Alyssa was screaming and crying from the moment when Handsome first jumped. She wiggled down from her highchair, underneath the tray. She ran to Handsome, petting his head and crying.

Jody made a quick call to 911. It only took her seconds to explain the situation. Following directions, she put down the phone without hanging up. Rushing to Alyssa, she took a quick look at the dead guy and the pool of blood forming around his neck. She kneeled between the dead body and Alyssa so Alyssa could not see him.

In about five minutes, the screaming sirens announced the cops' arrival. They came through the door seconds later, guns in hand. A few seconds later, they were followed in by two other cops.

"Jody," The head cop said, surprised to see her. He then inspected the dead guy, taking the knife from his hand. All the while, he was talking to Jody, asking questions. At last, he checked out Handsome, stroking his head. "You're hurt bad, boy."

"He's breathing, but he's bleeding a lot. I think he saved my life. We have to help him," Jody said. Looking up at the cop.

The ambulance arrived quickly. Two paramedics rushed through the door. "Get the gurney quickly," the head cop ordered. When it came in, they went to the dead body. "No, over here, guys. Now, the three of us are going to pick him up, okay?" When Handsome was safely on the gurney, he gave new orders. "Do you know where the Red Maple Vet is?"

"Of course," one of the paramedics said.

"Well, take him there. Get Doctor Modglin. Only Doctor Modglin to work on him."

As they were rolling him out, Alyssa was holding on to Handsome's fur. She would not let him go. "Take them, too.

Frank, follow them. Get Jody's statement. She was an DA, She'll give you a well-detailed statement."

He followed them out the door, seeing the ambulance off, he walked back into the gallery. Looking at the three other cops stand around. Then at the body, "Well, what do we have here?"

*

"Oh God, Mason. It is so good to hear your voice. Is Dana there?" Jody said into the phone the next morning.

"Yes, she's standing right next to me. What's up?"

"Okay, listen carefully and repeat everything I say to Dana. Do not interrupt until I'm done. Got it?"

"Got it." Mason looked at Dana and repeated what she just heard. Dana stood close to Mason, holding on to the payphone partition.

"First, I guess I'll start at the beginning." Jody went on to tell her story in detail. "So, the results right now are that Handsome saved my life and possibly Alyssa's. He killed the bad guy. He is at the vet's now. We were there till after ten last night. The head cop, David, is his name; he's really nice. He let us go with Handsome to the vets. Another cop, Frank, asked questions and took us home. Alyssa was a basket case; she could not go to sleep. Handsome is hurt really bad. But Dr. Modglin thinks he's really strong and has the will to recover. He was still under sedation when we left."

"Oh, God," Dana said as Mason repeated everything to her word for word.

"Anyway, I got a call from the detective, what's his name, he says he knows you. He's coming over soon to go over everything again." Jody waited for Mason to tell Dana. "Oh, they have the keys to the gallery, and my car is still there. I had to go with Alyssa in the ambulance to get her out of there. I tried to keep her from seeing the dead body."

Dana was leaning against the wall next to the phone, her arms crossed and her head down. Mason was leaning against the phone her head propped on one arm.

"You were not hurt? Alyssa was not hurt. Is that right?" Mason asked.

"Not physically. I think she's really distraught. A little scared. Well, so am I a little bit."

"It's a four or five-hour drive home. We'll see you as soon as we can get there. Anything we can do now?" Mason asked. As she stood up straight, Dana put both her arms around her and her head on her shoulder.

"Can I speak to Alyssa?" Mason repeated Dana's request to Jody.

"She's still sleeping. We were up till after one this morning."

"Okay. We're on our way. Love you."

33. THE RACE

As soon as Dana came through the door, Alyssa ran up to her. Dana lifted her up and held her tight. She kissed her cheek and her head. Tears were running down Dana's cheeks.

"Mommy, Mommy, Handsome is hurt. He was bleeding a lot. We took him to the hospital. Is he going to be okay? Mommy?"

"Yes. I'm sure he's is going to be okay," Dana said to her.

Mason come through the door after Dana. She and Jody clung together. "Are you okay?" Mason said in her ear.

"Yes, much better now that you're here. The detective had a lot to tell me." She kissed Mason. "I'm so happy you came home early."

They all followed Dana into the library, Alyssa clinging to her mom. Dana sat in the big chair and rearranged Alyssa in her lap. Mason and Jody sat together on the sofa, holding hands.

"Are you sure you're okay?" Mason asked one more time.

"Yes, I am. Especially after talking to Detective Longley. You know him, right?"

"Good cop and a better man. You're sure you're okay. Right?" Mason asked, shaking her hand.

"Jesus. Again, do you know how much I worry about you and Dana on these road trips? Do I constantly bug you? No! God, stop it now. I'm okay." Jody turned the back of her head to Mason but immediately turned back, squeezing her hand. "You're okay, right?"

“Yes, I got it. We’re both okay." Mason kissed her on the cheek. “We’re both good.”

Alyssa tugged on her mother’s arm. "Handsome is in the hospital. Is he going to be okay too?"

“I know, honey. Jody, do you have the number?” Dana asked.

“Yeah, give me a second.” She went to the hall and dug a card out of her purse.

Dana called and asked for Dr. Modglin. They spoke for a few minutes and hung up. "We're going to go pick up Handsome the day after tomorrow. He’s going to be really sore and tired. So, we have to be careful with him.” She kneeled to Alyssa level.

“Here is the rest of the story,” Jody said. “Detective Langley said they usually put dogs down after they kill somebody. But the head cop, David, loves dogs, especially protective dogs. So Handsome gets to live and not go to jail.”

“Really?” Mason asked. “Was he tall, with dark hair and massive hands?”

“I guess,” Jody said.

“Yeah. Handsome was safe.” Mason nodded.

“About the bad guy, he does this all the time, all over, and he usually gets away with it. He pays with different checks from different states. He works part-time as a bank clerk. That’s how he gets checks. He buys cars, jewelry, furs, paintings. Anything he can resell. They are all between three and five thousand dollars. The checks are always for a thousand or more of the purchase price. He’s not afraid of using that knife if the deal goes bad. He usually goes for the face or neck. He killed at least one jeweler in Kansas City. I was so lucky to have Handsome around.”

“Wow, you never know.” Dana pulled Alyssa closer to her, kissing her head, relieved she wasn’t hurt.

The next day, Detective Langley asked Dana and Mason to meet him at the gallery. Everything was very much the same, except for the yellow police tape which the detective quickly tore down. "I don't think we'll need this anymore."

Inside was a large pool of dried blood, a chalk outline of the body, and a much smaller dried bloodstain, with just the word *dog* in chalk on the floor. That was it. There was no other damage. Even the cold Mac and Cheese, it still looked edible.

"Thank you. You are wonderful—but everyone knew that already," Mason said to the detective.

He just smiled and shook her hand. "Thanks, chief." He turned and headed for the door. "Oh, how's the dog?"

"Picking him up tomorrow," Mason said.

*

Dana called the janitor firm they usually used. Mason came back the next day to supervise, also to explain why there was blood on the floor of the gallery a second time. The same afternoon, Dana, Jody, and Alyssa went to the vets.

Dr. Nancy Modglin came out as soon as the receptionist announced them. "He's good to go. He's limping and not very strong. He will probably limp for a month or more. Nothing to worry about."

A few minutes later, Handsome limped into the room. He tugged on his leash and wagged his tail upon seeing Alyssa and Dana. Alyssa rushed to him, putting her arms around his neck and got kisses all over her face.

His right side was almost completely shaven. He looked lopsided.

"Sixty-four stitches. Most were just skin cuts, but this one," she pointed to a long cut, looking up at Dana, "was bad. It went all the way into his lung. I think I repaired everything. I want to check that Monday. In the meantime, if he starts spitting up blood or has blood in his stool or pee, get him here right away. Don't let him run for at least a few weeks. See you both Monday." Looking over to the receptionist who had been listening in, she said, "Two-fifteen?" The receptionist confirmed the time.

Dr. Modglin handed the leash to Dana, who gave it to Alyssa. Jody patted Handsome on the head and scratched his butt. He always likes butt scratches because he can't reach his butt.

"You know, we're closed Sundays. But if you wanted to ask about Handsome, we could have lunch or dinner maybe." Nancy had a genuine smile on her face.

Dana looked interested. "Oh, I'm sorry. I'm in the middle of so many things right now. But can I have a rain check please?" She took out a business card, on the back she wrote her number, "I just got one of those flip phones. That's the number; call me anytime."

Dana took inventory of Nancy. She was as tall as her and had blond hair and blue eyes like her. A bit older, maybe mid-thirties. *Hmm*, she thought.

Handsome limped badly out to the car. Both Jody and Dana helped him into the front seat and strapped Alyssa into the backseat. As they walked around to the other side of the car, Jody said, "So, just to let you know, when you're going to dinner, let me know so I can spend the night with Alyssa."

Dana smiled, turning a bit red, "Sure thing."

*

The next Monday, Dana took Handsome back to Dr. Modglin. He was in much better shape, having slept a lot next to Alyssa. They both were exhausted.

"Just some pus on the big cut. Just squeeze it like this." Dr. Modglin squeezed a large amount of pus onto a large paper towel. "He will get some more, but it will be less each time. It should go away in a day or two. I'm giving him another shot to make sure he doesn't have any infections." Dr. Modglin patted Handsome on the head. She prepared a needle and made a quick injection into his shoulder. "There you go, boy." She handed the leash back to Dana. They were alone in the examining room.

"The other day. I should have asked if you were seeing someone. I'm sorry. I was out of line."

Dana got a big smile on her face. "Are you seeing anyone, Dr. Modglin?"

"No. Please call me Nancy."

"I'm Dana, and no, I'm not attached to anyone. I would love to go to dinner with you sometime. But like I said the other day, I am really up to my neck with projects right now. Give me a month or two."

"Deal, Dana," Nancy said. "Oh, bring Handsome back in about two weeks to get his stitches out." She opened the door to the waiting room. "He'll want to scratch them. Try not to let him."

Dana turned and headed to the door with Handsome.

"Wow, great ass," Nancy said under her breath.

Dana turned as she opened the door, ready to leave the building. "You have a great ass also," she said, smiling.

Nancy's face turned red, and she covered her face with the clipboard in her hand.

*

That afternoon, Mason drove up in the truck. Nashville was the next stop on the schedule because they had to scratch it on the last trip. So, it was first stop on this trip.

"You okay?" Dana asked, sitting at the small table in the trailer.

Mason had the plans and schedules out on the table. "I just don't like things out of schedule. We should have spent more time on this."

"Has anything else changed? I mean, other than the date?" Dana asked.

"Nothing that I can see. Fairview is a small town. There shouldn't be any more problems than the others," Mason said, pulling her papers together.

Fairview was built just after World War Two. It had deteriorated quite a bit, as most of the successful people had moved closer to Nashville or elsewhere.

It was three in the morning when the Red Bitch's Black Dragon was growling down the street, looking for a small house set back in the middle of a block in the development. It would have been easy to miss, except it had all the lights on, which wasn't unusual for a drug house.

The Red Bitch rushed the porch and kicked in the front door. The room was empty. She was expecting a guard moving toward the back of the house. The lights were on in every room, but nobody was home.

She was standing next to a bedroom when she noticed a stack of money in plain sight in the kitchen. She froze for just an instant. "Oh shit," she said as she ran into the bedroom. Grabbing a blanket off the bed, she wrapped it around herself, flying through the glass window. She hit the ground on her back and rolled next to the house's brick foundation at the same instant the house blew up. The brick saved her from the blast.

The kitchen went first, a split second later the bedroom followed by the front of the house. Dana jumped up and ran through the falling debris. Pieces of the house rained down on her head and shoulders, knocking her over, pushing herself up, she jumped into the Black Dragon, with debris falling from the car as she drove off.

Her ears were ringing so bad she could not hear the wheels squeal as she headed down the street. A blue pickup pulled out of the side street, blocking her way. She spun the wheel, pulled up on the hand brake, and hit the power. She spun around the other way just as two men were getting out of the truck. As she headed down the street, a red Camaro blocked the other end of the street, cutting off her escape. Two more guys started to get out of the Camaro.

The Red Bitch threw the wheel over, heading up a driveway between houses. There was a low wood fence protecting the backyard between the house and the garage. She burst through the fence and drove across the lawn next to the garage. Breaking through the wood fence in back, she hit the leg of a swing set. Swerving right, she got onto the driveway, clipping the fender of a car parked in the driveway and just missing the side of the house. She turned onto the street and hit the power.

The Camaro came out of the side street clipping the Black Dragon's back fender, sending it sideways down the street. She pointed the wheels down the street, downshifted to first, and hit the gas. That straightened her out.

Just as she was reaching the main street, she saw two squad cars blocking her way. The cops were out with their handguns drawn. The Black Dragon swerved up another driveway, going across lawns but staying partly on the sidewalk. The trees in the parkway protected her from some of the bullets fired at her. As she broke through a hedgerow on the street, several of the shots tore through the passenger window, spraying glass particles onto her right arm. Then one bullet put a hole in the drivers' side window. Her adrenaline hid the pain.

The Black Dragon powered up Main street. Dana reached for her flip phone and speed-dialed Mason. The explosion had deafened her, she couldn't even hear herself, but she yelled into the phone, "Honeymoon! Honeymoon!" She threw the phone onto the passenger seat.

"Oh shit," Mason said, hearing the words that meant *I'm in deep shit. Go to plan B*. Mason threw the truck in gear and sped west down Interstate 40 as fast as she could. There wasn't much traffic at three in the morning, just some eighteen-wheelers that she had to dodge. When she reached exit 163, she turned off and crossed the bridge and parked on the eastbound ramp.

The Camaro, followed by the two cop cars and the slower pickup truck, raced after the Black Dragon, the cops sirens blaring. She dodged late-night drivers on Main Street. They moved out of the way of the police cars, giving the pursuers a clear path. The Black Dragon turned onto Interstate 40 going west.

Dana flipped the switch, then pulled the trigger. The nitro kicked in, pinning her against the seat. In seconds, she was near two hundred miles an hour. She had to dodge the eighteen-wheelers. Her lights were off, so she had to rely on the trucks' light to keep on the interstate and from hitting one of them. After the thirty-second burn, the headlights of the chase cars were out of view, blocked by distance and the eighteen-wheelers.

Near exit 163, two trucks blocked each of the two lanes, one slowly passing the other. The Black Dragon swerved onto the shoulder, then up the ramp of the exit. Mason saw her coming and dropped the ramp. As the Black Dragon pulled in, Mason started down the ramp, closing the loading ramp at the same time. She pulled in behind an eighteen-wheeler, heading east.

Mason saw the Camaro and police cars racing down the street. She watched them in her rearview mirror. They raced past exit 163, going west. The blue pickup was a few miles back with its spotlight searching the westbound side of the road.

An hour later, Mason pulled into a campground east of Nashville near the Georgia border. She ran back to the trailer. Opening the door, she saw Dana with a bloody towel around her arm and a dish towel pressed up against the back of her head.

"Oh my God," Mason said, stopping in her tracks.

Dana gave a slight smile. "Well, this time, it is my blood."

"Let me have a look at that," Mason said, moving next to Dana. First, she removed the towel at the back of Dana's head and examined the wound. "Just a cut. Nothing serious. Head wounds bleed the worst. It's stopped bleeding, but don't move your head or neck."

"See what it did to my wig." Dana held up the Red Bitch's badly ripped red wig.

"From the looks of it, the Red Bitch saved your neck. Quite literally!" Mason said, looking at the wig. "Now, let's see that arm." She carefully unwrapped the towel. "Well, it's nice and shiny," she said, looking at the raisin-sized pieces of glass shards embedded in her arm. They had stopped bleeding, but Mason still saw blood running down her arm.

"Lift your arm." Mason inspected the underside of Dana's arm. "Good God. You've got a bullet hole. Looks like it went straight through your arm. It missed the bone, thank God."

Mason got up and retrieved the first aid kit out of the cupboard. She thought a second, then went into the bathroom and brought back a pack of sanitary napkins. She soaked the pad with peroxide and applied it to her arm around both bullet holes. "Hold that tight."

Dana bit her lip in pain squeezing her eyes closed.

"This might sting," Mason said.

"Now you tell me," Dana said, mashing her teeth together.

"Don't move your head. I'm just going to clip a little hair so your bandages will hold." Mason dropped the hair on the table and dabbed the wound with a cotton ball soaked with peroxide.

"You're supposed to say, *this is going to sting a lot.*" Dana winced again.

"You already knew that," Mason said as she attached three butterfly bandages to pull the wound tightly closed, then covering the entire wound with a larger bandage.

"Okay, now the glass." Mason took out a pair of tweezers and another cotton ball soaked in peroxide. "This might sting."

"Ha, Ha." Dana took a deep breath.

Mason pulled the glass pieces out one at a time and put them in a dish. Some blood followed the extraction of each, so she dabbed at them with the cotton ball and put a round bandage on each one. Some were deeper than others. In all, she removed fourteen pieces of glass.

"Save them. I might want to make a bracelet—or something—out of them." Dana looked at the pile of glass shards, glad they were not in her face.

Mason replaced the pad around the bullet holes with another, then placed another pad across the glass holes, wrapping Dana's whole arm tightly with gauze.

"Judging from the amount of blood on the towels, you have lost a lot. Don't stand up till I can help you. You're going to be dizzy." Mason got her a large glass of water. "Aspirin is all we got for pain, so take four." She handed them to Dana.

"Let's get ready for bed. We both need some sleep." Mason helped Dana off with her clothes and slipped on her long nightie.

Dana tossed a bit and fell asleep. Mason lay on her back, awake and wondering what had happened.

Before Mason fell asleep, Dana rolled over, putting her arm over Mason and her head on her shoulder. Mason put an arm around Dana.

Mason thought, *Oh god if they had killed her, I just couldn't take it.* As she fell asleep, she said quietly, looking over at Dana, *So, this is what it's like to be a mother. Fear, pain, and love.*

34. READY, SET,

Mason awoke around nine in the morning after only three hours of sleep. She made sure Dana was covered and asleep before cleaning the trailer. The bloody towels and cotton balls went into a trash bag, followed by a half-gallon of bleach. There were a few campers sitting in front of their trailers as she strolled to the campsite dumpster. No one took notice of her. She stood by the door of the truck looking around to make sure nothing was out of the ordinary. She climbed into the cab and drove off slowly, avoiding as many bumps as possible.

At her first stop Mason checked in on Dana, she had not moved but was breathing heavily. "At least she's breathing," Mason said as she checked Dana's forehead, it was cold and sweaty. She picked up some coffee and donuts and was on her way. Around noon, Mason pulled into the storage area and parked under the canopy. When she opened the door of the trailer, she was surprised to see Dana up, dressed and sipping a cup of coffee.

"Coffee?" Dana asked. "I just made it."

"How are you feeling?" Mason asked, stepping into the trailer. She checked the coffee pot. Like Dana had said, it was still hot. She poured herself a cup and joined Dana at the table.

"I'm really sore all over," Dana said. "I have a gigantic headache. I took a handful of aspirin, but they are not doing any good. My arm is killing me." Dana winced as she talked.

"So, what happened out there? I didn't learn much from you last night."

"They were waiting for me. It was a fucking trap. The goddamn cops were in on it. Jesus, they just about blew me up in the damn house. Then they chased me and rammed me. Then the cops shot at me. The Trans Am is a mess, poor baby. But she took care of me. God, she's fast. I hit the nitro, and she pinned me back. She's a strong girl. She didn't hiccup once. She really took care of me." Dana looked around. "Do we have anything to eat?"

"Just the coffee you made and donuts."

"Donuts, Where?" Dana turned her head around, then back quickly. "That hurt."

"Sit. I'll get what's left of the donuts. They're in the cab. I'll be back in a second."

"I've been thinking about what happened," Dana said as Mason set the half-full box of donuts in front of her. "The Red Bitch is now really a ghost," she said as she grabbed a powdered donut waving it in the air, "Looking at it, they tried their best to kill me. Then I just disappeared. Just like a ghost. That had to have scared them." Dana took a bite of the donut, leaving powdered sugar around her mouth. "Now, if I hit them again, that's got to really shake them up." She sat back, enjoying her donut and grabbing a second one. "I'm so hungry."

"Are you saying, what?" Mason asked.

"I'm saying as soon as the Trans Amis well again—and by that, I mean meaner than ever—we hit them and hit them really hard and fast. We take on the Alabama, Mississippi, and Louisiana drug lord—what's his name, oh, Sal. We take on the big money places." Dana looked at her donut. "What kind of donut is this? It's really good."

"Cinnamon and walnut nut." Mason said, "Enough with the donuts, give me the short version of what happened."

"All there is… is the short version." Dana looked down at her coffee cup. "Mind getting me another cup of coffee?" Then she went into a ten-minute, detailed version of what happened.

"Well, you're lucky. No shit. How did you think of driving through those houses' yards?" Mason asked.

"Only opening, I guess. There must be some very pissed people this morning," Dana said.

"Okay." Mason stood up. "First, you've got to get to a doctor and get that bullet hole looked at."

Dana looked at her bandaged arm, "I think I have someone I can see. But first I need Handsome, so you have to pick him up. Please don't tell Alyssa I'm home yet. I don't want her to worry about this," Dana said, pointing to her arm. "Not after all the shit she has been through."

"She's not going to like seeing me and not you." Mason emptied out the coffee pot into the sink.

"First, I've got to get the Trans Am to Eddie's Speed Shop. While I'm doing that, you pick up Handsome and pick me up there." Dana started to go to the Black Dragon through the little door.

"How are you going to shift gears with that arm?" Mason asked as Dana ducked down to enter the low door.

"Very carefully," Dana said.

"Whatever; it's your arm. By the way, there's one donut left. Do you want it?" Mason said.

Dana turned around, hitting her head on the door frame. "Ouch. Shit, that hurt," she said, holding her head and neck and reaching out for the last donut at the same time.

"Sorry," Mason said, stepping out of the trailer and into the truck. She hit the button, dropping the ramp. Dana fired up the Black Dragon and backed down the ramp.

Dana stood in the doorway of the small office at Eddie's Speed Shop. Nothing had changed, except for the calendar. It was now hot cars. "Do you call this work?" she asked.

Tommy turned and saw Dana. He jumped up and gave her a hug. She winced in pain.

"Oh, sorry. I didn't see that. What happened?" Tommy asked backing up, looking at her bandaged arm.

"Oh, just a little accident in the Black Dragon." She smiled. "What happened to the girly calendars?"

"Well, you see." He held up his left hand. "I got married. Molly doesn't like me looking at naked women. Except for her."

"Congratulations. Do I know her?"

"The cheerleader for the football team. Remember the one with the big jugs." Tommy made the gesture for big tits with his hands.

"Oh yeah. Molly, you said. How did you land her?"

"Charm, wit, and lots of alcohol," he laughed.

"The trifecta for seduction," Dana laughed. "Prepare yourself." She waved her left hand for him to follow her out to the front of the garage.

"Holy shit. What happened?" He walked around the Trans Am, assessing the damage.

"Road race. You should see the other four guys. I need her fixed up, including more nitro. I think I used it all." Turning to Tommy, her eyes were big as she said, "God, what a rush. She just took off like a rocket. A horse on fire. It was all I could do to handle the reins." Dana watched as Tommy poked and prodded the Black Dragon. He inspected the windows. "Gunshot?"

"Yeah, a couple of the guys had guns. They were mad that I was getting, well, in front of them."

"How did the fire work?" he asked, looking at the burnt and blackened edges around the fender.

"Fantastic. I used it a couple of times." Dana looked down at the burned paint.

"I can see that." Looking away from the car, directly into Dana's eyes, he said, "What do you want? I mean, besides getting her fixed up again."

"Make her meaner. And paint a dragon on both sides. Use just dark gold, dark blue, dark red, and gray, sort of like she's coming out of the paint. Make it look like the fire from the exhaust is coming out of its mouth."

Tommy nodded, "I know a guy that can do that."

"Now, here is the thing. I need her back in two weeks. Can you do that?" She stepped closer to him.

"Repairs, yes. Paint? That's a problem."

Dana took another step closer to Tommy. She was just inches from Tommy and she looked down at him. "Even for a ten-thousand-dollar bonus?"

Tommy had to look up six inches to Dana's eyes.

"I got a race coming up. I need her to be a badass."

Mason rolled up, waiting for Dana.

"Not for anyone else. Not even for twenty thousand dollars. But for you, sure."

Dana gave him a one-armed hug. From her, that was better than a handshake.

"Alyssa was upset that you weren't there," Mason said.

"I knew she would be, but Alyssa would be more upset seeing this." Dana held up her bandaged arm, now with blood seeping through the bandage.

"I have to pick her up at five. Do you think that's enough time?" Mason said as they drove off. Handsome leaned over the seat and put his head on Dana's shoulder. "

"It should be if Nancy doesn't call the cops." Dana petted Handsome's head. "I don't think she will."

Mason dropped Dana and Handsome off at the house. Dana switched to the Cadillac, loaded Handsome into the front seat, and left for the vets.

"Dr. Modglin please," Dana asked the receptionist at the desk.

"Hi, Dana," Nancy said, coming out a few minutes later.

"Stitches," Dana said, pointing at Handsome.

"Okay, come on back," Nancy said, patting Handsome on the head. She led Dana and Handsome to an examining room. Closing the door, she said, "You know it's a bit early. He's not due for at least another week."

"Okay," Dana said, turning her right side to Nancy.

"What's that? You're bleeding." That was just what Dana wanted to hear.

"Oh, I had a little accident this morning," Dana said, looking down at her bloody bandage.

"Let me see," Nancy said, pulling out a pair of scissors and cutting through the gauze. "Sanitary pads?"

"It's all we had."

"Well, it worked fine. Let's see what we have here." Nancy removed the pads, exposing the wounds. She started looking at the little bandages but then went right for the bloody parts. Cleaning the bloody part with a cotton ball, Nancy look directly at into dana's face, she studied her for a bit, "That's a bullet hole."

"Yeah, I know. Alyssa shot me. It's all my fault," Dana said with a not-real smile.

"You have got to tell me what happened."

"She found my pistol in my nightstand. The bullet went through the wall as I was putting my hair up in the mirror. Glass flew everywhere. And I guess the bullet went through my arm. That's all."

Nancy sat, staring at Dana.

"It scared Alyssa more than me," Dana offered.

"You need to see a doctor," Nancy said, moving her chair back.

"I can't. If a doctor sees a bullet wound, he has to call the cops. I can't have the cops questioning Alyssa. Not after that shit at the gallery. I just don't want her to have to go through that."

Nancy shook her head slowly, side to side. Without saying a word, she removed some supplies from her cabinet, and set it down on a stainless-steel exam table.

"Here, sit down here on the table." She motioned to Dana.

"Shouldn't Handsome be up here?" Dana said, sitting down.

"You need stitches. Handsome is fine. This will numb you," Nancy said, holding up a needle. She injected two shots on each side of Dana's arm. "I'm going make sure it's sterile," she said and went about her job as if Dana was a large dog. "Okay, no real problems. I'm going to give you two stitches on each side. That should do it." With no other words, she proceeded to stitch Dana up. When she finished with that, she took off all the round bandages that had the embedded glass in her arm. She inspected each wound, putting some salve on each one. With that finished, she dressed Dana's arm, from the shoulder to the elbow.

"I'll be back in a minute," Nancy said, leaving the room and shutting the door behind her.

Dana first thought was, *Oh, shit. She's calling the cops.*

Nancy came back and closed the door, which she leaned against, her expression impossible to read. "Here are some pills for pain. They are for Handsome. Make sure he only takes two, and no more than that every four hours. Then he'll need to lie down for a bit." Nancy handed her a bottle of pills. "Here is your bill." She handed Dana a folded piece of paper.

Dana unfolded the paper. It said, *Dinner tomorrow night at La Chateau, 8:30.*

Dana folded it back up and put it in her bra, saying, "This is one bill I'm looking forward to paying."

*

Alyssa charged Dana as she came through the front door with Handsome.

"Mommy, Mommy," Alyssa tried to get up in Dana's arms.

"Sorry honey, Mommy hurt her arm," Dana said, hugging her tight with her one good arm, kissing her on the head.

Jody was right behind Alyssa, "You look horrible. Food is almost ready. Eat, then go to bed. I'll take care of everything, and I'll spend the night."

Mason following behind Jody said, "so will I, if it's okay?"

"Of course, lover," Jody said.

*

"Coffee," Mason said as Dana came down for breakfast. Mason, Jody and Alyssa were sitting at the table eating breakfast. Mason poured her a cup of coffee. "Donut?"

"You're kidding me?"

"How about eggs, bacon, and toast?" Jody asked.

"Oh, thank you, God. And thank you to Jody."

Dana and Mason spent the next day in the hideaway, Jody's new name for the secret room. They were studying new targets and restudying old targets. They were putting in place plans A, B, and now C.

Dana looked up at the clock. "It's almost five. Jody has had Alyssa since ten this morning. Would you mind picking Alyssa up from the Gallery? I got to get ready for my date. Or should I say, pay my medical bill." Dana stood and made ready to head out the door.

"Date? Tonight? With who?" Mason asked.

"We're going to La Chateau. I've got to dress sexy." Winding her hair up. "Do you think I should wear my hair up?"

"Not with those bandages behind your head. Again, who?"

"My doctor." Dana turned to leave.

"Oh, the vet who sewed you up. Is she hot?" Mason smiled.

"She has a nice ass." Dana opened the door. "And yes, she's hot."

*

"So, mommy, when can I get my ears pierced?" Alyssa said, sitting on the side of the bed watching her mother getting dressed.

"Well, honey, when you get old enough," The standard answer.

"When can I get my own make-up?" before Dana could answer. "When can I get a bra?" Dana gave her a blank look, "when can I wear high heels? When can I..."

"Honey," Dana said, coming over to sit by Alyssa, putting her arm around her. "when, depends on how old you are, and what you want to do. And also, what you can handle."

It was Alyssa turn to have a blank look.

"Ok," Dana took a deep breath, not expecting this conversation so young, "If you want to get your ears pierced, we can do that for your birthday, ok?"

Alyssa nodded.

"Make-up. Well, you only need make-up when you get old like me, or especially like aunt Jody." They both giggled, "Heels, when you go to your first high school party. And," tickling her in the ribs, "a bra when you have something to put in a bra."

"Nancy, Wow, I don't know how to say this," Dana said over dinner.

Nancy gave her a blank look.

"You know I've been getting that blank look a lot lately," Dana said, "I wanted you from the minute I saw you. And I didn't even know you liked me."

"So, what's the problem?" Nancy said with her fist under her chin, "Certainly nothing on my end."

"Well, I was reminded tonight, in an indirect way," Dana said, looking sideways, "that I had made a promise to my Dad and Alyssa."

"Christopher, your dad, He brought Handsome in," she reaching across the table taking dana's hand, "I was at his funeral," Looking at her, "Of course you don't remember. Really why did I bring that up." She dropped Dana's hand turning red, with embarrassment.

"I want more to happen, I really do. But, I promised, I would not date in Atlanta until Alyssa dated. And shit here I am with someone I really want to be with... in every way. On a date in Atlanta."

"It's not a date. You're paying a bill. Well, that's an excuse you can use." Nancy said looking away.

"Oh," Dana looked down, shaking her head, "I'm sorry. No, I'm very sorry. You know I'll be free to date in a decade or so. God, that's wasn't much help!"

Nancy just looked away, disappointment showing on her face.

Dana's eyes lighted up, and she reached across the table to take Nancy's hand, "But no promises, there is no telling how many bills I have to pay, or how long you'll... How do I say this... take service in kind? Just paying bills, you understand? I can't date. No commitments."

"I'm not sure that's going to work for me," Nancy said, "I'm a commitment kind of girl."

"I understand, I'm sorry. I'm just trying to... you know... for my daughter, not confuse her with... you know, a love affair." Dana said, "Understand?"

"I understand." Nancy said, "But Handsome is my patient. So, don't you dare take him to another vet!"

"Deal," Dana smiled broadly.

*

The next day in the hideaway, they made more plans.

"That takes care of that. What's next?" Mason asked.

"Now we call Jess," Dana said, dialing.

"Hi, Jess. What's happening?" Mason asked.

"I'm sorry. I am having a hard time hearing you. Call back later." Jess abruptly hung up.

"Humm. What do you think that was all about?" Mason asked, hanging up the phone.

Dana looked up. "She thinks her phone is tapped." She looked at the wall covered in photos. They all now had names, addresses, some phone numbers, and a bio. All except for Ron.

"I'm going to Miami tomorrow," Dana said.

*

Dana timed her arrival at Miami International Airport for late afternoon. She drove down to North Miami Beach and parked next to a used car lot. She walked the three blocks to Jesse's house, going through the side gate to the patio. She searched around for the key and found it in the flowerpot.

She let herself in and started looking for bugs. The first and most obvious was the phone. It was in the extension in the bedroom. Another was under the refrigerator. Then one in the TV. She knew she was running out of time. She wrote a big note "The place is bugged."

Jess was startled to see Dana standing at the end of the hall, holding up the note.

"Holly Jesus, it's nice to be home," she said aloud and went into the kitchen and opened the refrigerator. Dana pointed under the refrigerator. Jess shook her head and mouthed; I know.

"Shit, nothing to eat. I got to go shopping sometime." Jess then signaled for Dana to follow her out to the patio, turning on the garden hose to make background noise, at the same time, leaning over and whispered in Dana's ear. "God, I'm so glad to see you."

"We got to talk," Dana whispered back.

"Get a room on Coast Highway. I'll see you at the Snap Trap around ten-thirty. And for God's sake, butch it up." They kissed and parted.

Dana stopped at Sears and bought men's work boots, white socks, Levi's, and two tank tops. She then stopped at a Motel 6 and rented a room for two days. She paid cash.

Dana removed all her makeup and put her hair up in a ponytail. She used a marker to write *Suck it up* on the wrapping on her arm. 'I think I'll keep my red nails, just to put Jess off a bit,' she thought.

At the Snap Trap, she sat at the bar and ordered a double Irish neat.

"Can I see your ID?" the muscle-bound bartender asked as he set down her drink.

"Fuck you," she said as she picked up her drink, dropping a twenty on the bar. She turned around and said over her shoulder, "Make sure I get the right change."

Twenty minutes later, Jess wandered in. She sat at the other end of the bar and ordered a beer. A few minutes later, she walked up to Dana. "What's happening, honey?" she asked as if meeting her for the first time.

"I don't know. I do know my drink is empty." Then she added, "Honey."

Jess ordered them both a drink. They sat and talked as if they had just met. After an hour, Dana got out her rental car keys and said, "I'll drive."

Once they were in the car, Jess turned and kissed Dana. "Holy shit. I don't think anyone was watching. But just to be safe, get out of here quick. Watch to see if anyone is following."

As they drove off, Jess checked several times to see if anyone was following. She was not running off at the mouth as usual. "The only place I can talk on the phone is in my office, and I'm not even sure my office phone isn't tapped. All-important meetings are in closed-door rooms and on different floors. Still, I have to watch who's around me."

After parking, they quickly walked to the room. Once in, Jess looked through the crack in the curtains to see if anyone was around.

Sitting on the side of the bed, she let out a lot of air. "I know who it is. I'm just not sure if anyone is helping him."

"Who is he?" Dana sat in the only chair in the room. She pulled off her shoes and threw them in the corner. "How do you wear those things?"

"How do you wear those six-inch heels?" Jess shot back. She was back up to speed. "Dan Wong is his name. He has a cubical on my floor. He's supposed to track Asians who we think might be spies. I've checked upon him. An extra five grand is showing up in his stock market account every week. Took me a while to figure that one out."

"So who's paying him? And more importantly, who's bugging you?" Dana leaned forward.

"The chief of police. I've got the evidence. By the way, I'm so horny," Jess said.

Dana gave her a kiss with a little tongue. "I'm horny too, it's been a long time." Dana shook her head, thinking about what almost happened the night before, coming back to present she looked at Jess. "We have got to talk. Time's short. I'm putting everything in position to pull the plug on Carlos. In a month or so, all three drug lords—Sal, Willie, and Eddie—will be against Carlos. Grandpa will have to support them and will pull his protection off Carlos."

"Good. I can't hold my team back much longer. I can't wait to nail Wong. My life is hell right now."

"You let me know when Grandpa has his meeting with the drug lords. That will be the trigger. We should act the next day." Dana pulled off her socks and threw them in the corner. "What's your plan?"

"We'll take them all at once. I have two and three-man teams on fourteen targets. I'll need police backup. That's going to be close timing. I need to bring them in without letting them know what's happening. I'm looking at using Orlando SWAT teams. They are the best." Jess had untied and slipped off her shoes and socks. "We will perp walk them into jail, maybe some of them into court. I don't know yet. I'll—or, I mean Windy Talker—will let the press know when to be at the jails. Lots of exposure."

"Make it late, like four to five o'clock. Better timing for TV and also for me. Pull all the cops away from Star Island. Don't let anyone close to the island till the next morning." Dana pulled off her tank top. She wasn't wearing a bra.

"Remember," Dana pointed at Jess with the tank top still in her hand, "Carlos is mine."

35. GO

"How'd it go?" Mason asked as Dana threw her bag over into the backseat.

"Let's get out of this airport. I'm so glad to be home," Dana said, settling in and buckling her seat belt. "It went really well. I paid cash for two nights. Rented the car for three. And disappeared after one. If anyone was watching Jess, I don't think they have a clue who I am. They probably think I'm just a slut lesbo."

"You do seem more relaxed. More satisfied." Mason winked at Dana, who just looked at Mason, pursed her lips, and then gave a small smile. That said everything.

"It's still a week before we can pick up the Mustang. A fiercer Mustang. What can we do to stir the pot till then?"

"You, mama, have to calm down Alyssa. I need to calm down Jody. We can work on stirring the pot in a few days." Mason parked in the driveway.

"What size shoe do you wear? I mean, in men's sizes?" Dana asked.

"Why?" Mason asked with a puzzled look on her face.

"I had to butch it up for Jess last night." She looked at Mason. "Don't ask."

"Size eight or eight and a half. Depends." Mason turned to look at Dana. "You were a dyke last night, weren't you?"

"Work boots, Levi's rolled up at the cuff, and a tank top. Quit laughing, Mason," Dana said, laughing, herself.

"You—I mean you—dressed like a dyke?" Mason said, punching Dana in the shoulder. "What color was the tank top?"

"Brown. Now quit laughing. Let's unload my stuff and go to the gallery. I can't wait to see Alyssa." Dana opened the car door. "On second thought, I think I'll keep the work boots."

The next week was quiet. Dana relaxed in the sheer luxury of a quiet week. No drama and no killing. Just planning.

A few days later before breakfast, Dana took her arm wrap off. Mason inspected it. She just had a few scabs and four stitches under her arm. "Not bad. Are you feeling better now?" she asked.

"Yep, time to call Dr. Modglin. Handsome and I need to get our stitches out," Dana said inspecting her arm.

"What kind of bill do you expect to get for that?" Mason smirked.

"I don't know, but judging from my last bill, it's going to be dinner conversation and nothing more." Dana looked away, "I think I'm ready for the dojo. I can't wait to get down there this morning."

Bobby and Tommy had been studying new positions and moves. They suppressed the smiles on their faces as they bowed to Dana on the mat. They were much more aggressive than ever. They really wanted to beat her. They had learned to combine several forms of martial arts, a technique they learned from Dana. They had her down once and went in for the kill. Dana's knee went into the side of Bobby's knee, sending him sideways into Tommy. In seconds, she had them both down and the Bo shaft across both of their necks.

"Guys, you're getting excellent. You almost had me there. Now, show me that move again," Dana said as she let both up. They spent the rest of the workout on the new moves, developing defenses and attacks around those moves.

Saturday late afternoon, Tommy from the garage called Dana. "You are not going to believe what I did. She is so sweet. Come by tomorrow around noon. I don't want anyone else to see The Black Dragon."

Dana and Mason showed up at noon the next day. Tommy greeted them at the door. "Just wait till you see her. Stand here and cover your eyes. Don't peek."

He went into the garage and opened the overhead door. They heard the *vroom* of the Dragon starting up, then the excited purr of an overpowered engine as Tommy backed her out of the garage. He got out of the car and walked around behind them, putting his hands on both their shoulders. "Now look."

Dana and Mason stood in stunned silence. "Oh my God," they both said at the same time.

The Dragon sat in front of them. Small flames came out of her side pipes behind the front tires. The painting was phenomenal, going from the tail of the car to the hood, turning as it went down to the exhaust. The head looked like it was breathing fire out of the tire well.

She was lower and sleeker. "I chopped and channeled the roof," Tommy said. "She's lower by four inches. I figured if I had to redo the door and windows, why not? I lowered the seats as well, just so you don't hit your head. And it's cooler. I can barely see over the dash. You're taller; you'll be okay."

Dana and Mason walked around the Dragon with their mouths ajar. Their fingers ran the length of her.

"The front and side windows are bulletproof. At least to a .44 Magnum. Bigger, I can't say."

Dana rubbed her healing right arm. "Cool."

"No rearview mirror. You don't need one. The spoiler blocks your view anyway. You'll have to use your side mirrors. I topped her off with nitro. But look in here."

Tommy pointed to the dash panel. It now had a combo of switches. "This switch is for the high beams. When I say high beams, I mean ninety million candle power. I also added a high beam in the back. Forty-five million candle power. Watch: Even in daylight, they are blinding." Tommy flipped the switch. The bright light blew into the garage. "I don't recommend looking in the direction of the Dragon with these lights on." He flipped off the switch. "Careful; you could blind someone for life—or at least fifteen minutes."

Dana squatted down on her haunches, just looking at the Dragon. A few minutes later, Mason tapped her on the shoulder. "We got to go."

Dana looked over at Mason, coming back to reality. "Tommy, I don't have words big enough to compliment you."

"Wait till you see the bill." Tommy handed it to her. It was nine thousand dollars.

Dana reached into her purse. "Here is ten thousand for the bill." Handing him another stack, she added, "The ten thousand bonus I promised." Then she reached into her purse one more time. "And ten thousand for your new kid."

Tommy looked at the pile of money in his hands. "Ten thousand for the kid? How did you know Molly was pregnant?"

"Tommy," Dana said, putting her hand on his shoulder. "Why do you think she married you? You didn't think it was your decision, did you? Now make her happy."

Dana got into the Dragon smiling, feeling the wheel and the lower profile. Tommy leaned in the window. "I almost forgot. See the knob? Turn it left, it reduces the flame. Turn it right, and you can get up to ten feet of flames."

"God, if you were not married, I'd take you home. And I don't do men."

Mason replaced Tommy at the window. "I don't think I have ever seen you this excited."

Dana was stoking the wheel, and petting the dash, she put her hand on the stick shift, "Oh, she is just power, pure power." Gunning the engine, she smiled widely, "See you at home. The Dragon and I are going to be busy tonight, I got to see a man about some pot," Dana said as she backed down the driveway and squealed her wheels as she took off. Mason was left standing with a questioning look on her face.

*

Mason parked in her driveway and went straight into Dana's house. "What's this about pot?" She cornered Dana in the hallway. "We don't do pot operations. Just hard drugs." Mason folded her arms, waiting for an explanation.

"We said we were going to hit them hard. They have millions in pot and money at Sal's transfer point. Sal, who runs the territory west of Carlos, he's known for pot. I need to know more about that operation and where to hit them. And I know just the man who can help me."

"You're going back down to Sylvan Hills, aren't you?" Mason asked.

"I got to see the boss. I haven't seen him in years. I'm sure he'll be happy to see me."

"I'm sure." Mason rolled her eyes.

At one ten in the morning, the Dragon rolled out onto the street. Dana drove down to Sylvan Hills and stopped at the corner where she used to see the brothers. It was a different crew on the corner. The Red Bitch had the flames on the Black Dragon dialed down. She stopped at the corner and got out. The Dragon rumbled her impatience.

The Red Bitch walked up to the main man. "Where's the boss?"

He looked the Red Bitch up and down and checked out the Dragon. He had heard lots of stories about the Red Bitch. He knew her reputation, and he knew he had to tell. "He's at club It over on Hamilton and Pine. He owns the place."

She got back into the Dragon. Out the window, she said, "Call him. Tell him to meet me outside."

The Dragon parked on the corner, just outside the door of the club. As the Red Bitch got out, the boss walked out of the club with three of his men just steps behind him.

"Long time no see," he said, walking up to the Red Bitch. She stepped forward and gave him a kiss on the lips, along with a little bite.

"Looks like you're doing okay," the Red Bitch said, looking him in the eyes.

"I'm doing good. I thought you were dead?"

"I am dead. I'm a ghost. I'm the Red Bitch's ghost." She kept her eyes on him.

He looked at the Dragon and then at the Red Bitch. "A real badass ghost. Why are you here? You always have a reason."

"The pot business. You're still in the pot business, right?"

"Ninety percent."

"Ninety percent. What's the other ten percent?" The Red Bitch stepped closer.

"Crystal meth."

She pounded her palm into his forehead not hard enough to hurt.

One of his men stepped up and went to shove her back. In a second, his wrist was broken and used to bloody his nose.

"Back off, you stupid motherfucker; this is the Red Bitch. She touches you. You don't touch her. Get the fuck out of my sight." He turned back to the Red Bitch. "Sorry about that. He's from New York. Dumbass."

She came close to the boss and whispered, "I know the main pot delivery points in Miami, New Orleans, and Richmond. I need to know the biggest transfer point to the west."

She stepped back staring him in the eyes, He leaned forward and whispered in her ear, "You missed Savannah. Upriver. The biggest transfer point to the west is a warehouse in Birmingham." He looked her in the eye and leaned in again. "You're not going to fuck with my supplier, are you?"

"Just the one. Make other arrangements. Pot's going up one hundred percent. I'm going to make you lots of money. What's a good time?"

"Nine, just as they're closing. Friday is always good," he said.

The Red Bitch stepped in and gave him a big, wet kiss. "Pot's okay. But, get rid of that shit meth. That will get you jailed or killed. Watch your ass."

The next morning, Dana came down late for breakfast. "Do I smell pancakes?" she asked, sitting at one end of the table. She always sat in Eve's chair. Christopher's chair was always empty. Handsome was lying next to Alyssa, catching dropped Cheerios.

Dana settled in with her coffee and pancakes. "Do you think Alyssa should be around some kids of her own age? She's four now. All she sees is us and art. Adult clients, maybe."

"Are you thinking that day school near the gallery? The one a block away?" Jody asked.

"Yeah, maybe just two hours a day or so," Dana said.

"Do you think Handsome can stand being away from her that long?" Mason asked, watching Handsome catch Cheerios, not missing a move that Alyssa made.

"I'll set it up. Handsome will get used to it," Jody said, patting Handsome on the head.

After breakfast, Jody settled into cleaning up. Handsome and Alyssa played tag, with Handsome rounding her up and herding her into the library. There was a lot of giggling.

"We got work," Dana said to Mason.

"You guys going to the hideaway?" Jody asked, picking up the syrup and butter off the table.

"Where else?' Mason asked, giving her a kiss and a pat on the butt.

*

"Here's our big hit. It's a warehouse in Birmingham," Dana said, standing in front of the map.

Mason went to her file cabinet. She pulled out a file and laid everything out on the table.

Studying the files for more than a few minutes, Mason nodded and looked up. "It should have millions in pot and probably a million or so in cash. I can't say how much. It says here cash pickup is Wednesday. Sometimes Friday also."

"Tuesday should be a good day to hit them," Dana said.

"You mean in two days? We got plans for Meridian on Tuesday." Mason went back to the map.

"The man says nine o'clock closing time on Friday is a good time," Dana said.

Mason went back to the files. "It says here it's open twenty-four-seven."

"I figured. So, we hit it around seven in the evening, just around dark," Dana said. "If my pot guy is going to send up flags, and I don't think he will, they won't figure Tuesday at seven."

Opening a floor plan, Mason said, "Look here—four loading docks in the back. This is where they drop off the big loads of pot and legitimate cargo. Next to that is a back door with steps. Here are the offices up front. No windows street side, also an iron door and steps, street side."

Dana was following her every word and memorizing the floor plan.

"They have a front drive-up door, and a door beside it. It's for pickups and cars. This is where the smaller dealers or mules pick up their stuff. Two guard booths back here by the loading docks, then one up here by the front drive-up. Probably two guards at that one. This is their weak spot." Mason pointed to the front roll-up door.

"Do you think if I just drove up and honked, they would let me in?" Dana asked.

"I don't know. Maybe." Mason shrugged.

"What about these offices?" Dana pointed.

Mason checked her notes. "Two offices and one bathroom. The front office has windows on the storage side. There is a front counter. There are usually three or four people up front." She read her notes for another minute, "here's something. In the front office, see this safe? Forget it. It's a fake, with just a little cash and books in it. See this back here?" Mason pointed to the back room. "See this door? I bet that's where they keep the real cash. Someone there has got to know how to open it."

"Ok, got it. Now, What about this place in Meridian?" Dana asked, pointing to it on the map.

"Well, we were going to hit it late. We still have time to hit it around maybe one in the morning. Two in one night." Dana smiled. "The Red Bitch's ghost is back. They will never forget us."

"Then what?" Mason wasn't sure about the plan anymore. Not with two in one night. What if the first job doesn't go as planned, what then?

"Then we hit the Jackson Mississippi job as planned on Wednesday night." Dana looked at the map. "Then, as planned, we hit this place in Slidell, east of New Orleans. Have you ever been to New Orleans?"

"Sure. Before I met Jody. Wild place," Mason said.

"I have never been there," Dana said, then she asked for the plans for Slidell.

*

Tuesday was like every other Tuesday. Dana picked up lunch at the Mexican restaurant. She handed her credit card to the girl at the bar. They made small talk. When lunch came, she thanked the waitress and gave her a big tip.

It had entered Dana's head that someone might be looking at the old Red Bitch killings in Atlanta. She didn't want to be tied to them.

At two that afternoon, Mason pulled up on the street behind the gallery. Dana kissed Alyssa and patted Handsome on the head, telling him to watch over them. A kiss and a hug for Jody, and she slipped out the back door. Standing on the trash can, she jumped over the fence and walked down the driveway of the condo behind the gallery. Knocking on the trailer, she signaled Mason she was getting into the trailer.

Dana had decided to ghost up the Red Bitch. Instead of the red wig and curls, she frizzed it up with pigtails coming out of the frizz.

She used a greasy white foundation on her face and neck, all the way down to her pushed-up cleavage. She used black eye shadow all around her eyes, so they looked sunken, and bright red lipstick that was overdone and bleeding around the edges. She used a little brush and had little red lines running down from the ends of her lips. She rubbed red lipstick into her teeth, so it looked like blood or meat between her teeth.

Dana looked at herself in the mirror. "Oh, I got to do this at least once," she said aloud. Then she said, "Woo!"

Mason dropped the ramp on a side street in the industrial section of Birmingham. She then went a few blocks to a new and used trailer sales yard. That was, in fact, the name of the place, New and Used Trailer Sales. She parked in the yard, behind the trailers on the curbside. No one was around, and she blended right in.

The Dragon rolled up to the door a little past seven. Dana tapped the horn. One of the guards looks out the side door. Dana made a gesture with her hands out, saying, "What? Come on."

He raised the warehouse door. The Red Bitch turned the fire knob on full and hit the gas. The guard standing in front of her with his automatic rifle had no chance to use it. It went flying out of his hands as the Dragon hit him, catching him between the Dragons headlights. His hands were on the hood and his heels dragging under the Dragon. She moved over to the second lane, heading for the first guard booth in the back.

Fire was blowing ten feet out each side, setting everything on fire. She hit the guard booth, killing the guy on the hood and crippling the guard in the booth. As she backed off, the dead guard fell to the floor. The guard in the second booth stepped out, fired a few shots, and ducked back into the booth as the Dragon came at him. She paused at the second guard booth and revved the engine. The next booth was consumed in flames. Squealing wheels turned down the next aisle as she hit the high beams. The ninety-million candle power high beams blinded the guard even before she crashed through the glass wall of the front office at the other end of the aisle. The guards at the counter were firing their AK-47s blind.

The Dragon backed off and turned off the high beams. The guards were still blinded as the Red Bitch came up the side. She pushed the one man's gun toward the other. The other man died from a dozen bullets. She swung her sword once and the first man's head landed on the counter and rolled off behind it. There were two people hiding behind the counter. One tried to push the head away.

"Hi, all. Who's the boss?" the Red Bitch asked. They pointed at each other. "You sure? Because I'm going to let the boss live." She laughed in a ghostly way. They looked at each other. "Sorry, Helen. I'm the boss," the man said.

"Okay boss. Open the safe." The man went to the big safe up front. "Not that one." She laughed again and signaled them into the other office. There was a door with a men's sign on it. "That safe." She pointed to the door.

"Sorry, Frank," Helen said, getting up and opening the safe.

"I smell pot. Do you smell pot burning?" the Red Bitch asked them, sniffing the air. "Is that what pot smells like when it's burning?"

They nodded their heads yes.

"You, Frank, is it? Please get that trash can. The big one. Now, empty it out and bring it here." She laughed again. "You're not laughing. Don't you think this is funny?"

They both faked a laugh.

"Fill up the trash can with the money. Hundreds first, please." They worked quickly with sideways glances at the Red Bitch's ghost.

When it was overflowing, the Red Bitch looked into the trash can. "Wow. Now, I need you two to take it out and load it into the Dragon."

When it was loaded into the passenger seat, she stood them over by the burning bales of pot. "Helen, you were a good girl. In fact, you were both good. Except for Frank. You know you lied to me. I'm going to have to slap your wrist so you will remember to always be honest. Now hold out your hand."

He reluctantly held out his hand. A half a second later, his right hand fell to the floor.

The Red Bitch took a moment, as she got into the Dragon, to look at the burning warehouse. "Now that's good work, girl," she said, patting the Dragon's dashboard.

The other guard in the front booth had been set on fire. He rolled outside as the Dragon entered the warehouse. Tearing off his burning shirt and flaming pants, in just his boots and tightie-whities, he got to his car as the Dragon left the building.

He tried to follow them but was more than a block back. The Red Bitch hit the high beam in the back, blinding him. He hit a parked car a block from the trailer sales lot.

The Dragon pulled into the trailer and Mason turned onto the street heading for the interstate. In her rearview mirror, she could see smoke from the burning warehouse pouring across the street. She could just make out the crashed car.

The Red Bitch called Mason. "Find a quiet spot to pull over. We got some adjustments to do and the Dragon has to turn around."

"I'll let you know," Mason answered back. About two hours later, she pulled behind a supermarket and dropped the ramp so she could go back to the Dragon. "What the hell!" she said on seeing the Red Bitch's ghost.

"Oh, forgot. I decided to ghost it up. Boo," she said.

"Damn, you're one scary bitch," Mason said as she was led around to the passenger side door. "What's this?" she asked.

"Forty gallons of mostly hundred-dollar bills. Don't just stand there. Help me get it into the trailer."

"How much do you think it is?" Mason asked, struggling with her side of the trash can.

"A couple million, maybe more. I have no idea. More, I'm sure." As it was dragged into the trailer.

"Where are we going to put it?" Mason asked once inside the trailer.

"Bathroom. Hurry, we got an appointment in Meriden."

*

At two in the morning, Mason dropped the ramp in downtown Meriden. The Red Bitch drove the three blocks to Mama's Pizza Parlor. She rammed into the front of the pizza parlor, then backed off a few feet. As she ran to the back of the kitchen, she saw three people run out the back door, into the alley.

"All righty then," she said. The coke had been cut and packed into individual bags, then packed into two larger plastic bags. She opened the brown paper bag sitting on the table. It had a stack of money in it. "Well, that was easy," she said.

"Oh candles, perfect." She took one off the shelf and lit it, leaving it on the table. On her way out, she cut the gas line to the pizza oven. "So long," she said to the empty room.

In the Dragon, she headed down the street and around the corner to the alley in back. She saw the three people running down the alley toward her. The Dragon revved up but only gave off a little fire as she raced down the alley. They saw her and turned and ran the other way. The Dragon passed them up, then she flipped the switch for the forty-five-million candle power rear high beam. All they saw was the Dragon disappear into a bright light. That's what they told Sal.

36. THE GOLDEN GUN

"Honey, I'm stone cold exhausted. You must be over the top dead," Dana said into her flip phone.

"Oh, I'm okay. I got my eyes taped open."

"Find a place. We got to get some sleep."

Mason didn't answer.

"Mom, you heard me. Didn't you?" Dana called Mason mom when she needed her attention or as a way of saying. "Alright, already." Then mom had two syllables.

Mason still didn't answer. Then Dana felt the truck slow downturn and come to a stop. A minute later the door of the trailer opened.

"I was parking the damn truck. We're at a rest stop," Mason said as she poured herself into a seat at the table. Looking up at Dana, said, "girl, you got to get that white shit off your neck and chest."

"I would, but the bathroom is full of money," Dana said, a little loud and a lot irritated.

Mason turned her head, then turned back. "We're both tired and grumpy. Screw it. Let's just get some sleep. You can clean that shit off tomorrow." Mason kicked off her shoes. By the time she had gotten undressed and, in her nightie, Dana was already asleep.

*

The next morning, Mason woke up to the smell of coffee. Dana had warmed up some water on the small stove and had wiped off the white foundation and was working on the red between her teeth.

As Mason jumped down from the bed, Dana handed her a cup of coffee, saying, "Sorry about last night."

"No problem. We were both exhausted." After a few sips, Mason set her cup down on the counter and opened the bathroom door. For the first time, she realized just how much money was in there. "Wow, that's a whole lot of moolah." She picked up a couple bundles of cash, holding up one pack. "this is ten thousand dollars." She read the band. "Doesn't seem that big."

"Think of a ream of paper. That's five hundred sheets of paper. A stack of hundreds that high would be fifty thousand dollars. In the space of one ream of paper, the three sets of bills that's a hundred fifty thousand dollars. A box of ten reams would be—"

Mason held up her hand. "One-point-five million. This has got to be ten million in there." Looking up at Dana in amazement, "At least." Mason put the money back. "What are we going to do with it?"

"Buy a Picasso. I don't know; we'll figure it out. I do know this: Sal is pissed right now." Dana sipped her own coffee.

Sitting at the table, Mason looked up. "Slidell tonight?"

Dana let out a lot of air. "How about tomorrow?"

Mason went over her notes in her head. "That won't work."

"Oh," Dana said, looking for her energy. She thought it must be hiding in the trailer somewhere.

"But," Mason said, looking up. "The pharmacy could be a target. It's a distribution point for illegal bootlegged or foreign manufactured drugs. The drugs were not FDA approved but Sal sell's them to legitimate pharmacies and drug stores as FDA approved. It was a profitable scam." Mason looked up, "We never really discussed it as a target. Still, it's Sal's baby. It's as close to a legitimate business as he has ever come. Plus, he uses it to laundry money."

Mason was going from memory. "It's not guarded like the drug houses, just an alarm system most of the time. Piece of cake. Besides, it's just east of Slidell just over the bridge."

"What are we going to get out of it? Besides some aspirin," Dana asked, she looked up at Mason. "You have been to New Orleans, right?

"I told you. Yes, before I met Jody. Sorry, just a little edgy yet," Mason said.

"Let's go!" Dana said, holding her coffee cup up to Mason.

Mason took a deep breath. "Why not?" They clinked cups.

*

They stopped around noon for breakfast at a Waffle House. Over breakfast, Mason quietly laid out the details of the pharmacy, sketching on napkins. All from memory.

When they got to New Orleans, they parked the truck and trailer on the roof of the multistory parking garage at the airport. They packed overnight bags, picked up a bundle of cash, and went down to the luggage area and waited in line for a cab.

They had the cab drop them off on Canal Street, right in front of Canal place, the multistory shopping center.

As soon as they got out of the cab, Dana grabbed Mason's hand. "Come on." She pulled her into the mall behind her. "Time to slut up."

"Oh no. I'm too old for that," Mason said pulling away.

"Mom, just this once." Dana put her hands together and begged.

"Oh." Mason rolled her eyes and allowed herself to be dragged into the mall.

They came out the other side in stilettos, miniskirts, expensive blouses, and new hairdos. They were carrying several bags each.

"How do you walk in these things," Mason asked, struggling to stay upright.

"Funny, I asked Jess the same thing. In your case, walk on your toes," Dana giggled. They ducked into one of the cabs waiting online. "Where to?" the cabbie asked.

Dana and Mason looked at each other with blank expressions on their faces. "Bourbon Street. A Bourbon Street hotel," Mason finally said.

The cabbie put one hand on the steering wheel and looked at them in the rearview mirror. "Which one?"

"Oh, you pick," Mason said.

The driver took them to the furthest hotel on Bourbon Street but still only one block from the action. He dropped them off at Lafitte's Guesthouse.

"We only have one room left, ladies. It's the attic room," said the guy behind a table that served as a desk.

"We're not addicts!" Dana quickly said.

"Funny, Dana," Mason said.

"Ladies, you have to walk up the last flight of stairs," he said with a little smile.

The room was large, with two dormer windows. They could see over the top of New Orleans, all the way down to the Mississippi River and the bank on the other side. It had turn of the century furnishings: Two old-fashioned chairs and a small love sofa, and vintage throw rugs on an old worn wood floor. It was perfect.

When they hit the streets, they were quite a sight. In their stilettos, they both were well over six foot six. Their miniskirts showed impossibly long legs. They got whistles and stares almost as soon as they stepped out onto Bourbon Street.

They stopped at the first bar with live music. "What will you two lovely ladies be having?" the bartender asked.

Dana again looked to Mason for an answer. "Hurricanes," Mason ordered.

"Hey, ladies. Looking good," a middle-aged man said, walking up to the bar and looking them up and down. "What are you doing tonight?"

"Leaving," Mason said, turning to the bartender. "Go cups, please."

A minute later, Mason was leading Dana out of the bar by her hand. They each had a drink in the other hand.

"You can do this? Take your drink on the street?" Dana asked.

Mason turned to her. "Honey, see that stand over there on the corner? They are selling Hurricanes. Now act like you know what you're doing."

"Yes, Mom," Dana said.

"Don't call me Mom tonight." Mason shook a finger in her face.

"Yes, ma'am," Dana smirked. Mason looked up and rolled her eyes.

The next bar they went into had a loud jazz band on a stage across from the bar. They walked up to the bar and ordered more Hurricanes. Leaning against the bar, their butts were quite a sexy sight.

"Girls, sweet girls. How are you doing tonight?" one of the three guys said, approaching them.

Mason turned around and put her elbows on the bar. She stuck out her breasts. Dana watched Mason, then copied her moves. "Just fine," Mason said, looking them up and down. She made them in their early thirties, probably here for a conference. She made it obvious she was looking them over.

"Can we buy you girls a drink?" another asked.

Holding up her full glass. "Got 'em."

"Well then, want to party?" the third guy asked.

“Sure, where?” Mason said.

The guys looked at one another. One finally said, “Well, we could start here.”

Mason gave Dana a kiss on the lips. "Sorry, guys. We were just leaving. Have fun with each other." With that, she took Dana's hand and led her out of the bar.

Dana looked over her shoulder as she trotted out of the bar behind Mason. “Have fun. We will.” Dana said.

When they got onto the street, they started laughing. "They actually thought we were lesbians," Dana said.

“We are.” Mason cracked up again. “Just not with each other.”

"Hungry?" Mason asked as she led Dana into a restaurant, finding two seats at the bar. "A dozen oysters on the half shell please." She said to Dana, "You're going to love these." Then back to the bartender, she said, "and a bottle of Dom.”

“What's Dom?” Dana asked.

“The finest Champagne in the world. We can afford it tonight.” Mason turned as the oysters were placed in front of them.

“What exactly are these?” Dana asked.

“Live oysters. You'll love them. Just put a little of this sauce on them and suck them out of their shell.” Mason demonstrated.

Dana reluctantly followed suit. Her eyes opened wide. "That's great. Tastes like the ocean." She went for another oyster. The tray was soon empty.

The Dom was brought in a silver ice bucket. The bartender popped it and poured each a tall, thin glass full, letting the bubbles settle before pouring some more.

“Gator bites.” Mason presented the next plate.

"Don't tell me," Dana said as she drove in.

The next morning, Mason pulled Dana out of bed and pushed her toward the bathroom. "Clean up."

A few minutes later, Dana stuck her head around the corner with her toothbrush sticking out of her mouth. "My tongue is red."

"That just proves you drank Hurricanes. Now get ready," Mason laughed.

The put on their new slut outfits and headed out. They passed a playground covered in laughing and screaming grade school kids. When they got to Jackson Square, Dana was drawn to the giant bronze statue of Andrew Jackson on a horse. It dominated the park. "Wow," Dana said. "Nothing like that in Atlanta."

She took more than a casual interest in the artists who had positioned themselves along a very wide sidewalk around the square. Some artists had their easels set up, offering to draw your portrait.

Mason pointed. "There that's Café Du Monde. Breakfast!"

From their table, they could leisurely enjoy a black man in a suit who was playing jazz on sax for change. The waiter soon set two cups of coffee on their table. "This is chicory café au lait. You'll love it," Mason said, sipping the frothy drink.

A few minutes later, the waiter returned with a plate of beignets, all covered in powdered sugar. "Donuts?" Dana asked.

"Beignets. Eat them while they're warm," Mason said as she took one off the top.

They wandered down Charters Street, looking in the windows and dropping in when they saw something interesting. The first art gallery they saw, Dana dived in, asking questions and having the attendant take notes for her. Mason was bored in fifteen minutes. An hour later,

Mason dragged Dana out. "This is not that kind of business trip. No more art galleries."

Dana stuck out her bottom lip.

They stopped at several vintage jewelry shops. More than a few pieces ended up on their fingers, wrists, and necks.

A few more doors down, they found a kid's shop. They both bought lots of toys for Alyssa. Dana walked out with her bag of toys and a skateboard under her arm. "You're not giving that to Alyssa, are you?" Mason asked.

"Hell no. She'd knock out her front teeth the first day. It's for me," Dana said, turning her head up.

"Yeah, I can see you going down Bourbon Street on that in your heels." Mason tapped her arm. "Let's drop all this stuff off and get an early dinner."

They passed a strip club on their way to dinner. The sleazy guy trying to talk guys into the club with fast talk and flyers looked at them as they walked by. "Girls, girls," he called to them. Dana stopped and looked at him. "Want some work?" he asked.

Mason just grabbed Dana by the arm and brought her down the street. "This is the court of the two sisters. Great Cajun food. Nice place." She stopped at the maître d' stand and asked for a table.

They were back at Lafitte's Guest House by six. After a few hours of sleep and a fresh shower, they packed up and slipped out before eleven.

"I think you should do that ghost bit again tonight," Mason said, packing the toys into the trailer. "How long does it take?"

"To put on or take off?" Dana asked.

"Good point,"

After Dana finished dressing, Mason said, "You know, that's really scary."

Dana turned and, with her claws in the air, she made an angry cat sound.

"Stay with *boo*," Mason laughed and signaled her over to the table. She had written down the details of the target again.

Dana studied them again. "Can't burn it. Sprinklers. Can't flood it. Everything is in plastic. Can't blow it up. No gas lines. Nothing we can take." She took a deep breath. "Time for the big bang."

She got up and went to the sink. Opening the doors under it, she got down on her knees and reached into the very back and pulled out a package.

"What the hell is that?" Mason never knew it was there.

"It's Jess a present. Get it? Jess a present."

"I get it. Ha Ha. Now, what is it?" Mason reached for the package.

Dana turned away, then set it on the table. "Don't touch. It's C4 with a timer. Jess gave it to me." Dana unfolded the package and presented it to Mason.

Mason examined it. "Why didn't you tell me?"

"I can't tell you all my secrets. Actually, I just did. Anyway, I figured strapped to one of those big propane cylinders up front, it would make an effective anti-pharmacy drug." Dana started for the door.

"Enough. We can't have a ghost wandering around the airport. I'll get the cylinder. It's not Halloween, and you might scare someone," Mason, said getting up. As she got to the door, she turned and said, "besides me."

Dana duck taped the C4 to the tank. "This is the full one?" she asked, looking up.

"Please," Mason said, sarcastically.

Dana then took the skateboard and taped the tank to the skateboard and attached one of Handsome's leashes to the tank.

"You were planning this all along, weren't you?" Mason asked, looking at the setup. "Just when did you figure this out?"

"Yesterday at the Waffle House; it kind of came to me," Dana said, shrugging.

"Now you're really scaring me." Mason looked over at Dana with a new understanding of her mind and thought, *I keep underestimating her. I have from the very start. She figures things out and waits for the right time; it might be years or just minutes. I really wonder what's next?*

Dana pulled the bomb around the trailer and made a few little adjustments. "Just what Dr. Jekyll ordered. Help me get into the Dragon."

*

Dana parked in front of the target. It was in a quiet industrial area, just a few trucks and cars were parked around several of the individual buildings. She unloaded the tank and pulled it up to the door, which was unlocked.

She Dana dropped the leash. Her shoto was tucked into the back of her bra strap. She tilted it so it was handy. *I guess what I'll do is just open the door and run in and see what I'm facing,* she thought as she quietly opened the door.

She was faced by two large men. One had already reached for his gun. The other was just turning to see the Red Bitch. She took two steps and flew into the air, so she was parallel to the ground. The thumbs on both of her hands went into the eyes of the guy pulling the gun. Her heel went into the other guy's throat. The force threw the two men onto their backs on the floor. She death chopped the now blind guy's neck. He would be dead in a minute or so, she thought.

As she got up, she put her weight on her heel, in the other thug's neck, driving it all the way to his neck bone. "Dead on arrival," she said, looking up to see a third man standing just behind them. A frail old man. The Red Bitch's ghost walked toward him. "You must be Sal. What are you doing here so late?"

"You're dead. Everyone said you're dead." Sal tried to stand still but took a step back anyway.

"Sal. My friend. Carlos says you're a nice guy. He said, however, that you still owe him money. That money I took the other day, that was Carlos's money. You were just holding it for him. And he said to thank you." The Red Bitch closed the gap.

Sal's hand was sliding behind his back.

"Sal, honey. Were you going to give me your gun? Is that what you're doing?" She stepped to within inches of his face.

Sal pulled out his gun. He didn't point it at her.

"Oh, thank you, and my God, is that what I think it is? A gold-plated nine-millimeter?" The Red Bitch took the gun out of his hand. "Thank you so much." She took a step back. "By the way, what are you doing here at this time of night? You should be home in bed."

"Inventory," Sal said, both hands at his side.

"Inventory. Of what? Money?" the Red Bitch asked.

"No, product." Sal waved his arms around the store, "Because of you, you fucking Red Bitch, I have to move product to pay the bills.".

She looked around at some of the boxes piled up around the place. "Mexico, Argentina, Egypt, India, Uruguay, and is this Vietnam? My, you have some, shall we say, unusual suppliers."

The Red Bitch turned to walk to the door. "You know I've been nothing but nice to you," she said, turning around, holding up the gun. "I even thanked you for your present, and you called me names. Not the Red Bitch part, the fucking part. Not very nice." She stepped through the door.

Sal took a deep breath and relaxed a bit—until she came back in, pulling her skateboard.

"Sal. Regardless. You did give me a nice present. The ghost with the golden gun. Nice title for a movie, don't you think?" The Red Bitch again held up the gun. Then she pushed a button on the timer and tipped the tank over onto its side. "So, I'm going to return the favor. My guess is you got forty-five seconds to get out of the building."

She then quickly walked out and got in the Dagon. She took off, leaving twenty feet of rubber. She could see Sal in her rearview mirror. He was standing in front of the building, shaking his fist at her when the building exploded: first one blast, then a bigger one a microsecond later.

Dana crossed over to the east side of Lake Pontchartrain. Pulling off, she found Mason and backed into the trailer. The ramp came up as Mason started back to Interstate 10. She was headed eastward and homeward bound.

Mason called Dana. "Wow. That was something else. I bet they saw it from Lafayette to Flora-Bama. Very impressive."

"A way bigger explosion than I thought. I hope Sal's okay," Dana said into the cell phone.

"We can be home by six or seven this morning if I drive straight through." Mason was anxious to get home. New Orleans, no matter how much fun, did bring back memories of a wilder life she would rather forget.

"Are you sure you want to do that?" Dana asked.

"When I'm on these trips, I'm like a bat. I sleep during the day and fly at night."

"Okay then, when you stop for gas, we'll get breakfast. By the way, what kind of bat are you? Do you eat insects or fruit?" Dana giggled.

37. THAT'S A LOT OF MONEY

Three hours later, it was only four in the morning. Mason said over eggs and coffee, "Honey, you have a little white under your ear and a little here on your chest." She pointed. Dana rubbed at it with her napkin.

"Oh, by the way, do you want this?" Dana put the gold plated 9-mm on the table. "Sal gave it to me."

"What are you doing?" Mason was looking around and pushing it back into Dana's lap.

"Well, do you?" Dana asked again.

"No. I got my own guns," Mason answered.

"Not a gold one like this." Dana started to pull it up again.

"Dana! No!"

"Okay. I offered." Dana finished her eggs and bacon. Mason shook her head. Dana wafted down her last piece of toast, then looked at Mason over the top of her coffee.

"It's started. Sal is broke. Why else would he be at the pharmacy late at night? Sal told me he was seeing what he could move quickly. He needs to do something. It probably takes time to dip into his foreign accounts. Willie and the other guy, what's his name, are almost as pissed as Sal."

Mason ate slower, and she picked up her coffee cup. They looked at each other over the tops of their coffee. "That was the point, right?" Mason asked.

"Right. I need to go to Florida and find out what's happening."

"When?" Mason picked up her last piece of toast.

"Sunday. I guess late Sunday afternoon." Dana drained her cup. "I'll ride upfront with you. We'll figure this out." Then Dana said with a smirk, "You got this?"

"Sure," Mason said, signaling the waitress. "Waitress, two large coffees to go please." She dropped a hundred on the table. "Keep the change."

The waitress looked down at the bill. "Are you sure? That's a hundred-dollar bill. Your bill is only about twenty dollars."

"That's the smallest I have. I hate change," Mason said, draining her coffee.

At the counter, the waitress had four cups of coffee waiting and two egg sandwiches. "Just in case you get hungry. And thank you so much."

"No problem." Mason reached over and pulled Dana's blouse over the gun in the back of her pants.

In the truck, Dana was grinning from ear to ear. "New Orleans was a ball. I still can't get over the look on the faces of the waiters when you dropped a grand on them and said keep the change."

"It wasn't all tip. And I only dropped a grand on the bartender at the oyster place and the waitress at The Court of the Two Sisters. I just said keep the change." Mason was now giggling. "I thought that the waiter at the oyster place was going to kiss me."

"He would have if he could have gotten to you. Don't forget you dropped a hundred on each of the bartenders." Dana pointed at her. "You are so generous. Oh, and don't forget Café Du Monde. Five hundred to the waiter and five hundred to that sax player. That was another grand."

"And you tipped the maid a grand. Of course, she deserved it with the mess you left." Mason was laughing.

A bit later Dana brought up the plan again. Things were changing. Even little changes meant having to go over the plan again and make whatever adjustments they needed.

They pulled into Mason's driveway, having dropped the truck and trailer off at the storage yard. It was near ten in the morning. As they came through Dana's front door, they were met first by Handsome, then Alyssa, and close behind was Jody. Dana dropped her bag on the floor and picked up Alyssa, giving her a big kiss and hug.

"You're just in time for breakfast. I know you like eggs, bacon, and toast."

"Love them," Mason said, following Jody into the kitchen, mouthing to Dana, "Not again."

At breakfast, Dana brought up what Mason was thinking. "I'm sorry, but we're dead tired. We need to get some sleep. Then we still have a lot of work to do. I know you've had Alyssa all week but—"

"No. No problem at all; we have a regular routine. Besides, Handsome watches Alyssa most of the time. Really, no problem. So, when will I see you? Before five, I hope?" Jody put up her hand. "No problem. I don't know what I was thinking. Never mind. Just have dinner ready."

*

Just after three, Dana was making coffee in Mason's kitchen. In about five minutes, Mason followed the smell down to the kitchen.

"You look like hell," Dana said, setting a cup of coffee in front of her. "your hair is a mess, your eyes are red, and when did you get those wrinkles." In return, she got an indiscernible grunt.

"Okay, eggs?" Dana asked.

Mason barely managed a middle finger.

Dana didn't say a word for a half an hour. She thought about running off at the mouth about nothing at all. She didn't, but she smiled at the thought.

A half an hour later, Mason spoke up. "What the hell are we going to do with all that money? More coffee please." She held up her cup.

"I have some ideas. First, we figure out how much money we scored. When you recover, we'll go back to the trailer. What am I saying? We'll do it tomorrow. You're in no shape to count," Dana said, leaning back in her chair. "And quite frankly, neither am I. "

"Okay, I'll just go up and shower," Mason said, placing both hands on the table, pushing to get up. She sat right back down. "In a minute." A cup of coffee later, she pushed herself away from the table and struggled into an upright position. "I'll be back in a while," she said, slowly heading for the stairs.

Dana dialed Jess. "Hi, you remember me?"

"Who?" Jess said, recognizing Dana's voice right off.

"You know. We met at that club, Snap Trap. About three weeks ago."

"No. Who are you?" Jess was smiling as she played along.

"The blond. Remember. Oh, come on, you could not have forgotten that night." Dana was hoping someone was listening in.

"Blond. Sorry. Who again?" It was all Jess could do from laughing into the phone.

"The tall blond. Who did…? Oh, never mind." Dana had to hold the phone away to keep from giggling into it.

"Oh, yeah. I remember now. Yeah, I remember." Jess was biting her lip to keep from laughing.

"Well, I'm going to be back in town. Maybe Sunday night. Same place, same time?" Dana put her hand across her mouth to keep from laughing.

"Sure, whatever," Jess said, waiting for the code word.

"Okay, then. It's a go. See you there."

"No problem. Later." Jess gave her the code word back. She hung up the phone. "God, I'm so ready," she said to herself.

*

"Look at that. I can get to the gallery around five. I'll keep Alyssa," Dana said as Mason come downstairs, looking much more alive. "And send Jody home. Please, can you and Jody make a home-cooked meal? I really miss that."

"Jody cooks. I'm the sous-chef. I just cut things up," Mason said.

"So do I," Dana laughed.

*

"Are you feeling better today?" Dana asked Mason as they got into Mason's car the next day.

"You can count on it." Mason faked a laugh. "See, I can be funny too." She said getting out of the car, heading for the trailer.

Dana pulled the trash can out of the bathroom in the trailer and slid it across the floor to the table. She had brought several large trash bags and boxes with her from home, plus a six pack of Coke.

"What we're going to do is make this look as big a pile as possible," Dana said, sitting down and handing Mason a Coke. "Take the band off the money and put it in the big black trash bags. Break them up, even wad them up. Put the bands over here." She pointed to a small box at the other end of the table.

"Try and get the fifty-dollar bills first."

They sipped their Cokes and talked about Alyssa, the gallery, and maybe taking a vacation. When the trash bag was almost full and the trash can half full, Dana got up and picked up the bag. "We need to double bag this. Give me a hand. Oh, where is the crack?"

Mason got up. Lifting the bench seat, she got out the two bags of crack. "Empty the bags into the trash bag."

Dana helped. She twisted the top of the bag. "I think I can handle this. I just have to carry it like Santa Claus," she said, leaning forward and countering the weight of the bag.

"Let's count up the bands," Dana said, each reaching in and grabbing a handful of money bands. They counted them up and put the amounts on a notepad. When they were finished, Mason added up the total. "Wow, two million, two hundred thousand. That's some Christmas stocking."

Mason looked sideways at Dana. "Okay, what's your plan?"

"I'm going to give this to Carlos. I'm not sure he'll appreciate it, though."

"That's some present. Are you sure Carlos isn't going to appreciate this pile of money?" Mason asked.

"Oh, I'm sure," Dana smiled.

"You're not going to tell me, are you?" Mason was not smiling.

"Don't forget the crack. He's getting that also." Dana picked up one of the big boxes and put it on the table.

"Tell me about your plan before you give this present to Carlos." Mason put her hands together. "Please."

Dana just smiled. "Count out what's left of the money and put it in the boxes. Don't unwrap them and stack them so we can get as much in as possible."

There was no conversation during this count, which went much quicker. Then Mason totaled the amount in the three boxes. She looked up, "Three million, two hundred and seventy thousand. Nice week's work."

"We'll put the plastic bag here, it in the back of the Dragon so it won't be in the way," Dana said.

The boxes were carried out and put in the trunk of Mason's car.

"What am I going to do with them?" Mason asked.

"Just put them on the shelf in the back of your garage. Mark the boxes *Winter Clothes*." Dana smiled.

Sunday evening at nine, Dana was sitting at the bar in Miami. The bartender came over. “You're Irish and soda, right?” he said, looking at her nipples showing through her white tank top. He had already mixed the drink and dropped it in front of her.

Dana dropped a twenty on the bar. “Don't forget my change. Your tip was looking at my nipples." She turned and put her elbows on the bar, sticking out her chest as Mason taught her.

In no time, a short, middle-aged woman in jeans and a short-sleeved blue men's shirt walked up to her. "Buy you a drink?"

“Got one.” Dana held up her drink.

“I'll buy you another one,” she said with a smile.

Dana just smiled as she watched Jess walk up behind her. Jess tapped the woman on the shoulder. "Mary. How are you doing? By the way, this sweet piece of ass is mine."

"Hi, Jess. It's Sunday. You're not usually here Sunday.” She turned and looked Dana up and down. “Want to share?”

“Her? Are you kidding me? I have to tie her down just to keep her from killing me. I'm not giving that ass up.”

Two hours later, they were sitting in Dana's Holiday Inn room. They had a bottle of Irish sitting on the round table between them and they were each sipping a glass of Irish neat.

“It's moving. What I hear from my sources is Sal has been given two weeks to come up with the money.” Jess was talking her usual speed, but her words were a little sloppy.

“Your sources?” Dana leaned forward. “Male or female?”

“Female. And for your information, she's fat and married.”

"When has that stopped you?" Dana splashed a little more Irish into each of their glasses.

"Dana! Stop! She's straight. She doesn't like her boss any more than I like mine. She's on the floor below me. We've got a connection. A friend connection, right!"

"I'm just giving you a hard time." Dana sat back. "Have sex with anyone you like. Just leave enough for me. Now go on."

"You're such a hard-ass bitch. I like you better as a goddamn lipstick lesbian."

"Hey, this was your idea. I'm just playing the part." Dana kicked Jess' shins with her bare feet.

"Sal's been calling Grandpa for help. Grandpa is not taking his calls. It's driving Sal crazy. The other two bosses are calling, and Grandpa is taking their calls. The guess is Grandpa is holding back to get a bigger piece of Sal's business. Maybe trying to get some of that offshore money." Jess took a sip of her drink. "You know your nipples are driving me crazy."

"Does this help?" Dana took off her tank top and threw it at Jess. "Now go on."

"Good Lord, help me," Jess said, looking to heaven. "The word is Grandpa is going to cut them loose to take what they can from Carlos."

Dana stood up and unbuckled her belt and slid out of her pants. Sitting down, she crossed her long legs and took another sip of her Irish. "When?"

"I don't know. A week, a month. But when it happens, it's going to happen fast, like all at once. That's when I make my move, on the same day. Like you said, at four o'clock. Maximum news coverage."

"Remember," Dana started.

"Yes, I know. Carlos is yours. No one will be near Star Isle till the next morning. Now, can I help you out of your panties?"

38. VACATION

"Mason, remember that vacation I promised you?" Dana called her the next evening.

"Yes," It was a very cautious, "yes."

"Well, it starts tomorrow. There's a trailer park in Hollywood. It's almost on the intracoastal. It's big, like a lake, but at one end is the intracoastal waterway. I got a slot right on the water," Dana said excitedly.

"I take it this has something to do with Jess," Mason said.

"Yes. Well, with what she told me. I got it for a month."

"A month," Mason said.

But Dana ran right over her. "Wait there's more."

"More?"

"Oh, yes, and this is sweet. I rented a twenty-nine-foot open speed boat. And get this: it's black, and it's got two big black engines on the back."

"You mean outboards," Mason corrected Dana.

"Yeah, whatever. They are one hundred and fifty horsepower each! I took it out this afternoon, only for about an hour. It's fun and fast," Dana said with even more excitement in her voice.

"Again, a month? What about Jody and Alyssa?"

"Yeah, I've been thinking about them. This probably won't take a month. My guess is about two weeks. But, then again, it could be a month. So." Dana measured her words.

"So?"

"So, I was thinking, if we like it, we could buy a real trailer and a boat. Take our vacations down here. Alyssa would love it." Dana was cautious with her words.

"I see. What about now?"

"Well, you need to explain to Jody," Dana said.

"I need to explain!"

"Well, I can't really talk to Jody. I'll talk to Alyssa." Dana had hope in her voice.

"You're damn right you will." Mason paused. "At most a month?"

"At most."

"We will have to get Alyssa into that preschool, we talked about. It's not fair to Jody. I know she loves her deeply, but she needs a break. She can't keep running the gallery and constantly taking care of Alyssa." Mason said.

"Can you do it tomorrow?" Dana asked timidly.

"Sure. Alyssa wants to talk to you."

"Yes, but one more thing." Dana was even more timid. "Can you pack up some of my clothes and makeup and load them into the trailer?

"Sure. Okay." Then Mason could not hold it back anymore. "Bitch."

"And just one more thing." Dana was wincing. "The gold gun. It's between my mattresses. Could you bring that also?"

"Yes, mistress. Would mistress like anything else?" Mason paused. Dana was silent. "Then I'll get Alyssa."

Alyssa had the talk with her mother and aunt about growing up and meeting new kids her age. "Why?" and "Do I have to?" she pleaded more than once. Finally, she gave a reluctant okay. Tuesday morning, Jody, Mason, and Handsome escorted Alyssa the two blocks to the daycare center. She held tight to Handsome's fur when they walked into the building.

"Really, she's in good hands. She will find lots of friends her age here. It's going to be okay," the director said. She reached out her hand to Alyssa, wiggling her fingers for her to come. Alyssa reluctantly let go of Handsome's fur and took her hand. The director turned and began to walk Alyssa down to the playroom. Mason and Jody, with Handsome walking behind them, began to leave, but Handsome jerked his leash and broke free. He ran to Alyssa and gave her a lick on the face. She wrapped her arms around Handsome's neck and gave him a kiss. "I'm going to be okay. Now go to auntie." She gently turned Handsome away.

He looked back and returned to Jody and Mason. Jody reached over and unclipped his leash. He walked between them back to the gallery.

At five that afternoon, Jody brought Handsome back to collect Alyssa. As the kids were let out running in all directions, Handsome zeroed in on Alyssa. He ran up to her, giving her a kiss. Alyssa gave Handsome a hug and kiss on the head. Handsome then smelled her up and down to make sure everything was alright.

Within a week, this was a regular schedule. Handsome and Jody walked her to school, and at a quarter to five, Handsome was waiting at the door of the gallery to go pick her up.

"This is a limited edition, Leroy Nieman. He sketched this out at ringside. I understand the original sold for almost two million," Jody was explaining the print to two possible clients. It was a quarter to five and Handsome was waiting at the door. Halfway through her sales pitch, he was scratching at the door.

"In a minute, Handsome," Jody said, turning to the noise. "Settle down."

"To hell with that. I got to go get Alyssa." Handsome though. Just then, the UPS guy opened the door with a large square box containing a painting in one hand and a clipboard under his other arm. Handsome rushed out. Fifteen minutes later, Alyssa opened the door of the gallery, letting Handsome and herself in. She gave Jody a hug and went to her drawing board and crayons.

"Does this happen every day?" one of the clients asked, handing Jody a check. Handsome was just settling down beside her.

"Yes, every day," Jody lied, but this became the truth going forward.

*

Dana was standing at the entrance of the trailer park in the guard shack. "Finally," she said as she stepped out of the guard shack. Right behind her was the seventy-two-year-old gate guard.

"Mason, this is Thomas. He was in the navy. See you later, Thomas." Dana waved as she got in the truck. "You'll never have to get stopped again at this gate as long as Thomas is there," she said to Mason. "There are three others I'll introduce you. But most of the time, it's Thomas."

"When?" Mason's one-word meant, when do we go home?

"Look it, I'm in communication with Jess and now Channel. Every day. When it's on, we'll know it's on."

"Who's Channel?" Mason turned to Dana.

"One of our sources. I had dinner with Channel and her husband last night at the Greek restaurant. Just over there." She pointed. "Well, you can't see it from here. But you can see it from our space."

Dana got out and directed Mason into the trailer space. As Mason got out of the truck, Dana could not wait to show her around the small trailer space, such as it was. "See here, I got a barbecue with charcoal and lighter fluid. I got these chairs. There are so cool and see? They just fold up." She opened one of the aluminum and webbed fabric chairs and sat down. "And they are so comfortable." She pointed to one. Mason opened it up and sat down. "What do you think?"

"I'm thinking ho, ho, home." Mason got up. "But it's not Christmas. All of this is not why I drove most of the night and almost all day. Again. When?"

"It's not up to us right now. We just have to be ready," Dana said, going around to the front of the trailer to unhook it from the truck. "Hey, you got a new propane tank," Dana said as she cranked down the front stand. She was wiping her hand as she came around the trailer. Mason had just finished locking down the back supports.

"Here, plug this in," Mason said as she entered the trailer and threw a power cord to Dana. "I brought everything you asked for. Your clothes, some red jewelry and," Looking directly at Dana, "accessories."

"Thanks. Want to get some dinner? You must be hungry after that drive." Not waiting for an answer, Dana said, "Lock the trailer up and follow me."

Dana led Mason to the last slip at the end of the last dock. "Ta-da," Dana said, showing Mason a sleek, twenty-nine-foot go-fast boat. She jumped into the boat, and in a nook next to the wheel were the keys. As Dana turned the keys, the outboards jumped to life.

"Well, don't just stand there. Cast off and jump in."

Mason looked sideways with her arms folded under her breasts. Then she looked back at Dana. "You don't know how much it hurts me to say this. Yes, captain." She then un-cleated each of the four lines securing the boat to the dock and jumped in, taking her place in the seat across from Dana.

As they headed out to the Intracoastal, Dana explained, "That's the restaurant we went to last night. Now, there are places we can go fast but other places that are marked *No Wake*, we got to just go slow."

"Yes, it's slow going until we get just north of Hullover Cut. Then we can go fast until"—The light went off in Mason's head. She looked at Dana—"until we get to Star Island." She punched Dana in the arm. "You bitch. Why didn't you tell me?"

"Why didn't you tell me you knew so much about navigation?" Dana smiled, rubbing her arm.

"I had a life before you and Jody. And how did you figure this out?" Mason asked.

"I had charts. Anybody can read charts." Dana was smirking.

Mason settled back and enjoyed the ride. When they got to the mangroves near The University of Miami at the top of Biscayne Bay, Dana pushed the throttles forward. The bow rose up in the air as the props bit into the water. Then, as they gained speed, the bow came down and the boat skimmed across the top of the water. The wakes from the other boats made the hull go *thump, thump* as it bounced on the water. No one was faster than them.

When they got further down the bay, they came to a group of islands on the east side. Dana pulled back on the throttles and cut between the islands. She turned and went down the east coast of Star Island. Her boat was at a quite idle.

"That's Carlos's," she pointed out. "That bridge is a barrier." She slowly turned the boat at the end of the island. "This boat might get under it, but that's highly questionable. That bridge," she said, pointing, "goes from that bridge to Star Island." Dana pointed to the long main bridge and then to the isle access bridge. "Getting under it is even more questionable. But it's the only way on and off the island except by boat."

Dana idled the boat back past Carlos's. They could see two guards playing cards on the back patio.

"Let's go eat," Dana said as they hit the open waters of the bay. The sped up the bay to a restaurant on the Intracoastal, La Tub. Mason jumped ashore and Dana tossed her the mooring lines.

As Mason was tying up the stern lines, she stopped in mid-stride, looking at the back of the boat. "You're kidding me? *Dragon II*? You got a boat named *Dragon II*?"

"Well, yes. She didn't have a name. So, I named her."

Mason draped the line around the cleat. "Why am I surprised?"

After a dinner of fish tacos and margaritas, they headed back to the dock. Opening the door to the trailer, Dana heard the refrigerator running. "Hey, the frig works when we're plugged in." She opened its door; it was cold inside. "I never knew it worked."

"That's because you never plugged in the trailer," Mason said, digging through the cabinets. She pulled out a bottle of wine and two glasses. "Let's go sit by the water."

They dragged the chairs around behind the trailer next to the water, then sat quietly, enjoying the quiet evening.

"Tomorrow's shopping day. We'll start in Coconut Grove and finish up by buying some groceries." Dana took a sip as she took in the glow on the water of the setting sun behind them. She watched as the streetlight along South Ocean Drive lit up, then the building lights began to turn on one by one.

Mason wondered what was next and when?

"Jess is coming over tomorrow night sometime. We got to barbeque something good. We set up a deal where she comes over on random days, never the same day of the week. That way, there is no real pattern. Don't you think we would make good spies?"

"No." Was Mason's one-word answer as she poured them more wine.

The next morning after breakfast in a diner, they headed for Coconut Grove. They walked around the shops. "This is the place I've been looking for." Dana grabbed Mason's hand before she could get away.

Mason looked at the sign. "Just Bikinis. That's a store?"

"Come on, sexy. Let's try some on." Dana pulled on her hand.

"I guess it's no use objecting. It's just like New Orleans—I'm trapped." Mason gave up. Dana bought ten bikinis and two cover-ups that didn't cover much up. Mason bought five bikinis and two cover-ups. They stopped in another shop and bought sandals and wide-brimmed hats. Still another store for sunglasses. By then it was lunchtime. They found a lovely outdoor café and ordered lunch.

Later they bought a cart full of groceries and headed back to the trailer.

*

"You're just in time," Dana said as Jess got out of her car. "The coals are just about right."

"A barbeque. Cool, what are we having?" Jess asked.

"Lobster, sweet potatoes, and zucchini," Dana said, pointing to the platter on the side of the barbeque.

"Beer?" Mason said, standing in the door of the trailer in her new bikini.

"Sweet mother of God. I've died and gone to heaven." Jess reached for her beer and brought one to Dana. "Lobster, barbeque, beer, and two sexy women in bikinis."

"This trailer doesn't have A/C. This is the only way to survive down here. Hell, I can see the water in the air, it's so humid." Mason made her way to one of the chairs.

They talked a bit about the plan. Nothing much changed. It was after midnight when Jess left.

There wasn't much to do for the next few weeks. They explored, relaxed, and enjoy the vacation. Every few days, they went by Carlos's. On one of their late-night cruises, Dana had Mason shut off all the boat lights and take her around to the bridge connecting Star Island to the main bridge between South Beach and Miami. Dana got up in the bow, and as they got close, Mason shut down the outboards. Dana pulled the boat under the bridge. There wasn't much room. She had to kneel to keep from hitting her head. She turned on her flashlight, and it didn't talk long to find what she was looking for, a supporting beam. Dana used duct tape to secure her package to the beam. Then she secured a second package to another part of the bridge.

Each day was about the same. They explored up to Ft. Lauderdale, going outside and racing down the coast to the Miami inlet. They checked out Hullover Cut. In the warm afternoons, they laid on the beach. Jesse's visits were always about the same except the barbeque menu varied each time.

On the day of Jess' fourth visit, Mason had caught a good-sized grouper near the furthest out channel marker at the Miami Inlet.

Jess pulled up, and Mason went to get the beers. "Grouper?" Jess asked, looking at the fish on the grill.

"Freshly caught," Mason said coming out of the trailer with three beers. "By me. It's not store bought."

After dinner, they sat around, watching the coal embers die out.

"It's been three weeks," Dana said. "Much longer and we're going to have to get new bikinis." She got up and went to the trailer. "More beer?"

Both Jess and Mason smashed up their beer cans and threw them into the trash can, the one they got in Alabama.

"I take it that's a yes?" Dana handed out the beers. She no sooner sat down than Jess's cell phone rang, she reached under her chair for her cell phone

Jess opened her phone and put it to her ear. She never said a word, but her expression froze. She closed her phone and looked at the others.

"It's on."

39. IT'S ON

Dana got to Coffee Joe's the next morning. She bought a cup of coffee and a *Miami Herald* and sat as far away from everybody as possible, with her back to the door, her newspaper open to the comics. Right on time, Jess entered and bought a cup of coffee and sat at the table next Dana, looking out the window.

"The three of them went to see Grandpa yesterday. Two left all smiles; Sal left fifteen minutes later. He was not smiling. We think Grandpa cut Carlos's strings last night. We're moving today. They will be walking up to the courthouse or jail at four this afternoon. Be careful; Carlos still has his guys. Good luck, honey. I got to run."

*

Jess walked into her floor of the FBI building with a big smile, a cup of coffee, and two agents walking behind her. She walked straight to Wong's desk and threw handcuffs on his desk. "Put them on. It's my pleasure to inform you you're under arrest."

"What the hell?" he said, looking around.

"Take good care of him, boys," she said to the two agents.

"You can't do this," he yelled as his arms were pulled behind his back and the cuffs were put on him. "I'll go to the police chief. I'll have you arrested, you fucking dike."

Jess flipped him the finger over her shoulder and kept walking.

They took him to the interrogation room. He would sit there till he was escorted to jail at four o'clock.

"Okay, guys," Jess said as she set her coffee down on the table. "The snitch is gone. But just in case, keep everything in this room. Pick up your targets starting at about three and handcuff them behind their backs. I want it clearly visible they are handcuffed. Then take them to the courthouse or jail, whichever you were assigned to. But don't get there till after four. Have them all in by five. Any questions?"

They began to cheer. Jess put out her hands to quiet them. "Cheer tomorrow. We got a lot to do. Make sure your arrest warrants are perfect. No loopholes." She sifted through the photos on the table, pushing five to the middle. "These guys could be dangerous. I've ordered down swat teams from West Palm Beach. Again, don't tell even SWAT who the target is, not till just before you take them. The rest of you should be able to handle your guys with just two or three agents, depending on your assignment. I want you to make it obvious they are arrested and possibly violent. I want an army of cops taking these guys in."

*

Dana got back to the trailer about same time Jess was giving the go to her teams. She signaled Mason to come into the trailer and told Mason what she had just learned. "We need to get some rest," Dana said. "It's going to be a long and wild night tonight."

Just before five, they walked up to the guardhouse. Thomas had a small TV to pass the time. "Hi Thomas, mind if we watch the five o'clock news?" Dana asked.

"Sure, I usually watch it anyway." The three of them crowded into the small shack to watch the news.

"It's five o'clock, and we are going to lead off with some really big news tonight," the male announcer said. "Let's go to Frank down at the courthouse. Frank."

Frank held up his mike. "In a surprise move, the FBI arrested the Miami chief of police with the help of a SWAT team." The picture zoomed in on the police chief in handcuffs being led up the steps to the courthouse. "Behind him is the Dade County head prosecutor, also in handcuffs. Sharon, what's happening at the county jail?"

"I'm here at the county jail. The SWAT teams are leading several judges and a number of Miami police offices into the jail, also in handcuffs." Sharon went on to describe the situation in detail.

"Wow. Looks like Windy Talker did her job," Dana said.

"Hold on," Sharon said. "I've just been told that the head of this FBI operation is going to say a few words and take some questions. Frank, take it away."

"I'm here at the courthouse. Inspector Rizzo is about to speak." The camera zoomed in on Jess as the reporter got closer.

Jess was standing on the steps in a black suit, open white shirt, a tight black skirt that ended just above the knees, and shiny black stilettos.

"My God. Look at Jess," Mason said, her hand over her mouth. "She cleans up really good."

Dana started laughing, watching Jess talk at normal speed.

"Shush, she's going to say something," Mason said.

"The men you saw brought in today were arrested for murder, accessory to murder, taking and giving bribes as elected officials." Jess was forceful and in charge, looking in turn into each camera on her. Her two FBI supervisors were standing behind her. They had been told from above to let her have the lead.

"She is speaking at a normal pace," Dana said. "She must have been practicing."

"Shush," Mason said with her finger to her lips.

The reporters were shouting questions. "What was the Miami chief of police arrested for?"

"All of the above," Jess answered. She took a few more questions, then held up her hand. "Thank you all. Now I have to attend to business in the courthouse." Jess waved as she led the group into the courthouse.

"Wow. I didn't think she had it in her. She really did pull it off," Mason said as they made their way back to the trailer.

"And I didn't think she could walk in stilettos," Dana said. "Okay, Mason. It's all come together. So, here is my plan," Dana said as she shut the door of the trailer. They sat across from one another at the table for an hour as Dana explained her plan in detail. "There are a lot of ifs, and's, or buts in my plan. So, are you in?"

"Are you kidding me? Of course, I'm in. I've been in since just after I figured out you were the Red Bitch. That was centuries ago." Mason smiled. "I always wanted to be part of the action."

"Tonight, you will get your wish. Just be careful," Dana said seriously.

Mason took Dana by the arm. "Listen to that, be careful. Coming from the Red Bitch's ghost." She smiled. "Let's get ready."

Dana dressed as the ghost of the Red Bitch. Then she did Mason's makeup the same way and pulled a red wig on Mason's head. "Aww, close enough," she said. Shortly after midnight, she pulled the Dragon out of the trailer.

"Okay, Mason," she said as Mason settled into the Dragon. "Let's go over this one more time. This switch opens the valve to the exhaust. This switch turns on the fire. This knob turns the fire up to the right and down to the left. Always flip the exhaust switch on before the fire switch. Always flip the fire switch off before turning the exhaust switch off. Lights. Don't forget the lights. Don't hit them till I tell you. Got it?"

"For the tenth time, I got it," Mason said.

Dana loaded the black plastic bag and her samurai swords into *Dragon II*. "One forty-two. Not a minute before or after," she said to Mason as The Red Bitch pulled away from the dock.

Mason gave her a thumbs up, then got into the Dragon, parked next to the docks.

The *Dragon II* raced down the coast to the Haulover Inlet, then over to Star Island. She pulled under the bridge and set the timers. Then she backed off and waited.

At one forty-two, Mason pulled up to the guardhouse. The guard looked at the Dragon breathing small blue flames, Mason gave the Dragon a little rev, spitting fire towards the guardhouse. The guard opened the gate, then closed the guardhouse door and laid on the floor.

At one forty-three, Mason turned the flame up on the Dragon. "Wow, I always wondered what pure power felt like?" she said aloud as she slowly drove down the street toward Carlos's house. Near his house, she turned the fire all the way up and drove by his front gates. She revved the engine, setting the Humvee just inside the gate on fire, as well as most of the bushes along the fence.

Two of the guards ran out of the house, firing their automatics at her. She smiled and waved at them. Then she blew them a kiss as the bullets bounced off the Dragon's windows. She pulled away down the street, turning down the fire.

At one forty-three, the first charge went off, blowing the power and communications to and from the island.

At the same time, The Red Bitch maneuvered the *Dragon II* to the dock. Dropping a line around a cleat, she pulled the black bag and her samurai swords from the bow. She tucked the golden gun into the back of her sash and the swords into the front. She hurried down the dock, dropping the black bag near some stairs on the patio. Adrenaline does wonders for strength.

Looking through the glass, she saw the four guards firing automatic weapons and handguns at the Dragon. Two thugs were racing up to the burning Humvee. The other two remained on the front porch, so she slipped into the kitchen on the far side. A Chinese cook was at the chopping block. Seeing the Red Bitch, he pulled a chef's knife and a cleaver off the chopping block and charged toward her, yelling. She took a step back, dropping her swords. Two steps later, he had a knife in his neck and a cleaver in his balls.

She had a good view of the two guards on the porch, through the kitchen's other door. The other two guards were at the gate, looking for the Dragon.

The Ghost of the Red Bitch slipped out the open front door. With her short sword, she slit the throat of the closest guard. Then she tapped the other on the shoulder. As he turned his head, she split it open with her long sword.

The other two guards were busy trying to put out the fire on the Humvee and move it away from the burning bushes along the fence and away from the gate. They were not paying attention to what just happened at the front door.

She slipped back into the house.

From the side of the entryway, the Red Bitch saw two other guards at the base of the stairway. A woman dressed in tight black leather pants, a black leather t-top, and black stilettos. Her leg spread holding an automatic weapon, pointing towards the kitchen, she directed one of the guards to check it out.

"Chink, where the hell are you?" The guard said, looking for the cook. The ghost of the Red Bitch slipped behind the wall separating the sunken living room from the dining room. As the guard came to the door, his head bounced on the floor then rolled into the sunken living room. His body took another two steps before falling forward.

"I've never seen that before," she said to herself in wonderment. She ran back to the kitchen.

His head had not even stopped rolling when automatic fire pulverized the wall between the dining room and the living room. The second guard was directed to check out the dining room. He edged his way along the wall, his automatic at the ready. All he found when he got to the dining room was blood spattered on the walls and a growing pool of blood on the floor where the dead guard's head once had been. In the kitchen, he found the cook lying on his back on the chopping block. He decided to go back to the dining room and check the front and back windows.

In the thin moonlight coming through the window, the Red Bitch found the service stairway leading up to the second floor. The stairway was pitch black, as was the hallway. She edged along the wall, her short sword in one hand and her long sword in the other. Toward the end of the hall, she could make out the profile of the woman at the top of the stairs. She was only three steps away.

The woman sensed the Red Bitch's ghost next to her. She turned to fire her automatic. One bullet bounced off the Red Bitch's rib. *Damn, not again*, she thought as she threw a kick, sending the automatic flying into the living room.

The woman turned to throw a chop at the Red Bitch's neck.

"Oh, fun," the Red Bitch said aloud. She took a short step back and dropped her swords, then a stance and, with her finger, signaled her to come and get it. The woman threw a kick, missing. The Red Bitch kicked her in the hip to move her into position.

The guard down below, on seeing them, fired at them both. They jumped in opposite directions. They both were at opposite ends of the stairway landing and both totally in the dark.

"What the fuck are you doing? You almost killed me," she shouted down to the guard.

"That's the ghost of the Red Bitch," he called back up.

"Go get the others. Guard the gate and the front door. Don't leave your positions," she called back down.

The Red Bitch could hear her flip open a blade. She could feel her, she knew her, she knew what the woman in black was going to do next. The woman in black stepped out, holding a blade visible in the faint light. She came at her as the Red Bitch flew into the air, kicking her blade down the stairs, their faint shadows but for a brief moment on the wall. They both disappeared in opposite directions into the dark hallway.

The Red Bitch whispered down the dark hallway, "You can turn and go to the kitchen and get out of here. Or you can die."

"Fuck you. I'm not dead yet," she whispered back.

"You tried with your thugs. You tried with your automatic. You tried with your blade. What do you think is going to happen next?" The Red Bitch knew her answer. But the offer was the Red Bitch's equivalent of a bow.

"Now," the other woman said.

"Okay," the Red Bitch said as they both flew onto the landing. The woman threw a high kick. The Red Bitch kicked higher, planting a heel in her ear. The woman in black died instantly. *No pain,* the Red Bitch thought.

Picking up her swords, even in the dark, she knew there must be double doors down at the end of the hallway. Behind it would be Carlos's office, his bedroom, and his sex dungeon room. She had heard about that room.

The Red Bitch knew Carlos was not alone and probably had maximum firepower. *Well, let's play,* she thought. She took her long sword, turned it around, and tapped on the door with the handle. "Hi. Anybody home?" She jumped to one side, hugging the wall.

The bullets flew at once, ripping the door to pieces. "I'll take that as a yes. Want to try again?" She heard two clips hit the floor. *Okay, two shooters,* she thought. One would be to the left. *That's the thug,* she thought. The other to the right, behind something, would be Carlos. She took a deep breath.

She reached over again and tapped on what was left of the door. "Knock. Knock. Who's there?"

The bullets flew again. The door was just flying sawdust, so the Red Bitch ran through the sawdust before they could reload. She jumped and planted a heels in the thug's chest. Then she tucked and rolled behind Carlos's oversized desk.

Carlos threw his empty gun aside and pulled out his handgun. "I'm going to kill you, you fucking Red Bitch," he shouted over the desk.

"Honey, you already killed me once. Or was that twice? I forget. Do you really think you can kill me again?"

He fired six shots out of his pistol and into the top of the desk, hoping the rounds would go through the massive teak and kill her.

"Oh, so you think you can kill me all by your itty-bitty self?" The Red Bitch's ghost stood up, her arms apart.

Carlos kept pulling the trigger on the empty gun.

"You can't do it. You never had the balls. Oh, but they would make nice earrings." She walked around the desk and hit him in the forehead with the butt of her long sword.

When he came to, he was in his bondage and sadism room, naked on the bed, strapped down—except for one hand that held the gold-plated 9 mm, which was taped down and pointing at his head.

"Well, you do have a hard head. You were not out that long. Okay, honey, this is how this is going to go. At any time, you can pull the trigger and end the pain. That's a much better deal than you gave Debbie," the Red Bitch's ghost said in a soothing and understanding tone.

"You fucking Red Bitch. I had you killed. I know you were killed."

"Yes, you did. Now it's your turn." She laughed. "Isn't this fun?"

Her cell phone rang. She pulled it out of her bra. Mason said, "The firetrucks are coming. What should I do?"

"What time is it exactly?"

"One-fifty-seven," Mason answered.

"Close enough. Are you on the other side of the open area, between the streets?"

"Of course," Mason answered.

"Okay, fire up the Dragon. Go full charge across the open area, full fire, full lights front, and back. Hit the nitro when you get into second. Hit the gate and keep going through the front doors. You got three guys to kill. Make sure you run them all down or burn them up. At two, the bridge blows. I need some more time. When you get in, the black bag is on the patio. Bring it up on the second-floor landing. Then go to the boat. Don't get fancy."

"Got it. Oh god, I think I'm having an orgasm," Mason said.

The Red Bitch turned to Carlos. "I hear you like nipples." She sliced off one of his. He screamed in pain. "Want to eat this?" She shoved it into his mouth. "Remember, you can pull that trigger at any time you want."

She turned and looked out the window. "Do you have any kids?"

"God damn you bitch, shit," he answered.

"Do you have any kids?" She asked slowly this time.

"God, no." slobber was coming out his mouth.

"The night Debbie died; I had my daughter. That was the saddest and happiest day in my life."

Walking back, she heard the Dragon crashing through the gate and into the house. It came to a stop at the end of the sunken living room, the engine still running, but it wasn't going anywhere. She turned; she didn't hear gunshots. "So, I guess she got them," she said.

"Anyway, as I was saying, you won't be needing these." She cut off his balls one at a time.

He gave out one long ear-piercing scream.

She gave him a big kiss. "Please don't pull the trigger till I get back." She went out to the landing just as Mason dropped off the bag.

"The place is on fire. What do I do now?" Mason said nearly out of breath. Just then, the bridge blew, falling into the bay.

"Ah, get out," the Red Bitch said. Picking up the bag as she turned, she said over her shoulder, "Oh, you better back the boat off the dock till you see me. I shouldn't be very long."

She headed back to Carlos. "Guess what, Carlos? You're going to die a rich man." She poured the cash and drugs on his bloody chest. "Nice drugs you got here. Well, now, you have all the drugs you want?"

Carlos looked at the cash on his chest, "Take it. It's all yours. Just let me live."

"Carlos, baby, I'm giving you the cash. It's a present from Sal. This is your money now." She gave him a kiss and took some matches from the night table. "Time to go." She lit several bills and dropped them on the pile of money. The money caught fire quickly and covered his chest in seconds.

Carlos's screaming didn't last long. He pulled the trigger.

The Red Bitch's ghost ran down the hallway and down the stairs. Mason saw her running down the dock and pulled up to the end. The Red Bitch jumped in and crawled into the passenger seat, holding her side, just now feeling the pain of the bullet wound.

As they were pulling away from the dock, there was a big explosion in the house—big enough to put out most of the fire. The two ghosts looked at each other wide-eyed, not knowing what happened. Mason got it first. "Nitro!"

The firetrucks were stopped at the bridge. They called for the fire boats. They had to come from the other side of the Miami Harbor entrance, so it would take them a while. As the *Dragon II* entered the Intracoastal, Mason opened the throttles. They could hear the fireboats coming up from the south.

Out of breath and bleeding from her side, Dana said, "Debbie, that one was for you."

40. DR. JENSON

"What the hell? Are you bleeding?" Mason asked, pulling the *Dragon II* into its slip. Dana was holding her right side, leaning to her right. Blood was between her fingers. It was a different kind of blood from the blood on her face, hair, and over her arms and legs and most of her body. The blood was not sticking, it was flowing.

"Well, yeah. I have been since that black devil shot me," Dana said.

"Who?" Mason asked.

"The dead woman at the top of the stairs. You saw her." Dana took a shallow breath. "She was excellent. I'm afraid you are going to have to help me back to the trailer."

"Why didn't you say something?" Mason asked as she lifted Dana out of her seat and onto the dock.

"Well, for one thing, I was kind of busy killing Carlos. And for another, if I said something, you would have slowed down and tried to help me. Then we might have been recognized or caught." Dana put her arm around Mason's shoulder. Her other hand still held her wound. They slowly made their way to the trailer.

"Help me undress," Dana said as they entered the trailer. Sitting at the table, Mason helped her off with her top and longline bra. The wound was along her lower right rib, just below the bra. "Okay, that's enough. Now get one of those beach towels and lay it on the floor."

Dana tried to lie down. Mason rushed to grab her arms and lowered her slowly onto the towel. "Now get the medical kit and lots of peroxide," Dana said. The medical kit was really a tackle box, filled with all sorts of medical supplies.

"Okay, doctor," Dana said.

"I'm no doctor. I don't know what to do," Mason said with a look of fear on her face.

"Oh, my dear. I've watched it being done before." Dana tried to chuckle. "Once." She raised her left arm and rolled on her left side. With pain in her face and her teeth clenched, she let out a small cry, "I can't really see it in this position. So, you'll have to tell me what you see."

"Lots of blood."

"First, just pour some peroxide on the wound." The pain caused Dana to hold her breath and clench her fists. "Now, what do you see?"

"It's long, maybe four inches. I can see your rib bone. It's a deep wound." Mason looked up at Dana.

"Anything sticking out?"

"No," Mason said, looking at the wound closely.

"Okay. Soak a towel in peroxide and clean around the wound. Make sure it's really clean." Dana lay quietly, not moving.

"Now see the bottle marked Anesthetic? I don't understand the names they give drugs, so I just write on them what they are for. Also, get a syringe."

Mason took the top off the bottle and unwrapped the syringe. "Now, what?"

"Just like in the movies. Hold up the bottle and suck the anesthetic out of the bottle into the syringe. Make sure the air is out."

Mason recalled the doctor TV shows; she played doctor and even tapped the side of the syringe. "Now, what?"

"Stick the needle in just under the skin and the meat line about a quarter inch. See those lines on the syringe? Slowly inject it but only for one line. Do this every inch or so on both sides."

Mason took her time. "Done."

"Now comes the easy part. First, pour some peroxide on the wound. Now, see those needles with the string glued to the ends? Take them out of the package. Starting at one end, squeeze the sides together and run the needle in below the skin. Pull it tight and tie it off. Do this every half inch or so. Don't worry. I won't feel any pain."

It took Mason about fifteen minutes to do the job. She was slow and as precise as possible. She had blood halfway up to her elbow. "There," she said, looking down at the bloody area on and around the wound. She then rifled through the tackle box, finding a bottle called pain killer. She gave Dana three pills, only one more than suggested.

"You're all bloody again. Don't tell me; I know. Wipe everything down with peroxide." Cleaning away the fresh blood, Mason said, "It's not bleeding much now."

"Good. Just lightly tape some gauze in place when you're done."

By the time Mason had finished, Dana was mumbling, "Now, I have matching left and right scars. Ha." She passed out.

Mason finished undressing her, partly using a pair of scissors to cut clothing away. She then, with a wet towel in one hand and an alcohol-soaked towel in the other, began wiping off the blood—Dana's blood and other people's blood. Her thick ghost makeup was the most difficult to remove. As she was moving her around, she slowly replaced the bloody beach towel with a clean blanket. When she had finished, she got a pillow and a light sheet and covered her up.

Mason sat watching over her. After a few hours, she put her head down and got a little sleep. When Mason woke up, a few hours later, checking Dana, she gently wiped some sweat away, with a wet towel. It wasn't till that afternoon, that Dana began to stir. She tried to roll over on her side, and her eyes flew open from the pain.

"Welcome back from the dead," Mason said to Dana's blank face. "That's supposed to be funny."

"Boo!" Dana said and winced. "Oh, I get it—the Red Bitch's ghost." Looking under the sheet, she peeled back the gauze.

"Excellent job, doctor," she said.

"You lost a lot of blood. Here, drink this orange juice. It will help." Mason handed her the glass, "Take this too." She gave her a vitamin C and B pill.

"I'll put on some new gauze." Mason got up from the table and kneeled to replace the gauze.

"Please get me a bikini. I want to get up," Dana said.

Mason helped her up and pulled up Dana's bikini bottom and tied her top in place. With one arm around her, she helped Dana out to the chairs in the shade of the trailer. They were looking out over the water. Mason handed Dana another big glass of orange juice and settled in beside her.

"Well, that came off almost perfect," Dana finally said.

"You are kidding me," Mason said, pausing between each word. "For starters, you got shot."

"Well, I wasn't planning on that. Shit happens," Dana said, taking another drink from her glass.

"The Dragon, the beautiful Dragon blew up. What about that?" Mason pressed.

"That was kind of on the edge of the plan. You did get an orgasm out of it," Dana chuckled, handing over her glass for some more OJ. "The whole thing went slower than I expected. That black devil really slowed me down."

By this time, hunger was taking over.

"I know just what you need," Mason said. "I'll go to the market and get some stuff. Here's the last of the OJ. If you need to pee, don't get up, just push your bottom aside and pee through the webbing," Mason said, getting up.

"Eww. I don't need to pee that bad," Dana said. "But hurry."

*

"More OJ," Mason said, coming back from the market and setting a gallon bottle next to Dana. She set down her bag of groceries and looked around. "Weren't you sitting over there?" Then she started to laugh. "By the wet spot."

"I spilled the OJ," Dana said sheepishly.

"I'll get the barbeque," Mason said, chuckling. After it was set up and the fire started, she unpacked her groceries.

"Liver? You're going to barbeque liver?" Dana looked to Mason for an answer.

"Sure. Why not? Besides, it's good for you. And I got asparagus," Mason said. Mason had stopped at Burger King and wolfed down a burger on her way back to the trailer. She didn't have to eat more than a bite of the barbequed liver.

"Not bad, but not my first choice. In fact, it's my last choice for a barbeque." Dana's hunger, not the flavor of barbequed liver, helped her finish her dinner.

Mason cleared the dishes and utensils, putting them into the sink. She opened the fridge and took out a beer. She thought for a second, then pulled out one for Dana. "Just one," Mason said.

Just as Mason was settling in, Jess called. "Hi, girls." Mason recognizing, Jess' voice, held the phone out so they both could hear her. "Did you see me on television? Wow, we got them all. Every last one of those assholes. It went smooth and just as planned. I didn't figure on the fire trucks going to Carlos's, or I would have slowed them down. Sorry.

But, hey, the bridge blew up in their faces. I went to Carlos's today. The place is all blown up. Funny, but almost no damage to the other houses, mostly just paint. They dropped a temporary bridge in place. You know you only blew up ten feet of the bridge. God, there were burnt bodies everywhere. Carlos is mostly ash. So that's where the golden gun went. I wondered what you were going to do with it. Poor Dragon, you can only see the engine. I got to run. Barbeque tomorrow night. Okay, bye."

"How did she ever slow down and talk like a regular person on television?" Mason asked, putting down the cell phone.

*

Dana had gained back some of her strength thanks to a sedative-induced deep night's sleep. They spent the next morning on the beach. Dana laid on her side with her stitches catching the warmth and energy of the sun. They walked down the beach, ankle-deep in the warm, welcoming small waves rolling in, then sliding back into the ocean where they came from. It was a short walk but relaxing. They found a restaurant along the boardwalk and settled in for an early lunch. Then they went shopping for Jody and Alyssa.

Jess showed up early. Mason was the first to get to her and to give her a big hug. Dana reached up from her chair and gave her a one-armed hug.

"So, you don't like me anymore?" Jess stepped back.

"Show her." Mason directed Dana, who turned to show her right side to Jess.

"Good God. What happened?" Jess said, looking at the wound as Dana pulled back the gauze.

"I got shot again."

"Did you kill him?" Jess asked, looking up.

"Her. You must have found her at the top of the stairs, on the landing," Dana said, putting the gauze back in place.

"Yeah," she said, signaling Mason to come help with the two ice chests in her trunk. "You mean Sheila."

Dana looked over at Jess with a puzzled look on her face. As Mason and Jess moved the chests over to the barbeque area, Jess's speed-talking took off.

"Yeah, Sheila. We found her along with a lot of other bodies. I told you about her, didn't I?" Jess raced on her hands waving, "Well, anyway, we could identify most of them. We are going to have to wait for forensic to identify some of the others. Those we found in the living room were definitely beyond recognition. Did I tell you that the houses next door got—"

Dana cut her off. "Wait. Back up. You knew this black devil, Sheila? How did you know Sheila?"

"Yeah, a real ball stomper," Jess said, handing Dana an open beer. "I mean that literally. She got into a fight with a couple of big guys in a bar. Beat the shit out of them and then stomped their balls with her heel. That was a couple of months ago. That's when we traced her back to Carlos. The DA refused to bring up charges. The cops didn't even take her to jail. I told you about her."

"No, you didn't. It would have been nice to know," Dana said.

"I thought I did," Jess said, opening the second ice chest. "Filet mignon and lobster."

Dana held up her hand, stopping Jess, "You know she's the one who shot me. I ended up putting a heel in her ear. It would have been nice to know she was that good."

"I knew about the heel part. I didn't know she shot you. We didn't find a gun upon the landing. Does it hurt much?" she asked, pointing to Dana's side.

"Yes, it hurts very much." Waving off Jess's question. "Start the damn grill."

"I didn't finish," Jess said, holding up a Tupperware container. "Onion slices and asparagus. Marinated in olive oil, balsamic vinegar, and garlic. I made it myself."

After dinner, they went over the events of the night before, and the investigation as it stood. "By the way, it would be a good idea if you guys slipped out of town. I think I got everything covered, but you never know," Jess said.

"You looked very much in charge on television. And I might say very feminine," Dana teased.

"Thanks, I think? Oh, my God, my feet still hurt. How do you find high heels that don't hurt?" Jess asked Dana.

"They don't exist. Get used to pain," Dana said.

"Now I got to go out and buy some suits and heels. Oh, I didn't tell you. I got no less than six calls from DC. And the FBI director called me himself. He said I did an outstanding job. He said that he was going to look after me. Whatever that means."

"Slow down, Jess. Take a sip of your beer. Now, did he say he was going to look after you? Were those his words?" Mason asked.

"Yeah. I guess?" Jess said, taking another, but this time bigger, swig of beer.

Mason and Dana looked at each other.

"That means you're going to get a huge promotion soon. Maybe even to the J. Edgar Hoover Building," Mason said.

They chatted about over dinner, in the end, they sat quietly, watching the coals die out and drinking the last of the beers.

Dana spoke up first. "I need you to pull some strings. I need you to find out where Ron is. He has fallen off the face of the earth. I hope he's not dead. I want to kill him myself," she said with clenched fists.

Jess sat quietly for quite a while. They all did.

"I'll do everything I can possibly do, and more. But I would like to ask a favor." This time, Jess was speaking at normal speed. What that meant was to listen. "Over time, and I don't know when or where I will need the Red Bitch to cut some strings for me. I promise they will all be drug distribution related strings." She now sat not saying a word, watching Dana.

Mason was studying Dana as well.

Dana looked up at the stars. She could see the Milky Way and made out the Big Dipper. Dana saw more stars than she had ever seen. *'Maybe I just wasn't looking before.'* Her mind now clear, Dana only said, "All I need to know is who and why."

41. CLOSING ONE DOOR

They pulled out of the trailer park the next afternoon, leaving behind the barbeque and the trash can. Then, in the boat, a thank you note for the owner of *Dragon II*.

Dana was quiet or slept most of the way home. She put her head on Mason's shoulder to relieve the pain but also because she needed comfort.

While they were unpacking the trailer and loading up Mason's car to the gills, Mason looked at the trailer in the bright moonlight. "What are we going to do with her, now that the Dragon is gone."

"Give it to Tommy at the garage. He's got plenty of room. He might be able to use it," Dana said, before getting into the car, over the roof, she said to Mason, "Keep the truck."

Mason asked, "Why?"

She just got a shrug.

Dana was unusually quiet for the next few days. Most of her conversation was reserved for Alyssa.

Mason and Jody felt that Dana was suffering from depression from the loss of purpose and the excitement of the hunt. Also, the adrenaline from the possibility of imminent death.

Until one day, after dropping Alyssa off at school, Dana asked Mason to join her and Jody at the gallery.

Dana walked in with Cokes and a pizza, the kind that Christopher loved. She opened the box, handed out the Cokes, and then sat down.

"Here's the plan. We are going to redo Dad's business plan," Dana said, looking around the table. "Completely," she added.

Mason and Jody looked at each other, then back at Dana.

"We are going to close the door to the public." Dana took a bite of her pizza. She waited for a reaction.

"How are we going to sell our stuff?" Jody asked.

"The question is *to whom* are we going to sell our stuff," Dana stated.

"Okay, to whom?" Jody asked again.

"Rich people. Rich people only."

"Really?" Mason asked.

"I have let our art slide into the middle class. That's all my fault. Shit, every foreigner in every major city, is selling shops full of *art*. We can't continue to compete with them. A lot of their stuff is copies and knockoffs, but people are falling for it. Look, our sales are down every quarter. We have got to do something." Dana put down her slice of pizza. She became very serious.

"At one time, we sold to only the top buyers. We're going to do that again but in spades. Nothing under ten thousand. Some up around a million or more." Dana took a bite of her pizza and sip of Coke.

Mason looked at Jody, then back at Dana. "How the hell are we going to do that?"

"The plan goes this way: Jody, first you're going to sell off as much as possible of our middle-class art. You'll put up for sale signs and do some advertising. I'll go through the gallery with you, and we'll figure out discounts, bottom prices, and most importantly the good stuff. We're going to keep the good stuff. The Wylands, for one. Got it?"

"I got it. I think?" Jody said.

"Then what? What's the next part of your plan?" Mason asked.

"You're going to redesign the gallery. An open, comfortable space is the key to the ambiance. A luxury private salesroom. A bar, which can be self-serve or with a bartender. Make it so it feels like a private party. Make them feel at home, but able to buy the art in front of them. It should be so that they can walk or sit. Oh, also a space for a band—small. A two to a four-man group. Soft background music, but live."

"A bar? We're going to sell booze?" Jody asked.

"No, we're going to give it away. But only top-shelf stuff," Dan said.

"Why do you think I can do this redesign work?" Mason asked.

"You're the only one with experience. The hideaway. You designed and built it. So, you're in charge," Dana said.

"I don't know," Mason said.

"I do," Dana said. Mason started looking around the space. She was getting it.

"Jody, take Dad's contact list, add it to mine. Go through it. Trim it down to millionaires only. Add to it where you can. You know, like the governor and whoever you can find of influence. You're going to make sales calls. Get addresses and private numbers if you can."

"Wait, you're asking a lot. What do I know about all this million-dollar sales stuff?"

"You're an attorney. You worked on high-profile cases involving millionaires. Clients with really high dollar numbers. You got the experience and the brains. You know how to get information out of people. When you talk to them, pitch it as a new kind of exclusive gallery. Viewing by invitation only. Try and get their preference for artists, type, and style of art. Anything about art and sculpting. Tell them to save some time for our grand opening; only the most important people will be there. Including some artist. Do not discuss money at all."

"What are you going to do?" Mason asked.

"What I do best."

"Kill people?" Mason joked.

"No, the other thing. I'll be in charge of the artists. I'll negotiate prices and/or commissions. Don't forget, I still have the first pick of the Wylands sculptures." Dana settled back and looked around the small table. "So, what do you think?"

Jody looked at Mason. Each waited for the other to speak up. "Is this why you have been so quiet lately?" Mason asked. "We thought you were depressed."

"I'm fine," Dana said, waving off Mason. "So, again, what do you think of my plan?"

"At best risky, at worst, a doorway into bankruptcy," Jody said. She looked to Mason for her answer. Words were not needed; they held hands, and each reached for one of Dana's hands. "We're in."

"Okay, we start tomorrow," Dana said.

"I'm starting today. I'm ordering For Sale, Art Sale, and Sale signs now," Jody said.

The next day, Dana and Jody walked the shop. Jody took the notes. "Twenty percent off on these. But take it as low as thirty percent." Then to another group of paintings, "Twenty-five percent. Go as low as thirty-five percent."

"What about this Larry Icart?" Jody asked when they neared the end of the gallery.

"That's not for sale to anybody at any price. In fact, I'm taking it home and putting it up in the library." Memories of Christopher and Eve lingered in her mind.

Mason did measurements, made out sketches. Remeasured, re-sketched. Finally, after a week, she caught up with Dana. "This isn't going to work. There just isn't enough room. I can't make it fit."

"I didn't think it would," Dana said.

"Then why in the hell did you make me do all this damn work when you knew it wasn't going to fit?" Mason asked, throwing the sketches down on the table.

Dana turned away and looked out the window. "So, you would agree with me," she said quietly to Mason's shouts. "See that new skyscraper? The one that just went up? I think it's sixty stories." Mason moved next to her.

"That one?" She pointed.

"Yes, that one. I don't think the top floor is rented yet. Let's see if we can buy it." Dana turned to her. "The whole top floor. Make sure the view is spectacular. You're in charge of construction, remember."

"Are you serious?" Mason asked.

"High-end means high-end. Besides, security will be easier."

Two weeks later, Mason led Jody into Dana's kitchen. "Pancakes, okay?" Jody said over her shoulder.

"Yeah. Make mine like Mickey Mouse," Alyssa said, climbing into her chair. Handsome settled in beside her.

Mason pulled her chair closer to Dana. "Here's the deal. We buy the top two floors, the fifty-eighth and ninth. Both are empty. There is nothing in there at all. Just a few posts and plumbing. The fifty-ninth floor has ceiling-to-floor windows all around. It also has four separate balconies, one on each side of the floor." Jody handed Mason and Dana cups of coffee.

"Thanks," they said in unison.

"The fifty-eighth floor does not have any balconies and smaller windows. If we own that floor, we control who's in there and what they do. That will ensure security." Mason sipped her coffee. "There is high interest in both floors, my source says."

"Wait. Who's your source?" Dana asked.

Mason leaned over close to Dana and, checking that Jody was busy cooking, said, "An old girlfriend of mine. She heads the inspection section of the building department. Okay?"

"Okay," Dana said without making a sound.

"Anyway. Two companies very much want those floors. One is a law firm. The other is an import-export company."

Jody set a pile of pancakes on the table and a plate with a pancake that had Mickey Mouse ears, banana eyes, and a banana mouth in front of Alyssa. "What's going on?" Jody asked, sitting down.

"I was just explaining to Dana about the new building. Mostly how we are going to get what we want."

"I assume you're going to have Sue—you know, your old lover—explain the facts of life to the owners. She is your former lover, right?" Jody said, stopping in the middle of pouring syrup on Alyssa pancakes.

"Most definitely yes. My way back, a former lover," Mason said with emphasis on *former*. "I can't keep anything from you, can I?"

"You better not try," Jody said, sitting down to her pancakes.

"So, how are we were going to get what we want?" Dana asked.

"My source, Sue, had a private talk with the owners last night. Mostly about how building inspectors go about their job. Also, the interested buyer of both floors is the former chief of police. You know, just in passing."

"That's really boring, Mom," Alyssa said, having finished her pancakes and milk.

"Yes, sweetie. I know it is. How did you do on your math test yesterday?" Dana looked over at Alyssa.

"Scheele mom, it was a spelling test. Pay attention," Alyssa said, slipping out of her chair. "One hundred percent, as usual."

*

Later at the gallery, Mason got a call. "Hi, Sue." Covering the mouthpiece, she whispered to Jody, "It's Sue." Jody waved her off as if she wasn't interested. The conversation went on for more than ten minutes with Mason taking notes. "Thank you! I owe you," Mason said, then looking at Jody. "Well, I do." Then louder, to get away from Jody's dirty looks, "Dana, where are you?"

Dana walked into the front of the gallery, carrying a painting. "I'm here. You don't have to shout."

"I just talked to my contact." Looking at Jody, she started over. "I just talked to Sue. Turns out the owners need money. And they need it quick. Here's the price." She held up a piece of paper. We can get a bank loan but need to give them one million down cash by tomorrow. That's no problem, but Jody, can you get a purchase contract together by tomorrow?"

"No, but I know someone who can." Jody reached for the note. "That's a hell of a good price. I thought it would be twice that. This is for both floors, right?" Jody looked up.

"This is what the owners want. Also, their information at the bottom," Mason said, handing the notes to Dana. Jody looked over her shoulder.

Dana and Jody studied it for holes or problems. Jody took it and, after a few notes of her own, handed it back to Mason.

"You know, Mason. When the reins are taken off, you do a hell of a great job," Dana said.

"High praise coming from you." Mason smiled. "By the end of the month, I'll have the fifty-eighth floor rented out to one or both of the companies who were interested. With some cash in advance."

"That will help," Jody said.

"We'll need to get an architect. I think I know just the guy. He's high-end, but I think I can make it work. Besides, he will get us some free advertising in architecture magazines. You know, he would be showing off his work at our place."

*

Mason oversaw the construction on both floors. Jody finished selling the remaining art and cleaned out the old gallery. Dana took to the road, finding and getting on board several excellent artists and sculptors. Some pieces, she bought; some, she negotiated a commission that made them both happy. Her commission structure was designed to keep them on board for years.

Jody made what seemed like a thousand calls. She picked out the most important people and got them lined up for the grand opening. Only the right people and also three writers from prestigious publications. She made sure they did not all come on the same night. The grand opening was scheduled on a Friday night, Saturday night, and Sunday late afternoon. The rest of the week was reserved for exclusive viewings.

Jody developed a catalog of the art, with Alyssa and Handsome in the picture, sometimes together and sometimes alone. She also brought in interesting people, some off the street, some from expensive clothing design studios, some just because it made the photo talk to her. It all depended on the piece.

The day the old gallery was emptied out, Dana stayed till late that night, sitting alone in a chair in the middle of the empty gallery, a bottle of wine sitting beside her on the floor, a wine glass held to her chest. She just let the memories come to her. Sometimes she giggled. Sometimes she cried as the ghosts of her mom and dad danced around her. Sometimes they were joined by the spirits of the paintings she had loved. The first painting she ever sold appeared to still be leaning against the wall.

Very late that night, Dana went to the door and, out of habit, set the alarm. She turned, seeing her mom and dad dancing, tearing up Dana said, "See you at home," closing the door.

42. UNCLE JESS

Three days before the grand opening, there was a knock at the door. It was near nine at night, too late for callers, Dana thought.

As she opened the door, Jess leaped into Dana's arms and gave her a big kiss. "I missed you so much. I'm on my way to DC. I'm moving there. I have just been put in charge of the national unit for corrupt officials, all the way up to Congress. But not the president. And guess what else?"

"Hi, Jess. How was your trip? Couldn't you have told me this last week on the phone? Never mind. Now, slow down and come into the library. Mason and Jody are here."

"This all happened in the last few days. Great, I can't wait to tell Mason and Jody the news." Jess had not slowed down. "Hi, girlfriends," she said as she rushed to give them a hug.

"And this is my daughter Alyssa," Dana said.

Alyssa stood up and held out her hand. "I'm so happy to meet you," she said.

"My, so formal. I am pleased to meet you too," Jess said, shaking her hand. "Now that we're properly introduced, can I give you a hug?"

Alyssa opened up both her arms. Jess gave her a great big hug and resisted the temptation to pick her up and swing her around.

Jess was speed talking. She was going into detail about everything that had happened since Thursday afternoon.

"Didn't I tell you, you were in for a big promotion," Mason said.

"The director called me up to DC. I mean, he called me on Thursday and wanted me there the next day. He has this gigantic office. I met him for the first time. You know, this is funny, I couldn't remember his name. But Mr. Thomas and Mr. Bennett, my DC bosses on the hit, were both there. The director himself offered me the job with the national elected official investigations unit. 'Well, sir,' I said, 'It is with great pleasure that I say yes.'"

A bit later, Dana said to Alyssa, "Honey, way past your bedtime. Go get ready for bed, then come down and give us a goodnight kiss."

"Okay. Come on, Handsome," Alyssa said as she headed out of the room.

"Was she talking to me?" Jess asked, looking at Dana for an answer.

"Jess, the dog's name is Handsome." Dana chuckled. "Now that we have heard all about your promotion, let me tell you about the grand opening." The three of them went over what they had accomplished over the last six months. The only interruption was when Alyssa came downstairs to say goodnight.

"Goodnight, Auntie Jody." She gave her the first hug and kiss. "Goodnight, Auntie Mason." She gave out another hug and kiss. She climbed into her mom's lap and gave her a big embrace and a kiss. "Goodnight, Mom," She said, climbing down. Turning to Jess, she started, "Goodnight. Hmm?" Alyssa said, thinking. She put her finger under her chin, eyeing Jess. "Who would you like to be, Jessica or Uncle Jess?"

Jess laughed with tears forming in her eyes. "Uncle Jess is excellent."

"Cool. Goodnight, Uncle Jess." With that, Alyssa jumped up in Jess's lap and put both arms around her neck. "I always wanted an Uncle." She gave her an embrace, cheek to cheek, and a kiss on the cheek.

Jess held her tight, gave her another kiss, and watched her and Handsome head out to the stairs.

Sitting in the library, with her only real friends sitting around her, she was starting to feel like a part of the family. She hadn't had a family since her dad threw her out at sixteen with a black eye, bloody nose, and just the clothes on her back. She tried several car's until she found one with an unlocked rear door. She slept in the backseat of a car. *Shit,* she thought, lying there in the chilly night. *Telling my folks, I'm a lesbian probably wasn't a good idea*. That was twenty-one years ago, September 12. That became her new birthday.

"Oh my God," Jess said, watching Alyssa leave, tears in her eyes. Dana had gotten up and poured four glasses of good brandy. She handed them out to the others.

"You deserve a celebratory toast." They stood and held up their glasses. "To Jess's promotion." They clinked glasses and took a sip.

Sitting down, Jess said, looking up the stairs, "I love her. And I love you guys so much." She wiped her tears with the back of her hand. She took a sip of her Brandy. "I would love to be part of this family."

"Haven't you figured it out yet? You are part of our family, Uncle Jess," Dana said. "You heard Alyssa. She gave you a choice, and you picked family." That called for another toast. "To Uncle Jess." Dana raised her glass. "Welcome to the family."

"She does have other uncles, you know, but she never sees them. The last time she saw them was at Dad's funeral. After a while, they quit calling every Sunday. Now it's special occasions only," Dana said with a sigh. As they sat back and relaxed, Dana had a thought. "Jess, I have a great idea. You wear heels now, right?" She sat forward.

"Of course. You know I can wear those heels for up to four hours at a time now. Hurts like hell. But I can take it," Jess chuckled.

"You are woman!" Mason said.

"Come to the openings. People will want to talk to you," Dana said.

"No, I don't think so. I'm kind of awkward." Jess backed off.

"Listen, there are going to be all kinds of influential, important, and rich people there. All these people have some political power. Money means power. The ultimate power is the power over politicians." Dana sat there. "Think about it."

They sipped their brandy, the three of them looking at Jess.

"By the way, I have a room for you. Your family now, so you'll always have a room here. Just no overnight friends. Do you get my meaning?" Dana nodded upstairs to mean Alyssa.

"Got it." Jess smiled.

*

The next morning, Mason and Jody were over early. Jody was putting together omelets. Jess came out of her room as soon as she heard a noise in the kitchen. "Can I help? What can I do?"

"Get the coffee ready. Oh, it's already ready. Pour yourself a cup and sit down," Jody said. She liked cooking breakfast. It was her favorite time of day. Alyssa was the next one down to the kitchen.

She was still in her pajamas. She rubbed her eyes. "Good morning, Auntie Jody. Good morning, Auntie Mason. Good morning, Uncle Jess." She gave out kisses and sat in her chair.

"So, what do you do for fun?" Jess asked.

"Oh, Handsome, and I play in the yard. I draw things. I look through the art books. At school, I play with my friends." Alyssa said.

"Oh, honey, slow down. You're starting to talk as fast as I do. How would you like to go to the park after school today? I hear they have a butterfly house there. We can just walk in with the butterflies all around."

Dana had walked into the room and poured herself a cup of coffee.

"Mommy, can I go?" Alyssa asked at once.

"Sure, but I don't think Handsome can go. They won't let him in with the butterflies," Dana said.

"Sure, they will," Jess said, taking out her badge. "Government business," she said with a grin.

"So, did you think about it?" Dana asked, sitting next to Jess. Mason and Jody both looked in Jess's direction.

"This Friday through Sunday?" Jess asked.

"Right," Jody answered.

Jess looked at Alyssa and around the room. "The rest of the week. Oh, yes."

"Do you have any cocktail dresses and heels?" Dana asked. Jess gave Dana a blank look. "Okay. Tomorrow, we're going shopping. Maybe to a spa," Dana said. Jess rolled her eyes.

The next afternoon, they shopped at Nordstrom, walked the mall, and finished shopping at Macy's. The results were four cocktail dresses and matching shoes and all new underthings.

Their next stop was the spa. After a relaxing steam bath and massage, Dana took Jess in her robe to a beauty chair. Holding her down with one hand on her shoulder, she called over a tech. "I know this is a difficult project: feet, nails, hair, and makeup. Make her beautiful."

"Oh, no. I can't do all that." Jess tried to get up.

“You’re not going to do a thing but sit there.” Dana pushed her back down. “I'll be back in an hour," she said, shaking a finger in her face.

The tech dropped a cloth around Jess’s neck. She took a deep breath and said, “You better make it two hours.”

Jess made a move to get up. Dana pushed her back down, threatening, “If I have any problems with you. I’ll handcuff you to that chair. Got it?”

Jess looked down and said, "Yes, ma’am.”

Dana came back two hours later. “Wow, you’re beautiful. You are the perfect lipstick lesbian. Now, just act like a lady.” Dana handed her a pair of wedges, a miniskirt, and a low-cut blouse. “You’re so flat, you don’t need a bra. In fact, I think you’re sexier without one.”

They walked out of the mall with arms loaded with new clothes and boxes of shoes. Jess had a great big smile on her face. For the first time in her life, she felt like one of the beautiful girls.

The grand opening went better than even Dana expected. The bartender served expensive wine, liquors, and liqueurs. Two servers in black waistcoats, white shirts, and black bow ties served caviar and other appetizers made by a young and talented sous chef in a minimal but efficient kitchen area designed by Mason.

Everything went great except, “I Nancy, how have you been. I’m glad you accepted the invitation.” Dana said to Nancy, the vet.

“I love this place, it’s wonderful. Out of my price range but, thank you.” Nancy signaled at a woman studying a painting. As she came over, Nancy put her arm around the woman’s waist, “I would like you to meet Jane.”

"Very nice to meet you." Dana put out her hand for a handshake. "Well, Nancy... Jane, I've got to get back to work. I'll catch up to you later."

Dana turned away, trying to put a smile back on her face, thinking, 'what did I expect? For her to wait a decade for me?' her smile now frozen in place she went to the other end of the room and began a conversation, about a Chagall painting with the people standing in front of it. Dana looked over her shoulder at Nancy and Jane, in disappointment.

Jess was lovely in her mini cocktail dress, strappy heels, new hairstyle, and makeup. She made more valuable contacts than she could believe possible. Business and personal card filled her clutch. Several were of particular interest to Her. No one guess she was with the FBI.

The last guest left around two-thirty in the morning. "Thank you so much for coming. Your Wyland sculpture of the mother whale nudging her calf to the surface is a great piece, I'm sure you'll enjoy it." Dana watches the elevator door close, then she joined the others at the bar.

Jess was sorting through her cards, sipping her martini, "He's dirty, he's a maybe, Oh, a good guy" She said as she stacks the cards in piles. "This guy, I have to watch, he's taking over from the city of Miami attorney. He didn't have a clue who I was. Wow," Jess said, "I could not get this much info in a year. And it's contacts all over the country. Shit Dana, I'm dressing up and putting on heels for each one of these." Jess looked puzzled for a moment. "You know I got asked out by four men all wearing wedding rings. One said he would take me to Monaco... Where's Monaco?"

"See you're irresistible." Dana laughed.

Mason studied Jess pile of cards. Then looked at Jody working with her sales sheets. "you know what we need? A spreadsheet. I can set that up on my computer. We'll get all the gallery stuff, name, phone numbers, preferred genre's, etc., and Jess you and I can work together to put a page 2 together with info that would be useful to you."

Dana and Jess looked at each other, "marvelous idea!" Jess said, Dana agreed.

Jody Had been quietly adding up the sales. "It came to over twelve million dollars. With commissions and some off for possible cancelations, I estimate our take is three-point-six million dollars."

"That's better than our take at the pot station," Dana said. "And it's legal!"

"And taxable," Jody said.

"Well, there's that," Dana said quietly.

*

Life evened out after that. Mason and Jody worked the gallery. They weren't open every day, only for special requests and for art openings for artist and special guests. It quickly became very popular with artists, who requested showings and hangings.

Dana spent more time with Alyssa and did the management. She worked with the artists and traveled every other week or so. Dana was soon amazed by how many young and attractive lesbian girls there were wherever she went. At first, she only had the one- or two-night stands. That would change as she got older. But for now, it worked.

Jess dropped by regularly. Making sure she was there for the showings. But then, early one Thursday morning, she knocked on Dana's door.

"Who the hell is that?" Dana said as she got out of bed. Glancing at the clock, it was just past four in the morning. Alyssa never knocked; she just came right in and crawled in bed with her mom.

Dana opened the door to find Jess standing in front of her. Jess slipped in quickly. "I parked my car in your garage.

If that's okay." She was talking at normal speed but out of breath.

"This isn't a pleasure call, I take it," Dana said.

"I wish." Jess took a breath, "Okay, I really wish. But no. Remember those strings I talked about?"

"Yes, I do. Like I said, who and why?" Dana sat down on the side of the bed.

"I drove here from DC. I already called in sick for tomorrow. I think I'm covered." Jess took Dana's hand. "I probably don't need to be this cautious. Just habit, I guess."

"I think you'll find caution an asset," Dana said.

"The McNabs. I met them at one of the openings." Jess took a breath, then nonstop said, "They called me. Well, Brenda called me. It gets a bit complicated here. Follow me. She was having an affair with the Illinois attorney general. He's married with three kids. You know she's married with two kids. The governor has been pulling all kinds of shit. He's taking bribes, doing shit with appointments, all kinds of illegal things. The attorney general wants to pull the plug and cut a deal for himself. He knows it's all going to come down on his head sooner or later. He doesn't want to do jail time. But the governor knows that he and Nancy have been fooling around."

"So? That doesn't sound like anything a divorce court won't solve," Dana said.

"But Brenda doesn't want to give up her family, and she says she still loves her husband. She doesn't want her husband to find out about her affair."

"And?" Dana said.

"So, here is the string. We have known for years that the governor is being controlled by a gang. They don't want anything to happen to him. The gang works out of a church on the southwest side. The preacher contacted Nancy. He told her if her boyfriend didn't back off and play nice, her kids would die first. Then his. Then her husband, then his wife. You get the picture." Jess flopped back on the bed. "That attorney bastard needs me. But he won't cooperate with this hanging over his head."

"That's the string. Okay, go to bed. Tomorrow, we'll work on something. Get some sleep. You look like shit." Dana walked her out of her bedroom.

"I need to know the Red Bitch is behind me," Jess said, turning to Dana.

"Don't worry. I said, who and why. Now get some sleep." Dana gave her a kiss and sent her to her bedroom.

The next morning, Alyssa was excited to see Uncle Jess at the breakfast table. "Where's Mason?" Dana asked Jody.

"She's sleeping in this morning. She's been tired lately," Jody said.

"Call her and tell her to get her ass out of bed. We got work to do," Dana said.

"Here, you talk to her." Jody handed Dana the phone.

Dana cupped her hand over the phone. "Red Bitch work. Jess is here."

"Okay. Meet you in the hideaway in what? A half-hour. Oh, bring coffee." Mason hung up.

"Let me guess. The hideaway and bring coffee," Jody said. "I'll take Alyssa to school and meet you guys in the hideaway. I'll give you something to take to Mason to eat. She needs to eat breakfast."

Jess gave Alyssa an extra squeeze and said, "Be safe. Love you."

In the hideaway, Jess looked around. "This is quite a place. Double glass panes." She tapped the window. "Walls?"

"Just insulation and corrugated aluminum. Sound and microwave proof," Mason said.

Jess went over with Mason what she had told Dana earlier that morning.

"It sounds like she trusts you, this Brenda. I assume she has told all this to the attorney general. What's his name, anyway?" Mason asked.

"Thomas Hung," Jess answered.

"We need to find out as much about this preacher as possible, and can I call them his thugs, his congregation?"

Jess dropped a large file on the desk. "Everything the department knows about this congregation is in this file, including pictures, names, addresses. Everything."

Jody brought another pot of coffee and, for Mason, another egg sandwich. The first one was sitting on the table with only one bite out of it. "Eat it." Jody dropped the new egg sandwich in front of Mason. "Don't push it aside," Jody demanded.

They went over the files about everyone: the governor, the attorney general, the preacher, and the McNabs. At noon, they went down and made sandwiches and drank Cokes.

"Okay, I think we can make a plan now," Dana said. "First, we have to be sure that this Thomas Hung is going to agree to work with the FBI. That's going to mean he has to feel safer talking with us than obeying the governor."

"If he does what we need him to do, he can stay out of jail. And Brenda's name and secrets would never be known," Jess added.

"You're going to need to talk to Thomas, Jess. You can't let him know you're with the FBI. He needs to think you work for an exclusive law firm. Only a few clients, one of which is the McNabs No other names. He must think their safety is what you're concerned about. That this only works if he cooperates with the FBI, and that that only works if the threat is dead," Mason said. She thought for a bit. "You need to get Brenda to introduce you to Thomas."

"That I can do," Jess answered.

"When you talk to Thomas, you're going to need to sound like an attorney," Jody said to Jess. "Let's work on that." They moved to the other side of the room to continue their discussion.

"We know about these four thugs. There might be more," Mason said.

"Good God. We need a lot more details," Dana said.

"I'm going to have to do some snooping around." Calling over to Jody, Mason asked, "Jody, can you handle things here for a week or so? I got to take a trip to Chicago. Oh, and by the way, can I get another sandwich?"

Jody smiled, happy Mason was hungry, "In a bit, honey. We're busy."

*

After dinner that night, Jess played with Alyssa and Handsome for a bit. Later, she said goodbye and left for DC.

The next day, she called Brenda. "I want you to back out of this thing as quietly and quickly as possible. Are you still seeing Thomas?"

"Hell no. Not for months. It was a big mistake on my part. I'm sorry I ever became involved with him. It's just that Roger was not paying enough attention to me..." Brenda said.

"That's an old excuse for an affair. Now I need to know where I can bump into Thomas. A club or a bar?" Jess asked.

"After work most nights, he goes to The Office, in Downtown. That's where I met him." Brenda said.

"Once I got his attention. I'm going to tell him you sent me. That should start things rolling. Back me up if he calls," Jess said.

The next day, Mason left for Chicago. The detective in her kicked in, and she was all over the southwest side. Homing in on the preacher and his small storefront church, she pretended to be collecting donations for orphans. That gave her a feeling of who lived around there. She watched who came and went to the church and checked out the local police patrols. In a week, she was back in Atlanta.

With Jess and Dana filled in, Jess was ready and left for Chicago the next day.

The next day, she casually walked in the office in her attorney suit, heels, and carrying an attorney-type briefcase. She saw Thomas at the bar, so she sat several chairs away with her back to him and ordered a sidecar. When her drink came, she turned and looked at Thomas. She gave him a smile. That was all it took for him to make his way over and start some small talk.

"Thomas, is it? Maybe we can get a quiet booth. It's much easier to get to know each other that way," Jess said, sounding as feminine as she could possibly muster.

Once seated, she took his wrist. "Brenda sent me to talk with you." Thomas went white and tried to pull away. Jess tightened her grip. "Come on. We're both attorneys. We know how to peacefully work things out. Now relax," she said.

"Who do you work for?" Was his first question.

"The McNabs, of course," Jess smiled.

"No, what law firm?" Thomas asked, looking in her eyes.

"It's a small DC firm. I really am not at liberty," She looked him in the eyes, "at this point to reveal that information."

"Does your firm's first name start with Kateland?"

"Maybe. Can we quit the bullshit? Here is what going to happen." They talked for a few minutes. She explained that the bad guys were going to be gone. Then he had to talk and cooperate with the FBI when they came calling. And they would come calling at some point. She didn't allow any questions.

She stood up. "Let me know your decision by ten a.m. tomorrow. I'll be on the third floor of the courthouse in the hallway, preparing for a case. Let me know if it's yes or no." She leaned forward on the table with both hands. "If it's no, or if you back out at any point before sending the governor to jail, you will wish that divorce was the only bad thing in your future." She dropped some photos on the table and left.

43. THE PREACHER

"Is this seat taken?" Jess asked the tall, attractive blond sitting by the window on the 96th floor of the Hancock Building. Her drink was on the ledge just next to the window.

"No, I'm saving it for a lesbian," the blond said with a smile.

"Well, you're in luck tonight," Jess said, taking the seat.

"Sundown is in half an hour. No matter what—clear, cloudy, rainy, or even snowy—somehow the sunsets over the city are always fabulous," Dana said, turning to Jess.

"What are you drinking?" Jess asked, pointing to her glass.

"Club soda. They didn't have and knife soda, so I had to settle for a club," Dana said with a little chuckle.

"You do know you're not always funny." Jess patted her on the leg. "But I love you anyway."

"How did it go?" Dana asked.

"As planned. I drove by the church as you asked. The hearse is parked beside the building."

"Good," Dana said.

"Tonight?" Jess asked.

"Sure, why not? Thomas's decision doesn't really matter. He'll talk one way or another, and this should convince him to cooperate. If not, you will have a reason to make him. The sunset is coming soon." Dana put her hand on Jess's leg. They sat quietly, a hand on each other's leg.

The clouds were streaks across the sky. The sun grew larger and larger as it neared the flat horizon on the west side of the city. As it touched the earth, it seemed to spread out along its lower edge. The underside of the clouds turned from pink to ruby as the white disappeared. The spaces in between the clouds went from light to dark blue, then to black. As the sun sank deeper into the earth, specs of lights appeared in the city. Just as the sun was about to give up the day, the streetlights pointed to the falling sun. The lights appeared as claw marks like the sun was scratching at the city, not wanting to go.

*

The Red Bitch left her hotel wearing a long raincoat draped over her shoulders. It was almost too large for her. Her arms were inside the coat, holding her long and short sword, and her hood was up. She had picked a spot that day and stood there for only a few minutes. It was just after nine o'clock. This was the time that the early diners were leaving, and the late patrons were coming in.

As the valet ran off to collect a car, another car pulled up. A driver got out of his new black Mercedes and opened the door for his date. They went inside, leaving the keys in the car for the valet. Dana just stepped in and drove off. It would be two hours before the owners found their car was missing. Another hour or so as the valet looked for it, and another hour with Chicago's finest, who were not going to look for the car anyway. This was just one of the dozens of vehicles stolen that night.

The Red Bitch drove over to the southeast side of town. She drove around the neighborhood to make sure she had the layout, then parked across the street from the church. She dumped her raincoat in the passenger seat, locking the doors and put the keys on top of the rear left tire. "Can't be too cautious in this neighborhood," she thought.

The church was dark, just as she had suspected. The hearse was not locked; no one would steal a hearse from this preacher. She got in and pulled down the visor and the keys fell into her lap. "I love this town," she said aloud as she started the hearse.

The drive wasn't far to a local bar, aptly named Love Bites. They stocked booze and whores. The Red Bitch backed the hearse up in front of the bar. Leaving it running, she burst through the front door and found four men at the bar talking to whores, their backs to the door. Two other hookers were sitting at a table smoking and drinking out of Champagne glasses.

Their heads turned as she entered. One tall, heavy thug turned and put his elbows on the bar. "Who—" Was the only word he got out before the Red Bitch flew through the air, planting a heel in his heart. As she rode him down, she pushed one of the hookers aside and slit the other man's neck with her short sword. Blood spewed in all directions.

As she pulled her heel out of the first guy, she covered the hooker's mouth as she started to scream. "Be quiet. No screaming. No talking. No moving." She took her hand away from the hooker's mouth. "I only got room for five."

She smiled at the whore next to her. She was Hispanic, with heavy makeup. She had a hot body for someone who could not have been over sixteen. The Red Bitch pinched her cheek and slapped her on the butt. "You're cute."

She looked around and held up two photos. "Where are they?" She looked around. "Please be nice. It's a sin to lie."

The girls pointed at a door at the far end of the bar.

"Thank you, girls. Now, don't anybody move or try to call out or try to make a call." Looking at the older woman behind the bar, she said, "Please do me a favor and put both your hands on the bar. As I said, I only have room for five. And believe me, you don't want to ride in a crowded hearse. Thanks again for your cooperation." She said all this as she walked toward the door. With that, she kicked it open.

Two big men screwing a small woman on her hands and knees, one in front and one in back. They never saw her coming.

Her long sword took off the head of the one behind, and then the sword went through the heart of the other one. They both fell backward, away from the woman. Looking down, she said, "Oh, I'm sorry. Thought they were through."

The woman on the bed started to scream. The Red Bitch put her sword to her neck. "Please don't do that. It hurts my ears."

She shut up.

"Follow me," she said to the naked whore.

The Red Bitch walked back into the bar. There was blood on her face, arms, chest, and left leg.

"Hi, all. I am so happy to see you all again. Now guys," she said to the two men still standing at the bar, "I have a little job for you." She looked at the woman behind the bar. "It's free drinks tonight, isn't it? I mean, with such a helpful crowd, helping you clean up the place and all. I think they deserve it, don't you?" The bartender's hands were still on the bar. "Yes." Was all she said.

"Good. Okay, guys, the hearse is outside. Please pick these dead guys up, one at a time. Oh, they won't be needing their rings, gold chains, watches, money, wallets, or whatever. Just take it all off them. Please just throw anything you find on the bar." The first man was stripped of most everything before he was taken out to the Hearse. The girls stripped the other men of their earthly possessions in minutes. "Now, now, girls. Be nice. You have to share. Now put all the loot on the bar."

They did as they were told but palmed as much as possible. After the fourth man was taken out to the hearse, the Red Bitch reminded the men, "Don't forget his head."

They ran into the back room and came out carrying it by its hair, then just threw it into the back of the hearse.

Just as they finished, the Red Bitch stood in the doorway, looking at the living and the loot. "You know the cops will want all that loot as evidence. They will just take it all for themselves. I'm not going to call the cops." Looking over her shoulder. "You can call the cops if you want." She shut the door.

She drove the hearse up to Waukegan. The Pastor had a beautiful lakefront mansion. By this time, it was past one in the morning. The hearse coasted into the driveway. The Red Bitch quietly got out of the hearse and walked around to the side door. It was locked. The end of her long sword cracked open a small windowpane, trying to minimize the glass falling on the floor. She pulled out a few large pieces of glass and reached in to unlock the door.

She walked into the kitchen. Light softly streamed in from the dining room. On her third step, she heard a growl coming from the doorway to the dining room. She opened the refrigerator; the light exposed a Doberman standing in the doorway, growling. Looking for something, she saw a package of steaks in the fridge. She took one out and unwrapped it.

The dog continued to growl and came close to her one step at a time. "You're a good boy. I bet you're a really good boy." She whispered softly and comfortingly to the Dobe, bending down to his level. "I bet you're a real well-trained boy. They probably don't feed you if you do something wrong. Here. You've been a real good boy." She held out the steak. He took another step closer, but he had stopped growling. "Here you go, boy. All yours." She laid the steak on the floor. He sniffed it and then hungrily went after it.

"Good boy." She stood up. The Doberman looked up with the steak hanging out of both sides of his mouth.

"Good boy." She patted him on the head. He lay down on the floor and, with the steak between his paws, enjoyed his dinner.

Leaving the refrigerator door open, she left the kitchen and closed the kitchen door behind her. In the dimly lit dining room, she could see the entry and presumably the stairway to the upper level. As she came around the corner to the entryway, a huge man in boxer shorts threw a punch at her head. Her arm came up fast enough to block the blow, but the force of the punch threw her against the wall. *Oh, damn, it's going to be six*, she thought.

He threw another punch. She moved, and his right fist hit the wall hard. She measured him; he was big but slow. He threw another blow with his left hand, but she moved aside again. His left fist hit the wall hard. He took a step back and took another swing with his right hand.

They never learn, she thought. In one blow, she crushed his windpipe. He finished his swing, hitting her in the side of the face. There was not much force behind the strike. He reached up, holding his neck with both hands, trying to get air. Seeing her standing just in front of him, he tried for one last blow. A quick kick to his knee brought him down. "Goodnight, lover," she said. Moving around behind him, she gave him one more kick. Her heel went into the back of his head, breaking through the top vertebrae and spinal cord.

"Now how the hell am I going to get you into that hearse?" she said to the body on the floor.

"Billy, what's going on down there?" she heard from the top of the stairs.

"So much for surprises," the Red Bitch said to herself. She slipped across the entryway, shutting off the lights as she went. The preacher fired two shots in her direction.

Sounds like an automatic. No way of telling how many shots he has, she thought.

"Billy, where the hell are you?" The preacher called down to the entryway.

The Red Bitch recalled seeing the breaker box in the kitchen. She slipped across the entryway again, just a quick shadow that was all the preacher saw. He fired four more shots. In the kitchen, the dog looked up at her. "You're such a good puppy. Do you need some water?" She grabbed a bowl from the cupboard above the sink and got him a small bowl of water. "Good boy." She patted him on the head and punched the breaker switches to their off position.

The preacher was still at the top of the stairs. The Red Bitch could hear him yelling even though she was still in the kitchen. "Billy. Fuck. Billy, where the fuck are you? What the fuck do I pay you for, Billy?" She slipped back into the darkened entry hall just as the emergency battery-powered lights came on. "Shit, I didn't count on that," She said aloud. *I just have to move faster,* she thought.

The preacher was outlined from the back by the emergency light in the upstairs hallway. The Red Bitch took a swing at Bill's head with her long sword and threw it up the stairs. It hit and went *thump, thump, thump* as it bounced down the stairs. It distracted the preacher, who fired six more shots at random.

I got to get closer, she thought again. *I can't hit him from here*. She looked around the entryway for an alternate way up the stairs. Dropping her long sword, she ran to a settee next to the stairway, using it to jump to the outside edge of the stairway while holding on with her left hand to the rail. She threw the short sword, catching the preacher in the gut. He fired another two rounds, then fell to his knees.

The Red Bitch dropped to the settee, then the floor, and picked up her long sword. The light in the entryway outlined her tall, sexy silhouette, as she slowly made her way up the stairs, her hips swaying in an exaggeratedly sexy manner.

As she came close to the top of the stairs, the preacher pulled his trigger one more time. The bullet missed by a mile and the Red Bitch did not stop or flinch. The second pull of the trigger, with better aim, went *click*. Empty gun.

Looking up at her blood-covered body, he said. "So, you're the Red Bitch I have heard so much about. I thought you were dead."

"I am," she said in a soft voice. "I'm here to take you to hell." His head hit the floor, then bounced down the stairway.

*

"How the hell am I going to get you in the hearse, Billy?" The Red Bitch looked down at the headless Billy. Even headless and with some bleed out, it was still an effort to drag him the fifteen to twenty feet to the back of the hearse.

She rested on the porch steps, wondering how she was going to get Billy in the hearse. Her eye caught a strap sticking out of the side of the hearse's door next to the bodies. Getting up, she looked closer at the back of the hearse. There was a strap on either side. Just inside the open door, she found a button. "These must be used to pull in the coffins," she said aloud. She pulled out the strap and tied it around Billy's legs, then pushed the button. The strap dragged Billy up into the hearse. "Cool," she said out loud. "Now for the preacher."

Shutting the back door of the hearse, she went back into the kitchen. "Hi, boy. Have you been a good boy? Of course, you have." She patted him on the head and took another steak out of the refrigerator. This time, she cut it up into smaller bites. "Sit!" she said, and the dog sat right down. She tossed him a piece of steak. He caught it in the air.

"Good boy. Now come." She walked out to the hearse with the dog following her.

"Come on. Get in," she said, opening the driver's door. The dog looked at the bloody Red Bitch and then jumped right in. He moved to the passenger seat, making room for the Red Bitch. Getting in, she gave him another treat, this time in her bloody open hand. He carefully took the treat from her hand. "Good boy. You're my good boy," she said, patting his head.

They drove together, playing the radio. It took her a few tries to find the right music. Soul music. *Appropriate*, she thought. About an hour later, she backed the hearse into Thomas's driveway and rolled down the window a crack. Petting the dog, she gave him the last treat. Leaving the radio on, she got out of the hearse. The dog lay down in the seat, probably waiting for her to come back.

Jess was parked across the street in the black Mercedes. "Need a ride, beautiful?" she called to the Red Bitch as she crossed the street. The Red Bitch leaned into the driver's side window to give Jess a kiss.

"Hold it. You got dried blood all over your face and hands. Probably everywhere else." She handed the Red Bitch a wet towel. "Good thing this isn't my car," she said as the Red Bitch wiped the blood off her face and hands while walking around to the passenger side. Before getting in, she took the raincoat that she had left in the front seat and threw it over her shoulders. She leaned her swords against the door. Then she gave Jess her kiss.

"Call your boys. Everything is set but tell them, to not hurt the dog or they will have to answer to me. He acts mean, but he's really a good dog." Dana waited as Jess started to make her call. "You need a good dog, don't you?"

Jess just looked at the Red Bitch. "No," she said before the team leader answered the call. She repeated the orders except she changed the part about taking care of the dog to "You'll answer to me."

She pulled away from the curb, turning on her headlights. A couple of blocks later, she passed two black SUVs. She flashed her lights. They flashed back.

Even at that early hour, the Stevenson Expressway was packed with cars on their way into downtown Chicago.

"I think I'll go to the Art Museum today. I got to look like I did a little work," Dana said, still wiping the blood off herself. "Want to go with me?"

"Sorry, love. I got to get back to DC ASAP. Boy, that's a lot of letters, even for me. I guess I don't have to meet with Thomas; my guys just picked him up. I got to go direct the operation from there. You know to stay out of the spotlight," Jess said. "Thanks, anyway. So how did it go?"

"About as planned." Dana pulled down the visor mirror and turned on the light. She checked the discoloration on the side of her face, wiping some last traces of someone's dried blood away. "Except for Billy."

"Who's Billy?" Jess looked over at the Red Bitch's face. "Where did you get that?"

"You mean this bruise? Billy. He's the fat one with no head. I guess he was the preacher's boyfriend-dash-bodyguard. I didn't count on him," she said, touching the red mark on her face. "I didn't see him coming."

"So, this all can be blamed on the Red Bitch's ghost?" Jess asked.

"Yeah. I left enough people alive at Love Bites for the word to get around to the right people," she said. "It's a lever you can use on Thomas. That son of a bitch. Whoops, I shouldn't have said that. Makes him sound like my son." They both giggled.

By the time they got downtown, it was almost sunrise. Jess parked the car just off Michigan Avenue.

"The sun will be up soon. Are you coming next month for Alyssa's birthday?" Dana asked, getting out of the car.

"Even you couldn't keep me away," Jess said as she got out of the car, throwing the keys into the Mercedes. They walked off in opposite directions.

44. GOOD NIGHT

Jess made at least monthly visits to Atlanta. She now had a real family, and she wanted to be with them, especially Alyssa, as much as possible.

"Please, go get Mason, Jody," Jess said, walking into the kitchen on Friday morning. "Tell her to meet us in the hideaway. And can I get some coffee, please? Where's Alyssa?"

Dana walked in behind her. "And something to eat, please. You're fifteen minutes late, Jess; I just dropped Alyssa off at school."

Jody smiled. "Another string, to cut?"

"Yep. Los Angeles this time," Jess said.

"Give me fifteen minutes. I'll get some breakfast ready," she said, pouring coffee for Jess and Dana.

This new mission helped revive Mason again. She spent a week in San Padro doing the scouting and detail planning. She was excited and energized upon her return to Jody. However, she started sliding downhill soon after.

Months later, Jess had another string to cut. Mason was up for the planning. Just as they finished their preparation, Mason sat back in her chair, her hands in her lap, her head down. "Girls," she said, not looking up. "I'm afraid I can't make it. Not this time, anyway." Her head dropped back down. "I'm sorry."

"Don't be. This is an easy one." Dana got up to put her arms around her from the back and gave her a kiss on the head. "Besides, we're going to need you at the gallery. We have three new artists coming in this week. All of them have super big egos. You're just what we need at the gallery this week. You're the controller!"

"Yeah, I'm the controller. Thank you," Mason said, kissing Dana's hand.

*

Later that afternoon, Dana walked with Jody and Handsome to meet Alyssa at the school.

"Have I been too hard on Mason? Is this all too much for her?" Dana asked.

Jody stopped and took Dana by the arm and turned her toward her. Taking both of Dana's arms, she shook her. "It's what has been keeping her alive. Once the new gallery was built, this was the only excitement she had left to look forward to. Just keep her involved as much as possible. If she doesn't have a purpose, she will die. Got it?"

"Got it," Dana said, and they gave each other a long embrace.

*

A few months later, they were all sitting in the library. Jess was getting used to reading rather than watching television. Still, she missed her sitcoms and football games.

"You guys up for Thanksgiving in DC?" she asked, looking up from her Hemingway novel, *For Whom the Bell Tolls*.

Jess got a unanimous "Hell no!"

"Let's do Thanksgiving at our house," Mason said. "We have a bigger oven. I know Jody is going to buy the biggest turkey she can find."

"Yeah!" Alyssa clapped her hands.

"Okay, then Christmas is here," Dana said. "Only one tree, and it's going over in that corner as always. We'll have Christmas Eve here and leave snacks for Santa, then open presents the next morning." Dana was insistent, "Okay, Christmas dinner is here."

"Yeah," Alyssa clapped. "Uncle Jess, this Christmas, please no more clothes. Last year, I had to take them all back and get a bigger size. I mean, I like them and all. But, no," Alyssa said, shaking her head.

"So. Clothes are out. What do you want?" Jess asked.

"A ten-speed bike. And a TV." Alyssa looked sideways at her mother. "And..."

"And no more ands. The rest will be a surprise. Nothing is guaranteed, especially the TV," Dana said.

"Then New Years in DC?" Jess asked hopefully.

She got a unanimous "No!" except for Alyssa, who said yes with her hand in the air.

"You don't have a TV," Jess said, to Dana. "Let's do New Year's Day at their house," she said, pointing at Mason and Jody. "We've got to see the Rose Parade and the Rose Bowl. I'm not missing that."

"If we're doing New Year's Day at your house," Dana started.

"Then we see the new year in at our house also," Jody said.

"Okay, we have a plan for the holidays," Mason said smiling.

*

Thanksgiving dinner was a huge success. Jody piled Mason's plate high. Turkey, stuffing, mashed potatoes, string beans with breadcrumbs. Mason picked at it, all the while smiling and talking.

Frank and Sofia, Debbie's parents, were invited every Thanksgiving. They usually brought a homemade pie, usually pumpkin, as it was Debbie's favorite. Talk of Debbie was kept to a minimum. They often left soon after dinner.

*

"Merry Christmas! Have you been a good girl?" Jess said, leaping into the kitchen wearing a Santa Claus hat. It was the Saturday before Christmas and Jess planned on leaving the Sunday after New Year's.

Jess helped Alyssa decorate the tree that first Saturday evening. Mason was the chief director for decorating and Alyssa happily followed her instructions for hanging the bulbs and tinsel. Jess overdid the higher parts of the tree. It was up to Dana to put the angel on the top of the tree. Mason enjoyed every minute of it.

The presents were arranged under the tree. Alyssa had a look of disappointment when she could not make out a ten-speed bicycle or a TV under the tree. She thought the only boxes she could make out were clothing boxes.

The cookies and eggnog were placed under the tree Christmas eve. "There. Everything is ready, except you're still awake. Santa Claus won't come if you're still awake." Dana led Alyssa upstairs to bed, with Handsome close behind. By the time Dana came back down to the library, Jess was drinking the eggnog, Jody had the plate of cookies in her lap, and Mason sat smiling with her eyes closed. Then, Jess and Dana brought in the red Schwinn ten-speed bicycle with a big red bow on the handlebars, followed by the console TV. Jess wanted to put up the antenna on the roof of the house that night. Dana wouldn't let her.

Jody and Mason were over early Christmas morning.

"Can I come down yet?" Alyssa called down to Dana every two minutes or so.

"In a minute. Let Jody and Mason settle in and get some coffee. You're peeping; back in your room," Dana scolded Alyssa. Handsome lay at the top of the steps watching the activity with his ears up, at alert.

"Okay, you can," Alyssa was halfway down the steps before Dana could finish saying, "come down now."

Mason laughed and clapped at Alyssa's reaction to seeing her ten speed. Then the TV.

"Now, can I put up the antenna?" Jess asked.

"Jess, after we open our presents. Oh, your present is in the backyard. You can open it anytime." Dana said. Dana had got Jess a blue ten-speed bicycle.

It was a wonderful Christmas. They got the TV going and watched parades. They all were hypnotized by movie *Miracle on 34th Street.*

Mason spent the day in the big chair in the library. She only got up go to the bathroom and for dinner.

Jess played like a little kid for the rest of the week. She and Alyssa rode their bikes together all over the neighborhood. Jess joined Dana at the dojo and found out she was not a black belt in that dojo.

Breakfast was sometimes at Mason and Jody's or at Dana's. Lunch was usually out somewhere. The five of them caught a movie one afternoon after they ran out of things to do.

"I get to stay up till midnight, don't I?" Alyssa asked hopefully.

"Sure, you do. You need to see the new year in with the rest of us," Jess said, looking up at Dana and getting a little nod.

A few hours later, Jess was shaking Alyssa awake. She had fallen asleep on the sofa. "Come on. It's almost New Year's."

They toasted in the new year with Champagne, and Alyssa got club soda in a champagne glass. They heard firecrackers announcing the start of the celebration and They rushed out to the front yard to enjoy the fireworks. By twelve-thirty, everyone but Dana and Jess were in bed and fast to sleep.

"Do you want to bring in the new year with a bang?" Jess asked, nodding up the stairs.

"Jess, I thought we were over that long ago? Besides, no friends. I told you that long ago," Dana said, but with a smile. "But, we're not friends. We're family."

"Eww, that's nasty. Forget I said anything." Jess corrected herself.

Two days later, it was Sunday. They all headed over to Mason and Jody's for breakfast before Jess drove back to DC.

"Where's the coffee?" Jess asked, sniffing the air. There was no smell of coffee. Dana followed Jess through the door. She took a quick look around.

"Jess, take Alyssa home and make her some breakfast," Dana said, turning Alyssa around and handing her off to Jess. "I'll call you," Dana said. Jess had a questioning look on her face but said nothing and did as she was told.

Dana walked into the living room, then up the stairs. "Hi," she said, tapping on their bedroom door.

"Come in," Jody said.

Dana slowly opened the door. Mason and Jody were locked in an embrace.

"She rolled over, hugged me, and told me she loved me. Then she just quit breathing," Jody said with tears running down her cheeks.

"Jody," Dana said, sitting on the side of the bed. "Jody, I'll take it from here." She gently took her arms from around Mason and helped her out of bed. "Please, go get dressed and go downstairs."

Dana walked her slowly into the bathroom with the attached walk-in closet. She then went back to Mason and rechecked her. Then she rolled her on her back. Dana covered her up to her neck and then put Mason's hands on her chest. Mason's eyes were closed, and she had a calm expression on her face. Dana gave her a kiss on the forehead. "I'm going to miss you so much."

Dana called next door. "Hi. Mason's gone." With a sob in her throat and tears in her eyes. "Take care of Alyssa. I have to tell her as soon as I can."

Dana started for the bathroom to check on Jody. She met her at the door. Jody took two steps into the bedroom and froze in place. She couldn't move in any direction. Jody just looked at Mason. Tears and sobs were her only words. Dana put her arms around her and did not try to move her. She just held her.

Then Jody managed to say, "I had not realized how thin she had gotten. God, I love her." Dana leaned in the direction of the door. Jody took a step toward the door. Then another. She stopped at the door. She looked up at Dana, then at Mason. "I love her so much." Then she went downstairs.

Dana then called the hospital. She explained the situation and requested an ambulance. "Please, no firetrucks and no sirens. Just a polite knock on the door. Take your time. We're in no hurry."

Once Jody got into the kitchen, she went on automatic. She did the first thing she always did in the morning: she made coffee. She just stood there, her hands on the counter, looking at the coffee pot. Tears were streaming down her cheeks. She then poured coffee for her and Dana. They sat together, Dana holding her hand. "Coffee is kind of salty this morning," Jody said with one chuckle, then wiped her eyes with a napkin. "We need to talk to Alyssa before the guys in the ambulance come to take her away," she said.

"I'll take care of it. In the meantime, I'll send Jess over here." Dana got up and gave Jody a kiss on the head before going next door.

Jess met Dana at the kitchen door. "Alyssa has been really quiet this morning."

"Go be with Jody." Looking at Alyssa in the other room, Dana took a deep breath. "I am not looking forward to this." Jess just stood there, looking at Alyssa. "Go. I don't want Jody to be alone. We'll be over in a few. Don't let them take Mason away till we get over there."

Dana sat down at the table next to Alyssa. She was drinking her milk and picking at a piece of toast with jelly. "Alyssa, remember when Grandpa went to heaven."

Alyssa reached over and held her mother tight. She answered, "Yes. Auntie Mason went to be with Grandpa, didn't she?"

"Yes, how did you know?" Dana had pulled Alyssa off her chair and held her tight.

"I had a dream." Was all she would say. Every other questions was answered with a shake 'no' of Alyssa's head.

She had quiet tears running down her young face. They walked back to Jody's hand in hand. As they entered the kitchen, Alyssa ran to Jody. Jody leaned over and held her tight.

"She's making biscuits and gravy," Jess said. "I couldn't stop her."

"That's okay. She'll do what she wants to do," Dana said.

"Alyssa honey, do you want some breakfast? I made biscuits and gravy. Here, sit down. I'll get you some." Jody juggled a hot biscuit in her hands as she pulled it in half. Putting it on a small plate, she added gravy. She put it in front of Alyssa. "Oh, fork. Where's my brain?" she said, turning around.

There was a soft knock on the door. Jody even offered biscuits to the ambulance guys.

*

Sally made it back for Mason's funeral. Lars had four dojos going and could not leave Spain. A week later, Sally headed back home. The funeral was attended by friends, well-known business owners, artists, and stars. Twenty-six squad cars and ten motorcycle policemen parked in front of the church and followed the hearse to the graveyard. With white-gloved hands, they gave her a final salute.

45. ALL IN GOOD TIME

On one of Jess's regular visits, she arrived Thursday night. The timing was a bit unusual but not surprising. The next morning over breakfast, she said, "I don't know how you feel about this. But I have another string to cut"

Jody put down a plate of toast and turned to go get the eggs she had made for breakfast. "After breakfast, I'll take Alyssa to school and see you two in the hideaway," she said on her way to the kitchen.

Jess looked at Dana. "Are you sure?" Then to Jody, as she sat down at the breakfast table. "Are you sure?"

"Sure," Jody said, "in about an hour." Then to Dana, Jody asked, "Is the Red Bitch back?"

"Sure," Dana said.

After the funeral, Jody spent most of her time over at Dana's. Her empty house just reminded her of Mason. Every time she turned around, she thought she saw her sitting at the kitchen table or reading in the living room. She would begin to say something to her but would just see an empty chair. It was just easier to not be there.

Jess and Dana were going over the file when Jody walked in with Handsome behind her. He had started limping on his left side, the side he had got knifed in. The pain was brought on by age.

"What do we have here?" Jody asked, pulling a few of the pages over in front of her.

"Three crooked cops protecting a city councilman in a small town in Kansas. We think they have killed one of the board members to keep everyone else quiet," Jess said.

"Can I see that?" Jody pointed at a layout of the police station and bar where they all hung out.

Dana passed the drawings over to Jody, who studied them for quite a while. "So, what are your thoughts?" she asked, looking up.

"The bar looks like the spot," Jess said, pointing out the floorplan.

"Did you think of doing it at the police station?" Jody said, looking up.

"We thought there would be too much firepower in the police station and too many barriers," Dana said.

"Well, they're cops, so they will always have two guns on them. So firepower is kind of irrelevant. They will have that at either place. Really, there are no barriers in the front, just a counter. This door here," Jody said, pointing to the blueprint, "could be a problem. But, don't you think whoever is up front would have the keys to that door? There is no back door. Everything has to come through the front door. So, keys or a button or something to make it easy to get inside has got to be there."

"What about the other cops?" Jess asked.

Dana answered, "only five cops. Can you pull up the schedule, Jess?"

Jess shuffled through some papers "Thursday at two in the afternoon. Just them and any prisoners in the lockup."

"Good! A daytime job. I am getting really tired of working nights," Dana said, looking up. "And I can let any prisoners that are there out of their cells, courtesy of the Red Bitch."

"Good call, Jody." Jess nodded her head.

"Looks like we got a new planner," Dana said.

*

The day before the Red Bitch left for Kansas, Dana said, "Jody, you're over here all the time. Why don't you just move in?"

Jody looked intently at Dana for a few minutes as she ran everything through her brain. "I think, if redone, your basement would make a great hideaway."

"Well, I guess you're right. So?" Dana waited for Jody to think about her answer.

"So, I guess I'll get right on it," Jody said, returning to her lunch.

*

Dana had a business trip scheduled the following month to Arizona.

In the meantime, Jody had cleaned out everything from both Dana's and her room. She had the walls repainted and ripped up the old carpeting and had new put in. Then she had the master bath redone.

She moved some of the furniture around. Some just worked better in their original rooms, but some had to be replaced.

Jody and Alyssa picked Dana up at the airport. "Can I help you with your things up to your room?" Jody asked, and Alyssa giggled.

"No, I can handle it," Dana said and headed up the stairs. Jody and Alyssa followed Dana up. Dana looked over her shoulder at them with a *What's going on?* Expression on her face.

At the top of the stairs, Jody stood with her back to the hall wall and her arms folded on her chest. Alyssa had her hands covering her mouth to keep from laughing.

Dana gave them a strange look as she opened the door. "Shit. What did you do to my room? It's beautiful," she said, putting down her bag.

"That's because it's now my room. It's not yours anymore," Jody said. "That's your room now." She pointed to the master bedroom.

Dana carefully opened the master door. "Wow," she said.

"I not only painted it and put in new carpeting; I also moved your things into here. God, did you ever think of organizing your stuff?" She opened the door to the walk-in closet. "Your shoes are sorted by color, jewelry's over here. Dresses are arranged by color on this side, skirts, and blouses on this side."

"Check out the bathroom," Alyssa said to her mom. Dana came out of the bathroom wide-eyed.

"If I'm going to live here, I need my own room," Jody said. Dana sat in a comfortable chair in her new room. Alyssa did not let her rest. Running over, she pulled her up by her arms.

"Come on, Mom. Wait till you see Uncle Jess's new room. It's just for her." She pulled Dana downstairs. "Isn't this just perfect for Uncle Jess?" Alyssa twirled around in the room, her arms out, a huge smile on her face.

*

Two years later Alyssa, now a freshman in high school, was invited to the Junior-Senior Prom, by a boy.

Dana sat up late in the throne on the patio. Her memories came flooding back. "God, has it been that many years?" Dana thought. She could still see Debbie's smile and her beautiful dress. She pushed the last time she saw Debbie alive out of her mind. Still, she dreamed about her that night.

Dana and Alyssa had a wonderful time spending the day shopping for a prom dress and shoes.

"I need a new bra, panties, and," Alyssa started in.

"Okay, why? Who's going to see them?" Was Dana's come back.

"Mom." Was Alyssa elongated answer.

*

"Oh, he's here," Dana said, answering the knock at the door. "Alyssa, wait up here and make your grand entrance down the stairway," Jody told Alyssa for the fifth time.

"Hi, I'm Mark," The young man held out his free hand, a corsage in the other.

"Welcome Mark," Dana shook his hand.

As he entered the house Alyssa started down the stairway, "Wow," Mark said, Dana smiled broadly. After the introductions, and the traditional photos in the entryway and library, the young couple held hands and headed for the limo. "Have fun. Be home by eleven, or else," Dana called after them.

Dana turned to Jess and Jody. "You know what this means?" she asked as she closed the front door.

"Our little girl's growing up?" Jody said.

"Nope. Well yeah, she is growing up. But what else?"

Jody and Jess just shook their heads in puzzlement.

"Jody, do you remember the pact I made with myself just after Alyssa was born?"

"No, not really," Jody said.

"I said I would not date in Atlanta till Alyssa did. She's on a date!" Dana said happily.

"What about me?" Jess said after the thought hit her.

"Find your own date," Dana said with a laugh.

"Good for you guys. Now, just don't teach our little girl how to be promiscuous. Keep it out of the house," Jody said, leading them into the library. She poured three glasses of brandy and held up her glass. "To our little girl growing up. No matter how old she gets, she will always be our little girl." They clinked glasses.

*

Alyssa came running into Dana's bedroom just three days after the prom. "Mom, Handsome just threw up."

Dana rushed to Alyssa's room. Handsome was lying on his side, his vomit on the floor next to his head.

"How are you doing, boy?" Dana asked as she petted him. "Come on, Handsome. Let's get you up and go see your doctor. Okay?" Handsome struggled to try and get to his feet. He could not do that.

Dana picked him up in her arms. Alyssa called down to Jody in the kitchen, "We're going to the vet's."

Jody shut off the stove and helped Dana with Handsome out to the car. "Call Dr. Modglin. Tell her we're coming. It's an emergency."

Jody tossed Alyssa her cell phone. "Call her, I I'll drive. I'm the only one dressed." Dana in her nightgown and Alyssa in her nightgown both got in the backseat with Handsome on their laps.

Dr. Modglin was waiting at the front door for them. She rushed Handsome into the nearest room. "Wait out here," Dr. Modglin said as she closed the examining room door in their faces.

Dr. Modglin came out to the waiting room. "He is dying. He was in a lot of pain. I have given him painkillers to make him comfortable." Alyssa burst into tears and sobs. Dana and Jody were also crying, the three of them holding each other.

"Please, come with me." Dr. Modglin led them to a small room with a sofa and soft lighting. "I'll bring Handsome in so you can say goodbye to him." In a few minutes, Handsome was wheeled in on a gurney and then placed in their laps. Alyssa was petting his head and kissing him. "When you're ready, let me know. He will just go to sleep, then quit breathing. He'll go quietly and comfortably." Dr. Modglin closed the door to give them their time.

"Remember all the fun we had playing in the backyard," Alyssa said to Handsome. He lifted his head and gave her a kiss on the face and put his head back down heavily. He closed his eyes. He began to barely wag his tail. Miss Dunn was petting his head; Debbie was petting him as was Christopher and Mason, "Come on Handsome, let's go for a walk," Christopher said to Handsome as his spirit got up off Alyssa's lap. As the spirits began to walk towards the door, Handsome stopped and turned to look at Alyssa. "Don't worry Handsome, you'll always be with Alyssa," Christopher said. "Remember, it's your job to always protect her."

*

Jess had begun to solidify her position at the FBI. She happily accepted more responsibility. She was offered promotions almost yearly. She never accepted any of them, it would have taken her away from her field agents.

Still, one to three times she a year, she needed a string cut. The Red Bitch was always available. No one in the Bureau ever made the connection between her family in Atlanta and the Red Bitch.

*

The gallery thrived. Their catalogs still featured kids, dogs, cats, adults, old people, and even a clown once. The catalogs alone were much sought after. Nothing in the gallery sold for under a hundred thousand dollars. Private parties or auctions were held only three to four times a year. When they had an exclusive buyer or a special piece of art for a unique client, private showings happened as required.

To be selected as an artist or client at Persson's Exclusive Gallery of Fine Art showed that you were now part of high society, no matter who your parents were.

Jody became the grand dame of the gallery. Dana became more involved in the daily operation of the gallery. Jody had a knack of discovering clients' wants and turning them into needs. Dana specialized in filling those needs.

Alyssa became a vital part of the gallery by sixteen. Like her mother, she found art as natural as breathing. All the clients loved her. All the artists discovered she was the key to access to the grand dame or Dana. Alyssa was not easily persuaded.

Jess finally found someone in DC she loved. Her name was Jessica. Jessica understood that they were going to make trips to Atlanta at least once a month and for every holiday and birthday. They shared a name, but Jessica was the exact opposite of Jess. That's just what they both needed.

"Dana, you have got to come to DC. I can't say anymore. No time. Love ya." Then Jess hung up.

Dana was sitting on Jess's balcony with a view of the Potomac. She and Jessica were having martinis when Jess got home. Jessica was an expert bartender. Jess had mostly drunk beer from a bottle before she met Jessica.

"Hi, lover," Jess said as she came home, dropping her briefcase inside the door and kicking off her heels. She came out to the balcony and gave Dana a kiss. Then, seeing the look on Jessica's face, went back, and put on her flats.

"Hi, number one lover," she said to Jessica and gave her a kiss before sitting down with Dana between them. "Sweetie, those martinis look fabulous. Can you make us a big shaker full?" All this time, she was writing in her notebook. Jessica saw nothing odd in that.

As Jessica left for the bar, Jess showed the note to Dana. "Meet me at the Club House Restaurant at one tomorrow." Then, just one name underlined many times. "RON"

46. LONDON

"Yes, ma'am, right this way." The receptionist said, leading Dana to a table. The Club House was classy and very loud and was full of congressmen and lobbyists. They all were on their second or third martini. None of the congressmen had remembered their wallets.

When they reached the table, the receptionist put down the menu at the chair next to Jess. The gentleman sitting on Jess' other side got up and offered his hand. "This is Craig. Craig, meet Dana." Dana silently shook Craig's hand. "I am so glad to meet you finally. You have the finest art gallery in the world, according to your big sister."

Dana sat down and did not say a word. She was waiting for answers. Her silence was more unnerving than if she shouted at them. Jess knew this and knew it was already getting to Craig.

"Craig, tell her what you do," Jess spoke up, settling back in her chair to watch the fun. She signaled for the waitress. "A bottle of Sauvignon Blanc, please. Thank you."

"First of all, this meeting never happened," Craig said. Dana just looked around at the full, loud restaurant. "None of these meetings are happening. If it weren't for no meetings, this restaurant would be empty."

Dana still didn't say a word.

"Craig get on with it," Jess demanded.

"Well, yes. I work for the US Attorney General's office. Normally I can't stand this bitch." He pointed to Jess. "She's pushy, demanding, and a pain in the ass. But she brings me so many airtight cases, I have to listen to her."

The waitress brought the bottle of wine, uncorked it, and poured out three glasses before putting it in a wine bucket beside the table.

"Don't stop now. Get on with it," Jess pushed Craig again.

"I try cases. I also oversee several programs, along with putting up with Jess's incessant questioning."

"Craig, tell her why I invited you to this little lunch and no meeting." Jess just kept pushing. Craig was being a typical attorney and not getting to the point. He was used to asking questions, not answering them. Especially with someone who was completely silent. Dana's eyes were fixed on his and did not blink. That made him very nervous.

Dana tasted her wine and looked at Craig.

"I sometimes work with the witness protection program," Craig said.

"Start at the beginning. Dana likes details. Don't leave anything out," Jess said.

Dana looked at Jess. The thought went through Dana's head, *She has something on this guy.*

"To begin with, all I do is oversee their files. But only if they start missing their monthly check-ins, or they are not where they are supposed to be during a surprise visit." He looked at Jess, then back at Dana. "Long before I came to this job, in fact, I wasn't even out of law school, anyway, before my time, there was a meth and coke lab in Ft. Worth, Texas. It was a big one. Mexican drug lords controlled it. I think the head guy was called Grandpa or something like that. I don't know; that's just what I read in the file. The lab supplied drugs to Texas, New Mexico, and Louisiana." He took a sip of his wine. "Years ago, something spooked this guy who ran the lab, really bad. So bad he turned state's evidence on the condition he was put deep in the witness protection program. He turned in his lab and a lot of contacts. He helped put a dozen thugs in jail."

"What scared him?" Jess asked.

"He would not tell us. We tried. We guessed. But we never really found out," Craig said.

Jess looked at Dana. They both knew what scared him.

"You left a part out," Jess said.

"You mean that stupid thing about a ghost? Come on; be serious," Craig said. "I want you to know that I was not involved in any of this."

"Okay, we know you were not involved. Now, what did you learn from his file?" Jess twirled her fingers for him to get on with it.

"I just got the file two days ago. As soon as I figured out who this guy was, I called Jess," Craig fidgeted with his glass.

"Craig!" Jess demanded.

"His prison record came with his file. That's how I knew, even with a lot of the file blacked out." Looking at Jess for support. "We relocated him to Whittier, California. We gave him a bookstore near the college. I got his file because he disappeared two weeks ago. He's the Ron that Jess has been bugging me about. He's going by the name Joseph Fine. He's not allowed to move around. If he's going anywhere else other than the Whittier area, he has to get permission."

Dana sipped her wine and looked directly into Craig's eyes. Her voice was soft and sweet, but her eyes turned chilly and evil as she said her first words. "So, you fuckers have been hiding him from me all these years."

"Not me!" Craig, his body stiffened up. Something about this woman was unforgiving. "Sorry," he said, looking at his watch. "I've got to go. I got a case in court," He chugged what was left of his wine and got up to go. "I'll see you around, Jess." He started to walk off.

"Your keys," Dana said.

"No, those aren't my keys. Don't forget the tab. It's on the table." Craig hurried out of there as fast as he could.

Dana looked on the back of the bill, It was from the same restaurant, but bore a different date. On the back were two street addresses.

"What can I do?" Jess asked. She knew the Red Bitch when she saw her.

"Find out what you can about Gina and her aunt. I gave you their addresses in London a while back. I don't think they have moved. See what else you can find out about Ron. Update me ASAP." Dana took another sip of her wine. She reached over and took Jess's hand and gave it a squeeze. "Thank you. I have a bad feeling about this."

"He's not allowed to have a passport. So, they should be okay. But you never know?" Jess said.

Dana checked her watch. Getting up to go, she took the keys and the bill and said. "Thank you again. Love you always."

"Love you too. Be careful," Jess said before Dana turned around and headed for the airport.

Alyssa picked her up at the airport. She complained about her new boyfriend to her silent mother most of the way home. A few blocks from home, she pulled over. "All right, Mom. What's up?" she asked, one hand on the wheel, the other on her mother's shoulder.

"I've got to go to Los Angeles tonight. I just need to pack. Then you can take me back to the airport."

"That's not what I asked," Alyssa said, looking her mother in the eye.

"It's just an old problem. I have to take care of, okay?" Dana said in a normal voice.

"Okay. Don't tell me," Alyssa said in her pissed-off voice. As she put the car in drive and pulled away from the curb, she continued, "Aunt Jody or Uncle Jess will tell me."

Dana got as much rest as she could on the flight to LAX. The first place the Red Bitch visited was Ron's house in Hacienda Heights. She let herself in and looked around. No one was there, and it looked like someone had packed in a hurry. Drawers were open, clothes were on the bed. She looked through his home desk next. Nothing, just household stuff. She went through the house, checking for hollow walls, under beds, and behind pictures. Any place she thought he might think no one would look. She found nothing special.

The bookstore was across the street from the college on Painter Avenue. She stood in front of it for a few minutes. It was closed. She used the key she found in the house and opened the door; she locked the door behind her. The Red Bitch searched around the counter. The cash register was empty except for change. Nothing else seemed to be out of place. Then she noticed on the wall behind the counter was a daily calendar. The last date on it was over two weeks ago. *Okay, time frame,* she thought.

She made her way to the small office at the back of the store and went through his file drawer first. She found a big file with pictures of him having sex with very young girls. Dropping them on the desk, she went through the rest of the drawer and found nothing interesting. Looking over the desk again, she saw a note pad with what seemed like a flight number and a time. Looking closely, she saw the impression from a pencil. She could just make out a phone number.

She called the number. "In Town Printing," a man said into the phone.

"Ah. I have a brochure I need printed. What's your address?" She jotted it down on the same notepad next to the number she had just filled in. She then called Jess.

Dana fed her the information she had just learned, "Find out about this guy, especially if he makes up phony passports. You know that bad feeling I had? It just got worse."

"I'm right on it," Jess said.

"I'm on my way to New York. I'll call you when I get there. Thanks, sweetie." Dana hung up. She dialed the airline and made a reservation. On her way out, she stopped. "Hmm," she said. Then she went back and got the sex photo file. She taped the pictures to the window, facing out. She locked the door, and on her way to her rental car, she threw Craig's keys in the sewer.

*

By the time Dana arrived at LaGuardia airport, it was after midnight. Dana called Jess from the lobby.

“Dana, after what I found out about the dirty son-of-a-bitch who owns the print shop, I sent a team into it. He is still in interrogation. He sold Ron a new passport and a New York State driver's license. He handed them over to him this morning. He left for London on a flight soon after. He's in London by now.” Jess was talking at people speed. She was serious.

“You know that bad feeling? It's really bad now. Okay, I'm still at the airport. I'll jump the next flight.” Dana started looking around.

“He changed his name to Rod Smith. I got you a flight tomorrow morning. I also got you a hotel room for a few hours' sleep. It's next to the airport. Get a little rest and shower. I'm sure you need it by now,” Jess said.

“Please call Gina and her aunt and warn them,” Dana asked.

"I tried that as soon as I found out Ron was on the move. I tried it several times. No answer. I tried Gina at work. She wasn't there, either. I called some people, and I'm trying to run them down now."

"Oh, shit. I hope we're not too late?" Dana said, depressed.

"Get some rest. You have a morning flight tomorrow. Baby, be careful. Be sure and eat something. Jody told me how you can be." Jess paused. "One more thing. Alyssa called yesterday. She wanted to know why you were going to LA. She also wanted to know why you took your swords. I told her you were on a little project for me. Nothing special. Now, get some rest and food. Your flight leaves in eight hours."

*

"Antiques," Dana said to the English customs agent as he opened the case holding the swords. "They are very old and very sharp. Be careful."

At the rental car counter, they gave her keys and a space number. She dumped her stuff in the trunk—"Boot," she silently reminded herself. Then she got into the car.

"Holy shit. What's the steering wheel doing over there?" This time, she said it out loud. She ran around the car and got in the other door. "Really, you're kidding me. Stick shift." This time, she almost yelled in frustration.

Jess had rented her a room at the Holiday Inn in Kensington. It was not far from West Brompton, where Gina and her aunt lived.

The first thing she did, after cursing out the car and remembering to drive on the wrong side of the street, was to drive by both Gina's and her aunt's places. Their homes were only two blocks apart and very similar. They were townhouses, the same as all the others that took up the entire block. Gina and her aunt's places were very similar except she had a low iron fence, more for decoration than protection.

She parked on the street and walked around, studying the area.

Dana then went back and checked into the hotel. The first thing she did after dropping her bags on the bed was to call Jess.

"Take a breath. Get some rest. They went to Belgium for a holiday," Jess said in her best English accent. "They won't be back for two more days."

"Any sign of Ron?" Dana asked.

Jess was more serious. "We got him landing. He didn't rent a car at the airport. We're trying to track down where he is staying, but nothing's coming up. He has just disappeared."

"Do you think he went to Belgium?" Dana asked.

"I don't think so. I'll give you any information as soon as I get it. Now relax a bit," Jess said. "Why is he risking all this for Gina and her aunt?"

"They are the ones who got away. Have you figured out how the hell he found them?" Dana asked, sitting on the edge of the bed in the small room.

"I'm looking into that. Oh, I sent teams into the house and the bookstore yesterday. They took down your window decoration. It drew quite a crowd," Jess laughed.

Dana took a hot bath, rolled into bed, and slept for eleven hours. The next morning, she had tea in her room and called Jess.

"Want to know how he found out where they are?" Jess asked, almost as soon as she picked up the phone. "In the bookstore, we found an airline magazine. There was a picture of Elizabeth, Gina's aunt. She had just retired. There is a picture of her leaning on her fence. Her address is clearly visible. They also gave her new last name. She's married now," Jess said.

"Shit. Ron must have been scanning the airlines for information," Dana said.

"Elizabeth won't be hard to find; Ron has names and addresses," Jess said. "Still nothing on him yet. Not a hotel or a car or anything. Here's what we think. He knows someone in London. He's with them. We're trying to run down any possible links."

Dana spent time in the area eating, having a pint in the pub and generally just hanging out. All this time, she never saw a trace of Ron.

She was at the ferry when it came back from Belgium. Elizabeth was with her husband. Gina had a small boy with her. Dana guessed him to be about ten or eleven years old.

The Red Bitch was now on guard. She spent most of her time in her car. The first night passed. Nothing happened.

Gina's aunt and husband came out of the front door early the next morning. She gave her husband a big kiss. He was dressed as a pilot. That meant he would be gone for maybe days. Dana followed Gina as she took her young son to school. Then she took a cab to the hospital. She figured they would all be safe for now. So, Dana went back to the hotel to get a hot bath to loosen up her stiff body. Then she called Jess, followed by a nap.

When she went back later that afternoon, she took her big raincoat to cover up her Red Bitch clothing when she had to leave the car for food or to take care of necessities. Later that evening, she saw Gina take her small boy to her aunt's. Then she went across the street to a pub. The Red Bitch drove over and parked near the pub. She figured this was Gina's regular hangout.

The Red Bitch was on full guard. She thought this would be the time Ron would most likely strike. Gina would be most vulnerable alone on the street at night. The Red Bitch sat quietly in her car, watching the front door of the pub. She could see Gina through the front window, drinking a pint and watching a football game, English football. She thought, *She probably speaks with a British accent*.

The Red Bitch settled in for a long night. About an hour later, she was startled by someone banging on her window. "How did I not see that coming," she thought. She looked over to see Gina, who was telling her to roll down her window.

"What are you fucking doing, following me?" Gina was holding a small wooden baton from the pub.

"Ah, I wasn't following you. I was just—" the Red Bitch stuttered.

"Wait. Look at me," Gina demanded. The Red Bitch slowly turned toward her. Gina looked more closely at her.

"I thought I knew that voice. Dana, what the hell are you doing here? Why are you stalking me?"

"Well, see?" she started to say, but a quick thought came to her. "How did you get out of the pub without me seeing you?"

"Back door. Don't change the subject," Gina demanded.

"I think Ron has found you and your aunt," the Red Bitch said.

"After all these years. Bullshit." She tapped her baton on her leg. "I'm getting my son. I'll meet you back at my place." She headed back to the pub to drop off her baton. "By the way, it's still nice to see you again."

Dana started to get out of her car.

"What are you doing?" Gina said.

"I was going to walk with you," the Red Bitch said.

"Dressed like a hooker? You're not," Gina said. "My place. Go!" She pointed.

The Red Bitch ground the gears and made a U-turn in the street and went back to Gina's. She parked and put her head back against the headrest.

Back door. Shit. The thought hit her. She jumped out of the car and ran the two blocks to Gina's aunt's block. Going down the side street, she found the narrow passageway that separated the buildings. The Red Bitch ran down the passageway. She came to the aunt's back door. *Damn. Forgot my swords*, she thought as she came to the door. It was partly open.

Stepping in, she saw steps going down to a basement and a coat rack and bench on her level. Then three steps up to the kitchen. That door was half-open. With her back against the wall, she looked in. There were two doors out of the kitchen, one to the dining room that then opened to the living room, the other to the front hallway.

In the living room, Gina's aunt was standing, looking into the hall. She had a bloody nose, a cut on her cheek, and another cut on her neck that wasn't deep. Her blouse was ripped and bloody. She was standing in front of the little boy. With both hands behind her, she was keeping him behind her, protecting him.

The Red Bitch inched open the door so she could see down the hall. Ron was holding Gina up against the wall with a knife at her neck.

"Both you and your aunt are going to pay for what you did to me! Pay big time," he was yelling with spit coming out of his mouth. Gina had a cut on her cheek.

Then Aunt Elizabeth saw the Red Bitch. The Red Bitch put her finger to her lips and mouthed, "Quiet. Don't move."

The Red Bitch quickly and silently made her way through the kitchen to the dining room, then the living room. She came up behind Ron.

"Oh, this is going to be good. It might even take me all night," Ron said, then licked the blood on Gina's face. "Yummy. Really good." Then he screamed in pain as the Red Bitch broke his little finger on his knife hand. He dropped the knife to the floor.

Turning to the Red Bitch, he spat out, "What the fuck? You're dead. I know you're dead."

"Really?" the Red Bitch asked.

Ron bent over to pick up the knife. She drove a heel through his hand. "Not a good idea, lover." She kneed him in the chest, sending him up against the wall. Ron tried to kick the Red Bitch. She drove a knee into his leg, forcing his kick to the floor. Then she ran a heel through his foot.

"You are so right. I am dead. You can never escape me. Remember when I hit your drug house in Atlanta?" She smiled and spoke softly.

"You're the Red Bitch. I know you're dead." Ron said wide-eyed.

"Hmm. Did you know it was Moses who gave me that nickname? The Red Bitch. Just the day before I killed him." She pulled off her red wig. "Do you recognize me now?" She was smiling, just inches from his face.

"You. You." He pointed at her with his left hand. "You're that kid who broke my finger. Me and Moses had to spend four years in jail because of you. Yeah, you're that bitch."

"Red Bitch to you." She stepped back, then said, "Okay, lover. I want to remind you like I reminded Moses." She then drove her heel through his heart. His eyes opened wide. "It's not a good idea to kill my mother."

Just as she pulled her heel out of his chest, and as he was taking his last breath, she whispered, "Moses is waiting for you in Hell." He fell to the floor, dead. His mouth was open, his eyes wide. *That surprised look again*, she thought. She tilted her head, looking at Ron and then took a deep breath.

She turned and looked at Aunt Elizabeth, then turned back to Gina.

"Hi, Stump. I'm Godzilla." Dana kissed Gina on her shocked lips. "I'll give you a call sometime. Call the cops. Oh, what do you call them here, Bobbies? Take your time. Take lots of time. Now, make sure everyone's okay."

Gina rushed to her son and aunt, hugging them, asking if they were okay. Turning back to Dana, she didn't have time to say anything. Godzilla was already gone.

*

Dana landed late in Atlanta. She did not have time to call Alyssa to pick her up. She just took a cab home. Alyssa heard the front door open and rushed to the top of the stairs. "Mom," she said as she came down the stairs two at a time. She grabbed her mom and they wound themselves around each other. Then she stepped back to put her arms across her chest. "Where have you been?"

Dana put her arm around Alyssa and led her into the library. "To hell and back." Dana sat in the middle of the sofa, where she had sat as a little girl. Alyssa sat next to her. Dana could hear the records playing and could see her mother and father sitting in their big chairs reading their books. She put her arm around Alyssa and kissed her. " We'll talk tomorrow. I've got jet lag. I need to sit up a while. Go to bed. Oh, how's Aunt Jody?"

"She sleeps like a log. I'm sure she never heard you come in," Alyssa said as she headed for the stairs. Aunt Jody was standing at the top of the stairs. She went back to bed with a smile on her face.

Dana poured herself a glass of her dad's good brandy and went out to the patio. She sat next to the throne. She put her hand on the arm of the throne and spoke to her mother. "You can rest now. You and Dad." Sipping brandy and wiping tears away. "And now, at last, so can I."

THE END

EPILOGUE

"I'm sorry, honey. But I need to get some away time. See the Pacific Ocean again," Dana said to Alyssa.

"Well, I guess Hawaii is in the middle of the Pacific Ocean. So, I guess you can't miss it. But do you have to go now?" Alyssa was taking inventory at the gallery bar.

"I know, but you and Jody can handle it," Dana said, looking out the window with its view of the city of Atlanta.

"Please, Mom. Auntie is trying, but she is getting so forgetful. I can't trust her." Alyssa dropped the clipboard on the bar.

"I tell you what. I'll find some artists or shows or something in Hawaii. I know a couple of buyers who might go for some of that art. At least it will look like I'm working," Dana said, turning to Alyssa.

"Sure," Alyssa said in a frustrated tone. She could never tell her mother anything. "When are you leaving?"

"Tomorrow," Dana said quietly.

"Figures." Alyssa looked away. "When do you want me to drive you to the airport?"

*

Hawaii was warm and friendly.

Dana parked herself in the Hilton on the Beach. She had a beautiful room overlooking the ocean with a balcony. The first night she went to Club D. The guy at the desk said it was a mixed club, straight and LGBT. She met Mabel there. She was from San Francisco, so Dana called her Fran.

A few days later, she met Lucy. She was young, cute, hot, and horny. She had a small apartment near the Hilton. She said she was an art student. The second night, the phone rang at five in the morning.

"Hi, sweetie." She sat up on the side of the bed, her naked back to Dana. "Sure, I'm so glad you're home early. Give me an hour. Love you." She hung up. "You got to go. My husband came back from Korea early."

"You're married?" Dana sat up in bed.

"Yeah, didn't I tell you?"

"No," Dana said slowly. "It would have been nice to know." She was dressed and out the door in less than ten minutes. No kissing was involved.

On her walk back to the hotel, she questioned herself. "Why didn't I catch that?" Followed up by, "I can't do this anymore. These young chicks are just too scatterbrained for me." Her eyes were drawn to the sunrise over the ocean. Lifting her heart, it reminded her of Pismo Beach, long ago, except that was a sun setting then. This was a sunrise. "Maybe a new awaking," she said softly to herself.

Walking into the hotel, she saw a blond, a little younger than her. She was walking through the lobby with sandy feet, legs, and butt. She was wearing a long t-shirt and carrying her thongs. She had a smile on her face. She was walking like the world had been lifted off her shoulders.

Lucy called later that afternoon. "You got to help me. My husband found one of your credit card receipts. He thinks we had sex. He's standing right here. We're coming over; you can explain to him nothing happened." Click.

Later, standing at one end of the bar, Dana was trying to calm down the situation. She really didn't want to be there. Looking around, Dana saw the woman from the lobby. She was drinking a martini and eating chicken wings. "What a mess," Dana thought. "She has sauce all over her face, even on her forehead and in her hair, not to mention down the front of her white blouse."

Dana turned away and back to the confrontation in front of her.

Why am I attracted to her? God, she's such a mess, she was thinking. She called over the bartender and sent the messy woman another martini.

The woman looked up as the martini was placed in front of her. Then the bartender pointed out Dana. The messy woman gave Dana a little tip of her glass and went back to her wings. "Well, that usually gets me an introduction at least. She's probably straight. Oh well."

Lisa downed her second martini. On her walk out of the bar, she gave Dana a little wave and mouthed, "Thank you."

Coming soon, "Angel the Assassin" and then "Love and Revenge."

ACKNOWLEDGMENTS

Paula Lehman—She followed along with me, reading chapter after chapter as I completed them. She not only gave me input but also encouragement.

Jay Lipscomb and Chandra Corley—My Beta readers. They showed me when and where I was off course.

Susan Helene Gotfried of westofmars.com—Her advice on content drove me in the right direction, plus all the other things she helped direct me with to become a better writer.

Humbert Glaffo at 99Designers—He designed an outstanding cover.

Robert Lewis at Southern Editing & Cover Design—He gave me fast and cost-effective editing.

Finally—All the bartenders who kept my wine glass full and gave me space to write.